Eclipsing

The Zoe Eferhild Chronicles: Book 2

E.C. Lawton

First Edition: April 2024

Names: Lawton, E.C., author.

Artist: Xenia

Title: Eclipsing, The Zoe Eferhild Chronicles, Book Two/ by E.C. Lawton

Description: First edition.

Audience: Ages 18 and up.

ISBNs: ebook: 979-8-9885648-2-9; paperback: 979-8-9885648-3-6; hardback: 979-8-9885648-5-0

Printed in the United States of America.

Contents

To every wounded inner child who has never felt captivating, I
hope The Zoe Eferhild Chronicles helps you feel seen.
You are wanted. You are needed. You are wholly dazzling.
All of my love,
-E.C. Lawton

Author's Note

This story contains material that may be uncomfortable for readers. This work is intended for readers eighteen and older. While Zoe's story is one of hope and designed to empower those struggling with mental wellness, reader discretion is advised.

Content Warning: allusions and references to suicide; sexual assault (non-specific or graphic- flashbacks); self-harm scars; recovery from alcohol abuse; drug abuse; domestic violence; death of a family member; Post Traumatic Stress Disorder (PTSD); depression; anxiety; violence.

KINGDOM OF CANIS
EARTH
COURT OF CANOPUS
Realm of Carina
Lord Astral Abel
Lady Astral Aura
COURT OF ALGOL
Realm of Perseus
Lord Astral Oleander
Queen Hesperia
SIRIUS
Queen Farron
King Aldrich
COURT OF VEGA
Realm of Lyra
Lord Astral Elvy
COURT OF RIGIL
Realm of Centaurus
Lord Astral Terran
Lady Astral Sierra
COURT OF ARCTURUS
Realm of Bootes
Lord Astral Kai
Lady Astral Seraphina

Kingdom of Canis Quick Reference

<u>**Kingdom of Canis**</u>

King Aldrich

Queen Farron

<u>**Court of Vega**</u>

Lord Astral Elvy

Lady Astral Zoe

Star Elemental Realm for Water

Realm of Lyra

Delmira—Second

Clodovea—Third

Blaz—Emissary to Canopus

Imelda—Emissary to Arcturus

Finnian—Emissary to Rigil

<u>**Court of Algol**</u>

Lord Astral Oleander

*Queen Hesperia

*Tiergan—Sublunary Leader

Star Elemental Realm for Spirit

Realm of Perseus

Zadie—Second to Oleander

Court of Rigil

Lord Astral Terran

Lady Astral Sierra

Star Elemental Realm for Ground

Realm of Centaurus

Court of Arcturus

Lord Astral Kai

Lady Astral Seraphina

Star Elemental Realm for Fire

Realm of Bootes

Court of Canopus

Lord Astral Abel

Lady Astral Aura

Star Elemental Realm for Air

Realm of Carina

1

Prologue
THE ARCHER

"They will cease to remember the ways of old," my father said, standing in their celestial form before me. Darkness rippled around them, creating the illusion of a being with a sentient form. Ebbs of light flickered within their hazy body, growing brighter the closer they were to the celestial's core.

Life always craved death in the end. And that's what my creator was—death.

I called Algol father because they preferred it, but they were simply my architect. I came from their very spirit. There was no mother, no love in my absolution. I did not yet know my purpose.

All the celestials convened around an elaborate table, made up of the five elements. Each essence was displayed equally, none overpowering the other in this domain. In the realm of Nova, they were equals and represented themselves as such.

Nova sat at the head of the table with my father—Algol—on her left and the celestial Vega on her right. Nova was ancient compared to the celestials and provided a neutral party for them, not that they ever listened to her. Her cosmic eyes and pale, nearly translucent skin had always unnerved me, and I did not know the language that was marked on every surface of her smooth skin. Yet, I trusted her implicitly.

I'd done as they'd asked in linking their realms together with my bow and string. That purpose had been served... but I'd given more to the immortals of the star realms than what had been decreed by their council. I'd made it so that the immortals didn't have to choose one or the other. I'd given them the autonomy to love freely and be who they wanted—a concept I didn't fully understand myself.

For that gift, I had been punished. I still heard their cries in my nightmares, begging to feel the magic that had once filled them with joy and hope. My heart shattered for them, broken into five pieces. One for each bond I had to break between them.

The other celestials, Rigil, Canopus, and Arcturus, sat along the table, looking bored. Vega and Algol had always been at odds. I could only guess that the life and death they both served hated each other. In my core, I felt their disdain ran much deeper than what I could speculate. They were both important—essential. If they lost their lust for power, they'd be able to see that. I would find a way to make them. No matter the cost.

"Be careful, Archer," Nova said, staring at me with those never-ending eyes. She spoke through my mind, so that only I could hear. *"Some prices are too high."*

"What they made me do is unacceptable," I argued.

"So it is, child," she said, pausing. *"She will burn. That will be the price."*

"Who?" I asked.

"It is not yet time," she answered. *"When you start to feel peace, it will be ripped from you. You will regret your haste, and you will lose everything, Archer."*

"I already have," I returned. The blinding cry of rage enveloped me, but I had nothing left to give. No. No more tears would come.

"There is always more to lose, Archer."

I gazed into her eyes as Vega and Algol continued to argue around us with their volume increasing. Her eyes were sad, as if lamenting a future that had already come to pass for her. I was gifted in the *sight,* but I was still a novice with it. If I'd been able to *see* what Vega and Algol were going to make me do… I would have found a way around it. I'd have to practice—learn to be better than even the *sight* of Algol.

"You are mistaken," Nova said aloud to Algol.

"And in what way is that, Nova?" they responded with a superior air, even though Nova was much older than even my creator.

"There will be those who are untouched by the evocation of your blood magic. They will never forget."

"What can a few do?" Algol asked, scoffing at the warning. Not me. I would use it to my advantage.

"You should heed my warning, celestial. For you will suffer the worst. You will beg for the help of whom you deem your greatest enemy—whom you deem most beneath you."

Algol turned to the other celestials, fearing one of them would betray them and the agreement for the immortals to only serve one of the elemental stars.

"Which of you will deceive me?"

None of the celestials answered. I realized it would not be one of them. Whether Algol's paranoia realized this was lost to me.

"An Emerging," Nova said, only to me through my mind. *"An Emerging of Legends and Realm-Healer."*

"He will save us?" I asked.

Nova shook her head slightly.

"She will either save us," Nova paused with significance. *"Or destroy us. That remains to be seen."*

"I will find her," I swore. *"I will pay whatever price."*

"So you will," she said, bowing.

2

New Moon

ZOE

Red. The hue of death had morphed into the seduction of the black shadows that lived within my heart.

Elvy—my flame—had once told me I could forge my fury or my fear. Right now? My blood ran hot with vengeance. Hesperia had slaughtered my parents. Well, my mother and stepfather. My actual father felt like some mystical illusion that was determined to piss me off further by sending me on some quest to right the wrongs of the stars. Maybe it was time the stars got off their thrones and cleaned up their own mess.

A pain shot through my hands, and I realized they were bleeding. Elvy was at my side at once, tenderly caressing where I'd been clenching my nails into my callused palms.

"Let me," he whispered, as the blue glow of his healing magic quickly repaired my damaged skin.

His magic was connected to the Court of Vega—the water elemental star realm. His real magic had only recently been revealed to me, and I had half a mind to ask him to use it to annihilate those I wished death. I couldn't ask that of him, though. Not only was he the Lord Astral of the immortals of Vega, but he hated his family curse—death. It went against the very thing Vega was known for—life.

Elvy and I had joined our flames together only three days ago. Flames—soulmates—were rare amongst immortals, and I'd had to fight like hell to get back to him when I was an Emerging mortal. I completed the trials in the star realm of Nova to prove that I was worthy to Emerge as an immortal. What the stars didn't count on was my sheer willpower to choose myself above all else. The celestials of Algol and Vega had wanted me to pick between them, and I'd refused. Instead, I'd forced them to choose me. I knew a price would come with showing them up on their home field, but I had other things to worry about now.

The day our flames had joined as one was supposed to be a time of love and life. Instead, Hesperia, in her delusional need for power, had killed every mortal there. Even while human, I'd never been one to dream of a grand wedding day, but when I'd seen Elvy standing there at the end of the aisle waiting for me, joy had encompassed every molecule of my immortal body.

Dark fury had eclipsed our love—our moment.

"She took everything from us, Elvy. And she's just getting started."

He cupped my cheek, turning my gaze away from the starlit ocean from the window of our manor.

"Don't let her take that moment from us, Zoe Eferhild," he whispered.

Moments were an important thing to me and Elvy. I believed that life was defined by the seemingly insignificant moments that coaxed our spirit into the darkness or the light. I wasn't sure that either way was good or bad.

"All I can see is my mother's face," I answered, voice breaking. My tear ducts heated with a desire to spill, but I had nothing left to give them. Instead, I turned my emerald green eyes from the calm of the ocean waves to face the storm-gray eyes of my flame.

"I love you," he said through our joined bond from the flames. *"Endlessly."*

"I don't know how to move forward."

"Together," he promised. *"With one breath at a time, if we must."*

I let him wrap me in his sturdy arms, pulling me close. He swayed our bodies to music that wasn't there, and I allowed the strength of him to carry me in this moment that felt too big to bear alone.

Jelly—a simargl—which was basically a fire-wielding dog with wings, nudged our swaying forms with her cold nose. Jelly had been my service dog when I was a mortal living on Earth. She was still a beautiful black and white border collie, but she now possessed angel-soft wings that allowed her to fly and transport between realms. We were still learning things about her, as most of her ancient lineage had died off in the Court of Arcturus—fire realm.

We had plans to visit there soon, as well as the other two elemental realms that were new to me. The Court of Canopus was the star realm for air, while the Court of Rigil was the star elemental for ground. Combined with water in the Court of Vega and spirit in the Court of Algol, these five elements were tethered to the main star Sirius in our Kingdom of Canis. These bonded stars provided these essential sources of life to the mortals on Earth. Hesperia had destroyed the balance when she'd severed the tether in Algol, damaging the spirit element for not only mortals of Earth but the immortals whose life source came from the star itself.

I'd solved that minor problem temporarily when I'd healed Algol with my magic from Vega and bonded Algol's life source to my very own. I was still deciding whether that was a dumb decision or not. Either way, there was no changing it. Not yet anyway.

Bending down on the plush gray rug of our bedroom, I stroked Jelly's soft fur and placed my forehead next to hers. Elvy joined us on the floor next to the blue-green flame of the fireplace and motioned for us to move closer to him. Jelly and I both snuggled into him, knowing that this was the last night we would get to be like this for a while in our ocean-side home in Vega. I wanted to let go of the worries and heartache of what had happened and what was to come. Even if it was just for a little while.

Elvy seemed to know this. Of course he did. He knew everything there was to know about me, and that was before we'd officially bonded. He clicked a few hidden buttons, and the skylight pulled back, revealing the magnificence of the cosmos. The realm of the stars was like living underneath the Milky Way every night with a stunning light show from an even grander aurora borealis. The sun never rose in the realm of the stars, and I found that I didn't miss it most of the time. Now that he'd open the skylight, the sound of the ocean brought me comfort with each wave that crashed on the shore.

"My girls," Elvy said, contentment in his voice. He let out one of his aqua blue transcalent but still substantial wings to safely encircle us in his embrace. "No matter what comes with tomorrow's rising moon, I will fight to get back to this moment." The conviction in his voice was an oath. One that seared itself in my very soul.

"You have so much faith that we will win," I mumbled with sleep in my tone. I'd been exhausted over the last three days but had rarely slept.

"The stars brought me you," he said, undoing the braid of my dark brown, wavy hair. "You are my eternal moment, Zoe."

Gently, he began massaging my scalp and humming some song I didn't know. He trailed his fingers down my exposed back, tracing the map of the stars that rested there. Every immortal Shadowed had wings and a tattoo of the Kingdom of Canis on either their chest or their back. Mine was across my shoulder blades and slightly different from all the rest, which triggered even more bitterness inside of me. Nothing was ever simple.

"I'm so angry," I tried to argue, but it fell flat. The ember of my fury had burned out for the night.

"It's not anger, Zo. It's grief," he countered, and I knew he was right. "Sleep, beautiful. You are safe tonight."

Elvy's arms had always equated safety to me, and before I could protest any longer, my consciousness flew to the world of dreams.

***

"Little bear," a warm voice spoke to me through my dreams. The Archer had revealed himself to be my biological father last year, and he was the direct descendant of the celestial Algol. Prior to that, he had never been a part of my life, and I still wrestled with the idea of truly letting him in. Trust was not something I easily gave.

His voice was filled with concern, and what I felt sounded like sorrow.

"I'm not in the mood," I said sternly into the abyss. My father had never shown me his true form, always cloaking himself in shadows.

"Vivian—your mother—she deserved better."

"You were the one who got her wrapped up in all of this the moment you met her," I accused. "She'd still be alive if you had just left her alone."

"Believe what you must, little bear, but I loved your mother. Dearly. I did not know this would be her fate…"

"Lies," I said. "You have prophecy in your veins."

"The future is subjective. You know this with your own sight. I did not see it coming until it was too late. I sent word to June immediately."

June had been my boss when I was still mortal, and I hadn't known at the time that she was part of this world at all until the day of my joining ceremony with Elvy. I still didn't know what she was, really. I just hoped she'd taken care of my mother's body.

"Is my mother at rest?" I asked.

"Yes, June has cared for her physical form. Her spirit…" he trailed off, but the glare I gave the shadows must have kept him going. "Her spirit is gone. Whatever Hesperia did, I can't feel her in Algol."

I'd suspected this, but it broke me all over again to hear it confirmed. My knees crashed onto the wet sand beneath me as I buckled over in pain. I'd experienced the agony of seeing my sister die. My failure began that night when she perished and I lived. I still hadn't figured out a way to bring her back from the spirit world. At least she still had a soul to bring back. In the meantime, she was stuck with Oleander, the Lord Astral of the Court of Algol. Mom would never get that chance, and I guess that was supposed to be the natural order of things. She shouldn't have died yet, though. We never should have had the joining ceremony in my hometown of Saint Andrews, Florida. I'd just wanted to give my mother a good memory to hold on to before I left for the star realms.

A rough but gentle hand brushed the hair from my eyes and tilted my chin up. The man before me resembled me in many ways. His skin was dark, as if he'd spent too much time in the sun. His hair was silvered, but was clearly once as dark as mine. It was his eyes, though, that did me in. They were the bright green flames of my own. If there had been any doubt left that he was my father, it was vanquished. There was no question.

"Little bear, you are not *a failure," he said, cupping my cheek. "You are ferocious, just, and kind. Hard times are ahead, yes. But you are a true Daughter of Algol. You will mend that which was broken, child of the cosmos. We will see this through. You are never alone."*

An odd feeling came over me. I wanted to hug him. Seeming to read my mind, he cradled me in his arms, whispering words of encouragement. He was being the father I'd always wanted—needed—him to be. I knew he'd been watching over me in his own way with June, apparently, and the mysterious woman who had given me the first prophecy last year—Phoebe. But to have him actually hold me… my inner child clung to him with all the years she'd missed out on with her father. Emma, who had been my therapist for the years following the night I tried to end my life, was hopefully smiling down—proud. This moment was the least I could give her after Hesperia had taken her life, too.

"Life has been unkind to you, little bear. You must remember the glimmers against the shadows, too. The times that kept you alive."

"I don't know how to control this darkness inside of me," I whispered, almost afraid to admit it.

"The more you try to shove it down, the worse it will get. It's a part of you that you must learn to embrace, or someone or something else will control it," he said seriously, but I feared who I would become if I allowed

that. Hesperia had almost put the darkness in my brain's driver's seat, and I shivered, remembering how sinfully good it felt.

"What must I do now?" I asked.

"You know you must find that which was lost."

"Your bow," I confirmed, and he only nodded.

"Any idea where to start?" I asked.

"You must find it on your own, little bear. But remember your creed. Let it guide you as my true Daughter of Algol," he answered. "Now, go back to sleep and dream of happier things."

For the first time since The Archer had started visiting me, he didn't send me away into the abyss of sleep. He continued to hold me in his arms until the sound of the waves lulled me into a deep slumber.

***

I woke to my favorite smell in the world—coffee. Emerging as an immortal had not dampened my love of the elixir.

"Courtesy of Octavia," Elvy said, handing me a cup, but I saw the pot behind him on the desk. We'd merged our two bedrooms together before the joining ceremony and had fashioned what had been my room into a private study. I hadn't gotten to enjoy it very much, but I mostly used it for reading or strategizing where to start my search for The Archer's bow. Sometimes, I used it to be alone in my grief.

"Whatever you're paying her, it isn't enough," I said, taking the cup gladly. Octavia and I had grown fond of one another. She was a Keeper in the library downstairs. I'd never seen her outside of there and wasn't sure where she went after her shift.

"How are you feeling today?" he asked, eyes full of concern. "You were restless in your sleep. Moreso than usual."

Jelly laid her head in my lap, seeming to worry about me, too.

"The Archer came for a visit," I answered and explained the rest of the dream to him.

"I wonder why he revealed himself after all this time?" he asked.

"For once, I don't think it's calculated. I think he was trying to be a father."

"Are you okay with that?"

"He's the only parent I have left… I feel like maybe I need to give him a chance."

"Maybe," he said, gray eyes distant. I knew he was thinking of his parents, whom Hesperia had killed long before I came into the picture.

"We keep your parent's spirits alive in us, Elvy," I promised him through our bond.

He gave me a soft kiss. "We need to meet with the Luminaries and finalize our movements."

I nodded, resolved that I must go on. The Luminaries were our inner court members. As much as I wanted to wallow in the unfairness of life, I was called to a greater purpose. Life moved ever forward. It was up to me to move with it.

Elvy's jaw lingered near my neck, and the traces of his hair skimming the sensitive area sent a shiver through my body. His silver-brown curls had gotten longer, nearly enough to pull back in a hair tie, and I bit my lip, suddenly hungry for something only he could give me. Getting lost in his distractions seemed a good way to spend my time, and I couldn't ignore the desire to surrender my worries to him.

"Do we have time—" I started, and he answered with the crushing force of his lips.

I barely noticed Jelly seeming to roll her eyes as she trotted off to find the others.

He slipped off my midnight-blue nightgown in one fluid motion, exposing my naked flesh to him. His stormy, gray eyes devoured me, and every part of my body heated with his smirk and darkening eyes. He was just as ravenous for me as I was for him. I made quick work of the buttons on the front of his coal shirt as he skimmed his tongue up my neck, biting gently as he made his way to my ear.

He trailed his gloriously soft lips further down to my collarbone, then lower, and a sigh escaped me as he drew pleasure with his tongue. I gripped his curly brown-silver hair, demanding more from him. I felt the smile on his lips as he trailed his fingers to the most sensitive part of me, moving at a twisting rhythm.

My flame called to him in desperation, needing to fill the endless void of darkness within me. Grinding into him, I couldn't stop the moan that penetrated the room. No... he wasn't filling the void—he was pulling the shadows to the surface, reminding me of who I really was. Powerful. And a convulsion in his arms.

"Mine," I said, voice desperate—claiming my flame. I clung to his shoulders, trying to keep my magic from erupting entirely.

We were a beautiful cataclysm, designed for each other by the stars themselves.

"Yours," he agreed, biting down on my neck as he continued driving his fingers, making me hold my breath in anticipation.

The buildup was like a hot coal burning in my core, and I needed more of him. He placed one of my thighs on his shoulder to give him better access to my apex of pleasure, and his tongue invoked noises from me I couldn't contain. My skin burned beneath the touch of his other hand as it explored my hips, then higher... the stimulation was overwhelming in the best kind of way, and my body went rigid—bracing.

"Let me remind you that we're alive, Zo," he murmured.

At those words, I broke for him, as he saw me through the pulses of my bliss.

I didn't know when he'd taken his pants off, but I felt feverish taking in the sight of him. Pushing against his starry, tattooed chest, I flipped him onto his back so that I straddled him. I gasped at the fullness of my flame. We began moving as one, and he expertly used his fingers to bring me even more pleasure. My body rocked with euphoria, and I used my hands to grip his chest so that I didn't collapse in pleasure as he continued his rhythm. His hands locked around my hips, and my eyes found his. I could barely operate my legs, but I rose, exploring my body with my hands.

"Zoe," he growled, and my center warmed, ready to break for him again.

"Together," I panted, and screamed in bliss as he spilled into me, finding his own release.

I lay on his chest, committing this memory to my heart. His heartbeat slowed to match mine, and our flames called each other home. The gentle trailing of his fingers down my back settled my restless spirit for now.

"I love you, Elvy."

"For the heart of the new moon," he answered.

"And the life in the starlight," I promised.

3

The Luminaries

ZOE

After taking much too long in the shower, savoring every touch of each other, we eventually emerged from the safety of that moment. He'd kissed what used to be a jagged scar on my left forearm from the night I'd tried to end things as a mortal. The remnant of the scar was still there, but there was a swirl of the cosmos inside when I removed the glamor around it. In fact, both of my arms were lined with patterns of the stars. They'd shown up after I'd healed Algol from the brink of death. On my wrist, my immortal mark resembled an eight-pointed star, with the four cardinal points slightly larger than the others. When it wasn't glamoured, it glowed brightly with blues and blacks—unusual for immortals to have more than one color.

Elvy brushed out my hair, helping me braid the silver and brown strands down the length of my back that had also been marked by the stars. Not only did every Shadowed immortal have a map of the Kingdom of Canis on their back or chest, but we were all marked by silver streaks in our hair. My tattoo was a little different, with Vega and Algol being larger than the others. The Archer's constellation also rested just above the kingdom as a permanent reminder of who I was—a true Daughter of Algol. We helped each other into the uniform of the Shadowed Legion for the Court of Vega. It was a leather-like material, but much more durable and flexible. The leathers were a midnight blue with gold accents—the colors of our court.

Before leaving the comfort of our room, Elvy clasped my hands in his, displaying the retelling of our story on the back of our hands through the stars. The record was only complete when we held our hands together, and it was much like the legends of the constellations in the mortal night sky. I just hoped ours did not end up a tragedy.

Leaning his forehead against mine, he whispered, "You and me, Zoe. This is what we fight for."

He squeezed our palms together tightly, as if he could force us to always be together, no matter what.

"We will always find our way back to each other, Elvy," I promised.

"I know," he said, gazing into my green eyes. "The stars will always guide me home—and you are my home, Zo."

I kissed him softly, sealing our words as vows.

Satisfied, he led us through the ocean-side mansion. I liked to think of the manor as a beacon of hope, as the stars seemed to be interlaced into the moonstone. No matter where we were in the city, the glow of our home could always be seen. Inside, there were hints of gold and the different shades of blue of our court. I was still getting used to *our* court and not *his* court.

Jelly joined us in the hallway, brushing her wing against my thigh to let me know she was with me. I scratched behind her ears before continuing up to the secure room on the roof that had become our meeting room. We would have to make our final decisions today on where and how to utilize our forces—both seen and unseen. All the plans we'd made prior to our joining ceremony were void after what Hesperia had done. Adjustments had to be made.

As soon as we crossed the threshold of the room, a familiar force crushed into me with a bear hug.

"Blaz, I can't breathe," I said, only half-joking. Blaz was a devilishly handsome immortal with black-silver hair and dark eyes. He was also the general of the Shadowed Legion and emissary to the Air Elemental Star Realm—the Court of Canopus.

"I trained you better than that, Lady Astral," he said, releasing me and giving me a once-over. I caught the gleam of the silver pendant that was infused with my healing magic tucked away beneath his uniform and around his wrist. The pendant was a simple orb with the water mark carved into it, and I had gifted each of the Luminaries one on my joining day. "Where are your weapons?"

Before we'd left our room, Elvy had placed his swords across his back, as well as a variety of knives sheathed in hidden places. Glancing around, I saw that all the Luminaries wore their weapons.

"I've barely trained with them, Blaz. Do you really think I should?"

In the brief training we'd been able to do, I'd found that I'd taken a liking to the smaller blades—knives—versus the swords. The knives felt more natural, while the hefty swords felt awkward.

He rolled his eyes at me. A common thing for Blaz. "Yes, Zo. I do. The pointy end goes into the enemy. I know you're a supercharged immortal with unmatched power, but knives help in a pinch. We'll train as we can."

"Alright, alright, you mother hen," I said, strapping the knives he handed me into the sheaths of the uniform.

"Blaz is a big softie, isn't he?" Imelda asked, slinging an arm around him. Imelda was emissary to the Fire Elemental Star Realm—the Court of Arcturus. She was Clodovea's partner, who was Elvy's third in command.

"I like the new hair," I commented. Imelda usually sported her natural, full hair, but she'd shaved the sides of it and looked feisty.

"I did it for her," Clodovea said, joining us and kissing Imelda. She still wore her black-silver braids that were much longer than mine.

"What are we talking about?" Delmira asked, joined by her twin—Finnian. The twins both had strange violet eyes and matching lilac hair with silver streaks. They were also the only other immortals that I knew who had gone through the Emerging trials.

"Clove shaved Imelda's hair," Blaz said, nodding towards her.

"That's kind of sick. You've got to do that for me before we leave," Delmira said, eyes pleading. She was Elvy's second in command. Well—*our* second in command now. The twins had telepathic magic from Vega. Delm could influence the thoughts around her, while Finnian could take memories from others.

"Sure thing, Delm," Clodovea said easily, leaning into Imelda.

"Are we ready?" Elvy asked, drawing our attention to the map of the star realms hovering above the table like a hologram.

Delmira nodded, leading us to our places around the table. She sat to mine and Elvy's right, while Clodovea sat to our left. The rest gathered around in accordance to the court they represented.

"Where's Zadie?" Elvy asked Finnian. Zadie was the second to the Lord Astral of Algol—Oleander. He had become a close ally to our court. More than that—he was an important friend to me.

"I'm here," she said, flaming red-hair blowing in the non-existent wind as she walked through the doorway. Two of the Vega Shadowed escorted her. I'd started remembering some of their names. The male closest to her was a captain named Evander. "Sorry, I'm late. Hesperia is becoming increasingly difficult to dodge while leaving Algol."

"Freyja?" I asked, concerned for my sister.

"Safe," Zadie promised, moving her bright hair from her brow. Finnian gave her an endearing look that seemed to promise privacy later. I didn't know to what extent they were seeing each other, but the connection between them was obvious.

"Thank you," I said sincerely. I knew Oleander would do all that he could to ensure her safety.

"What's the plan?" Delmira asked, ready to get on with the proceedings.

"There are three things we must accomplish at once. It's going to require us to separate. There's no other way to make it work logistically," Elvy began.

"What do you need from us?" Clodovea asked.

"We need to petition the other courts to our side, protect Vega, and we must find The Archer's bow," I stated. "Nothing else we do will matter if we don't find his bow to reconnect all the tethers. We do not know how long my magic will hold Algol to my own life."

"It could make you weaker," Delm said, thinning her lips.

"Or stronger," Finnian disagreed.

The only answer I gave them was my silence. The only thing I knew for certain was that I felt more unstable than ever before, but stability did not necessarily equate more power.

"And we have to find a way to kill Hesperia in the process before we reconnect the bonds," Blaz said, pulling me from my thoughts.

"Yes, if we reconnect the tethers before she's killed… I'd hate to imagine what her madness would do to the mortals of Earth," Elvy said.

"There are fates worse than death," I agreed.

"So we protect them," Clodovea said, eyes narrowed in concentration. "And we remember that our actions here have consequences. If the entire Kingdom of Canis is at war… the effect this could have on the mortals of Earth would be unprecedented."

My thoughts briefly drifted to my mother, but I swallowed that memory down quickly. I desperately wanted to go back to Earth to see June, but I knew that wasn't a priority right now.

"What about you becoming the face of the rebellion in Algol?" Blaz asked.

I shook my head. "Logistically, it's not feasible for me to be in Algol for a host of reasons. Hesperia being there being the least of them."

It was clear he wanted to argue, but he didn't press the issue.

"I will do what I can for them," I said, nodding towards Zadie.

"So we divide into three parties?" Blaz asked.

"No, two," I responded. "I need to search each court for the bow. I'll be able to *see* more clearly once I'm in that realm. That's the best strategy until I have something more concrete on where to look."

"What's the order?" Delmira asked both Elvy and me.

"Delmira, Finnian, Imelda, you will stay behind in Vega to defend the immortal lives here. We need stability in our court. It's too risky to travel between realms as frequently as Delmira and Clodovea did during our time on Earth," Elvy explained. "Finnian, we need you in the Hall of Memories researching how Hesperia might use dark magic to reverse the tethers without the bow. We need to understand what she's capable of."

I hadn't known that Clove and Delm had been traveling to Vega while we'd been on Earth, but, of course, they had. Someone had to be here. That must have been exhausting to keep up that rotation.

I'd expected Delm to argue about staying behind in Vega. She liked to be in the action, but she only nodded, taking her assignment seriously.

"Blaz, Clodovea, Zoe, and I will go to the Court of Rigil first. Sierra and Terran have been allied with our realm for a long time. They are already expecting our arrival."

Rigil was the ground elemental star realm. Despite the horrific reasons for going there, a part of me was excited to see a new star court.

"Should I go to Rigil as the emissary to the ground elemental?" Finn asked.

"No," Elvy shook his head. "You need to be with Delmira for your powers to be effective."

"And I am closer with the Astrals there," Clodovea said.

Finnian nodded, seeming unbothered by this.

"What do we need to do in Algol?" Zadie asked.

"Keep pressing on," I answered.

"No disrespect, Lady Astral," Zadie began. Blaz's nostrils flared, but he didn't make a move towards her. "You are now the only thing keeping Algol tethered to life. Wouldn't it be safer for you to stay guarded? If something happens to you, all the immortals in Algol will die. Your sister's spirit will be lost forever."

The others shifted uncomfortably at her words, but she spoke the truth. It was her job to protect her court, and I didn't begrudge her that.

"That consequence was greatly weighed," I responded. "However, I am the only soul alive who can find The Archer's bow. I have no choice but to go."

Zadie bowed her head, accepting that this was the only solution. That didn't mean she had to be happy about it.

"We will need Oleander to dispatch the Sublunary as we move through the courts," Elvy said. "We need every advantage."

"How many do you need?"

"As many as you can spare. We will be sending some of our healers back with you."

Zadie sent me a curious glance. I'd kept the devastation in Algol from the rest of the Luminaries after I'd healed the refugees who had been suffering from their star's sickness. Their life force had been fading, so their lives had been disintegrating, too. With Algol tethered to me, they would not need as much healing, but there were so many uncertainties about this magic.

"I only told him what was necessary. Please do not turn our help away," I said.

"Oleander will accept," she promised.

"Can you get our healers to Algol safely?" Delm questioned. Delmira and Zadie tolerated each other at best.

"Of course I can."

"Are you sure we shouldn't go to Queen Farron and King Aldrich first?" Clodovea asked.

"It would be better to have at least one of the other courts backing us," Finnian pointed out.

"We will assess our visit to them after we meet with Terran and Sierra. The King and Queen will have heard about Zoe and me joining. They will be curious why they were not invited and why she has not presented to register her magic as the Lady Astral of Vega. I'm honestly surprised we haven't heard from them yet."

"Do you think they know Zoe is of two stars?" Imelda asked.

"I don't know," he admitted. "We'll need to be careful what we reveal to them until we know they are on our side."

"And the magic that gets recorded there…" Finnian said, verbalizing what Elvy and I had already discussed privately.

"I am working on obscuring my magic with my shield."

"The archives should only read her healing power from Vega. Its power alone should cover it if it comes to that."

"I know I can't hide forever," I said, sighing. "My wings are a dead giveaway… and Hesperia already knows."

"But you can hide what Algol gifted you by using your shield… so if it picks up on any magic from Algol, it'll just be your shielding magic. That's kind of brilliant," Finnian said excitedly. A high praise from our resident historian and researcher.

His enthusiasm was infectious at times. Blaz was far more practical.

"We'll need to be careful then," Blaz said.

"We move out in one hour," Elvy decided, fists on the table, still analyzing the playing field. "Whatever you need to do to get ready, now's the time."

The Luminaries dispersed, leaving me alone with my flame. Jelly lay in the corner, ears perked in our direction.

"Do you trust Sierra and Terran?" I asked him, circling my arms around his waist from behind his unforgiving frame.

"I do. They've been my personal friends for a long time."

"Do you think we will ever get to enjoy our lives together? Without the threat of death always lurking?"

"We will know peace," he said, gripping my hand tightly. "Whenever you doubt that, look to the stars and remember the hope you've always had in them. You are their creation, not their destruction."

Even I believed the conviction in his voice, despite the tendrils of doubt and darkness that wanted to tear down my armor of hope. I had to keep fueling the ember of life deep within my soul. It was buried underneath the rubble of despair, but I'd been through hard things before. I'd died and lived. I'd burned and risen as a phoenix. This was my fate to bear. And bear it I must. For those who couldn't. I would cling to the wildness of hope when the abyss tried to entice me into self-doubt. For a healed world.

I was Zoe Eferhild, Realm-Healer—Emerging of Legends. I was worthy of this fight, and I would go to battle for the peace of realms until there was no longer breath in my lungs.

"There's my warrior," Elvy said, turning to pull me into his embrace. I hadn't meant to project my thoughts into him, but I must have. Or he'd seen the resolve in my eyes. He just knew me that well.

I kissed him with passion, sucking his bottom lip into my own. He gripped my braid in his hands, pulling my body flush against his. There was something desperate in our kiss, as if our flames knew something dreadful that we didn't. As soon as we left this realm, the crushing weight of reality would demand to be felt. And this was war—there was no guarantee that everyone I loved would get out of this alive. I jumped into his arms, wrapping my legs around him, deepening the kiss. I would not let death or fate have him. He was *mine.*

He met my fervor and trailed kisses down my neck. He was right here—real and safe.

"I love you," he said it like a promise.

I gripped his face in my palms. I didn't know if it was my gift of discernment or prophecy, but I had the uncontrollable urge to tell him my next words. My stomach dropped with the familiar feeling of intuition.

"I will always find you. No matter the realm I have to cross or the blood I have to spill, I will find my way to you," I said with fear in my shaking voice. It rocked with a rage I couldn't place.

"What is it, Zoe?" he asked, reading the emotion in my voice. "Did you *see* something?"

I tried to lean into my gift, but it was fuzzy. Nothing was clear.

"No, but I feel…" I said, still holding him close to me. I rallied my gift of sight—it would answer my demand. I received no images, but I spoke my next words with conviction. "We are bonded in more ways than one, flame. It's how we'll find our way back home. Always."

"We're not leaving each other's sides. Never again," he swore.

"You don't know that," I said, shaking my head, eyes begging him to remember this moment, even if neither of us understood what it meant. "Promise me you will remember my words."

"I swear," he said, solidifying his vow with one last kiss.

4

Court of Algol
FREYJA

I'd never gotten used to how I feel—a soul between worlds. The pull to go back to the realm of the dead grew stronger daily, but I wasn't ready to go when the fate of my sister was still so fragile. And Mom—her burning light was gone from existence entirely. And Dad had never seen the killing blow coming. How could he when Hesperia hadn't even touched him? And I did nothing but stare in dismay—unseen. What more could the universe take from me—from my family? I shook the thought from my mind, not wanting to tempt the stars to do just that.

The viper inside me, though? It wanted to tell the stars to screw off.

Zoe had looked so beautiful—happy. Even though only a select few could see me, the tears that fell from my eyes as I stood by her on her joining day were nothing but joyful. She deserved to feel that way after bearing the shame of the night I died for so long on her shoulders. I hated that I'd pushed us to go out that night. I knew it was neither of our fault. We'd just come across bad people at the wrong time. Still—I hated how weak I was now. My older sister always referred to me as the strong one, but strength mattered little once you died.

I was only a mirage of an existence. Only the immortals from Algol could see me—touch me—if I could manifest my form substantially enough to allow that, but even some of those in Algol were not gifted in seeing the dead. It grew more difficult with the passing of each day. Some exhausted part of me was ready to rest. A deeper, secret part of me believed my sister could bring me back. She was stubborn enough to get it done, but now with war on the way to the realms, my own desires had to take a backseat. I understood that, yet I wasn't ready to give up hope. Not yet.

I stood outside on the balcony of Oleander's palace in Algol. I'd come to watch the snow fall and blanket the ground below. We were protected here at the moment. With Algol bonded to Zoe, Oleander's magic was even stronger now. He would protect those who relied on him with his life. I kept him at arm's length, though. Letting someone close to me was selfish. I was nothing more than a nuisance in this form—a liability. Hesperia was a genuine threat to my existence, as she'd shown with the way she'd burned my mother's spirit away.

Everyone here had enough to worry about, so I'd tried to make myself useful. I spent most of my time in the refugee camps, helping where I could. Most of them were accepting of me, but were curious. A loud handful were leery of me, though. So, I'd stopped going there, too.

That was the problem with death. I didn't belong anywhere.

"You must be cold," a smooth voice said from beside me—Oleander.

"The weather means nothing to me," I retorted. "I never get cold or hot anymore."

He stepped closer, so he was standing beside me, gazing at the mountains in the distance. I swore I felt his warmth, but it was just an illusion. Nothing more than a feeble wish.

"Have you not warmed to me?" he asked, with a pouting lip. I kind of wanted to bite that lip, but I'd never tell him that. His silver-blonde hair and sparkling blue eyes made me weak at the knees. Having him think I hated him was easier for both of us, though.

"Sorry, Oleander. My heart is made of ice."

He leaned in closer, and I didn't flinch away. My libido was a traitorous little thing. I didn't even know how sex would work in this form, but she didn't seem to care.

"Ice melts, sweetheart," he whispered, a breath away from my ear.

I turned my head so that I could meet his piercing gaze. Smile full of charm, I said, "Don't hold your breath."

His brilliant grin lit up his face, ready to go to battle with my banter. Thankfully, Zadie interrupted before I did anything stupid, like fall for the Lord Astral.

"I'm back from the delegation," Zadie said, sauntering in with a walk that would put mortal models to shame.

"How did it go?" Oleander asked. He hadn't moved an inch from my side, and I tried not to notice.

"It's freezing out here," Zadie responded, hands on her hips. "Can we go inside?"

"Sure," he responded, holding his hand in front of us. "After you."

I rolled my eyes, following Zadie's brilliantly red hair into the small library. It was an intimate room with a stunning fireplace carved from varying shades of gray stone that went up the length of the black walls. I perched on the red chaise, and he plopped down beside me, pouring himself a drink. It smelled of cinnamon.

If there was anything I particularly missed about my mortal life, it was the food. My spirit had no need for such sustenance now.

"Go on," Oleander instructed.

"Elvy, Zoe, Blaz, and Clodovea are leaving for Rigil. I assume they will arrive soon. Delmira, Finnian, and Imelda are staying in Vega."

"I assume Zoe is looking for The Archer's bow?" Oleander asked.

"Yes. Delmira is in command of Vega in their absence. Finnian is working on understanding the magic that vile witch plans to use."

"Good. I'm sure Finn will find something. Why are they going to Rigil?"

"Elvy is close with Sierra and Terran. Zoe will try to *see* the bow there. It's as good a plan as any," Zadie said, shrugging.

"Yes, we are a little out of our depth here," Oleander agreed.

"What should we do?" I piped up, wanting to help my sister in any way that I could.

"Elvy and Zoe sent healers with me to help the refugees," Zadie said. "They also requested we persuade the Sublunary to go to each of the courts."

"For what purpose? I imagine each court's Shadowed Legion has capable warriors?"

"We can't be certain that all courts will align with us," Zadie suggested. "The rebels will know where the other realm's weaknesses are, and they're valuable reinforcements."

"They're incredibly secretive," Oleander said, but I also saw the resolve in his eyes. "We don't really know what they're capable of.

I don't know if it's a good idea to send them off to the realms, and I can't get a true read on the unallied."

"Yet, you allow them in your court, Lord Astral," Zadie countered.

"Because I had no choice," he spat.

"Wrong," I disagreed. "You could've reached out to the Court of Vega. They would've helped you."

There was anger in his eyes, but he didn't disagree either. I'd learned that his mask could be a weakness for him.

"I'll talk to the Sublunary leader tomorrow," he conceded.

"I can't believe Zoe is risking her life and the lives of every immortal in Algol by going to Rigil or any of these realms," Zadie muttered in frustration.

Now my icy anger flared. "Zoe has sacrificed more than you know. Whatever she chooses to do, she does it with others in mind first."

"You trust her with your life?" Zadie asked.

"Yes." It wasn't me who answered, but Oleander. "Zoe knows the risks."

"I hope you're not wrong," she responded with sincerity.

"We haven't trusted others outside of you and me for a long time, Zadie," Oleander said, stepping towards her. He brushed a hair out of her face, comforting her. "It is time we learned to trust others, or our immortals will suffer the consequences of that."

Zadie nodded with silver in her eyes. I turned my attention back to the snowy mountaintops through the window. If Zoe failed, I would cease to exist. All spirits would be gone, just as my mother now was.

"Penny for your thoughts, sweetheart?" Oleander asked, sitting close to me. Zadie was gone for the night.

"Zoe has found her way… it's time I find mine. With whatever time I have left, I want to make it count."

I wasn't sure if he noticed the twinge of desperation in my voice, but I did. It reminded me of how Zoe and I had lived life on the edge with every spontaneous decision we'd made. It's like we both knew we'd die young and liked to tempt fate to greet us as soon as possible.

"Freyja… don't speak like we've already lost," he said. "I'm supposed to be the doom and gloom one."

"Regardless if we win this war, Ander," my ivory cheeks would have flushed with embarrassment at the slip of my tongue if they were capable. It was confusing the amount of times he crossed my mind in a day. "Oleander."

"Oh no, I quite like Ander," he said, slipping an arm around me. He grinned as if he'd won a point in our never-ending disagreements.

I only rolled my eyes and continued, "Win or lose—I am dead. I can't stay forever. You all seem to forget that."

"I will hold on to hope for both of us then," he said, simply. "Life would be dull without the bite of your ice."

My body betrayed me and leaned in just a little closer to him. Regrettably, he noticed it. Before he could speak words that would endear him to me more, I said, "I have to go."

"Are you hiding from me?"

"I guess you'll never know. Your magic doesn't work on me," I said, stepping further away.

"It is infuriating," he purred. "Do whatever you need, Freyja. Run for now if you must. I'm not going anywhere."

Before I could shoot back into his arms, I darted down the hall to what Oleander had designated as my quarters. He would never come here unless invited to do so.

The walls were the same black stone throughout the rest of his palace. A fireplace burned and acted as a focal point in the room. Across from the fire was my black canopy bed, and I flopped down onto the gold comforter. It didn't feel soft or hard. It just existed as I did. At times, I felt as though I was haunting this place.

I glanced at the mirror beside the armoire in the corner and didn't recognize the girl who stared back. I was the exact same as the night I'd been assaulted and killed by the worst kind of humanity. If I allowed it, my form could revert to the moment I died—bruised, scraped up, bloody, *broken*. It took energy to make sure I didn't look like that. I'd hate for Zoe or anyone to see me in that state. I was dead, and I needed no more looks of sympathy.

Exhausted from the energy I'd been exerting in keeping my form substantial, I allowed it to dim a bit—more transparent. I assumed the surrounding air was now much cooler, but I couldn't feel that for myself.

Another con of being dead? No sleep. Which meant no dreams—no distractions from my mind.

Even in this form, I had to clench my legs, squirming in want—need—of Oleander. I mean, ghost sex? The universe was cruel. My mother had raised us on the eighties and nineties movies, so Swayze was a prominent figure in my mortal teenage years. Swayze managed to get it on while a ghost, so maybe... but that movie also ended with him staying dead.

Sighing, I closed my mind to that train of thought and resigned myself to flip open a smutty romance novel. I might as well get my vice from somewhere, since sleep wasn't an option. I was soon lost to the world of a nonsequential story about forbidden love, and I let the weight of the world drift from my shoulders with every turn of the page.

5

Court of Rigil

ZOE

We flew in formation through the swirling portals of the cosmos that bridged the realm of the stars together. Elvy and I were in the center with Jelly to my right. Clodovea was to Elvy's left, and Blaz was on the other side of Jelly. I was finally in enough control of my massive wings to handle realm travel. Jelly kept up easily with us as we moved hastily to the Realm of Centaurus where the Court of Rigil was located.

My wings were a beautiful mix of turquoise and black against my shoulders. They were also marked with the same swirling cosmos that lived on my arm, which made little sense to me, but the celestials were nothing less than mysterious. Elvy, Blaz, and Clodovea all had similar translucent wings that were different shades of blue, representing their source of life in the water element.

We weren't sure if Hesperia would try to attack us while traveling, but we didn't want to chance anything. We all had our immortal marks shining brightly against our wrists to give us as much power as possible if needed. A break in the tunnel of starlight was just up ahead. Just a few more seconds and we would cross the barrier to the Court of Rigil.

I couldn't feel Hesperia anywhere and knew we were in the clear for now, at least.

"Now!" Elvy shouted as we all dove for the break in the cosmos.

As soon as we crossed the barrier, the sound of the whirling wind silenced, and we were met with another star-filled night sky in the realm of the stars.

I wasn't sure what I'd been expecting, but out of all the traveling I'd adventured to while on Earth, I'd seen nothing quite like this realm.

There were floating pieces of… the ground big enough to hold a small mortal suburb that seemed to all connect, creating bridges to the cities. We flew lower, gliding past them and over the water below us, approaching a vast landmass with glittering lights scattered throughout. While the ocean was not nearly as magnificent as Vega's, the breeze felt just as calming. The buildings seemed to be made up of nature itself, but there was still a sophistication to them. Some of the taller buildings looked like smooth metal, while others were more like the adobe homes I'd seen road-tripping through New Mexico. Even still, I caught glimpses of light in the trees, and upon further investigation with my immortal eyes, I found stunning treehouses with lanterns along the wooden bridges.

Elvy seemed to be leading us to the city center. Below us, the paths were mostly ground and stone, but completely smooth at the same time. Just as in Vega, there were no vehicles. Immortals seemed to either walk or fly, but I didn't see any train or public transportation. That didn't mean it didn't exist, though. The closer we got to what had to be the home of Sierra and Terran, glowing fauna started sprouting as we crossed above the surface.

"An alert system," Elvy said, flying close to me. Vega had similar iridescent plants, but I'd never seen them do that before. "It's time."

I nodded, banishing my wings, while he caught me in his waiting arms mid-flight. We'd decided to wait until we landed to display my markings from Algol. We may trust our friends more than other courts, but we couldn't be too careful.

The building we descended on seemed to comprise a combination of various materials found within the ground. There were diverse stones, clay, wood, and jewels. The elements were used to create some semblance of a work of art that I didn't want to look away from. It reminded of intricate mosaics that were also functional.

A circle of Rigil's Shadowed Legion waited for us down below. Blaz's stiff posture let me know he was on high alert, but Clodovea seemed more at ease as a smile crossed her face at whom I assumed were Sierra and Terran.

Sierra had skin as dark as the night sky above, with striking silver hair that contrasted beautifully. Her dark gaze was piercing, but the friendly smile across her face was only inviting. Terran was a handsome male with brown-blonde hair. The silver scattered in his hair marked him as a Shadowed. Both of their immortal marks on their wrists glowed emerald green.

"Elvy—brother—it has been too long," Terran spoke, holding out his hand. Sierra followed closely behind him.

"Indeed, it has," Elvy agreed, motioning towards me. I noted Blaz and Clodovea stepped just slightly closer to me. "This is my wife—my flame—Zoe."

I held out my right hand to shake Terran's, and he glanced down at my wrist in confusion. "Where's your immortal mark?"

"Can you keep an open mind?" Elvy asked, jaw clenched slightly.

"Zoe is special," Sierra stated. "I can feel it. Go on. Reveal your truth."

My court looked to me for confirmation. I closed my eyes, leaning into my gift and found no ill intent before us.

I opened my eyes, calling my wings forth. Sierra did not so much as flinch. I held out my left arm, displaying the mark of the immortals that was so different from every other one. I wore long sleeves to keep the rest of my scars and tattoos covered. Traditionally, an immortal's mark was on their right wrist. But me? Nope. The celestials just had to make something else different about me and put it on my left. It was admittedly the least weird thing about any of my immortal features. So much so that it was one we had easily glossed over when I'd first Emerged given that everyone thought I'd died when I'd turned to stardust.

"You aren't here on a casual visit," Terran stated.

"I'm afraid not," Elvy answered. "We don't wish to bring harm to your realm, Terran, but war is here. We must prepare."

Jelly inched closer, sniffing the Lord and Lady Astral. They looked at her curiously. When Jelly wagged her tail, my muscles relaxed. I trusted Jelly's instincts above all else.

"And you brought a simargl," Terran said, shaking his head in disbelief. "What have you been up to, Elvy?"

"Follow us," Sierra said, turning towards the entrance of their home.

Clodovea moved to Sierra's side after looking to Elvy for approval. He nodded, and I held onto his hand for dear life, and followed behind our hosts. Jelly brushed her wing against me, letting me know she would protect me. That had become a new thing for her—to use her wings to communicate with me.

"Clodovea, it's wonderful to see you again," I overheard Sierra say, tone kind. "I trust Imelda is well?"

"She's keeping me on my toes," Clove laughed easily with the Lady Astral. "Couldn't do life without her. Nor would I want to."

I refocused my attention on my surroundings, letting the two friends catch up. I gazed in wonder at the living trees that created a hallway down the center of the home. Lanterns kept the place brightly lit. Our entourage continued down similar passageways, and my ears popped, indicating we were well beneath the surface. I'd never been claustrophobic, but I wasn't sure I liked the idea of being underground in what felt like a labyrinth. In the corner of my eye, I noticed a group of immortals loading wooden boxes marked for Arcturus onto a larger crate, which I hoped was a good sign for the fire realm.

Elvy's thumb circled my hand softly, reassuring me. I could no longer hear the ocean and relied on the comfort of my flame to regulate me. However, as we got closer to our destination, the familiar sound of a roaring river soothed me. A smile broke across my face as we crossed over a beautifully carved bridge, intertwined with vividly green vines. I felt like I was in some underground terrarium. The grotto smelled of dirt and freshly cut grass, but still felt like a home.

We stopped on the other side of the bridge, and Sierra spoke. "Your rooms are just around that corner. Follow the river that way. Elvy, Zoe, and your companion, you all are in the first. Clodovea in the next. Blaz in the last."

"We will meet in the dining room through there as soon as you have time to freshen up from your travels. An hour?" Terran asked.

We all nodded, banishing our wings.

"You will be safe here. No one can cross this bridge without my or Sierra's approval," Terran promised. "I'll leave you to it."

"Blaz, you've been so quiet," I mentioned, nudging him with my shoulder. Jelly bumped her head against his other side. Jelly may be my guardian, but Blaz and Jelly had a special bond all their own.

"I can't afford any distractions," he said simply.

"The carefree Blaz that we all know and love is for our eyes only," Clodovea explained. "He is always like this around others."

"Does that bother you?" I asked.

"No. The safety of my court is my top priority," he said simply.

"No one could ever doubt your dedication, Blaz," Elvy said, nodding to his oldest friend.

We'd arrived at our door and agreed to meet up in a bit.

"Go on with Uncle Blaz," I said, scratching Jelly's ears. "He needs your help."

Blaz almost protested, but he saw the command in my eyes.

"Yes, my lady," he said, smirking. "Let's go, Jelly."

I turned to follow Elvy into our bedroom for the duration of our stay. It was larger than I'd expected and uniquely beautiful. The room had a wooden bath, large enough to fit two immortals with their wings out off to the side. A smaller bathroom was through another door. The wooden canopy bed was the focal point of the room. The vines and trees that made up the posts were clearly still alive. Twinkling lights were interwoven throughout. This magic was incredibly charming. I had a feeling that was a deception. Mother Nature was a powerful mistress.

"Are you tender?" he asked, checking my back. I was still getting used to my wings. Since Elvy was born immortal and Shadowed, he couldn't even remember learning to fly, but he still made a point to make sure I was okay first.

"A little," I admitted, rolling my shoulder blades to sprout my wings. "That's the furthest I've traveled with them. It didn't hurt while flying, but now…"

Elvy was already starting the bath. "We have time to take care of you."

I sighed, grateful. I didn't think there was any primal hunger from either of us at the moment.

He began stripping off his clothes and helping me out of mine. The bath filled quickly, and he gently placed me in front of him.

"Should I let my wings go?"

"No, I'll work on them. Just because they aren't visible doesn't mean they hurt any less," he explained, and I agreed. I was all too familiar with invisible pain.

He worked a kneading oil into my translucent but still substantial wings, and I groaned, curling my toes. How could something hurt so badly, but feel so euphoric at the same time? Not that long ago, I would have scoffed at the idea of any man, or person for that matter, massaging the back of my neck, yet here I was—craving more of it. The back of my neck had been the biggest trigger point in my body for my flashbacks while still mortal and struggling to heal from PTSD and the trauma that had caused it. With Elvy? I wanted more. More touch. More of him. More time. Just… more.

I feared that all of my trauma symptoms would come back after everything that had happened on our wedding day, but I would face them if they did. I only wished I could heal my brain the way

I could provide the same release for others. Wishing only made my pain worse, so I shook the thought from my mind and focused on Elvy's touch.

"Vega, that feels incredible," I said, smelling the fresh lavender of the oil.

"It'll get easier the more you use them," he said, moving those magic fingers to another part of my wing. I yelped in surprise, and he unsuccessfully tried to stifle his laugh. "Sorry."

"No, you aren't," I teased.

"Perhaps not," he mused.

"Are we going to tell them everything?" I asked.

"Everything they need to know," he responded. "I was hoping we could use your gift to decide what to tell them."

"I didn't get any bad vibes from them, but I'll keep my *sight* open. I'll send word through the bond if my gut says we are broaching an unsafe topic."

"I have always been able to count on Terran and Sierra, but with everything going on—I hate to even think I can't trust them," he said, voice laced with fatigue.

"That's what Hesperia wants us to believe. That we are isolated—alone. We've got to be willing to let others in. That's what will help us win—the belief in the goodness of each other." I tasted the truth of my words and knew the celestials had placed that on me.

"And we have to believe we possess that goodness, too, Realm-Healer," Elvy said, pulling me against him, and I let my wings go for now.

"Just a few more minutes," I mumbled, wishing nothing more than to stay here in his arms. "Thank you for that."

He kissed the top of my hair and held me until we could wait no longer to meet our fate.

6

Knives

ZOE

The rational part of me knew that I was underground, but the emotional part of my brain truly believed I was beneath the starlit sky. I felt as if I were having dinner in an enchanted forest. The trickle of the underground river provided a soothing song as we gathered together around a wooden table that still seemed to breathe life into the surrounding air. Branches of trees created a canopy above us, and peeking through the leaves was an illusion of the cosmos. Terran and Sierra had incredibly powerful, elegant magic.

Our meal consisted mostly of fruits and vegetables prepared in a variety of ways. There were no meat options, which was just as well. The food was mouth-watering as it was. Jelly seemed a little miffed that she would not be getting any meat slyly given to her by Blaz tonight. Nonetheless, she didn't turn up her nose at the sweet potatoes he was slipping her, so she'd survive.

"Dare I ask the urgency of your visit, Elvy?" Terran asked, taking a drink of his wine. He hadn't batted an eye when I'd asked for something without alcohol. I sipped my delicious, fruity concoction happily.

"Things have gotten worse with Hesperia," Elvy started. "We need to prepare the Shadowed Legions of the courts who will stand against her."

"We thought Hesperia was contained in Algol?" Sierra asked, chewing on some colorful fruit I'd never seen before.

"The damage was more severe than we'd initially thought when she severed the bonds between Sirius and Algol," Clodovea said.

"Algol was dying," I clarified. "Leaking its poison to Earth. To my home."

Terran cocked a head at me curiously. "You are an Emerging." It wasn't a question.

"Your scent… it's different," Sierra said, crinkling her nose.

I looked at Elvy, and he nodded his head in confirmation. Blaz flanked my left as I stood from my seat. Jelly circled me protectively on my right. Vega help anyone who tries to make a move on me now. Jelly hadn't incinerated anyone yet, but I felt like she could. My little fluffy dragon.

I rolled my shoulders back, exposing my wings to them again for all the glory they were. I waved a hand over my mark so that it glowed in the colors of Algol and Vega. A phantom caress from my flame brought me comfort from across the room. His stormy gray eyes burned into mine. For the briefest of moments, I let him in, and he showed me the way he saw me. Ethereal. More than his equal.

Terran and Sierra studied me longer than our brief greeting outside their home. I saw it in their eyes when my true identity clicked.

"You brought an immortal of Algol to my home?" Terran questioned. He hadn't left his seat, but the stiffness in his jaw indicated he was on edge. Jelly and Blaz moved in closer. Clodovea remained by Elvy.

"No, Terran," Sierra disagreed. "She's both. Algol and Vega."

"Not possible," Terran muttered in disbelief.

"Your eyes do not deceive you, husband," Sierra said with a soft smile on her lips. "Tell us what you need."

I looked at Terran, and he nodded for me to continue. It was clear he trusted his wife implicitly.

"Hesperia must be killed," I stated bluntly. "We believe she aims to bond back to Earth and reverse the elemental tethers into Algol. We cannot be sure what she really wants, but we know she desires to have the five elemental realms at her mercy."

I allowed my invisible magic from Algol to expand from my consciousness into the Lord and Lady Astrals. They had shields, which was to be expected. I easily broke through them, *seeing* their intentions. Their auras were pure. They had no plans to meet with Hesperia, and there was no sign that they would easily sway to her side. I couldn't *see* anything specific, but I got a sense they were *good*.

"That's impossible," Terran said, repeating himself.

"I would remove that word from your vocabulary when it comes to my Lady Astral," Blaz said, speaking for the first time. Terran was about to comment, but Sierra held her hand to stop him. I took that as my cue to continue.

"Once she has killed the mortals of Earth, we assume she will try to bond to another mortal plane. We don't know where. But I doubt she will care whether the elemental realms survive her pursuit of power."

"Can she actually bond back to Earth? Why would she sever the tether in the first place?" Terran asked. Fair questions.

"She can't permanently align Algol back to Earth, no. But we know she plans to come for each of you. It's some kind of perverse magic. We have our best trying to figure it out."

We couldn't tell them about The Archer's bow. This fear is exactly why she must die before we weave the realms back together.

"We simply won't help her," Terran stated.

"I don't think she is taking 'no' for an answer," Blaz retorted. He was sassy today.

"She will take what she needs," I agreed.

"So you must prepare for battle, brother," Elvy advised. "We don't know what she needs from The Astrals, but she will come for you both."

"How do you plan to stop her?" Terran asked.

"We kill her. Working on the details of how to do that."

"If she can bleed, she can die," Blaz said.

"Then we bond Algol permanently back to Earth, restoring spirit properly. Oleander will rule as Lord Astral," Clodovea said.

I paced around the room, Jelly following my every move.

"Oleander is poison," Terran said. How wrong he was. His misplaced hatred kept him from asking the obvious question: how do we plan to weave Algol back to Earth?

I paused in my pacing. "Do not say one negative word about Oleander. He is far braver and more selfless than you could imagine." There was venom in my voice, and the darkness swirled within me. I wanted to rip off Hesperia's vulgar hands for the things she'd made him do.

"I can see we misspoke," Terran said apologetically.

I breathed deeply, listening to the river.

"Your eyes… they went black for a second," Elvy said through our flame.

"I don't know if it's the shadows or Algol anymore. It's becoming difficult to tell them apart. I'm holding too much in," I said, on the verge of a spiral.

Jelly nudged me with her wings. I had a mission. I couldn't lose control every time someone said something stupid.

"How will you restore Algol back to Earth and the other star realms?" Terran asked. I sighed. He was full of questions.

"You'll just have to trust me," I said, voice steady.

"Again, I ask you, Zoe Eferhild. What do you need from the Court of Rigil? You shall have it," Sierra said.

"I need to search your realm for something that belongs to me. Don't ask me what it is. I cannot tell you that. I am bound by that oath."

Sierra and Terran both nodded their heads, giving me their permission and their respect.

"There's one more thing," Elvy said. "We need to plead our cause to the King and Queen. We don't know if Hesperia has gotten to them yet, but if the courts should fall, Sirius is the last hope."

"It will be done," Sierra swore. "We will provide you with horses to aid in your search of our realm with the rising of the morning moon."

"Rest," Terran said. "Sierra and I have preparations to make with our Shadowed Legion."

"She will go for your wards around the power source for Rigil," Blaz said.

"Let us know if we can be of assistance," Clodovea offered. "It will take all of us to win."

"Thank you," Sierra nodded, standing from her seat. Terran led his wife away, with hushed whispers following them.

"What now?" Blaz asked, arms crossed. "I'm too amped up to go to sleep."

"I agree. Let's train," I suggested. Blaz had once offered to bear whatever I needed. I would do the same for him.

After we'd all changed into training gear, Clodovea led us expertly through the underground tunnels until we came upon what seemed like a state-of-the-art training room. It was similarly equipped as Vega's with cardio machines, weights, rope courses, rock walls, and my favorite—a punching bag.

I moved towards the punching bag, but Blaz pulled me to a set of dummies instead. Elvy gave me a swift kiss on the cheek and a wink before he made his way to the climbing wall with Clodovea, and I was a little jealous. That seemed kind of fun.

"You need to learn to work with your knives better," Blaz said.

"I thought you said that I just needed to put the pointy end into the bad guy, and I was golden," I said, with a whine to my voice that was out of character for me.

"That works in a pinch, but I know you, Zo. You need this," he said, positioning the fake opponent.

My eyes landed on the bow behind Blaz.

"Shouldn't I learn to do that first?" I asked.

"Bows are great for long-ranged attacks… but you need to know how to defend yourself in the heat of battle. Besides, I have a feeling that The Archer's daughter will know what to do with a bow. A knife? Doubtful."

"Fine," I said, placing a hand on my hip. "What do I need to learn, oh wise one?"

"It helps if you know where to put the sharp end."

I unsheathed my knives and pointed to the throat and heart. "Those seem like obvious choices."

"That's part of the problem," Blaz said, sliding his knife to the heart of the dummy. "The heart is well protected, and not the best for a knife fight. You have to get through too much bone and tissue, and the angle has to be right. The neck is usually more exposed. Go for the jugular, though, to make them bleed the most."

He brought me to the back of the dummy, slicing through the spine. "This is also effective if you have the strength to do it, and I think you do."

I swallowed, taking my stance back in front of the dummy. I briefly glanced over to see Elvy and Clove halfway up the wall. There was no backing out of this.

"Begin," he directed.

I dug my knife into the side of the neck, and fake blood spurted out.

"Nice. Now, incorporate some kicks—roundhouse, single-legged, and punches. Then we'll move to training against each other."

The hum of energy flew through me, and my soul loved the violence and sweat that dripped down my back. This I could handle. It was like dancing with purpose, and I relished the feeling of expending the pent-up magic inside me.

Soon, I was lost in the art of combat, soaking up every word Blaz said. I blocked out all other distractions except the commands of Blaz and my target. When I faced Hesperia again, I would not fail.

It didn't take long before I was landing my throws with precision, as if I'd been throwing knives at people my whole life. Maybe if I had been, things would be different and Freyja would still be alive. I shook the thought from my head. What's done was done. I would bring Freyja back. Somehow. In the meantime, I would make myself strong enough to do what was impossible.

I could tell Blaz was fatigued by his unsteady movements, but he said nothing, willing to go as long as I wanted to. He would be and do anything for me. My adrenaline was coursing high, but beneath it, I felt myself tire.

"That's enough for tonight," I said, sheathing my weapons.

Blaz nodded, patting me on the back. Elvy stood off to the side, looking concerned, but he hid it well. No one else would have noticed it. Jelly bumped her head against my leg, and I reassured her with head scratches. Clodovea was nowhere to be found. How long had we been going for?

"Hours," Elvy answered through our bond.

"I didn't realize…" I trailed off.

"It's okay, my starlight. We will give you whatever you need."

He walked over, kissing me feverishly.

"I didn't realize how late it was," I murmured, eyes heavy.

"No kidding," Blaz said sarcastically. "Even I am going to be hurting in the morning, Zo."

I gripped his wrist, finding the water pendant I'd given him, and sent more of my healing magic.

"That should help," I said, smiling sleepily.

"You didn't need to do that," he said, holding onto the magic seeping from the pendant.

"I know," I said, as Elvy swooped me into his arms, and I fell asleep before we'd even made it out the door.

But my dreams were not peaceful. Flashes of death permeated my nightmares. One after the other, those I loved perished, and there was nothing I could do to save them. The corpse of my mother seemed to blame me, and I let the shame of my failures sink in. What petrified me most of all was Elvy's lifeless face staring back at me. Everything was red again, and I couldn't tell the difference between my *sight* and my trauma. I didn't trust myself to discern what was real, so I rode the waves of torment, praying I'd wake and find it all to be a bad dream, but I knew my reality… and I would burn.

7

The Sublunary

FREYJA

We sat in one of the central buildings in the refugee village, hidden by magic and the forest near Oleander's castle. The Sublunary leader had agreed to meet with us around dispersing the unallied to the other courts to help the established Shadowed Legions. It wasn't going well so far. Oleander kept his face cool, but the telltale signs of his frustration were showing—a death glare and left brow raised. His clenched fists showed he was almost at his breaking point.

"Tiergan, I'm not sure what is so difficult to understand," Oleander said, voice leveled.

"Why should we help those who serve the celestials? We are not bound to them."

"Yet you are here," the Lord Astral responded in exasperation.

"The immortals of Algol are innocent."

"So are the other courts," Oleander said, voice rising. "I don't think you understand. If we lose this war, these realms cease to exist, which means you no longer exist."

"Our life forces are not tied to the stars in the same way as yours."

"You cannot leave the star realms," he countered with knowing eyes. He wouldn't state it if he wasn't absolutely sure.

"We want things to change," Tiergan responded, clasping his fingers together.

"Don't we all?" he muttered, then shifted his voice louder. "What are your demands?"

"Please, Oleander. You make us sound unreasonable."

He closed his eyes, taking a deep breath. "What kind of changes would you like to see?"

"We want it to be as it once was. To freely choose which star to serve, or to serve multiple stars and keep the magic within us at our birth. We do not want to be forced into choosing a part of us over the other."

I understood their sentiments. Zoe had only wanted the same thing. The freedom to choose, so she had. She'd chosen herself, forcing the celestials to choose her instead. I'd never been more proud of her.

"I cannot control the celestials!"

"Maybe you can't," Tiergan said. "But Zoe Eferhild, Realm-Healer—Emerging of Legends can."

My eyes shot up at the mention of her name.

"We saw her true potential when she healed us during her visit to your realm. We believe she has the authority of the cosmos to do this."

Well, he wasn't wrong.

"I give you my word that she will do everything in her power to make this possible."

"Not good enough," the Sublunary leader shook his head. "We want to hear it from her."

Oleander stood and let the rumble of his power roll from him. I didn't think it was intentional, but I feared he'd blow if he didn't release some of his power soon.

"It's incredibly risky for Zoe to travel back to this realm with Hesperia as completely unhinged as she is now," he said.

Tiergan paused in his argument, as if weighing the pros and cons. I secretly and selfishly hoped for my sister to come back here. I missed her. Reading the letter she sent me when she'd first arrived in Vega could only do so much.

"We will show you a… let's call it a back door to this realm. Zoe comes and swears she will do this, then we will answer to her and her—alone."

"Fine," Oleander said, understanding that Tiergan was not budging on this. "I will go fetch Zoe. Though since you do not know Zoe Eferhild, there is no 'fetching her.' I ask that a handful of your Sublunary travel with me. Realm-travel is not safe right now."

"You shall have them." Tiergan bowed his head, finally agreeing to something.

"Great," Oleander said, voice still tense. Out of the corner of my eye, Zadie fumed.

"A word, Lord Astral," she said pointedly.

"Not now, Zadie. Please coordinate with Tiergan and prepare the Shadowed Legion for departure."

If looks could kill, Oleander would be dead by the way she stared at him, but she didn't argue and got to work. An irrational part of me wanted to move between them. He was only doing what he thought was right.

He stepped towards me, hands running through his perfectly styled hair.

"Walk with me?" he asked.

I nodded, following him out of the building. He guided us along a quiet path in the forest that smelled richly of pine. A creek flowed with the music of nature, creating a moment of calm after such an intense meeting.

"I'd watch your back. I think Zadie's had enough of you."

"She means well," he said with a small smile. "She's practically my only family, and I am for her, too. The thought of me dying is rather irritating to her, I think."

"I think Zoe would be pissed at you. Best avoid it then."

"And you?" he asked, looking more vulnerable than usual.

A smile played on my lips. I paused at a tree, leaning against it and crossing my arms. I wore a dark sweater and jeans that seemed appropriate in the snowy weather, though I supposed I could wear shorts and be fine. That was one cool thing about death, if there was such a thing. I only had to have enough energy to 'change my clothes.' With little thought, my modest sweater turned into one with a plunging neckline.

My body instantly screamed, 'abort mission!' Too little, too late.

"I don't know who I'd fight with if you were gone, Ander." I used the nickname that I knew would make him smile. My mouth simply would not shut up.

I wasn't expecting him to move closer, teasing me in a whole different way. He placed one hand above my head and leaned in close enough that I saw the black flecks in the blue of his eyes. His jaw rippled as he took in the sight of me.

"I want to be the only one you fight with, sweetheart," he said, breath smelling of peppermint. "I already told you—I'm not going anywhere."

He was so close that it clouded my judgement. *Crap.* I wanted to pull his lips to mine, but I couldn't do that to him. Leading him on would devastate us both in the end. I was dead. He was alive. He had an entire existence ahead of him if we won this war. If he wouldn't be reasonable, then I would have to be. Reasonable and responsible are not words that I thought I'd ever associate with myself. I thought death would mean I didn't have to try so hard.

"I can see that brain of yours turning, Freyja," he said, stepping away. The moment he did, it was as if the fog had washed away from me. "One day, you won't talk yourself out of what you feel."

"You don't know what you're talking about," I said, voice ice again.

"Oh, I see you, sweetheart," he paused, making me stop. "The moment you're ready, I'll be right here."

He kissed me on the cheek, and I could almost feel the heat of him, or at least, let myself believe I did.

"Please be careful," I said seriously.

"I will bring Zoe back safely," he promised, even though that's not what I'd meant. I didn't bother to correct him, though.

I watched his dark figure fading away into the forest, and I let myself pretend I was what he'd try to come back to.

There was a faint tug to what I'd dubbed 'the land of no return.' It was seductive in its own right, promising eternal peace, love, and light. I seemed to inherently know that door would not stay open forever. If I didn't go to it soon, it'd be lost to me.

Why did dying have to be so complicated?

8
The Search Begins
ZOE

We were still below ground, but we stood in the personal stables of Sierra and Terran. I'd never ridden much as a mortal, but these horses were much bigger than I'd ever seen. The reasonable part of me was a little afraid of them based on size alone. My sleep had been restless despite how tired I'd been after the training session with Blaz. Elvy had scrounged up some coffee for my caffeine-addicted self. Immortal or not, I refused to give up this vice. He didn't mention the circles under my eyes that I was certain were there. He didn't need to. Our flames felt my distress. He'd sent his healing magic through the flame, but his magic had no effect on the kind of exhaustion I was experiencing. This was in my soul and had nothing to do with a physical injury.

My eyes burned with fatigue, and my body felt like it was in a different time… in a different world. When the world felt unsafe and the faces from my nightmares lurked behind every corner. I took a few breaths, trying to remind my body of what my present truly was. On instinct, my nails dug into the soft flesh of my palm, but Elvy discreetly laced his fingers in mine before they broke skin.

"I'm here. This is real. You and me," he said through our flame.

My gravity.

I mentally shook off memories best forgotten and refocused my attention on our hosts.

"Have you ridden before?" Sierra asked me as she brushed a beautiful black stallion. His mane shimmered in the moonlight, with piercing blue eyes gazing at me intelligently. I focused my senses on him, taking me further away from those terrors.

"A little," I answered. "I'm certainly no expert."

"Damek will make you an excellent rider," she said, strapping a saddle onto the stallion. "Come."

Letting go of Elvy's hand, I cautiously tiptoed towards Sierra and the horse—Damek.

"Hold out your hand, Zoe."

I obeyed, and Sierra placed my palm on his pink nose. The coolness of his snout surprised me, but even more, the gentleness of Damek settled me. My *sight* flashed through my mind, and I received a brief image of me riding Damek across the lands of Rigil, arms spread wide—wild and free. Such a juxtaposition from what I'd felt moments ago. I couldn't help but wonder what my late grandmother would think about the horses of Rigil. She loved horses, and I hoped she was seeing all of this.

"Alright, Damek," I whispered. "You've got me."

He seemed to nod his head, and Jelly perked up her ears in wonder at her new friend. Damek leaned down, sniffing Jelly, and seemed to grunt in approval. She licked his nose, and he whinnied in response. They were fast friends, apparently.

"You ready to strap in, my good girl?"

Since Jelly couldn't ride a horse and her wings wouldn't allow her to keep up with us in the air just yet, she would ride strapped to me in a harness system. We'd attempted nothing like this, but

I trusted the bond between us. Jelly folded her wings back, and I buckled her straps around her.

When I finished, Elvy hoisted Jelly up onto my back and strapped her in, so I wore her like a backpack. She rested her head on my shoulder, content.

"Where are we going, my lady?" Blaz asked, already astride his silver horse. Clodovea was also ready on a brown and white spotted mare.

Closing my eyes, I leaned into the gift of Algol, trying to *see* The Archer's bow. My gut clenched, letting me know that something was here that I needed. I just wasn't sure what it was yet. A glowing white light emitted in front of me, guiding the way to our destiny.

"North," I said confidently.

"We will not pry," Terran said. "But be careful. We will begin working on our visit to King Aldrich and Queen Farron in Sirius."

"Thank you, brother," Elvy said, leaping onto his gray-spotted horse.

I heaved myself up onto Damek in one smooth motion and nodded my thanks to Sierra and Terran.

"Follow the tunnels. The horses will know where to go," Sierra offered.

I nodded as Damek trotted towards our target.

Before I could cross into the tunnels, Sierra called, "And Zoe?"

Pausing, I halted Damek in his tracks.

She slid a golden ring off her finger with the symbol for ground and gave it to me.

"What's this for?" I asked.

"It's infused with my magic… it packs quite a punch. Consider it a sign of my good faith," she said, backing away.

"Thank you." I bowed slightly and returned my attention to Damek to push on.

I had no idea how far away we would need to travel, but something told me this would not be a quick trip. Part of me regretted the intensive training last night, and I prayed I wouldn't get sore from riding. A good night's rest would have been useful, but fate had other plans.

We emerged from the underground tunnels, and the cosmos shone brightly above us. The cool breeze tossed my braid in the wind, and determination swept through me. I would not fail.

"North, Damek," I said, and he snorted, throwing us into a gallop.

***

We'd traveled across varying planes of glowing wildflowers with snow-capped mountains peeping in the moonlight. This realm smelled like the fresh dirt of Earth, and a twinge of sadness for my mortal life ran through me. I'd always been one to go on adventures, and they were almost always with Freyja. I did not know when I would see her again, but I knew she was safe as long as I was breathing and keeping Algol alive with my own life force. Here we were living in the most epic adventure of our lives, yet we could not do it together. Not yet.

I hadn't noticed too many differences yet in my body since tethering Algol to me. I felt a little more unstable, quicker to anger, and I craved more of the shadows within me. There was a part of me that feared that I would drown in them one day if I wasn't careful. I had to always remember that an entire realm depended on me to survive. I could not be so willing to sacrifice myself as I had once been. Then again, that was like telling water not to be wet.

Our entourage had stopped to let the horses rest. Jelly ran around them, and the horses seemed just as interested in playing with her.

"Any idea where you're leading us?" Elvy asked, sitting down next to me on the soft grass.

"Somewhere North. The path hasn't changed. Whatever we're looking for is there."

"Do you think we'll be lucky enough to find the bow on the first try?" Blaz asked, flopping down on the ground. His movements were smooth, as if his muscles weren't too sore, and I hoped my magical pendant had gifted him some relief.

I shook my head. "I don't think luck has much to do with it. Whether it's the bow or not, The Archer wants me to retrieve what is here. Maybe once we see what it is, we'll figure out the rest."

"Do you *see* any danger?" Clove asked.

"No, but that could always change. Right now? It feels like someone is stopping time—protecting us."

"The Archer," Elvy guessed.

"He's more mysterious and powerful than the legends said. He does nothing without intention," I said. "I mean, he even had June watching over me. I had no idea…"

"We didn't either, Zo," Blaz said, and I saw through his easy half-smile. It bothered him that he hadn't realized what June was. I'm sure it made it worse that we still didn't know everything about her. With everything going on in the star realms, there was such a lack of closure on so many things. We all had to take it one day at a time.

"I don't know why, but I have a feeling she's still at that rescue. I just can't picture her ever leaving—no matter what she is or isn't."

I munched on some dried fruit and took a swig of water. Stretching, I called Jelly back to me. Luckily, when we were riding, her body weight was held by Damek.

"We're getting close. I can feel it," I said.

Elvy helped strap Jelly onto my back and kissed my cheek before we all got onto our horses.

"Just a bit further, Damek," I said, stroking his mane. He nodded and put us into a fast cadence, heading North under the realm of stars.

★★★

We'd ridden another two hours, and my gut sent a piercing plea that I could not ignore. Instead of fighting it, I embraced it, allowing discernment to fill me. We were in the valley of a looming mountain. A seemingly unnatural fog hovered over us, and I checked my shields, making sure my mind was protected. Oleander had only been able to briefly show me how to extend my shield to others. I was only versed enough to extend it to one other person for now, so I covered Elvy. Not that he really needed it with his own impenetrable shield. My flame still demanded that I protect what was mine.

Flashes of images of an intricate cave system flew through my mind, but I didn't see an entrance anywhere.

"Look for an opening in the mountain. We're looking for a cave," I stated.

Damek and the horses he led navigated the rocky terrain with precision. When a flat surface revealed itself amidst the rubble, I jumped off Damek and let Jelly out. The gut instinct coursed through my body like a tsunami.

I circled around, trying to *see* what I needed to, but nothing came. I suddenly got the urge to go the opposite way I'd been traveling, and I bit my lip in confusion. The others seemed to have the same thought. Then, I remembered the magic that Oleander used to protect the refugees in Algol.

"Stop," I panted against the magic. "It's glamor."

The three of them blinked rapidly, seeing that I spoke the truth.

"You will stay here?" I asked Damek, and he nodded.

I ran my hand along the rough grooves of the mountain and found what I was looking for—something that didn't belong. Carved into the stone was the mark of the immortals—the same mark on all our wrists. Swallowing my fear of what might happen, I let my mark's magic shine brightly with blues and blacks. With a final steadying breath, I pressed my glowing wrist to the immortal mark, and the entire mountain rumbled.

Elvy and Blaz slung me behind them, shielding me with their bodies while Clodovea unsheathed her sword, ready to slaughter any who came near. However, once the dust settled, there was nothing but a cave entrance revealed to us. It was darker than the night sky above, but we had to enter.

The three of them cast a swirling ball of blue light that hovered above us, and it was a reminder of how little I knew about this world.

"Starlight," Elvy breathed. "Here, let me show you."

He patiently instructed me how to cast the starlight above me by pulling on the strings of magic connected to our source of power—Vega. Without too much difficulty, I summoned the orb of light for myself.

"Big breaths, everyone," I said, walking with purpose into the shadows.

9

Feather

ZOE

The air was stale inside the cave and smelled as if there was a spring somewhere nearby. The drips of water coming from the stalactites echoed like thunder throughout the intricate cave system. We relied on my gut to lead us through, and I prayed it rang true, or we may never get out of here.

We moved in silence, weapons at the ready and prepared for anything that might come our way. Jelly moved silently beside us, hackles slightly raised, as if she were on edge. Her flames stayed extinguished, but I wouldn't put it past her to ignite them if she felt we were threatened.

I didn't feel any other presence with us as we moved, but I couldn't shake the sense of dread either. We came to a part of the cave that required us to squeeze through a tiny crevice, and I tried to quiet my trembling frame. I'd never been claustrophobic before, but something about getting stuck in a cryptic cave for the rest of eternity freaked me out. My chest could barely expand for a full breath as I shimmied to the other side of the narrow rocks.

Eventually, we all came through and found ourselves in an enormous cavern with the moon shining high above. We might be able to fly out at the top, but we couldn't see how narrow it truly was.

There was nothing out of the ordinary about the cavern until I looked at the floor. There was an intricate design—a star with four cardinal points. In the center, there was a grooved circular pattern, and the moon shone directly on it.

"Any ideas?" Blaz asked, circling around the markings.

"Four points… four elements?" Clodovea suggested.

"We only have two represented here," Elvy said, thumb resting on his chin in concentration.

I tried to lean into my gift, but the stars were done helping me for the night and provided no further explanation. We would have to figure this out on our own.

Bending down to one point, I wiped away dirt from the years of zero disturbance and found the symbol for water.

"Check the other points," I instructed, and they did.

"Ground," Blaz said.

"Air," Clodovea added.

"And fire," Elvy confirmed.

I dusted off the circle in the center of the star and found the symbol for spirit beneath the layers of dust.

"Spirit," I whispered, but it echoed off the cavern.

The ring Sierra had given me glowed in my starlight, and I took a guess at what we needed to do.

"Elvy, stand over there on water," I instructed, and he obeyed.

I placed Sierra's ring that was infused with her elemental magic on the point for ground.

"That's two," Clove said, nodding her head in understanding of where I was going with this.

"Jelly," I called her to the fire element. "Sit."

She listened adamantly, and I was sure she understood me. "We'll need your flames in a bit, okay?"

Her only response was to pant happily, which I took as understanding.

"What about air?" I mumbled to myself.

"Would this work?" Elvy asked through our bond.

I looked in his direction and found his semi-translucent wings unfurled.

"Take a feather," he said.

I shook my head. *"We don't know that it'll work."*

I knew feathers represented air simply because I'd read many occult books trying to figure out what Elvy was while I was still mortal.

"Whatever psychic conversation you two are having, please clue us in," Blaz said, arms crossed and brows raised.

"Elvy wants me to pluck one of his feathers for the air element."

"No," Clodovea replied. "We don't know what kind of magic is here. It could take everything from you for trying to deceive it."

"We must try," Elvy said, resolute.

"Then I will do it," she answered.

"Oh, hell no," Blaz said, stepping in front of her.

"Logistically, I'm the best choice. You need to be ready if anything happens, Blaz."

Too quick to argue, Clodovea plucked a feather from her wing and winced at the pain only slightly.

"What now, Zoe?" Elvy asked.

I stood over the circular pattern in the middle of the cardinal star, trying to find the path to unravel this task.

"It's always about the beginning… and The Archer said I had to accept the truth of my blood. Only a true Daughter of Algol can wield his bow."

I unsheathed my knife, flipping it over in my hand.

"I know what I have to do," I told Elvy.

Before he could respond, I said, "No matter what you see. Do not cross the barrier once I start the process. I'm not sure what will happen to you or me if you do. Blaz, make sure Jelly stays put."

"I love you," Elvy whispered through our bond. *"Endlessly."* He said it like a warm embrace.

"Always," I responded.

I hovered above Sierra's ring and slit my palm open. With one final breath and a silent prayer for the celestials to be with me, I let a few drops of blood collide with the ring. The moment my blood made purchase, the ring sizzled and a path of starlight followed the marks on the floor to Elvy.

He allowed his water magic to splash on his element, and I once again let my blood drop to the floor in payment. Did everything have to come at a price? I knew the answer to that, though. The starlight moved towards Jelly.

I moved to her next. "We need your simargl fire, little dragon."

She bowed, allowing flames to scorch the symbol for fire. I had to cut my hand again and repeat the process. The starlight flowed to Clove's feather, and I prayed this would work.

Allowing my blood to fall on her feather, I sent one last plea to the cosmos. The moment the splash of blood reached her feather, Clodovea buckled to her knees, wailing in pain. The magic I had gifted in her pendant was of no use to her with this amount of destruction.

My initial instinct was to run to her, but the starlight continued its path to the circle around spirit. It trapped me inside the symbol as starlight shot up to the opening of the cave. I could no longer hear Clove screaming.

"The only way is through," I said. I sliced my poor hand open yet again. Elvy tried to heal it through our flame, but it was like the starlight created a barrier. Letting my blood flow down to the circle, I let a few tendrils of Algol's darkness touch the symbol. Starlight flooded through the mark of spirit, and the circle began spinning upwards. Stone ground against stone, and it took every ounce of willpower not to reach out my hand before it had finished moving.

An opening was carved into the rock, but it wasn't a bow. I almost didn't want to touch it, but this was what we'd come for. This was what Clodovea was enduring horrid pain for. I gripped the wooden structure, and it fit nicely in my hand, as if it were made for me to hold, with grooves fitted to my measurements.

The starlight vanished, and we all rushed to Clove's whimpering frame. Her beautiful blue wings, which reminded me of the glow of bioluminescence, were ravaged. My wings hurt just from using them… the amount of pain she was in… I couldn't imagine.

"We've got you," Elvy said, placing a hand on his third.

Blaz and I joined him, and all three of us sent our glow of healing magic into her. Jelly whined behind us, disliking seeing Clove in distress. Slowly, Clodovea's wings healed as the magic flowed through her. She sighed in relief as we repaired the worst of it. I imagined her wings would be of little use to her for a few days.

"Vega, that hurt," Clodovea said, but there was laughter in her voice, which put us all at ease.

"Imelda would have killed me if something had happened to you," Blaz said, grinning.

"Please tell me you got the bow," she said, sitting up. She couldn't hide the painful shudder in her movements.

"Come on. Let's get out of these creepy caves, and I'll show you," I said, leading the way out. Blaz swept her up in his arms, and Elvy clasped my hand in his as we walked back to the entrance.

"It was terrifying not to feel you—feel this," he said in our bond.

"We've got each other now," I reminded him, kissing his palm.

We eventually all surfaced from where we'd entered the cave, mostly unscathed. Damek and the other horses were where we'd left them, and they seemed disinterested in whether we came back as they munched on the plants they favored. However, he did whinny in acknowledgment that Jelly had made it out alive. She circled the horses, trying to taunt them to play. They seemed to find their small friend amusing.

"Let's see it," Blaz said, setting Clodovea gingerly on her own two feet.

I pulled the small wooden hand-like thing out and showed the group. Upon further inspection, there seemed to be two circular holes at either end, as if something was supposed to go there.

"Is that…?" Elvy asked, turning to Blaz.

"Oh yeah, that's a grip," he confirmed.

"A what?" I asked, turning it over in my hand.

"A grip for a bow," Elvy explained. "So it's part of The Archer's bow, I assume."

I took in the object more deeply and noticed the constellation carved into the wood.

"Of course, it couldn't already be put together," I groaned. "How many parts are we looking for, then?"

"Two limbs and a bowstring," Blaz informed.

"Where do you think…" Clove started, but my yelp put them on high alert.

I ripped my jacket off as searing pain went down what used to be my scar as a mortal. It felt like molten lava trickling down the scar tissue, and I clutched it in agony.

"What the fuck?" I yelled into the night sky.

Elvy was instantly at my side, and I cried out more. He was rubbing my back, sending healing magic through our flames, but it was no use. Whatever force in the cosmos wanted to burn me was going to do it.

"You will burn, Zoe Eferhild." Nova's words rang through me as a warning. She'd told me that during the star realm trials, and her words had been true in too many ways.

"Hilarious," I said through gritted teeth.

Eventually, it faded away, and the marks on my arm had changed.

"Can I see?" Elvy asked gently, holding out his hands.

I nodded as he sent cooling water over my arm, relieving some of the pain. He gently twisted my arm, examining the slight changes. What had been a swirling cosmos within the scar had changed into a more solidified line with cardinal stars along the length of it. The rest of my arm remained the same, marked with varying patterns of stars.

Elvy's forehead formed a worry line as he thought through the new marks. He held our hands together, moving his finger over the map of the constellations that told our story. Then he looked back over my arm again.

"Interesting," he said, clarity visible in his eyes. "It's a map."

I scrutinized my arm as he began pointing to the cardinal stars along the mark.

"This is the constellation for Centaurus, and the cardinal star is filled in. The next one is the Realm of Bootes—Court of Arcturus."

"That's our next target," I agreed, feeling the truth of my words.

"Do we still go to the King and Queen first?" Clove asked.

"We'll check in with Delmira and the rest back in Vega and decide from there. If Finnian has learned anything about how Hesperia plans to enact her plan, we'll need every bit of information he can give us. We'll also need a relic from the Court of Canopus for air before leaving for Arcturus. I don't think the trials will let us do that again," Elvy said, pausing and changing directions. "It's only a matter of time before Hesperia figures out Algol is bonded to another life source."

"Meaning me," I said.

"She won't touch you," Blaz swore.

"Agreed," Elvy promised. "Let's head back to Rigil for now."

"She doesn't have to physically touch me to harm me," I reminded them, voice shakier than I meant. "Not if she can get to Algol. Our bond is reciprocal."

Both of their eyes darkened in hatred, and I knew it terrified my flame to know this.

"Good thing you can heal me, flame," I said lightly, trying to bring him back to me.

"If she harms you ever again, she is dead," he promised. *"Screw the consequences."*

I didn't have the heart to argue with him, but a sense of foreboding filled me at his words. We all had to recognize that our actions had consequences. He and I most of all. In my heart, I knew he would be there to heal me if and when that time should come. Most likely when. Like he said, it was only a matter of time before Hesperia learned the truth and exploited it in the star's only knew what way.

I slipped Sierra's ring back on, feeling the pulse of the elemental magic infused in it. My gut instinct wasn't screaming at me, but it made itself known. I silently infused more of my magic into Clodovea's pendant, and stood up from where I'd been sitting.

My gut clenched tightly in warning. Everything was…quiet. Much too quiet.

"Let's move with caution," I said, strapping Jelly back into her harness. "Something doesn't feel right."

Elvy quickly helped me onto Damek, and Clodovea rode in front of Blaz, too weak to ride on her own.

"Move silently, Damek," I whispered. "Off the main trails."

He nodded his head and seemed to communicate this to the other horses. They moved soundlessly as if commanding the ground to muffle their noises. I wasn't sure what we were racing to, but we'd meet it head-on.

10

Gemini

DELMIRA

"I've never wanted to stab something so badly in my life. My hand is feeling twitchy," I said, twirling a knife in my fingers. My twin—Finn—promptly ignored me, and I was a minor inconvenience away from accidentally throwing it at him.

How Elvy kept up with the daily running of Vega was beyond me. I found it dull, but I forced myself to do it. He and Zoe both trusted me to take care of this realm, so I would. Never said I wouldn't complain about it, though.

I stared at the map before me, looking for any weaknesses in our defenses. Our link to Vega was as secure as I could make it, but our immortals were vulnerable. I had the Shadowed Legion on varying patrols, but we only had so many. The right magic could slip past us undetected, though our wards should give us a heads-up if anyone crosses. So far, it's been quiet, which makes me all the more anxious. Knowing what's out there...

Finn and I had been exhausting our magic. We had been using a low-level amount on as many immortals as we could, but that quantity depleted our reserves quickly. I'd been working mine to keep the Shadowed Legion calm and in order while my twin had been scanning for any traitors. He didn't pry unless needed, and his magic worked almost like a filter. He could align the vibrations of the psychic field to search for something specific—like keywords. My magic was more like sending distinct vibrations out into the universe, and I decided what the pulses felt like.

We'd both been charming kids growing up in the mortal world before our Emergence in the star realms. We had to be captivating living on the streets of New York City in the late 1800s. Skirting around the budding foster care system was our most treasured activity, and tricking foul old men out of money was a favorite pastime.

It'd always been us against the world, but even we couldn't outrun our past forever.

"I think I found something," Finn said, standing up from his seat beside Imelda and pulling me out of thoughts better forgotten.

They'd been in the Hall of Memories since Elvy, Zoe, Blaz, and Clodovea had left. They'd barely rested, and the food I'd sent them had gone largely uneaten. I'd forced them to come up for some fresh air, with much protest from both of them.

"You figured out Hesperia's magic?" I asked hopefully, though I knew he would have let me know the instant he'd learned something.

"No, the Hall of Memories is being coy about it," Finnian said, sounding a bit hurt. He'd always had a special bond with that sentient place. He was really the only one I knew of who actually enjoyed being there. I was impressed with the time Imelda had been spending there helping him.

"We're not sure what we found," Imelda admitted. "But we think it's worth checking out."

"Alright," I said, bouncing up from my chair. I wouldn't admit it to anyone else, but I wasn't far from going stir-crazy. "Lead the way."

I triple-checked my weapons again before following them out into the hall and down the stairs.

Just before we crossed the threshold that would lead us into the courtyard, Octavia waved us down from just outside the entrance to the library.

"Hello Octavia," Finn said in a friendly tone. My twin was a private male, but I was pretty sure they'd dated before and had remained good friends afterwards. A concept I didn't understand but respected… the thought of being friends with any of my exes made me want to vomit. Not that I really had exes. More like previous hookups that were never quite satisfying.

"Hi, Finn," she said, cheeks rosy. "Imelda, Delmira."

"Hey," I said, tone firmer than I'd intended. I'd never been good at small talk.

"Did you need something?" Imelda asked, with a perfectly kind delivery.

"I was wondering when Zoe—the Lady Astral—would be back?" she asked, correcting herself, though I doubted Zo cared about titles.

"That's classified," I stated.

"Sorry, Octavia, we aren't sure about that," Finnian offered. He'd always been far kinder than me. I was full of mistrust and baggage issues for days, which often led to concise deliveries that missed the mark more times than not. "Can I pass on a message when I speak to her again?"

Her cheeks reddened with embarrassment. She hadn't realized she was asking something she wasn't supposed to, which meant she was innocent.

"I found some more information on simargls. I thought I'd give them to her," she said, holding out a decrepit-looking thing. Book was too nice a word.

"We'll make sure she gets it," Imelda promised. "I know she'll appreciate it."

"Of course, let me just log where the tome is going," she said, writing something down with the Keeper's magic-infused pen. When finished, she handed it to Finnian, who tucked it into his satchel securely.

"Thank you," he said sweetly. "Take care."

She bowed slightly and scurried back off to the library.

"Well, that was nice of her," Imelda said as we walked to wherever they were taking me. We'd exited the manor and seemed to head toward the beach.

"Octavia is always nice," Finnian said.

"Then why did you break up with her?" I questioned.

"Geez, Delm," he said, exasperated. "It just didn't work out."

I'd been rude again with my blunt delivery, but I'd actually been sincere. I was trying to navigate my own feelings for a certain someone who shall not be named. Feelings during war made you stupid, and I was not.

"I miss them," Imelda said, sighing heavily.

"You mean you miss Clodovea," I said, laughing.

"Of course," she admitted. "But I miss Elvy, Zoe, and even Blaz."

My heart paused for a moment at the mention of him.

"I didn't think anyone could miss Blaz this soon," Finnian joked.

"He's just a presence you notice is gone, you know?" Imelda asked, nudging me.

"Yeah. It's easy to notice when he's gone… things are suddenly peaceful," I said, deflecting with humor as always. I was the queen of unhealthy defense mechanisms. Zoe and I should really form a club.

They both laughed. But the truth was that things were much less peaceful for me when he was gone. I didn't know what it was specifically, but he just understood me. He was my best friend. I hadn't exactly been the easiest new immortal to get along with, but Blaz had stuck it out with me through it all. He was easy to miss.

We stopped just outside the main lighthouse in Vega. I hadn't been up here in ages. I dismissed the Shadowed on duty, and he seemed relieved to be free of the boring post for a little while.

Finn pulled out some notes and led us inside, but ignored the staircase leading up.

"Help me find this symbol," he said, holding out the scribbles to Imelda and me.

"The water element?" I asked.

He nodded, scrutinizing the walls, so I started scanning the floor.

I cast my starlight so I could see better and found a raised portion of the dark rock floor against the glitter of the stones embedded in it.

"Over here!" I called.

A grin crossed Finn's face as if he'd found a precious treasure.

He cast some of his water magic on the mark, and a spiral staircase opened below. A cloud of dust greeted us, which I could only assume meant no one had been down here for a while. It was musty, but the smell of the ocean wafted through the air, comforting my spirit.

We had our starlights hovering above us as we descended the stairs, which felt solid beneath my feet despite their decrepit appearance.

"Where are you leading us, Finn?" Imelda asked.

"I'm not sure yet," he admitted.

"Comforting," I said.

We reached the landing at the bottom of the staircase to find nothing but darkness.

"This isn't creepy at all," I said, wondering what the hell my twin had gotten us into.

"Come on," he said, leading us down a tunnel that seemed to be made of glass.

"Are we... underground?" Imelda asked.

"No," Finn responded. "Can't you feel the ocean?"

"I can," I agreed. "We must be below the surface of the ocean."

"Why is it so dark, then?" Imelda asked. "Our waters are usually much brighter with the stars."

"Maybe some kind of cloaking," Finn suggested.

"I feel like a target," I said, a little uneasy. "Our starlights are giving away our position."

"To whom?" he asked.

"I don't know... a hungry sea monster?" I suggested.

They both laughed easily, but I was on high alert. I'd never seen one in all my time here, but even Vega had legends of beasts.

We came to a massive door at the end of the tunnel with the words 'Musterion' carved above it.

"Musterion?" I asked.

"Mystery?" Finn muttered to himself. "I'll have to look into it."

"Where do we think this leads?" Imelda asked.

"I'm not sure, but the stars led us here for a reason. Let's see what they want us to know."

"How do we open the door?" I asked, looking for a handle, but Finn was reading some more scribblings.

"Entry demands payment that will make those who enter weaker," he said finally.

"Safety measure," I said, nodding. "Not a bad idea."

Finn slit his palm open and laid it against the seam in the center of the door.

With great effort, the heavy gate opened before us, revealing a secret that had been lost to time itself. I held my breath, petrified of the echoing sound that seemed to travel miles before us unseen.

Moments later, the starlight of the ocean lit up the scene before us. My mouth wanted to collide to the floor, but I held myself in resolute wonder.

"This changes everything."

11

Rebel Alliance
ZOE

The discernment within me was blaring to cease our pursuit back through the underground tunnels and into the heart of Rigil. Even though Damek was a massive horse, far larger than the ones I'd seen while still a mortal on Earth, he moved with stealth. I wasn't sure if he'd felt the danger ahead and instructed the other horses to silence their footfalls, or if they were just all that intuitive. Either way, I didn't think Damek was going to stop. Much like Jelly would always come to my rescue, Damek would go to Sierra and Terran.

Elvy, Clodovea, and Blaz rode in formation with the apparent intention that I was not to be harmed. For once, I simply allowed them to protect me. It wasn't just my life at risk if something happened to me, but all those who depended on Algol for their life source.

"Damek, I know you want to get back to them," I said, rubbing his beautiful midnight mane. "We will have a better chance of helping them if you give me just a moment to *see* what's going on."

He slowed, stopping just before the hill that would send us to the underground stables. I wasn't sure that was the best plan of action, though. The rest of the group circled around me as I went into a trance, calling on the gift from Algol.

Leaning into the dread, I saw flashes of images. Hesperia was here, and she hadn't come alone. Her black eyes were wilder than I'd ever seen them. She had such a calm air about her, even as she tortured me with a knife. It was strange to see her this way. *Desperation.* It consumed her. That made her even more dangerous. Desperate people would do anything to achieve what they needed. Her rage was like a black cloud all around her, following her every movement.

"She's here," I whispered under the night sky. "She won't find the underground tunnels. I don't *see* her there. She's heading straight for the palace front door."

"Bold move," Blaz muttered.

"We could leave," Clodovea said, eyes down. It pained her to even suggest it. "We will get you out of here, Zoe. Our duty is to you first."

I shook my head. "No. You know I will not leave. We will fight."

"The star realms will not standalone," Elvy agreed. "If we get a kill shot, we take it. But no unnecessary risks."

We all nodded in agreement, even though we did not know how to kill her for sure.

"Let's cross our fingers that Oleander comes through with reinforcements… sooner rather than later," I said, directing Damek back to the palace. "Ride, Damek. With the power of the ground beneath you."

He stood on his hind legs before taking off at a furious pace.

★★★

We greeted Hesperia and her Shadowed Legion in the middle of the battle. Sierra and Terran surrounded Hesperia on both sides as she unleashed dark tendrils of magic. I still didn't quite understand her gift, but I knew those wisps of darkness did nothing good. The field was flooded with immortal marks flashing mostly green hues of the Court of Rigil. The bioluminescent green glow of the wings would have been beautiful if not contrasted so grimly with the cries of pain coming from both sides. Shadowed immortals used their magic artfully, and I wished I had time to appreciate it fully.

I briefly noticed tangles of vines holding Hesperia's legion to the ground as Shadowed soldiers gutted their enemies. Craters opened in the ground, swallowing immortals whole as the weight of the rocks closed in on them. Yes, nature was beautiful, and she was mighty.

Damek raced straight towards Sierra and Terran, and it was a good thing. Just as we were upon them, Sierra cried out, whirling her head around as if she were looking for something. Hesperia crept behind her, and Terran was distracted as he fought off another assailant.

Without hesitation, I unsheathed a knife from across my chest and threw it, aimed at Hesperia's heart. The cry from that miserable queen let me know I'd hit my mark. It couldn't be that easy, right?

She turned, glaring at me with a hatred I felt in my soul. Ripping the knife from her chest, she pointed a death mark at me. It appears I only angered the little beast lurking beneath her. Blood seeped from the wound, and I remembered Blaz's wisdom. If she could bleed, she could die.

Sierra had seemed to recover from whatever Hesperia had done and was now helping Terran with the onslaught of foes.

"There you are," Hesperia purred. "I've been looking for you, Zoe."

"Can't say the same," I said sweetly.

"I wasn't finished with you," she said, stepping towards me. I leaped off Damek, and he raced towards Sierra. She smoothly wrapped around his neck and was atop him in one swift motion.

I released Jelly from my back, and she ignited in flames, morphing into her true form. Out of my periphery, Elvy battled his way towards me, but he was outnumbered ten to one. We both knew he had the power to end all of this with one nod of his head, but the likelihood that he could control which souls he vaporized from existence was little to none. Not to mention the burden of taking that many lives—especially the innocent souls of Rigil.

Blaz and Clodovea were lost in their own battles, too. We were outnumbered and outmaneuvered. I hadn't *seen* it go down like this, but I got the sense that we were waiting for something—stalling. I hoped my gut was right.

"It's you and me, little dragon," I murmured to Jelly, unsheathing two more knives.

"The great realm-healer has come to fall from legends so quickly," Hesperia taunted, circling.

I didn't dare look away from the snake before me.

"I know how this ends, Hesperia."

"Have you forgotten? You see what I want you to see," she mocked. "It's only a matter of time before you see things my way. We are far more aligned than you believe."

If what she said was true, then she was a blind spot to my power, but there was no way I would ever be on her side. She was more delusional than I'd thought. Her hidden magic was certainly a complication, but one I couldn't figure out right now. Live today. Fight tomorrow.

"Let me see the real Zoe," she teased, stepping closer. A wall was behind me, so I couldn't step back.

"She's right here," I stated, looking for an opening, but she covered herself well.

"I have no interest in the facade you wear," she responded. I swallowed.

She was referring to the monster that lived within me. She'd coaxed it out of me before. For whatever reason, she needed me to become a slave to that part of me, so I couldn't allow it out. No matter what.

"Come, let me see those dark eyes," she said, invading my personal space. I sliced upward, nicking her across her face. Blood glistened on her cheek. "That was rude."

"How does it feel to need me, Hesperia? To know that you aren't powerful enough to achieve your greatest desire without me?" I smiled villainously.

Her wicked sneer faltered some, and I took the opening, carving deeply into her gut as Jelly locked her jaw around her left arm. They weren't killing blows, but they'd hurt. The smell of burning flesh engulfed me as Jelly continued to attack Hesperia.

"Jelly, no!" I shouted, rolling away from the flames.

Elvy joined the fray just as she stabbed Jelly viciously in the jugular, and my heart sank. Jelly yelped, and I lost all reason. Elvy and I advanced on Hesperia, as Jelly lay limp to the side of her. Time stood still for a moment as my little dragon's breath labored and blood stained her white fur burgundy.

That's it. The female was dying tonight. Elvy sheathed his long sword and drew two shorter blades. He moved as if battle were his favorite dance, anticipating every blow his opponent was about to make.

Seeing that I would be more of a liability than helpful with how skilled Elvy was, I rushed to Jelly's side, finding her heart beating beneath her soft fur. Without hesitation, I called on the power of Vega, healing my protector. She let loose a sigh of relief as her wound threaded back together. If there was one promise to the universe, it was this—under no circumstances was my dog dying. I didn't care if she was some mystical, ancient beast now. She was my responsibility. And she would never die for me.

"Thank you for saving me, my good girl," I whispered. I knew the throes of battle sounded all around me, but for a moment, it was just Jelly and me, as it used to always be.

Elvy moved with grace and purpose, deflecting every attempt Hesperia made against him. Apparently ready to be done with this fight, the dark mist of her magic moved like a fog, emitting from her hands.

"*Move!*" I screamed through the bond.

He didn't waver, rolling backward toward me. Her tendrils followed us, but they were thwarted with darker coils of magic coming from another source—Oleander. He'd caught her off guard, and she withdrew her magic.

"Poison," she spat with a fiery dark gaze aimed at the Lord Astral of Algol. "You dare defy your Queen."

"Please, Hesperia," Oleander responded, rolling his eyes. The male had a death wish. "Your antics have grown tiresome."

This only angered her more.

"You suddenly have a pair of balls," she said, moving closer to him.

"I have the Emerging who will be your end on my side," he said, shrugging.

Elvy and I moved in on her. Jelly reignited her flames, closing in on her with us.

"Let's finish this," Elvy said. The rumble of his power, which could move mountains, made the battle still for a moment. Even Oleander raised a brow, curious at the magic emitting from my flame. Perhaps he knew the danger that would ensue if he unleashed it, but I knew he truly did not understand just how dangerous my flame could be.

"This would all be so much more pleasant if you would embrace who you really are, Zoe. This is far from over," she promised, disappearing into the shadows. Whatever of her followers weren't dead, transported between realms after her.

I whirled on Oleander. "Could you not piss off the one immortal that could end my sister's existence?"

"Freyja is perfectly safe, Zoe. No thanks required."

I wasn't in the mood for his sarcasm.

"You're sure she cannot get through your wards?" Elvy clarified.

"Yes. Let's just say I reinforced them before coming here to collect you all."

Blaz and Clodovea were with Sierra and Terran in the distance. It looked like they were counting casualties and reinforcing the magic around the city. I prayed that the numbers were low, but the amount of bodies lying motionless on the ground was many. My itch to reach out to them was strong, but I couldn't bring the dead back. Whatever healing needed to be done, they would have it from me.

"What do you need, Oleander?" I asked.

"I've run into a bit of a snag in convincing the Sublunary leader to come to our aid," he responded.

"And what terms have they set for us?" Elvy asked.

"Oh, you know, just a little something," he said, laughing. "They want Zoe to swear she will change the magic to the old ways—no more choosing which celestial to serve."

"You've got to be kidding," Elvy said, running his fingers through his brown-silver curls. His eyes went dark for a moment, and I felt his power begging to be unleashed through the bond. My flame gently caressed him, and his shudders settled, bringing him back to me.

"How do they expect me to make such a promise?"

"Didn't you know? You are Zoe Eferhild, Realm-Healer—Emerging of Legends. Anything is possible for you, apparently." The sarcasm was rich in his smooth voice.

"Then I guess I'll just have to make it happen," I said, as if it were perfectly reasonable.

"They want to hear it from your own lips," he informed.

"Hesperia could be lying in wait for us the moment we crossed into Algol," Elvy said, shaking his head.

"They showed me a 'back door,'" he countered. "That's how we got here."

Elvy clasped my hand in his. I think it was more to regulate himself than anything else.

"Your call," he said through the bond.

"We must go."

"Then we will," he said, kissing me softly on my hairline.

Jelly licked my hand and wagged her tail. She seemed to know we were going to see Freyja. My desire to chastise her for putting her own life in danger was strong, but I didn't, understanding that was her calling—her very own moment. I scratched her ears, needing to feel normal for a second. I'd been so worried about Elvy's death power leaking from him I hadn't noticed how close my own had come to joining us.

I took a moment to extend my water magic to her stained fur, washing away any trace that Hesperia had harmed her. The reminder almost sent me into another spiral, but I reined it in.

If I ever let my shadows out around Hesperia... I shook the thought from my head. No, I never would.

"We will come, Oleander," I said. "But first, we have to heal everyone here who is injured."

"That might take a while," Blaz said, joining us. He was bloody and bruised, but alive. Clodovea was in about the same shape.

"Most of the dead are Rigil," she informed, voice tight, as if she was trying not to cry. "Even more are injured."

"How many?" Elvy asked, as if it was for him to bear.

"We're still getting the final numbers," Blaz answered, voice steady. He was in warrior mode.

"Then there's no time to waste," Elvy responded, striding towards Sierra and Terran. We all followed him. It didn't matter how tired we were. We wouldn't rest until every immortal that we could save was healed.

To whatever future, this was a gift we could give them.

12

Reunited

FREYJA

Zoe's presence filled me with warmth even though she was tired, magic nearly depleted from the healing she'd done by the looks of it. Her eyes were a little duller than the brilliant green flames they'd become since Elvy entered her life. Her smile still lit up the entire room, despite the darkness around us all. She really was life, and my spirit seemed to know that a part of me was tethered to her eternally.

"Zoe," I said, racing towards her. Elvy, Clodovea, and Blaz circled behind her, eyes searching for someone they couldn't see.

"Freyja," she said, smiling, embracing me fiercely. Her arms seemed stronger, more muscled.

"We have to stop meeting like this," I joked.

"Ah, yes, sister. It would be nice if the turmoil of life would end."

Jelly yipped at me, wagging her tail happily.

"Hello, Jelly," I said, bending down to scratch her ears. "I hear you were a brave girl."

Her tongue hung out, which made it look as if she were grinning at me.

"I think she misses you," Zoe said, sitting next to me on the red rug beside the fireplace. She seemed to wince, but the expression was gone as soon as it'd come. The rest of the crowd had dispersed elsewhere, giving us the needed space.

"Think you're going to convince Tiergan to send the Sublunary?"

"Failing isn't an option," she responded with fatigue in her voice.

"What's going on, Zo?"

"I just feel like I'm playing chess, and you know I'm crap at chess. I have to plan ten steps ahead. One wrong move, and we'll be checking to that vile queen. But even more than that... I don't have all the pieces. I'm blind to her."

Her eyes darkened so quickly that I almost thought I had imagined it.

"She wants me, Freyja. And... some part of me is called to the darkness inside of her—like it recognizes a kindred spirit."

"Hesperia has you afraid," I stated, a little surprised by the vulnerability in her expression. She really was scared, and I think it was more about what her wrong move could mean for the rest of the realms.

"I'm no expert on the star realms, but I am on you," I said. "The more you try to shove something down, the more it eats at you."

"So, what are you saying?"

"Stop being afraid of what's inside of you. Use it. Mold it. Weaponize it if you have to."

"Forge my fear..." she murmured. "The darkness doesn't have to be a bad thing. That's what Elvy has always told me. The Archer also said I had to learn to embrace it, but Freyja... the times I've let it out, it feels so good. Exquisite. What if I get lost in it? What if I am... bad?"

My sister was inherently good. I refused to believe anything less, even if some of her actions were wrong.

"No, Zo. Don't spiral down that path. That's what she wants you to do. Doubt your goodness," I said, pausing. "Didn't you and your therapist do exposure therapy before?"

She winced at the memory of Emma. Hesperia had somehow found out about her and had slaughtered her at the joining ceremony just because she could. A death that weighed heavy on Zoe's shoulders.

"Yes," she said, nodding. "I could gradually expose myself to it…"

"And Elvy could bring you back with the flame, right?" I asked.

"I think he will always be able to reach me," she agreed. "But I get the feeling that something is going to test that. I have a sense of dread around it."

"You are soulmates," I said, holding her close to me. Jelly laid her body across us, and I pretended to feel her warmth. "You will figure it out."

She leaned her head against my shoulder, sighing. If the chill I gave off ever bothered her, she never complained. I sometimes forgot what I was when I was with her.

"I'm sorry I haven't figured out a way to bring you back yet," she said, voice sorrowful.

"Saving the realms comes first, Zo. If you're going to bring me back, I need something to come back to."

"Are you happy here?" she asked, voice hopeful. "Is Oleander being annoying?"

"Ander is…"

"Ander?" she asked, sitting up.

"Sorry. Oleander."

"Oh no," she said, eyes mischievous.

"I am not talking about this where anyone could hear us!"

Zoe held up a finger, silencing me. Closing her eyes, she focused on something within. I felt the hum of magic spill from her, and I wanted to chastise her for using any magic after exerting so much just hours ago. She opened her eyes, satisfied.

"No one can hear us," she promised. "A little trick of Anders," she said, emphasizing the first three letters of his name.

This seemed so silly and… *human.* It was a moment that used to be.

"Are you sure this isn't weird for you?"

"Why would it be weird for me?" she asked with a puzzled look.

"Well, didn't you…" I trailed off, blushing at the ridiculousness of my own brain.

"No," she said, laughing. "Nor him me. If anything, he saw me as a savior to Algol. It's always been Elvy for me. *Always.*"

I nodded, knowing that to be true.

"I guess I've grown fond of him," I answered, rolling my eyes. "I annoy myself."

"Freyja, you really like him, don't you?" she asked with knowing eyes.

"It doesn't matter how I feel," I dismissed. "He's alive. I'm dead. We have no real future together. I couldn't do that to him."

The fire in her eyes burned brighter.

"I vow to bring you back, Freyja. I don't know how, but that future will be made possible for you."

"Can you *see* any chance of that happening?" I asked.

She closed her eyes in concentration, and the song of her magic filled the air. The vein on her forehead showed the strain she put herself through. I gently caressed her arm, pulling her back to reality. Jelly's ears perked up in concern, and she just as quickly laid back down after ascertaining that all was safe.

"See? Even you can't guarantee this future, Zo."

"I'm not giving up," she promised. "In the meantime, give Oleander more credit. You can't decide for him. Sometimes, you just have to put it all out there and see what happens."

"I have to protect him," I disagreed.

"Your protection could do more harm than good. Trust me. I know from experience," she said, nudging my shoulder with her own. "Besides, you told me to *live* when I was Emerging. You should take your own advice."

I didn't have the heart to point out that it simply wasn't the same thing, so humor it was.

"I have half a mind to disappear on you right now," I joked with her, lightening the mood.

"I just want you to be happy, Freyja. You sacrificed yourself for me. Let me try to find a way."

"Okay, Zo," I agreed, knowing there was no stopping her.

Footsteps echoed through the halls heading our way, and Zoe snapped her fingers, dispersing the shield around us.

"What are you ladies up to?" Oleander asked, sitting next to me. Elvy followed behind him and plopped down beside Zoe.

"Wouldn't you like to know?" I asked, lips sealed.

"I would indeed," Oleander responded, leaning closer to me. "Seeing as Zoe put up a shield to keep your conversation secret."

"You nosy betty," Zoe said, leaning into Elvy.

"We hate to interrupt," Elvy began, but Oleander interjected.

"Speak for yourself."

Elvy rolled his eyes, plowing through, "I'm afraid Tiergan is ready to meet with you, Zo."

"No sense in prolonging the inevitable," she agreed, standing up to stretch. "I need a cup of coffee and a long rest afterwards."

"You know, those two things rarely go together," Oleander pointed out.

"Don't come between an Eferhild and her coffee," I said. Oleander and Zoe laughed, but Elvy's lips formed a tight line, frustrated that he couldn't hear me.

Zoe laced her fingers through his and followed Oleander out the door. I caught up to him, leaving them behind us. We walked on one of the hidden paths in the treeline down to the village that he tirelessly protected.

"Don't feel like you have to be silent just because others can't hear you, sweetheart," he said seriously. "I'll make sure they hear what is needed."

"I think it would get annoying constantly being my translator," I murmured.

"Quite the contrary," he smiled. "Finding reasons to be around you is becoming my favorite thing."

"Vomit," I said, but the smile betrayed my heart.

"Such bite, viper," he said, voice deepening, as if he liked the idea of me wicked.

The others seemed chilled by the snow-covered ground, but I couldn't feel it. I longed to experience the frigidity of nature on a winter morning with nothing but the backdrop of a mountain and the moon shining above.

I wouldn't be opposed to a cinnamon whiskey and honey right about now. I knew Oleander had some stored. Curiosity had gotten the better of me. He had a vast collection of various wines and bourbons, but I'd never seen him indulge more than taking the edge off his stressors. He'd explained that too much affected his ability to do magic properly, and he couldn't afford to have his powers compromised with everything going on now.

"I'd still love to know where that mind goes," he murmured.

"It's not all that interesting," I replied.

"I doubt that," he smirked.

We passed by the tree he'd put me up against, and my core heated at the memory. I'd wanted him. He'd wanted me… and I had a feeling he would know how to persuade me to talk.

"Like that. Right there," he said, leaning just a breath away from me. If I wasn't careful, I would get lost in those sea-blue eyes, and Zo would see more of us than she cared to.

I bit my lip, trying to bring myself back to reality.

"Not helping," he said, turning his gaze back to the path ahead of us.

Zoe and Elvy held each other's hands, looking like a Hallmark movie. They were completely lost in each other's presence. Their silence made me think they spoke through their bond. There wasn't envy from me, and I wished for that easiness with someone. I knew it was a facade, though. This may have been one calm moment, but what they'd been through and where they still had to go… they'd earned this peaceful walk.

We stood outside the door that would lead us into the informal meeting room of the leader of the Sublunary—Tiergan.

"Ready?" I asked Zo.

She nodded her head, expression confident, and with the heart of the warrior that lived in her, she strode in without a second thought.

13

Mustache

ZOE

Tiergan was the king of mustaches. I mean, it was glorious, and I had mad respect for it. I blinked rapidly, trying not to let it distract me from the seriousness of the conversation we were about to have.

"Zoe Eferhild, Realm-Healer—Emerging of Legends."

"You must be Tiergan," I said, nodding a respectful distance away. If Blaz had taught me anything, it was to assess my opponent first. Clodovea and Blaz stood against the wall in the shadows, barely seen. Zadie had not joined us for this meeting.

"It's nice to formally meet you, Daughter of Algol," he stood, smiling. Mustache and all.

I met him half-way, holding out my hand to shake his. His grip was calloused and firm. Elvy stood a few paces behind me with Oleander. This was my fight. My actions would secure the course of fate in this war.

"Likewise," I nodded. "I hear you are in need of my aid?"

"We just want things as they once were," he answered, eyes a little sad. "How they should have remained before the celestials took it from us… from you."

His eyes were knowing. I discreetly opened up my discernment towards him and sensed… grief. Genuine sorrow. And beneath the trenches of regret was a small ember of righteous hope. An ember I planned to stoke with my very own flame. Tiergan had a story to tell, but he would not give it easily, and something in me respected that. Perhaps it was my own lived experience. Not everyone deserved the right to know those parts of me, and I would give this male that same courtesy.

"You want the freedom to choose," I stated.

It was no secret that I had to choose between Algol and Vega. Knowledge of my Emergence would spread across the realms in time. Fortunately, the realms interacted little with each other now. They would not understand how I'd defied the stars. Even I wasn't certain. My will was unwavering, but I doubted it alone resisted the celestials.

"Is that so much to ask?"

"I don't know how to give you what you seek…" I started, pausing to find my truth. "But I vow that I will not yield until I find the answer and restore the realms to the way my father intended."

Tiergan's eyes sparkled with the infectious power of faith. It was simultaneously humbling and terrifying to see how much he believed in me.

"I cannot do this alone. *We* cannot do this divided. You must answer the call to battle in the other realms that require aid. There will be no restoration until Hesperia is dead."

Tiergan stood from his seat and walked closer to me. Blaz and Clodovea surrounded me quickly. Elvy, Oleander and Freyja moved behind them. Jelly's wing brushed against me. I stood resolute in my conviction. Discernment was on my side. Tiergan would choose wisely today.

"Is that all, Zoe Eferhild?"

"I have no time for empty promises. You choose to trust me or not. Decide."

A small smirk played beneath his mustache. Tiergan kneeled on one knee, bowing his head in his own pledge to me. The other Sublunary followed suit.

"You have my sword," he promised. "All that I have is yours to use, Realm-Healer."

I joined him on the ground, kneeling in front of him.

"Together, Tiergan," I swore, holding out my hand to him.

"Together," he agreed.

I pitched my voice so low that only he could hear it. "I feel your pain—your grief, Tiergan. My magic doesn't always know the difference between physical and emotional pain. You don't need to tell me who you miss… but know that we keep them right here," I said, placing my free hand over my heart. "To whatever future."

He said nothing, and he didn't need to. I hadn't said those words for me.

His grip tightened on my hand, and he nodded slightly.

We rose seamlessly—a united front.

Cheers and clapping surrounded us, breaking the trance of our private moment, but I'd felt the smile from the threads of fate. It was a small victory, but a win nonetheless. After the attack on Rigil, our spirits needed this.

"We will await your order," Tiergan said, and I nodded in thanks.

"How should I call for you?"

"Take this," he said, pulling out a small stone that resembled a crystal. A rainbow seemed to form in the center.

"What's this?" I asked.

"Immortals have forgotten the old ways," he answered with a heavy sigh. "But we Sublunary have not. These are communicators between realms. We call it an iris. I have its sister star. They are linked. Use the magic in your mark to light your iris, and the message will get to me."

I nodded, placing the stone in my pocket. Undoubtedly, Tiergan was a wealth of knowledge. One we should take advantage of, but I could not be the one for this mission. I'd have to learn to delegate.

"I'll be in touch," I promised. "In the meantime, I trust Oleander to be my liaison. I don't know the rumors you have heard, but he is a good male."

"We have been guarded immortals for a long time, but I will concede to the Lord Astral," he agreed.

"Take care, Tiergan."

"You have my word, Realm-Healer."

***

Clodovea, Blaz, Oleander, Freyja, Elvy and I left the meeting in high spirits. Jelly and Blaz rolled around in the snow, and I couldn't help but join in their fun. It took no time at all for us to erupt into an unnecessarily intense snowball fight. It was a perfect moment. The evergreen trees and snow-capped mountains created a picturesque backdrop to the scene unfolding under the starry sky and brilliant moon. Faces were flushed with rose-colored cheeks from the chill in the air. Even Freyja seemed to enjoy herself, though she kept giving Oleander death glares when he threatened her with a snowball.

Before long, we were all piled in front of the fireplace, warming the ice blocks that had once been our hands and feet. Freyja stood off to the side, letting those of us who were not immune to the snow warm up first.

"That went surprisingly well," Oleander said. "Tiergan's never been that kind to me before."

"You better learn to play nice," I said. "You need to earn his trust. He's going to be invaluable in this fight."

"Why?"

I rolled my eyes in exasperation. "He may know more useful things that you all have forgotten." I kept the rest of my gut instinct to myself. My discernment told me he was important.

"I don't think he's going to warm up to me," Oleander said, smirking.

"Can you blame him?" Elvy joked.

"If I've learned anything, it's never to doubt what Zoe says," Clodovea said.

"Alright, love. I'll try, but I'm telling you. I'm the wrong male for the job."

I scratched along the shield of his mind, and he begrudgingly let me inside.

"Don't think so little of yourself, Oleander. I trust you," I said seriously, then left him to his own thoughts.

He gave me a slight nod, but I felt the eye roll he truly wanted to give.

Jelly slept peacefully in Blaz's lap as the crackling of the fire surrounded us. Blaz seemed ready to join Jelly in the world of dreams. I knew he was tired. We all were. We not only needed that win, but we also desperately needed a good night's rest before we realm-traveled again.

I sipped my coffee, allowing the warmth of the liquid to ground me in this moment. I hoped there would be a future where all of my friends and family were around a fire without the threat of some dark destiny looming over us. A future where Freyja and Elvy could laugh together, and she could freely be with Oleander if that's what she wanted. I'd fight for it. I'd come so far, yet still had so much further to go.

"Where will you go next?" Oleander asked.

I tapped on the map of the stars that adorned my forearm. "The Court of Arcturus—Fire."

"Have you found the bow?"

"The less that know that, the better," I said, and he didn't argue, knowing the truth of my words.

"I think we should go to Vega first and check in," Blaz said. "Communication has been scarce… nothing feels safe anymore."

Elvy nodded in agreement. "We need to see what progress Finnian has made. I hate being away from home when Hesperia's movements are so uncertain."

"Whatever she's doing, she's evading my gifts," I said, frustrated. "Whatever read I can get on her future… I feel like it is only what she wants me to see—an illusion."

"It's been much the same for me," Oleander agreed.

"Can Tiergan show us a backdoor to Vega?" Clodovea asked. "I don't want to risk being followed." I knew she was worried about Imelda's safety.

"Maybe Imelda should come to Arcturus with us," I suggested.

"She is the emissary to the fire realm," Elvy nodded in agreement. "We'll decide when we get back."

Freyja had moved closer to Oleander. I wondered where Zadie was, but kept the thought to myself.

"Can we see the rock Tiergan gave you?" Elvy asked.

I nodded, plucking the iris from my pocket.

"He said that immortals had forgotten the old ways. Whatever that means."

"See, Tiergan gives us useful things," Freyja said, chastising Oleander.

He winked at her in response, and I returned my attention to my flame.

Elvy held out his hand, and I plopped the crystal into his palm.

"I've never seen one of these before," he said, twirling it in his hand. "You?"

"No," Oleander answered, brows raised. "Tiergan is a traditionalist to his core. He's likely got an arsenal of ancient weapons we aren't aware of."

"Which is why we are going to play nice, Ander," Freyja said, hovering right beside him. I smiled secretly.

"How would something like this cease to exist in our memories?" Clove asked.

"Maybe something to do with The Archer? When the celestials made him undo the bonds to the other stars?" Blaz offered.

"I'm sure there was history lost once we no longer shared knowledge with one another," Elvy agreed. "There is likely much more that was lost. Hopefully, it will come back to us when our mission is complete."

I didn't miss the hope in Freyja's eyes, and I let that fill me with purpose.

"Maybe Finnian will know something about it from the Hall of Memories," I suggested, as a yawn crept over me.

"Let me show you to your rooms for the night," Oleander said, standing.

The feeling had finally come back to my hands and toes. Elvy helped me up, and we followed behind Oleander's retreating figure after I gave Freyja a hug goodnight, promising to see her before I left the next day.

Oleander paused outside a room and gestured towards it.

"I'll see you all at moonrise," he stated, but I caught his arm.

"Actually, we need your help with something first," I said, pulling him into the room with my flame.

"We do?" Elvy asked, not using our bond.

"Yes, come on," I said, slamming the door behind them.

I concentrated for a moment and threw up a shield of steel around the three of us. I was getting stronger, not weaker, with Algol bonded to me, it seemed.

"Please don't tell me you have some roguish idea," Oleander said, genuinely puzzled. Elvy looked just as perplexed.

"Ew. No," I said, rolling my eyes. "This is serious."

"I'm all ears," Oleander said, waving his hand around.

"It appears Hesperia needs my darkness to take control of who I am, though we really don't understand it yet," I started. Elvy had the same issue, but I wouldn't give him away. His struggles with his power were for him to tell. "Freyja and The Archer suggested I try to embrace it. In small doses. You know, like exposure therapy."

"What do you need me for?"

"I need you to coax the darkness out. In a controlled environment. I refuse to believe that part of me is bad… but I think it can be corrupted. I need you here to keep me contained while Elvy helps me come back through our bond."

Elvy clutched his hand in mine.

"I may be overly prepared, but I'd rather be safe than sorry since all those of Algol are tied to my life force right now."

"Thank you for the consideration. Shall we, love?" His eyes were now playful, full of mischief.

"Make sure I come back," I told Elvy.

"Always," he vowed.

"Let's get started then," I said, closing my eyes, digging deep into the pit of my being, allowing all that I am to envelop me. My darkness was part of me and answered to me alone. It was not a tool for Hesperia to manipulate.

I felt Oleander place his fingers on either side of my head, and I let him in through my shields.

"Hello, little darkness. Come out to play."

The swell of discernment flooded my core, and I smiled at the pleasure it brought me. Elvy's hand squeezed my own, and I relished the feel of him there. Even now, my heart knew its flame.

"Open those eyes, love," Oleander whispered, and I responded immediately.

"Beautiful. Even still," Elvy whispered, and I turned to face him. I knew my eyes had gone dark, and I sought the abyss lurking within him, too. My shadows had never met Elvy's before… not even on the beach of joining day. And she wanted him. Now.

"I can't do that, starlight," he murmured, voice deepening. Some part of him wanted it, too.

I was briefly aware that Oleander was studying us, but he seemed insignificant right now. My shadows didn't want to be alone.

"Come, Elvy," I leaned into his waiting arms. "It feels divine."

I let out black tendrils from my palms and moaned at the euphoria they provided me. They wanted blood, and I wanted to answer their call.

Someone coughed, and I whipped my head around, forgetting for a moment that Oleander was there.

"Zoe?" Oleander asked.

I reached out my tendrils towards him, caressing his cheek. It would be so easy to end him.

"That's enough for tonight," Elvy said through our bond. His voice was shaking.

"Vengeance," I responded.

"You will have it," he promised. *"Hesperia is not here."*

I growled angrily, circling the magic around Oleander's neck. He did not move, but his eyes seemed to sparkle with some delight.

"You're getting stronger, Zo."

"Come back to me," Elvy said, pulling my face towards him. His lips crushed into mine, and his tongue invaded my mouth.

With every second that he claimed me, I let the darkness seep back into my core, hiding her away for a while.

"I think you should go," Elvy said to Oleander, as he trailed his lips down my throat.

Oleander grunted something I didn't care to hear and shut the door behind us. I felt that he put up a shield around us, probably to keep our rumblings silent.

"Mine," I said, staring into the storm-gray of his eyes.

"Always yours," he agreed, slipping my sweater over my head and unclasping my bra in one swift motion.

His teeth teased my body as he expertly pulled my pants and underwear off. This felt messier than ever before. Fervent. Picking me up, he backed me against something hard. I was too invested in him to be bothered by what it was. The coolness was a wonderful juxtaposition to the heat he emitted.

I vigorously pulled his shirt off as his tongue sent me over the edge. One hand held me up while his free hand undid the button of his dark jeans.

"I need you now," I demanded, biting his shoulder.

He didn't hesitate, filling me in the way my body demanded. I gripped his curls in my hand, pulling his mouth to mine, sucking on his lower lip.

The groan that radiated from him got me closer. Elvy moved his finger against the most sensitive part of me, creating a pleasure so intense that my entire frame trembled. If that were even possible. My strength had left me, and I knew the only thing keeping me up was his own deadly power.

"Come for me, my starlight. I need to know we're here. Together."

The darkness had scared him. I felt his own desire for the shadows, and it was just as intense as my own. I'd provide him every reassurance that I was his—that I was right here and so was he.

I shouted out my release as I moved with Elvy through the convulsions that fluttered through me.

"I love you," I whispered. "To whatever future."

His powerful arms picked me up as he continued to move within me, placing me on my back on top of the bed. He pulled out, greedily taking his fill of me. His tongue moved from my neck, then lower until a gasp escaped me as he fueled my desires.

"Endlessly."

His fingers teased more pleasure from me, and my body braced as my desire for him built back up. Elvy did not yield until bliss engulfed me again, and he smothered my cries with his lips, clinging to them like his favorite delicacy.

"This is real, Elvy," I whispered, sweat drenching us both, but I didn't care. I needed him to feel that truth.

He shifted, filling me again. I moaned at the swell of him stretching me until I could not take anymore.

"I need you with me, Zo," he whispered, holding my hands above my head as he continued his unforgiving rhythm.

Curling my toes, I bit my lip as I felt the release growing again. Elvy nipped my neck, and that was my undoing. I yelled again, and he followed me into euphoria.

He collapsed on my chest, listening to my heart.

"Ethereal," he murmured through the bond, and I gently stroked his curls as we let our restless spirits settle, satiated for the night.

14

Lost City

ZOE

"You'll be careful?" I asked Freyja before we left for Vega.

"I'm already dead. What else can they do to me?" she joked.

Oleander looked less than pleased at her humor, and so was I.

"I'm serious, Freyja. Stay with Oleander."

The longing in his eyes suggested he wanted nothing more than to do just that.

"Promise, Zo," she agreed, scratching Jelly's ears. "You come back in one piece, alright?"

"I will," I swore. I didn't know how to keep that deal, but I'd try.

"The Sublunary have agreed to escort us on an obscure route back to Vega. We'll regroup there and head to Arcturus in a day or so," Elvy stated. Clodovea and Blaz were behind him, packs ready to go.

Zadie had come from wherever she'd disappeared to yesterday. Her mood was cordial, but I wouldn't call it pleasant. I knew I wasn't her favorite immortal at the moment, but I didn't take it personally. If I died, so did her realm. She disagreed with the risks I was taking. Fair enough.

"Can you give this to Finn?" she asked me quietly, handing me a book.

"Of course," I answered, and she gave a small smile.

"Are we ready?" Blaz asked.

We all nodded and said our last goodbyes to those of Algol.

Before I left, Oleander caught my shoulder.

"Be careful with that magic, love. There's something… different about your shadows around him," he said, nodding towards Elvy. "More than that… your tendrils feel dark. Like nothing I've felt before. Foreign from shadows I've felt in Algol. You may only be a means to an end for Hesperia. There's a reason she's after yours specifically. She's taking a risk to take on a magic that rivals her own power. Keep practicing, but take precautions, okay?"

"Your concern is endearing, Oleander," I said, giving him a quick kiss on the cheek. "Win Tiergan over. I'll focus on the magic."

He rolled his eyes. "Ever I aim to please."

Freyja smiled, waving as we headed to the transport zone.

I committed that moment to memory, vowing never to lose sight of those I loved.

***

We swirled through the cosmos, flanked in rank. I hadn't expected the Sublunary to have wings, but I guessed they could, just like any other immortal.

No attacks came as we traveled through the realms, and somehow, that made me even more nervous. The Sublunary made entrance to the North of our home, and the sounds of the bustling city put me at ease. Quiet usually meant something was wrong. Noise hopefully meant that it was business as usual.

To our surprise, a squadron of the Vega Shadowed Legion descended upon us quickly. Even the Sublunary seemed surprised by this.

"Sorry, Lord and Lady Astral," one of the captains bowed—Evander.

"How did you know we were here?" Blaz questioned. He was an expert on our wards. Apparently, this was supposed to be out of bounds for what they typically did. Clodovea seemed curious, too.

"I believe it will be better if Commander Delmira fills you in," he stated.

"Lead the way then," Elvy responded, and we all followed behind them.

As we flew back over the city of Vega, the scattering of lights created a beautiful glow against the waves crashing along the shoreline. Our ocean-side home glistened beneath the moonlight as we descended onto the secure rooftop where Delmira, Finnian, and Imelda waited for us.

The moment our feet found purchase, Imelda rushed into Clodovea's arms, embracing each other with fierce love. Delmira strutted forward with something in her eyes that told me she had something big to reveal. Even Finnian's eyes cast a knowing glance towards us. Jelly circled them both as Blaz stayed flanked by my left side and Elvy to my right. The Shadowed Legion had escorted the Sublunars to the training center for now.

"I'm glad you all made it back," Delm said, smirking. "There's been a development."

"Of epic proportions," Finnian agreed.

"Evander said as much," Elvy said. "Is Vega okay?"

"Yes," Delm admitted. "More than okay. Our ancestors may have provided a way to keep us safe until Hesperia is vanquished."

"What do you mean?" I asked.

"It'll be easier to show you," Delmira informed. "Evander, you are dismissed. I'll send word of new movements when we are ready."

"Yes, Commander," he responded, turning away.

Blaz moved from one foot to the other. He was typically in charge of Vega's Shadowed Legion, but we all had to sacrifice and become roles we'd never thought possible. Deep down, Blaz knew the legion was in good hands with Delm at the helm.

"Follow me!" Finnian said excitedly.

Elvy took my hand as we all trailed behind him. Jelly pranced beside me, wings closed on her back. Finn led us down to the harbor's black stone lighthouse. It seemed to glitter in the moonlight underneath the cosmos.

"Going up?" Blaz asked.

Delm shook her head. "Down."

"Down?" Clodovea asked, still clinging to Imelda.

"The Hall of Memories revealed this place to me. I'd been looking for a way to stop Hesperia's magic, but they showed me this instead."

I subtly extended a silencing shield around us as he continued to explain. We couldn't be too careful.

"Which means two things," Delm added.

"One—there's no way to stop Hesperia's magic if she is successful in her plans. Two—the stars have shown us a safe harbor to keep the immortals here protected, which I hope means the stars still have hope in us to defeat her."

Elvy squeezed my hand. It wasn't the news we wanted, but there was some silver lining in it.

"Let's go," Elvy said, not wanting to waste any further time.

Finnian nodded, leading us into the base of the lighthouse. There didn't seem to be a way down, but he paused over the center of the floor. Discreetly, the image of the water sign was carved into the black-glittering stone. You wouldn't have known it was there unless you knew to look for it. He conjured his water magic and placed his hand against the carving. Within a few moments, a spiral staircase appeared, leading down. The cavern smelled of the ocean itself.

"We've secured the entrance to only open to the Luminaries and, of course, the Lord and Lady Astrals," Delmira explained.

My discernment engulfed me. Whatever we were about to enter would be a significant change in this war and, perhaps, the future of the star realms.

We descended the staircase with blue-green torches, providing enough glow to light the way easily. The stairs seemed to be made of the same material as the lighthouse—what must once have been a beacon of hope for the immortals of Vega.

Once we hit the bottom, a dark tunnel appeared before us with the same carving of Vega. We cast our starlight, trusting Delmira and Finnian not to be leading us towards our demise. It was an eerie feeling, but my curiosity kept one foot in front of the other. At the end, we came to a stone door that had the texture of coral reefs. This one was much grander than the secret door to the stairs and had the word 'Musterion' carved above the entrance.

"Musterion?" Elvy asked.

"Sacred secret," Finn explained. "I don't know how this place disappeared from our history. I'm still working on understanding our lost past."

Finnian conjured his magic again and slit his palm, letting his magic and blood fill the mark of Vega.

"This city requires a sacrifice to enter," Delmira added.

"City?" Blaz and I asked in unison.

Slowly, the doors opened, revealing a glass tunnel with the swirling cosmos of the ocean lighting the way. Sea creatures that I had only read about it fairytales surrounded the outside of the tunnel as if to welcome us home. Jelly turned her ears curiously, wondering what to make of these new beings. I was right there with her. Beneath the creatures lay the most beautiful coral reefs I'd ever seen. They glowed with the stars themselves, and there was a variety of fish and ocean plants with every color of the rainbow represented.

"Beautiful."

Right along with the more identifiable marine life, like dolphins, jellyfish, manta rays, whale sharks, and sea turtles, there was also a horse-like creature with skin like seaweed and fins that glistened in the glow of the moon above. This had to be where the mythology of the kelpie and hippocampus came from.

"If a mermaid pops out, I'm going to lose it," I muttered to no one in particular.

"If there are any, they have not made themselves known," Finnian said diplomatically.

Imelda seemed to enjoy the wonder on Clodovea's face. I was in full-on tourist mode myself. Even Blaz couldn't hide the smile spread across his face.

"There's more," Delmira said, guiding the group onward. I could've sat in the tunnel for ages staring at the sea-life. A twinge of longing rattled through me. My job at the rescue may have been mundane, but I loved working with the animals.

Elvy pulled me along the path, and the closer we got to the end, the brighter it became.

"Welcome to Musterion," Delmira said, opening the glass door to a sprawling city.

I thought the first time I laid eyes on Vega, nothing would ever compare. This—whatever this was—made my jaw drop.

Below us, a city made of various ocean rocks with all the vivid colors of the coral reefs greeted us. There seemed to be a city center with a capitol building and remnants of a bustling market. There were townhomes lined along the streets with second and third-story balconies that reminded me of the French Quarter in New Orleans.

"How could we not know of this?" Elvy asked, squeezing my hand, grounding himself to this reality.

"I'd say you were all lying if I wasn't standing here looking at it myself," Blaz agreed.

Finnian, Delmira, and Imelda stood patiently with the rest of us as we took in the mesmerizing sight.

"There's evidence of an art district, theater, training grounds, schools, courts, markets, and a throne," Finnian said excitedly. "The immortals of Vega once lived here. I don't know why they moved above ground or when. Everything is still in pristine condition, as if frozen in time."

It was eerie to think about why they'd left. From the looks of it, the previous occupants just got up one day and left everything behind. Why would anyone leave all of their belongings?

"Security?" Elvy asked.

"Completely undetectable from the outside. It's some creative magic camouflaging it," Delmira said. "It's like a mirror to anyone who looks at it."

"But the sea creatures can see us?" I asked.

"We think it may be only to those who have ill intent," Finn said, shrugging.

"How long could our immortals survive down here?" I asked.

"Indefinitely. There are gardens on the far end, just before the forest begins. The immortals who built this thought of everything. It is its own ecosystem down here. Quite advanced as well," Finn added.

"With the Lord and Lady Astrals' permission, we would like to begin evacuation to Musterion immediately."

"Is there enough room for everyone?" Blaz asked.

"Yes. It'll be tight, but they will be comfortable enough until this is over."

"Won't there be a risk if Hesperia breaches the wards to find Vega empty?"

"She won't be able to find this place; however, we suggest that most of the Shadowed Legion remain above ground for extra protection and to guard the bond to Sirius."

"They would be putting themselves at substantial risk," I pointed out.

"They serve at the pleasure of the Lord and Lady Astrals," Delmira said with conviction in her voice. They would do this, so our immortals would be safe.

"We all must make sacrifices in war," Elvy said through our bond.

"Hesperia could strike at anytime. If we are going to do this, we need to begin," I agreed.

"Begin phase one of the evacuation," Elvy said, looking over Delmira's plans.

She bowed. "It will be done."

If I ever had any doubt about leaving Vega behind in search of The Archer's bow, Delm's confidence dried out any lingering doubt. She would take care of this realm.

"Finnian, Zoe and I require your expertise on our mission," Elvy said. "Is there somewhere to talk securely down here?"

"Yes, in the central building."

An idea came to me, or my gift influenced the sudden gut feeling that was consuming me.This was an ancient city when immortals could embrace more than one star. Something from the air elemental realm was here. I could feel it—the pluck on the thread of fate gnawed at me to embrace it.

"Have you seen the symbol for air anywhere?" I asked.

"The five elements are represented in the town square, right in front of the capitol building. I haven't really noticed anything else."

"Zoe and I will meet you there in a few hours?" Elvy asked, understanding me the way he always did.

Finnian nodded, and I instructed Jelly to stay with Blaz, which they both seemed eager to do.

Elvy laced his fingers through mine as we walked through the ancient underwater city together. Some buildings resembled shells and rough corals, while others were smooth stone as if they had been under the power of a river for many years. Some homes were made of the familiar patterns of driftwood. It was beautifully unique, and the different textures worked together in the way only water can. I bet June would love it here. My heart sank, thinking of her. I hoped she was okay. Should I ever make it back to Earth when all this was said and done, I would offer her a place here—if she would take it. If we all made it through this alive.

"I want to take this as a win," Elvy said, pulling me closer.

"I feel the 'but' in there."

"We could be a liability to it…"

"If Hesperia ever gets to us. If we can't learn to embrace the darkness."

Elvy pulled us into one of the charming townhouses that was not unlike my sea bungalow on Earth.

"Let's practice," he suggested.

"We're supposed to be looking for the air element," I countered.

"We've got time for both," he reasoned.

"The last time put us both into a… frenzy," I pointed out.

"I've got you," he promised. "You don't need Oleander to call on your magic. It answers to you. Just a little. Enough to feel the shift."

"Oleander said that he noticed my shadows feel weird around you," I said, trying to make the puzzle pieces fit together. "It's like I can feel you, but it's more than our flame."

"I feel it, too," he admitted. "It's… intense."

"I don't think it's a coincidence that we found Musterion—that the past is revealing itself."

"What are you looking for?" he asked, eyes full of concern.

"I don't know," I said, frustrated. "It's like the answer is on the tip of my tongue, but I just can't *see* it."

"Breathe, Zo," he said, pulling me flush against his body. "We will figure it out. Let's focus on what we can control right now."

I nodded, closing my eyes, asking the shadows to come forth. They wanted to crash through the floodgate, but my will was stronger. I only needed a few of them. They seemed to crawl up my skin, caressing me like a lover. I tasted the delicious need for retribution. My dark eyes reflected in the storm of Elvy's. My shadows ached to meet his.

"Zoe," he murmured, kissing along my neck. I was more in control, but I was only dealing with a fraction of the shadows. His touch was grounding me to this reality. Even with the ocean all around me, I couldn't hear it, so I focused on his beating heart—my gravity. I listened to his rhythm as the shadows continued to taunt me to their side. I knew they had their uses, but they had to exist for me, and not for Hesperia.

"I want blood," I said with a bit of dissatisfaction.

Elvy's eyes eclipsed for a second, and it was like I could see the obscurity that lived in him begging me to bring them out. I pulled a knife from its sheath, slicing his neck softly. His hands gripped my hips tighter, which seemed to thrill my shadows even more. I wondered what he tasted like... Just as I moved to find out; he pulled away.

"I don't think that's a good idea, Zo," he said through our flame, even though his arousal said otherwise. *"We don't know what that could do to either of us. Mixing blood magic and shadows."*

The part of me that was in control knew he was right, but the wildness in me wanted to see what happened.

"Breathe, Zoe. You can still taste me, but you have to banish those shadows first," he teased, pressing into me harder.

Closing my eyes, I took three deep breaths, thanking the shadows for the purpose they served. I let them know I no longer needed them in my space, and they relented. This gave me hope we would come to know each other as allies in the end.

"How did that feel?" Elvy asked, holding me against him.

"I was more aware, and so were my shadows somehow. It's hard to explain."

"See? Progress," he laughed, exposing his teeth, and the sound was glorious.

"But I still *wanted* you," I said, brushing a hand against the paper-thin cut on his neck, healing it instantly. I used my water magic to clean the remnants of it away.

"You had me," he said, brushing a stray hair from my eyes.

"No, I wanted all of you," I said, referencing his true power, but a sly smile came to me as I slid to my knees, unbuttoning his pants to expose his arousal.

The amusement was gone, replaced by hunger.

"I said I wanted to taste you, flame," I whispered through the bond, and he groaned as I did just that.

★★★

We'd cleaned each other up and had gotten back on track in finding the one thing we needed to continue recovering pieces of the bow without one of us going through torture again. It was moments like these that made me truly appreciate the cleverness of water magic.

"I love you," I whispered, nuzzling his neck, as his arms wrapped around me securely.

"I love you, Zoe," he said, holding me even closer.

I pulled back, leaning into my magic.

"Concentrate," Elvy whispered, holding my forehead to his.

"Your proximity is distracting," I said, grinning.

He kissed along my neck, playing with me. "A good warrior can work through any circumstance."

I clasped his wandering hands in my own.

"Behave for a moment," I ordered, and he stopped his explorations, smirking.

I closed my eyes and called on my gift from Algol to guide me where I needed to go. With little effort, a path of light emitted from me, guiding us forward.

Grabbing his hand, I led the way as we continued to take in the forgotten city that had once been so full of life. We spoke little, just enjoying each other's company. It was easy to pretend the war was over and we were taking a midnight stroll underneath the ocean, beneath the cosmos that still glimmered above.

We came to the end of the path of light and found a few vases that were on a windowsill outside of what I assumed was once someone's home.

"That one," I said, pointing to the white vase in the middle. There was nothing special about it other than a feeling my gift gave me.

Elvy handed it to me, and I opened the lid to find a necklace inside. It was a silver chain with a feather carved out of moonstone hanging from the base. The symbol for air was carved into the feather.

He helped me put the necklace securely around my neck, next to the necklace I always wore. The pendant that he'd given me in Saint Andrews felt like a lifetime ago.

I twirled the ring Sierra had given me from Rigil around my right ring finger. Both relics emitted a small amount of power from their elements. It was like a warm trickle of energy when I touched them.

"Are you ready to head back to Finn?"

I nodded. "Let's take the scenic route. Just a little longer."

That's all I would ever crave with my flame. Just a little longer—a little more. Never enough.

***

We were in the central building with Finn to brief him on our mission and what we needed from him. The structure was regal, resembling the ancient temples of the Greek gods. I felt even smaller standing next to one of the massive columns that circled around the entire structure.

"Did you like the tour of the city?" he asked, leading us inside to a secure room. The interior was just as breathtaking as the outside.

Elvy and I laughed at each other. "Something like that."

Ever the professional, Finnian ignored the comment and continued on to the objective. I told him about the bow grip that we'd found, and that we anticipated finding the other pieces along the map that had manifested on my forearm.

"So you need me to figure out how to put it together and use it if The Archer doesn't come through?"

We nodded.

"No pressure," he said. "Anything else?"

"Yes," I said, pulling out the iris that Tiergan had given me to contact him. "Have you seen anything like this around Musterion?"

Finnian grabbed the crystal and flipped it around in his hands.

"Yes, we have. I did not know what they were, though."

"Tiergan showed me how to use one. They're called an iris. They are some sort of stars that you charge with your immortal mark. If you have the sister stars, you can communicate across realms," I explained.

"Seems simple enough. This would have been useful in recent years," Finnian said, nodding. Personally, I found it all complicated, but then again, I'd never understood how Wi-Fi worked either.

"Do you think you can get a few going for us before we leave for Arcturus tomorrow?" Elvy asked.

"I'll get on it after dinner," he answered.

"Thanks, brother," Elvy said, placing a hand on his shoulder.

"I'll meet you before you head to the transport zone."

"Are you getting any sleep, Finn?" I asked seriously.

"Just when I blink," he said. "Oh, Octavia wanted you to look through some tomes on Jelly. They're in your room."

"Send her my thanks. I'll try to find her before we leave," I said, pausing to take the book Zadie had given me out of my satchel. "From Zadie."

"Thank you," he said, placing the book on a desk that was below a massive star map.

"What's this?" I asked, pointing.

"Oh, I guess you two missed this when you were… exploring the city," he said, stifling a laugh. He flipped a switch, and the map lit up with swirling magic. Some markers I could identify, but others I couldn't.

"This is how Evander knew where we'd shown up?" Elvy asked. "Are those all transport zones?"

"Yes, that's how we knew, but no. Not all of them. We are still investigating them as we have the resources."

"You all really have been busy," I said, holding my stomach. The hunger was getting to me. Or fatigue. Probably both.

"We shouldn't keep you waiting, my lady," he said, shutting down the map with a couple more switches.

We continued in easier conversation as we headed back to have dinner with the rest of the Luminaries and Jelly to review our plans. I was just looking forward to sleeping in our own bed tonight.

15

Bravery

FREYJA

"**I** have a surprise for you, sweetheart," Oleander said, pulling me from my thoughts.

I'd felt the pull again to what lies *beyond.* Some days, my spirit was tired of being here… tired of dreaming for a better tomorrow. Zoe kept me on solid ground. Against every odd, she always pulled through, but my soul was still jaded. It feared the word *hope.* Dreaming opened me up to disaster.

And Mom wasn't there waiting for me in what lay beyond the veil, and I equally hated the thought of Dad being there without her. Either way… I was disappointing as a daughter.

"Little surprises me anymore, Ander," I said, with no hint of amusement on my face.

"Then perhaps a little joy?" he asked, with brows raised. I saw through the playfulness in his beautiful blue eyes. There was concern in them. I'd lost my light these last few days. I'd struggled to keep up with his banter, which was very unlike me, and he knew that.

He sat on the black-leather couch, leaning into me, and my form seemed to solidify at his touch. Some deep-rooted part of me called to him, and it was hard to shove her back down when she felt like she belonged to him. I concentrated on the comforting sounds of the fire crackling and the steady rhythm of his breathing.

"What do you have?" I finally asked, smirking at his excitement.

He pulled out a little clear rock that seemed to glimmer with the hues of the rainbow.

"What's this?"

"An iris. I managed to sweet-talk Tiergan into giving me one. It's a way to communicate with Zoe more often. I convinced him she would be more amenable to him if she could speak with you more."

I was glad he was slowly getting the Sublunary leader to warm up to him. He dropped the rock into my semi-full palm, and I rubbed the stone around in my hand, waiting for something to happen.

"How does it work?"

Ander's brows furrowed in frustration. "It takes magic to make it run… I'm afraid you'll have to communicate through me." He seemed to hope that me holding it would make it magically work.

Determined to keep the gloom from his face, I hugged him fiercely. "Thank you, Ander. Really, it's great."

I gave him a swift kiss on the cheek, which made my core light up.

"So, how do we call her?"

"I'll use my magic to charge it, and we'll speak the words over the stone. Once I let go of the magic, the rainbow will find its mark."

"How soon can she respond?"

"Pretty immediately, if she's available. Want to try it?"

I nodded my head enthusiastically, and the crystal hummed with the song of Oleander's magic—such an exquisite sound.

"When the streetlights come on," I whispered to the stone. It was an inside message between sisters who felt so far away in my memory. He looked at me curiously but said nothing.

We only had to wait a moment for Zoe's voice to come through with the glow of the rainbow.

"I'll be home," she said back to me, and I couldn't help the smile on my face.

"Thank you for that," I said to Oleander.

"Anytime, Freyja," he responded.

If I were human or immortal, my skin would flush pink, but alas, my form stayed ivory and transparent.

"You look more tired than usual," I pointed out, ignoring the piercing gaze he so often gave me. It was an accurate description of him. It wasn't just the circles under his eyes. His entire energy was depleted. He seemed as fatigued as my soul was.

"I always have time for you," he said, shrugging his shoulders.

"Maybe you should go to bed."

"Is that an invitation?" he asked, smirking.

"You know I don't sleep," I said matter-of-factly, ignoring the heat radiating in my core.

"Ah, but I do."

"You want a ghost watching you while you sleep?"

"I'd be flattered," he chuckled, then turned more serious. "I'm not afraid of you, Freyja."

"Maybe you should be," I whispered, barely audible. I wanted to tell him he had nothing to fear from me, but that wasn't true. I could leave this realm forever. The ways of the *otherside* would not allow me to remain on this plane in this form eternally. Luckily, fate had bigger things on its mind right now.

"Tell me what's going on inside that mind of yours."

"Zoe said I shouldn't decide for you," I began, testing out how brave I was truly willing to be tonight.

"What kind of decision is that?" he asked, leaning in so close his scent overwhelmed me. He smelled of fresh mountain air tonight.

"I feel… protective of you…" I said, looking away from him to the blue-green fire.

Oleander pulled me onto his lap, turning my head to meet his gaze. *Why* did he have to do that?

"Keep going, Freyja," he said, voice deepening.

"What if this is all I will ever have to give?" I asked, gesturing to my semi-solid form. "What if I'm forced to go to the otherside, and it's over before we even began?"

"Sweetheart, we never know what tomorrow holds. All I know is that I can't get you out of my brain, just as you are right now. You, Freyja. Just you."

The fiery ember of life burned a little brighter within me at his words and the conviction I heard in them. He meant what he said, and he will risk it all just to try.

"Don't fall in love with me, Ander," I whispered, a breath away from his mouth. He responded by locking his lips with mine, and I could almost feel how soft they were. My body reacted as my hand gripped his hair, pulling him closer. It was an odd sensation to feel everything and nothing at the same time. I momentarily let myself forget that I was not fully there, and gave in to the desires I'd been shoving down for far too long. Anger was easy to hide behind, and I didn't feel like staying hidden tonight.

Oleander swept me into his arms without breaking the kiss. I didn't care where he was taking me. I just didn't want this moment to end. Some part of me knew that he'd brought us to my bedroom. Gently laying me on the bed, he finally broke free of my lips, eyes shining with desire.

And fatigue. He was tired. I didn't want him to go.

"Stay," I said simply.

He nodded, slipping out of the black dress shirt he always wore. He was… hot. Whatever training he had done with the Shadowed Legion was paying off. My traitorous libido wanted to lick the ripples across his abdomen. Ander was not shy in slipping off his dark jeans, revealing just how much he enjoyed kissing me against his black briefs. Before I could launch myself at him without thinking, Oleander slipped underneath the comforter and pulled me close to him.

No words were said as I lay beside him while he drifted off into a peaceful sleep and left me with distracting thoughts. *How many muscles does this guy even have? Why does he smell so good? What the hell have I started with the Lord Astral of Algol?*

Nothing. I chanted to myself. I warned him not to fall in love with me. Now, if only I could take my own advice. We were just two lonely souls in the middle of a war. That's all it was. That's all it could be—because more likely than not, I will complete my death. The *otherside* will call me home eventually, and I'll have to pay up.

For now, in this moment, I'd listen to the way he breathed and watch the rise and fall of his chest, proving that poison does, indeed, have a beating heart. I'd notice the way I seemed to fit perfectly into the cradle of his arms… I was so screwed.

16

Point

DELMIRA

Everyone else had gone to bed after dinner except for Blaz and me.

I was too keyed up to even think about lying down anytime soon.

"Are you going up?" I asked, cracking my knuckles for the hundredth time today.

"Where are you going?" he asked, avoiding the question. The purple circles under his eyes showed his fatigue, but I knew Blaz better than most. His mind could overcome what his physical body didn't think it could, and he would always put someone else above his own well-being.

"Thought about going for a few rounds of training. Want to come?" I offered. Maybe he needed to punch something, too.

"Sure," he said nonchalantly.

We walked in comfortable silence to the mostly empty training field. The only souls out here were those who had the unlucky draw of overnight watch duty. Most of our forces were centralized around our bond to Sirius or were on patrol of our ward's borders, trying to understand the new map from Musterion. These Shadowed had the dullest assignment by far.

"How are you dealing?" Blaz asked, wrapping his knuckles with tape.

"Are we sparring?" I asked, deflecting. I didn't do vulnerability. At least I wasn't doing it tonight.

"Answer the question," he demanded.

"Who the hell do you think you're talking to?" I asked, following suit despite how pissed off I suddenly was.

He pinched the space between his eyes and took a couple of deep breaths. We were constantly at each other's throats, but he was my best friend. Always had been.

"I'm fine, Blaz," I said. "I'm dealing."

He nodded his head and stepped into the sparring circle.

"What's dealing look like?" he asked.

"I don't know," I said, shrugging. "Lots of meetings, little sleep, caffeine, and yelling at idiots."

"So, a usual day for you then?" he asked, smirking.

Humor I could do.

I lunged, and he dodged me easily.

"You're easy to rattle, Delm," he said, grinning fully now, but I didn't take the bait this time.

"I could easily distract you, Blaz."

He circled me, assessing for a weakness, but I had none now. I would win this on pure spite if I had to.

"I'm never caught off guard," he disagreed, rolling into a round-house kick.

But he had trained me. I knew all of his moves, which also put me at a disadvantage. He knew all of mine.

The Shadowed on patrol had lost interest in the fight already and went to a different area of the training center, looking for something more entertaining, probably.

"We do this every single time we spar," I pointed out, holding up both arms securely. I wouldn't let him in close enough for a point tonight.

"Yet we keep doing it," he said. "Why is that?"

I didn't answer because I didn't know. Fighting with Blaz was somehow comforting to my soul. Knowing I'd always have him when times got hard. He wasn't always nice about it, but his intentions were good.

"Come on, Delm," he said. "Make a move. I can't always be the one on offense."

I don't know where the impulse came from, but my body was moving before my brain could tell it to stop. A dangerous thing in battle.

Circling around him again, I lurched towards him, but instead of going in for another punch like he expected, I pressed my lips to his.

I felt his surprise against my lips, and just as he was about to pull me in closer to deepen the kiss, I reared my head back, head-butting him hard. I didn't waste time on whether the adrenaline was from finally gaining a point on him or the fact that he'd wanted to kiss me, too.

"What the hell, Delm!" he roared, holding his head in pain. It took every ounce of resolve I possessed not to clutch my own forehead. There were no winners with that maneuver, and my head was throbbing.

"Point," I said, delivery shakier than I'd intended.

Before he could say anything else, I turned around, leaving the training room.

Perhaps we were the most entertaining thing here tonight.

And what the hell did I just do?

17

Court of Arcturus
ZOE

We'd decided to head to the Court of Arcturus before visiting the King and Queen of the star realms. We hoped that having the support of a majority of the courts would look better and help them move into swifter action. I just hoped Arcturus would be on our side, or we were losing a big gamble.

True to his word, Finnian had gotten the iris crystals working. One for each of us. He also said he had a theory about the bow, but he'd need to do more research to be certain.

"These stars are all connected, fragments from one larger star. Zoe, you'll carry the one Tiergan gave you to communicate with him, and this one," he said, handing me a second iris. "This one connects to the stars the rest of us have."

Freyja had sent me a message on the iris Tiergan had given me. Oleander must have worked a deal with Tiergan for an additional iris for her, which I was thankful for.

"Are we all ready?" Elvy asked, strapping his swords to the length of his back.

"All here, boss," Blaz said, standing with Jelly and Imelda.

Imelda clung to Clove with a fierce grip. Clodovea was staying behind this time since Imelda was emissary to the fire realm. She knew them best, but no one in our court had a great relationship with the fire realm. None of us wanted to travel right now, but with the help of the Sublunary, we had a better chance of not running into Hesperia's minions on the way to Arcturus.

Delmira was noticeably absent. I assumed her duties had called her away, but the frustration in Blaz's eyes told a different story. I decided not to pry.

"Kai and Seraphina are unpredictable at best," Imelda said. "However, they can lust for power as strongly as their dragons."

"I'm sorry… did you say *dragons*?" I asked, looking down at Jelly, as if to say, 'Can you believe this?' Her lopsided tongue seemed unbothered by the prospect of beasts that could eat her whole.

"It is the fire realm, Zo," Elvy said, with a hint of a smile on his face. "Arcturus is home to the dragon riders. We just have to convince them of our loyalty and that what we seek is the bigger prize than what Hesperia can offer."

"Will they see Jelly as a threat?" I asked. "When I first transformed her… you all mentioned that the last of the simargl died off in the fire realm."

"I'm leaning towards they will be extremely fond of Jelly," Imelda said. "Hopefully, the dragons see that as a sign of respect. The riders take counsel with their dragons."

"Alright, Jelly. No fire until I say, okay?" I asked her and she barked, as if she could understand me. Maybe she could.

"It's time," Elvy said, guiding us to the transport zone.

We all wore our Shadowed Legion uniforms, and I had knives strapped wherever I could place them. They all seemed fairly optimistic that it'd go well, and I had to trust them since my discernment wasn't telling me much.

"Zoe?" Elvy asked.

"I *see* no danger. All I can *see* is that going is not optional. We must enter this realm to collect the next piece. I *see* Seraphina and Kai meeting us at the border on… dragons. They won't turn us away, but…"

I shook my head. "There's something fuzzy around it all. Something is hanging in the balance."

"That's enough to go on," he said, kissing my hand.

Imelda gave Clodovea one last kiss before we all unfurled our wings, shifting into our Shadowed forms as we launched ourselves into the swirling cosmos.

Jelly flew right below me with Elvy on my left and Blaz on my right. Imelda was behind me. We were soon joined by a handful of Sublunary flanking us. We'd all agreed that they would not cross into Arcturus until we'd finished negotiations with the Astrals.

Much like our flight to Rigil, no one tried to attack while traveling, and none of us knew what to make of it. The moment we crossed the barrier to Arcturus, Kai and Seraphina greeted us astride gargantuan dragons.

I was so distracted by the giant lizards in front of me that I couldn't take in the rest of the realm. We descended upon a grassy plain, and unlike Rigil, Vega, and Algol, the sky was different here. It was still a cosmos of night above us, but there was a bright glow that almost gave the illusion of daylight. I quickly realized it was the power of fire, and I returned my focus to the literal dragons, staring down at us as if we were a tasty treat.

Jelly stood protectively in front of me, but her hackles weren't raised. The rest of the Luminaries flanked around me protectively.

I would be annoyed if it weren't for the fact that an entire realm rested on the fate of whether I lived or died.

One dragon was as black as the night sky above him. He was massive—like fifteen stories high. Seraphina was astride him… or her? I didn't know how to tell male and female dragons apart. Next to the midnight-black dragon was a slightly smaller brown dragon with a scary-looking tail that resembled a ball with spikes on it. Well, everything was petrifying about them. Kai was atop the brown dragon. Both beasts leaned their heads to my eye level, and it took the feel of Elvy's hand to keep me from bolting as their smoky breath blew my braid around.

I tried to find a source of water to ground me, but there was nothing I could hear over the loud rumblings of the dragons in front of me. So, I listened to the steady beat of Elvy's heart and focused on the feel of Jelly's soft wings against me. This was real. Whether my brain wanted to embrace this reality or not. This was all real.

"Seraphina, Kai," Elvy said firmly. "It has been too long."

"We've heard strange whispers throughout the realms," Seraphina said, just loud enough for us to hear.

"Let us speak as the allies we are," Elvy replied. "We will tell you what you want to know."

"The Queen of Algol said the same," Kai responded, gaze bored with the situation.

"Tried and failed," Seraphina confirmed. "We are not interested in war."

Lie. Or not a full truth. Something about that statement was off.

"It seems you are on friendly terms with Algol," Kai said, motioning towards my wings and immortal mark. I didn't think trying to deceive them would end well for me, so I'd forgone the charade altogether. My *sight* had warned me of that.

"I am of both," I said, voice steady.

"You cannot serve both," Seraphina said.

"Yet, here I am," I replied.

I was growing tired of being told what I could or could not do. My empathy for Tiergan and his cause only grew.

"War has come," Blaz said, catching Seraphina's gaze and refocusing on the conversation. "What side of history will you be on?"

"The side of peace," Kai said. "We've lost too much in meaningless battles of old."

"Our dragons will protect us," the Lady Astral said. Her dragon breathed a plume of smoke as if to drive home the point.

"Even your dragons will die without the power of all five elementals," Imelda challenged. "Please hear reason."

"We're losing them. They are hiding something," I said through our flame. *"New tactic."*

I leaned down next to Jelly and felt the four pairs of eyes watching me closely. They could sense I was different—unfamiliar to them. Unknown meant danger. I had to play this card, or we would never win them over.

"Light it up, little dragon," I whispered. She cocked her head and barked excitedly as flames engulfed her. She turned to the two dragons in front of her with a fierce look in her eyes. Jelly had the heart of a hero, and I hoped these beasts respected that.

The monster of a black dragon leaned its gigantic head towards us, but we all stood resolute. I was certain moving unexpectedly would be the wrong move and would result in us all getting burned to stardust.

The black dragon seemed to inhale the scent of Jelly through its ridiculously large nostrils that I was certain I could probably stand in. Then the dragon did something *gentle*. The beast nudged Jelly's nose ever so softly and seemed to turn its colossal head in fond familiarity.

"The dragons are communicating with their riders," Elvy said through our flame.

"One of the simargl have returned to us," Seraphina said with silver in her eyes. She was crying. Even Kai seemed moved by the power of my little bundle of joy with wings. Here she was. Saving me again, as she always has.

"You're her master?" the Lady Astral asked.

I nodded.

"We will hear what you have to say," Kai said, bowing to us, and we returned the gesture of respect.

"Good girl," I whispered to Jelly, and her flames disappeared.

"Follow us," Seraphina said, launching her dragon into the air. The thing may be huge, but it was still incredibly fast.

We all unfurled our wings again and flew right after them.

I took the time to take in the landscape below me that I could easily see with immortal eyes. There were mountains in the background. Wait. No. Not exactly mountains. Volcanoes that were spurting out bits of lava. I'd always had an irrational fear of them, but at least I could fly away now should they erupt. No one else seemed fazed by this, so I swallowed down my worry.

The grassy plains turned to black stone that seemed to make up the streets and most of the buildings. It was kind of dull and monochromatic. Oleander would dig it.

Despite this, the city bustled with immortals, and the glow of their red and orange wings showed their allegiance to their star. I didn't focus on them for too long as just beyond the city was a grassland of dragons... What do you call a pack of dragons?

"Flight or wing," Elvy answered through our flame. My thoughts must have been loud.

My ramblings continued. There were various shades and sizes. They all had four legs and massive bat-like wings. Their razor-sharp talons did not escape my notice, nor did their unnecessarily large teeth. There were green, blue, red, orange, brown, and black dragons with varying spikes and intimidating features. I just hoped we didn't fly too close, and they misjudged us for a snack that needed to be deep-fried first.

"Deep breaths, flame," Elvy coached. *"We're almost there."*

I glanced back up at the Lord and Lady Astral to find that they had started a descent towards a cave on the outskirts of town. This did not calm me down. We were absolutely about to become dragon food in there.

"I'll protect you," he promised, but there was a hint of amusement in his voice that set me at ease.

Part of me was kind of excited about dragons, but they were *so* big. It's like the first time I went riding on a horse. They were freakishly larger than I'd anticipated. It took a while for the horse and me to accept each other, but I eventually loved it. So, that's what I'd do. Picture the dragons as slightly bigger horses.

"You are ridiculous," Elvy said, laughing out loud.

"Do I even want to know?" Blaz asked.

"Please share," Imelda chuckled along with them.

"Don't you dare!" I shouted back, and Elvy zipped his lips up and pretended to throw away the key.

I blew him a kiss and landed softly on the stone that led into the dark cave. Jelly circled me, checking me over.

"Your guardian admires you," Seraphina said, standing in front of me, having dismounted from her saddle.

"And I her," I said seriously.

"Follow us," Kai directed, leading us up a flight of stairs that went over the cave instead of through it.

"Let's go," I said, taking Elvy's hand and following the silent vibrations of destiny forward. Ever forward.

18

Sleeping Beauty
FREYJA

Oleander was not a peaceful sleeper.

He seemed to carry the weight of the realms on his shoulders, even in the world of dreams. His eyes fluttered beneath the thin skin of his eyelids, and I wanted to take his worries away. This was the second night he'd slept in my bed, and I hadn't psyched myself up enough to touch him while he slept.

I wanted to ease away those woes. One caress. Just to see. I gently lifted a palm to the strong line of his sharp jaw and rubbed my thumb across his cheek. Closing my eyes, I made my hand as solid as possible, soothing away his troubles. Ander responded almost instantly with his worry lines relaxing, but he didn't wake.

The crinkles on his face smoothed into the marble structure they so often were. He turned his face towards my palm, making my thumb slip to the softness of his lips. I bit my own in return.

"Don't fall in love with me," I whispered to his sleeping form. He seemed to frown at this. I wasn't sure my own heart got the message. It was leaping off a cliff at Mach 7.

Normally, and by normal, I mean if I wasn't dead, I'd be happy to leap. Enthusiastic even. Zoe and I had always been wild spirits, but this… I couldn't control the variables here, which meant this couldn't possibly be safe. I couldn't be selfish. I couldn't hurt him because… no. Stop. Thinking ten steps ahead would change nothing. While I would like to be his in a lot of different ways, this could only be fleeting. Eventually, fate would call us—call me—to the *otherside*.

I pulled my hand from his face, and his features abruptly went back to the distress of the world. Sighing, I began soothing him again. If nothing else, I would give him a night of peaceful sleep. So I did.

★★★

"Good morning, sleeping beauty," I said as Oleander's blue eyes met mine.

"Beauty? You mean stunningly hot sex god?" he responded in mock offense.

"Nope. I said what I meant."

"I'll take it, sweetheart," he said, pulling me so that my head cradled his bare chest. Breathe, little libido. Breathe… no. Don't breathe. He smells too good. I'm a ghost. I don't need to breathe!

"Are you ever going to tell me what you're thinking without me having to pry it out of you?" he asked, stroking my dark hair down the length of my back.

"You may not like what I think."

His lips nuzzled against my hair, breathing me in. "I highly doubt that, Freyja."

"Is it frustrating that you can't read me like other immortals?"

He paused for a moment before answering.

"No, it's refreshing—it keeps me on my toes."

I involuntarily scooted closer to him. This was the opposite of what I was supposed to be doing.

"Tell me what you're thinking. I promise you, my imagination is far worse," he teased.

He had a point.

"I was thinking… you smelled good. And I didn't know how to feel about that."

"Would you rather I smell bad?" he asked, a grin dancing on his lips.

"No. It's not that," I said, not offering a further explanation. Turns out. I didn't need to.

"Oh. You're trying to keep yourself at a distance," he said, tilting my chin back to meet those blue eyes. "You don't have to do that, you know? I get to decide, too."

I wanted to argue with him. Tell him that *I* was trying to protect *him*. I could list all my very reasonable explanations on why this was a terrible idea, but something held me silent. Perhaps it was fate. Ander ever so gently kissed my lips, and I got the odd sensation of feeling him and not feeling him. What I would give to have him solid beneath me. I kissed him back in fervor, and he moved his mouth to my neck, trailing kisses up and down. If I could get goosebumps, I would be flooded with them.

A knock came at the door, and Oleander paused, leaning over me.

"Go the hell away," he ordered. I couldn't believe he just said that. Now everyone would know he was here. He seemed to see the thought on my face. "I don't care who knows how I feel about you, Freyja. Never doubt that."

Before I could question him about these alleged feelings, the knock came again, and he slumped in defeat.

"I'm sorry to interrupt, Lord Astral," Zadie began through the door. "I'm afraid you are needed in the village. Hesperia is right outside the wards."

"Always in the way," he said, leaping into action. I followed suit.

It took less than ten seconds before we were flying over the forest and descending into the refugee village. She'd never breached the wards before, and I prayed to God that she wouldn't start now.

The refugees had all gone into hiding until it was safe again. Tiergan, the Sublunary leader, stood on the other side of Oleander. Tiergan may not truly like him, but he hated everything Hesperia stood for. That gave us a common enemy. Zadie stood to my right, almost protective of me.

"Can she see us?" Tiergan asked.

"No," Oleander said confidently. "But she knows we are here."

"Won't the Lord Astral come out to play?" she purred, sickly black hair blowing in the wind.

No one moved. The air was so tense around us that I wanted to choke on it, but I stood unyieldingly next to Ander. He would not do this alone. The Sublunary surrounded us, poised to fight. The Shadowed Legion, loyal to Oleander, unfurled their wings, ready to protect the refugees here with their lives.

"I've come in peace, Oleander," she said sweetly, as if she knew him. It made my skin crawl to be reminded of what she'd made him do. "Can't two old lovers have a civil conversation?"

Ander stood still, hands in pockets. His stance may be casual, but a trained eye saw how uncomfortable he was. I wanted to claim her death right there. I knew Zoe would call for it, though. That was her destiny.

Hesperia's smile never faltered. I just now noticed that she stood alone. She hadn't brought anyone with her, which meant… distraction.

"This is a stall," I whispered.

Ander nodded. He seemed to be aware of it, too. Yet, he could not leave, since it was his magic that kept the wards strong. Should they fail, he was the only one who could heal them.

"Very well then," she said, shrugging her shoulders. "I tried to do this graciously."

She raised her hands and started pulsating her dark magic around the wards, looking for a weakness she would not find.

"Warn Zoe," he commanded. "They're probably heading for her… or Vega. Who the hell knows?"

He slipped the iris out of his pocket and charged the stone for me, and I relayed the message to my sister, praying that she was safe and unharmed. There was no time to wait for a response, as Hesperia was using her power as a battering ram against the protective magic after finding no weaknesses to exploit.

"Showtime," Ander said. "She won't get through, and she knows this. Try to figure out what this is all really about," he instructed both Tiergan and Zadie.

Zadie bowed, and Tiergan nodded.

"Please go with them," he requested. I wanted to argue, but this was no time for that.

I gave him a swift kiss on the cheek and murmured, "Don't die. It's not all it's cracked up to be. Speaking from experience here."

He laughed. "Don't worry, sweetheart. Life's just getting good. I'm not going anywhere."

With those parting words, he lifted his palms to the sky and sent his own magic to the wards, reinforcing their stability. Zadie pulled me with her into what they'd made a command headquarters. There was movement all around me as the immortals tried to figure out Hesperia's play here.

"I'm going to contact Finn," Zadie said, moving us into a corner, pulling out her iris.

"Where did you get one of those?" I asked.

"Hadn't you noticed my absence the last couple of days?"

I looked away sheepishly. I hadn't, but to be fair, I had noticed little else outside of the Lord Astral.

Zadie rolled her eyes, but there was a smile on her lips. "I'd gone to see Finn. They found a bunch of them in Vega. He wouldn't tell me where. Realm security and all."

"Makes sense."

Zadie charged up the iris and whispered her message over the rainbows. We both watched in amazement as the shimmering lights disappeared to deliver the communication. Now we waited.

"What are your intentions with Oleander?" Zadie asked, ignoring the fact that we were quite literally in the middle of a battle.

"Um—" I said, turning up blank.

She looked at me expectantly. I didn't know what to say, so I said nothing.

"Just don't hurt him, okay? He's nothing but marshmallows underneath all that melodramatic persona."

She was right. He was.

"I have no plans to hurt him," I promised, and I guessed she saw the sincerity in my eyes.

Before she could question me further, Finn responded with four words that I won't soon forget.

"We are under attack," Finn's voice echoed within my very soul. I wasn't sure if Zoe was still on Vega or if they'd already left for Arcturus. Neither scenario was good.

Zadie leaped into action and looked Tiergan square in the eye.

"Vega calls for aid!"

That was not technically true, but I didn't feel the need to point that out.

Tiergan paused for a moment and looked around at the other Sublunary.

"And we will answer," he nodded.

Less than five minutes later, the Sublunary were in formation to take the back door out of Algol and into Vega. Oleander and I had to stay behind. Me—because my soul was no longer allowed outside of Algol and the *otherside* linked to it. Oleander—to keep Hesperia out of the refugee village. He was pissed, but knew where he was needed the most. Half the Shadowed Legion would follow Zadie into battle in Vega. The rest would stay here in case the wards failed.

"Go," Oleander commanded while still exerting his magic to strengthen the wards.

Zadie and Tiergan did not hesitate to launch themselves from the transport zone and into the cosmos above.

"Please be okay," I whispered to the universe.

19

Allies

ZOE

The more we ascended the treacherous stone stairs, the more my gut felt unsettled. My *sight* wasn't telling me what to look for in our hosts, but something didn't feel right. There was a sense of teetering. Jelly revealing her true form seemed to push fate more to our side, yet… something was wrong.

"The dragons stay below in the caves," Seraphina offered for casual conversation as we came upon a castle within the mountain itself. It reminded me of Petra in Jordan, which I'd only ever seen in the third Indiana Jones movie. Again, my mom loved the eighties. A twinge of pain flooded my heart at the memory of her, and I swallowed the lump in my throat down.

My travels had never quite led me to that part of the world, but it wasn't lost to me entirely yet. Unless we fail. Then everything was lost. Until then, I would keep my mother's spirit alive in me.

This stone was much darker than the red of Petra. Maybe a better reference was the White Mountains that Gimli, Legolas, and Aragorn traveled to before the final battle for Gondor. That sense of foreboding sliced through my gut, but the same force screamed that I must enter.

"Stay guarded," I whispered through the bond. Elvy nodded, sending a discreet hand signal to Imelda and Blaz, who had never relaxed since crossing the border.

"Do the dragons have names?" I asked curiously.

"The names are only known to their bonded riders," Kai said.

"My apologies," I offered, but Seraphina shook her silvery hair.

"No need. The ways of dragons are riddled with secrets."

I only nodded, observing the pair up close. They were both tall—at least six feet. Kai didn't have a strand of silver in his hair, but Seraphina's was nothing but silver. The star tattoo that peeked across the V-cut of her chest was the only sure sign she was Shadowed. I assumed Kai was not.

I guess it didn't really matter if you had wings when you had an entire dragon at your disposal.

"How did you come across a simargl?" she asked, a little too curious.

I offered little. "She's been with me for some time."

"Yet, you are newly Emerged?" Kai asked. "And of both Algol and Vega."

Imelda and Blaz both stepped a little closer to me. Jelly still trotted right beside me with Elvy on my left. Neither Kai nor Seraphina seemed to care much about my alliance to the stars. Their eyes were on Jelly most of all, and my magic felt on the verge of letting loose if they tried anything.

"Yes, my flame completed the trials of the Emerging during the last solstice."

"So you found a simargl when you made Vega your home? The realms know the simargl belong to Arcturus. I do hope you weren't keeping this one hidden, Elvy," Seraphina said, smile tight.

I weighed the options. Start a civil war between Vega and Arcturus, or take a leap of faith in telling the truth. It sure would be nice if The Archer would show up right about now. No—that would most certainly not help our cause. The discernment within me urged me to pull on the thread of destiny.

"Jelly was my creation," I said with confidence. "And the simargl belong to themselves." Octavia's records had come in handy after all, not that I'd gotten to explore them very much.

The Lord and Lady Astrals hid their startle well, but I'd caught it.

"You're powerful enough to create life?" Kai asked, understandably skeptical.

"My full powers have not been tested," I admitted. I was no necromancer. The balance would not allow that—but adjustments I could do.

Kai and Seraphina led us into what I assumed was a meeting room deep within the walls of the castle. I felt a little suffocated, but the ceiling opened up to the stars and a brilliant red moon hung over us. The strange glow of the fire from the volcanoes created an eerie illusion. There were no rumblings within these walls, however. Not even from a dragon, though these walls were enormous enough to accommodate even the largest beast's size.

Our hosts shared the head of the table. Elvy and I sat on their right while Blaz and Imelda sat on their left. There were no guards from the Shadowed Legion around. It was just us. Somehow, that made it more suspicious.

"What have you come to demand from us?" Kai asked bluntly.

"Not demand," Elvy disagreed. "We have a common enemy—Hesperia. She threatens the peace of realms."

"No," Seraphina countered. Blaz grew rigid across from me. Imelda's composure was much more practiced. She was used to the stubbornness of this court. "She threatens the peace of your court, Elvy. Not ours."

"Have you been made aware of the gravity of what she has done to Algol?" Imelda asked.

"What's it to us if Oleander dies? I didn't think you would care so much about his life, given the history between the two of you, Elvy," Seraphina said.

"I was mistaken about the Lord Astral of Algol. He has been nothing but honorable."

We weren't winning them over with this tactic. They saw forgiveness as nothing more than a weakness.

"What about our sovereign duty as the elemental star realms in protecting Earth?" I asked. "We are sworn to safeguard the peace of that mortal plane. The damage has been catastrophic… the realms as we know them will cease to exist if she is not stopped."

"You dare to speak to us with familiarity? You are but a child," Kai scoffed. Jelly growled.

"You know her name," Blaz said. "The rumors are true, Lord and Lady Astral. Zoe Eferhild, Realm-Healer—Emerging of Legends. She will bring peace, but she cannot do it on her own."

Seraphina and Kai looked at Jelly again, who stared fiercely back at them.

"The simargl chose her," she said to her husband. "You know the law."

"How do we know it is not a ruse?" Kai asked, as if we were not here. They must not be flames and had no ability to talk through a bond.

"Listen to your dragon," she murmured. "We have been made fools."

Kai paused, closing his eyes. Whatever he heard made his nostrils flare with anger. This was another turning point on the thread of fate.

The moment Kai opened his eyes, one of my pockets warmed, demanding my attention. It was my iris from Tiergan. I swiftly shielded the Vega court and sent my magic to charge the crystal in payment to the rainbows.

Freyja's frantic voice called over the pulsing light, "Vega is under attack!"

Nothing else.

We all seemed to simultaneously direct our gaze towards Seraphina and Kai, who had the audacity to have apologies in their eyes and waiting on their lips. I guess they favored excuses when it served them.

"Hesperia… she got in our heads… promised us things," Seraphina said. "I'm so sorry, Elvy."

"She used the dragon lust against us," Kai explained.

I turned my head and leaned into my gift of discernment, and plucked the thread of magic that tied me to Algol.

"Why is Hesperia waiting for you?" I asked, speaking with the conviction of a judge, jury, and executioner. I would assume whatever role was required of me now.

"She said you would come and gave instructions to stall," Kai informed.

Jelly transformed into her burning simargl form in a protective stance around me. She was angry.

Then, the unexpected happened. Kai and Seraphina kneeled in front of Jelly, who seemed ready to set them ablaze.

"We will help your master," Seraphina said, slicing her palm in a blood oath. Kai followed suit. Jelly circled around them and seemed to grow to the size of a great dane instead of the height of her usual petite border collie. Even her features transformed into something more vicious and wolf-like.

I realized that Jelly was far more powerful than I'd ever understood. The immortals of Arcturus revered her.

"You will answer the call for aid," Elvy said, getting up from his seat. Blaz and Imelda followed him. "You will ride with us to Vega and allow us back to search for the item we need."

"What item?"

"You don't get to ask questions," Blaz spat. "You dishonor the title of the Astrals."

They didn't argue, resigned to accept the punishment for their actions.

"I want everything you have on the simargl," I added. "When we get back."

Seraphina nodded. "You shall have it."

"We've wasted enough time with these lies. We must fly," Imelda stated, growing anxious. Clodovea was an exceptional fighter, but that didn't mean there wasn't danger.

"Come, we will take the Alpha Wing of Dragons in the Shadowed Legion," Kai said, wasting no more time. The pair hurriedly led us down passageways that I assumed led to caverns below their castle. They must have given some silent command because their Shadowed Legion was ready with five riders saddled on their dragons. The rest would fly and had their own red and orange wings unfurled, ready for launch.

"We ride to the aid of Vega!" Seraphina shouted, mounting her black dragon.

Less than ten seconds later, we were traveling through the cosmos with dragons on our tail. Words that I never thought would cross my mind in any sense of reality. The wonder of it all.

20

Storm of Justice

ZOE

We descended upon Vega like a storm, threatening to destroy anything in its path.

"The Sublunary have arrived," Elvy said through our flame.

The fiery red-hair of Zadie and the mustache of Tiergan greeted us in the distance. Yep. I could see that sucker from all the way up here. Delmira and Clodovea led the charge against Hesperia's supporters. Finnian was nowhere to be found, and I hoped that meant he was stationed down below as a last line of defense for our immortals.

There were no signs of Oleander or Hesperia, which gave me a sinking feeling. That meant they were likely in the same place... fighting each other alone, which meant Freyja was on her own. I shook the worry from my face. I couldn't let that affect me right now. There were innocent immortals below me who did not deserve to be casualties of this war.

The moment the dragons descended right along with us, time seemed to stand still just for a moment. Hesperia's legion seemed confused, assuming the Court of Arcturus would be there to aid them.

Wrong.

Jelly flew by my side, and the dragons began... burning. Their riders were skilled, battling from all parts of their beasts. The dragons avoided the immortals from Vega, focusing their breath of death on Hesperia's army. Those in the path of their flames didn't stand a chance.

Before I could so much as unsheathe a knife, Hesperia's army called for a retreat. I wanted to go after them. No—not me. The dark revenge writhing in my bones desired to see what their insides looked like.

"Your eyes!" Elvy shouted, but they had already gone dark. I swam in the bliss of retribution—of justice—as I embraced the shadows.

My black tendrils shot out towards the cowards fleeing from the battle. I couldn't let them go back to Oleander and Freyja, so they had to die. I was briefly aware of my flame following behind me. He wasn't going to let any harm come to me, but I wasn't sure he would let me ensnare my prey. One of my tendrils reached out towards him, but his voice stopped me.

"We can have some fun, flame," Elvy promised through our bond. *"Then you have to come back."*

Maybe I didn't want to come back, but he didn't need to know that.

My web of black magic had captured a few of Hesperia's immortals, and I circled them like a predator. Because that's just what I was—an apex predator.

"You three have been wicked," I said, voice low but firm.

There was fear in their eyes, and I fed off it. I moaned at the pleasure coming from the shadows feeding me.

"You're just like her," one male said. Sweat drenched him, and the vein in his forehead strained violently. Something snapped inside me. The euphoria was gone, but the shadows remained. This was darker... like the second trial in the star realms. I demanded retribution.

I lifted the man into the air with my magic alone.

"What did you say to me?"

The reflection of my dark eyes shined through the terror in his own.

"You will come to her side in the end. Everyone does," he said through labored breathing. My shadows slowly suffocated him. "She has plans for you, Zoe Eferhild. Plans for you both."

"My name may stand for life-bringer, but I'm afraid it will not stand true for you," I whispered as the threads of fate sang a sorrowful melody. They did not want me to end their lives, but the darkness called for justice, and it was ravenous.

Time paused for a moment, and my soul recognized the male before me. He'd watched Hesperia beat me the night I'd healed Algol, and he'd winced...

But he hadn't stopped her. He'd given me no mercy.

Just before I dealt the killing blow, the man choked out, "She's watching... waiting."

With those parting words, my shadows ripped him and the other two captives into ribbons.

"Let her come," I whispered.

I leaned back, embracing the power as a gentle hand pulled on my arm.

"It's time to come back, starlight," the voice said.

Turning to the voice, my black eyes found the gray of my flame, but I wanted something deeper.

"Join me," I whimpered, cupping his cheek with my palm. He leaned into it, kissing my hand gently. "We don't have to go back there."

I didn't want to shove this part of me back down into the vaults deep within me. I didn't want to face what I'd just done and the consequences that would surely come.

"I'll help you face it," he promised. "Every part of you I love."

Tears flowed down my flushed cheeks, and for a moment, his eyes darkened, mirroring my own.

"Join me," I said again, voice breaking, and it felt like my insides cried out.

Elvy's eyes blackened, but I did not fear him. I was consumed with nothing but love.

A dark mist closed in on us in the distance, and my eyes caught sight of The Archer's constellation above me, brighter than usual.

"My bond," I said, voice affectionate. A multitude of emotions flooded through me, and I couldn't make sense of it. My spirit spiraled, lost in the darkness, but part of me wanted to stay hidden in them forever with him.

But I couldn't.

Slowly, like molasses dripping from its tree, I let go of the shadows and allowed the light of Vega to fill my soul. I shuddered at the weight that still held firmly on my shoulders. Elvy's dark eyes withdrew into the familiar storm gray I loved.

"That was incredibly reckless," he murmured, still leaning into my palm.

"I have a feeling I just failed a test," I whispered.

"We," he corrected.

"I'm sorry," I said. "With Algol's link to me… I just feel out of control."

"I know," he said, kissing me gently. "I was raised to feel nothing but shame for that part of me. To let someone see it willingly…"

"Thank you. For sharing that with me… I shouldn't have pushed you."

The mist grew closer to us, like a dark fog rolling in.

"I don't think you were entirely in control there," he said.

"I wasn't afraid. At least, not of you," I said seriously. "My shadows recognized you."

"I felt it, too."

There were so many questions, yet I did not know what they were.

My stomach soured at the destruction I'd caused the males lying on the ground. Their flesh was unrecognizable, and my knees threatened to crash to the ground, but I formed my heart into ice. I'd chosen to end their lives. I didn't get to wallow in it now.

"Come on. We need to get back to the others," I said. "The weather looks like it's turning for the worst."

"Yes," he sighed.

"Where's Jelly?" I asked.

"She stayed with Blaz. With the magic so unpredictable…," he trailed off, but I understood. He knew I'd never forgive myself if something happened to her at my hands. Or at anyone's, for that matter.

"Are you ready?"

"I am," I said, but I didn't really believe it. That was radical acceptance. Whether I was ready, life happened. Fighting the waves would just cause me to drown.

Elvy pulled me in for a kiss, moving slowly, helping me ground to this moment.

"I'm still here. I see you. All of you. And I love you," he murmured like a prayer.

When I was centered, he clasped my hand solidly in his and guided us home.

★★★

We'd all gathered back in our ocean-side manor, leaving Musterion untouched. Zadie hadn't asked about the lack of immortals, though I was certain her watchful eyes noted our sudden population decrease. We would likely tell the Court of Algol about Musterion eventually, but not until we were ready. The safety of our immortals came first.

Delmira handled the Shadowed Legion with striking expertise. They held their own before the dragon wing descended upon Vega, incinerating the enemy swiftly.

Blaz aided her in regrouping the squadrons. His eyes kept turning back towards her when he thought no one would notice. I smiled, looking down, resigned to keep whatever was going on between them to myself. Clove and Imelda kept stealing secret touches, moving fluidly with one another as they conducted post-battle work. I grimaced. Immortals had yet again died needlessly. My immortals.

Most had been evacuated to Musterion but not enough. The most vulnerable had been moved first, but any life lost to war was one too many.

"Why did the wards fail?" Elvy asked, helping the Luminaries with their tasks.

Evander—Elvy's favored captain—provided his own theory.

"I took my squad along the perimeter of the wards five minutes before the attack. We just checked them again, and the wards were still intact."

"The backdoor we took into Vega last time?" I asked.

Evander shook his head. "We extended the wards to cover that area."

"I'll talk to Tiergan. See if he knows anything," I offered, and Elvy nodded.

Seeing the devastation wrought from this attack that seemed to have no rhyme or reason had unsettled my flame. No one else seemed to notice, but his eyes kept flickering between his storm gray and the black hue of death.

"Settle, flame," I whispered through the bond. *"Letting loose of that power now will only kill innocents. Breathe."*

Elvy closed his eyes, listening to my soothing chant. With a bit of concentration, the darkness cleared, and his body trembled with the release of what he'd deemed his curse. I never saw it that way. It was a part of him that he feared, yet a part of him that was designed to protect him. It was hard for me to dislike anything that would protect the one who forever held my heart.

Evander winced, holding his arm. The midnight blue of the uniform hid the blood well, but it could not hide from my magic. The healing power sang within me, needing to help. Acting on instinct alone, I brushed my hand over the wound, healing it instantly. His sigh of relief was payment enough.

"You needn't do that, Lady Astral. The healers could have handled it," he said.

"I am a healer," I countered.

"Thank you for your generosity," he said, bowing. "I'm sure the medics would appreciate your assistance with the wounded."

"Of course," I agreed. "I'll be there as soon as I am able."

With those parting words, he left as the rest of the Luminaries, including Finn and Jelly surrounded us. Seraphina and Kai waited on the Shadowed Legion's training field with their dragons.

"You brought dragons?" Delm questioned. "The dragons haven't left Arcturus in… I don't even remember when."

"Well before our time, sister," Finn offered.

"They owed us," Imelda shrugged.

Zadie and Tiergan walked up just then. It was better to have all our allies on the same page, but we weren't quite ready to let in Seraphina or Kai just yet. One act of righteousness does not dissuade the act of cowardice and betrayal to the star realms.

"Why did they owe you?" Zadie asked, looping an arm through Finn's. Delmira's gaze wanted to burn her hand right off, but she kept silent, which was a grand stride for her.

"They knew Hesperia would attack Vega, though she never did join the battlefield," Elvy said curiously.

"Oleander is taking care of her," she answered, shifting her weight to her other hip.

"By himself?" I asked, heart fluttering.

"He's behind the wards, and she was alone. She won't get past him… she'll drain him—maybe."

"This doesn't make any sense," Clodovea said, sighing. She twirled her long braids in a frustrated movement.

"Doesn't it?" Tiergan suggested.

"What do you mean?" Blaz asked.

Jelly nudged her head into my palm, trying to focus my attention on her.

"Hesperia is chaos," Tiergan said. "That is her power—her gift. To never be seen clearly, yet project what others want to see. It would drive an immortal mad trying to figure out her moves."

I felt the truth of his words in my heart, but it didn't feel… complete. This may be one of her gifts, but it was not *the* gift. The threads of fate urged a deeper understanding of Tiergan, but I could *see* he would not give freely yet.

"I've never heard of magic like that," Zadie said. "But the ways of Algol's power manifestations have always been shrouded in mystery, less finite than the other elemental realms."

"I'll say it again… immortals have forgotten the ways of old," Tiergan said, eyes twinkling with amusement.

"Do you know of another way into Vega? We don't know how they got in," Elvy said.

"There are many," Tiergan confirmed, as if that wasn't concerning.

"I think I've found them when I was down in the archives in…." Finn trailed off, not saying Musterion. He and Zadie may be an item, but his loyalty was to the immortals of this court. "I have a theory about the map. I can go out with a squad to test it."

"Go," Elvy said. "There's nothing left to be done now."

Elvy ran his fingers through his dark, silvery curls—a sign he was frustrated. He wasn't alone in that feeling. We were all drained and would likely remain so until this was all over.

"We need to get back, Tiergan," Zadie said, but her expression seemed to want to stay right here with Finn. My heart softened. When all of this was over, I hoped things would be easier for them in whatever way they deemed fit.

Tiergan bowed slightly and followed her retreating form.

"I'm going to tend to the wounded," I said. "The more severe cases."

"I just want to be alone for a little while," I confessed through our flame.

Elvy kissed me on the back of my hand, smiling that one-dimpled smile. *"I'll come collect you before we go to the dragons. Call if you change your mind. I'll be there instantly."*

"I know," I said, waving goodbye to the rest of them while Jelly followed dutifully beside me.

After I was a good distance away, I allowed my attention to focus on the crashing of waves hitting the shoreline and breathed in the scent of the saltwater. A pod of kelpies followed us as we walked along the shoreline to where the wounded were. They were curious creatures, and I revered them.

I slipped out my iris and charged it with my magic, wanting to let Freyja know I was okay. That we all were.

Moments later, the stone warmed with a message of her own, which meant Oleander wasn't completely depleted.

"Tired but okay." The rainbows delivered her words across the realms.

"Freyja is safe," I said, petting Jelly, and her lopsided grin seemed to hear me.

"Just you and me, like old times," I said, splashing through the ocean water with her, craving some sense of normalcy.

"Hard to believe this is our life now, isn't it, girl?" I asked her, staring up at the infinite stars above.

Earth felt so far away. Jelly laid her heavy head on my lap, sensing my emotions were turning dark. I tried not to let myself think of my mom or the way she had sacrificed her own life to save mine. Her last act had been one of true bravery—a mother's love. I was afraid to allow myself to think about her. I feared never rising from the abyss of that grief. Then, there was Emma's horror-frozen face in the end. My therapist had been so kind—so patient with me. She was gone much too soon in life. Grant's lifeless body flashed through my mind, too, and I shuddered. My dreams were still often plagued with that day, but here lately, it was just a dark void.

The flashbacks just kept coming sometimes, which was why I tried not to think about them. Not until this was all over. That didn't stop the waves of grief that teetered on the edge of sanity. I couldn't afford to check out right now when so many depended on me to… save the realms. Heal them. Beat Hesperia's chaos. That was part of being a warrior. We shoved all that stuff down until the mission was done. No breaking until then.

But part of me felt broken already after what I'd done to the three males. Why had he winced? Why did that moment feel so significant to me? Why had I gone through with killing them after feeling the urge to pause? I glanced at my palms, expecting them to be red with the shame I'd felt at failing, but they weren't.

I would honor every innocent blood spilled by defeating her. Then I would truly grieve—wallow. Not before then. Until then, time moved forward, and so would I.

"Let's go, Jelly," I said, turning my gaze from the sky above. A secret part of me had been hoping to hear from The Archer. He hadn't shown, though. There were no signs that June or Phoebe were around either. I swallowed down my longing and headed to take care of a problem that I had a solution to right now—heal what was broken.

21

Intention

FREYJA

Oleander had faced Hesperia alone, and she'd never come close to breaking through the wards, which was concerning to everyone involved. Why would she exert so much energy when it would inevitably amount to nothing? Chaos at its finest, or maybe she just wanted us to know that she knew where we were hiding. Fortunately, the shadows to transport other Shadowed to other realms were within the village boundaries. We could—they could—get out if needed. I might forever be stuck here.

I shook the thought from my mind. That was not something I could control right now.

After Hesperia finally left, and we'd heard from Zoe that Vega wasn't decimated, Oleander finally relaxed some. He sipped cinnamon whiskey while we listened to the fire and waited for further instructions. He felt certain the courts of Algol, Vega, Arcturus, and Rigil would pay a visit to King Alrich and Queen Farron before continuing on with the mission from The Archer.

I was sure the delicate balance of the decision between potentially life-saving politics and obtaining the ultimate weapon weighed heavy on Zoe's shoulders. I wished for my sister to have an easier life, and I wanted the same for myself.

A tug ripped through my core, and Oleander noticed the wince in my expression before I could hide it.

"What was that?" he asked, moving closer to me on the red sofa.

I shook my head. "Nothing."

"Nothing made you clutch your side?" he asked. "I didn't think spirits felt much physically."

"This isn't physical," I replied, swallowing down the pain as it settled down again. This one was more violent than previous callings to the *otherside*. It seemed anytime I longed for peace, the keeper of the *otherside* called me home, promising the peace within. I had a feeling that it was, in fact, peaceful there. I could be with my dad again and see him in a blissful form instead of the tragic face he bore when he died.

I would be forever lost to this world, never seeing my sister again or Oleander. That thought was my own secret that I held fondly in my heart.

His piercing blue eyes never left my gaze. Somehow, he seemed to have my secrets bared to him, and maybe I didn't mind being known. That thought was paralyzing.

"You don't have to do this alone, Freyja."

I put on the mask of the warrior who protected Ander… and hurt him at the same time.

"The world of the dead is no business of a mortal," I snapped.

"Sweetheart, I'm not mortal."

He smiled. Greedily. I wanted to fill my psychological armor with knives to twist… to protect him. It sounded much crueler in my head, but I knew deep in the abyss of my spirit, it was I who needed protecting. If I truly let him in how I wanted to, I'd never stop falling for him.

"You can bleed. You can die," I countered.

"It's been a while since we've truly played," he said with adoration in his voice.

He liked it when I pushed him. Why?

"It means you're here. Fighting to stay," he said, seeming to respond to my thoughts.

"You don't know that," I replied, shaking my head. Was I trying to convince myself or him?

"Oh, but I do," he said, pulling me into his lap, and I didn't resist.

I suddenly felt guilty. He'd just expended an exorbitant amount of energy that I truly had no comparison to understand. Yet, here he was. Focusing his attention on me. Soothing me. It should be the other way around. If my cheeks could flush, they would flare with the shame I felt. So, I looked down, away from his eyes.

"Now we can't have that," he said, lifting my chin up to meet his gaze. "No hiding from me, Freyja."

I swallowed, soaking in his features.

"Tell me what that pain was, sweetheart."

One deep breath and a leap of bravery. That's all I needed to get the words out.

"The *otherside* has been more aggressive in calling for me to come home."

"Do you want to go?" he asked. The subtle strain in his voice told me just how much he thought of that idea, but he asked anyway. It wasn't about what he wanted or needed. This was about what I wanted.

"No," I answered honestly. "Sometimes I think it would be easier, and I'd be with my dad. I don't think he'd want that for me, though. If there were another way. What I would leave behind is too much."

"Then we fight it," he said. "Until Zoe figures it out."

"Promise me something," I said with urgency lacing my words.

"What?"

"If Zoe fails to bring me back… forgive her. Don't resent her. Your friendship is important to her."

He didn't seem happy about it, but he slowly nodded.

"I promise," he agreed.

Oleander seemed settled now, but he still twirled the iris in his fingers while we held each other, waiting for our next move. The crackling of the fire and the steady beat of his heart would have lulled me to sleep if ghosts did that sort of thing.

And then pain like I had never recalled experiencing, mortal or dead, ripped through me.

I shot out of his lap, trying to escape his presence because I knew what was coming next, but fate had other plans for me.

My spirit collided to the stone floor, and I could do nothing but embrace the waves as my image flickered.

"Leave!" I shouted, barely getting the words out as my body continued to violently convulse on the floor, but Ander only moved closer, hovering over me with fear in his eyes.

"What's going on, Freyja?" he asked frantically.

"Please go," I whimpered as the last of my energy left me.

"I'm not going anywhere, sweetheart," he murmured, as my form became steady again.

My arms circled around my body, trying to hide what I knew he now saw—my body in the same state I had been when I'd died. I wore bloodied jean shorts and a torn white blouse. Bruises and slashes were scattered all over my body, but the worst wound was the deep gash in my neck that had ultimately ended my life.

"I told you to go," I whispered, eyes down. "No one should see this."

He sat beside me on the floor, and his shadows circled all around us.

"May I?" he asked. "If you really want me to leave, I will. But for the record, I don't want to."

"If you're just staying to say how sorry you are that I went through this, I really don't want to hear it," I said, voice bitter.

He moved his body closer to me, but I couldn't bring myself to look up from where I sat.

"May I?" he asked again.

Finally, I let my gaze meet his, and he outstretched his hands for me with a blanket in one hand. His eyes were soft, but I knew Ander. They also promised a death he couldn't hide.

I scooted into his waiting arms and he placed the blanket around me, though I couldn't really feel it. I couldn't feel much of anything with my energy this depleted.

"I've got you, sweetheart," he murmured, and I broke.

He said nothing as the memories I'd shoved down for so long surfaced and the tears of shame flooded me.

★★★

I had no idea how long Ander held me, but it was long enough for my energy store to come back enough to shift my form into something less morbid. He said nothing as I shifted, and he gazed out the window—calculating.

"You have enough to worry about right now," I said, turning his head so that he had to look at me.

"Yet you are all that seems to really matter," he said, voice low.

"Don't go do anything stupid, Ander," I said seriously.

"I won't," he promised. "For now."

Before I could protest further, Zadie, Tiergan, and the rest of our Shadowed Legion, and the Sublunary arrived back in the Court of Algol. They seemed a little tired, but nothing serious. There didn't seem to be many casualties on our end, either.

We both rose from our spots on the floor.

"Lord Astral," Zadie bowed.

Oleander moved to stand by the window, gazing out at the snow-capped mountains. I could only imagine what was going through his mind. It was just the three of us in the parlor. The rest must have gone to clean up and recuperate.

"Report?" he asked.

"As we suspected. Hesperia came here as a distraction to launch a formal attack on Vega, but they didn't accomplish much, which is odd. Why the risk? We were taking losses until the dragons arrived."

That seemed to get his attention. He turned more fully towards Zadie.

"The dragons of Arcturus came to Vega?"

She nodded. "Zoe, Elvy, Imelda, and Blaz had already left for Arcturus. It appears Hesperia had previously paid Seraphina and Kai a visit. They had initially chosen to side with Hesperia. You know the lust for power that dragons and their riders can have. It can be a sickness, making them blind to the bigger picture."

"I'm familiar," he replied, waving a hand for her to continue.

"Apparently, they were swayed when Jelly revealed herself as a simargl. They respect the simargl above all else, calling them the guardians of life. For one to pick Zoe meant that she was pure of heart."

"We're not being foolish and completely trusting their word, are we?"

"No, but I believe them," Zadie conceded.

"Casualties of the attack?"

"Minimal," she informed. "It would have been worse without our aid and the arrival of the Court of Arcturus."

"Thank you for going," he said with a small smile. "I apologize that I could not fight alongside you all."

"You were needed here, Lord Astral," she said, bowing again.

"I was," he said, glancing toward me. "Is Finnian okay?"

"Yes, Lord Astral."

"What's the plan now?" I asked, speaking for the first time. Zadie and I hadn't quite warmed up to each other in any serious capacity, but I didn't dislike her.

She turned, acknowledging I'd spoken.

"The courts of Algol, Vega, Rigil, and Arcturus will head for Sirius at twilight."

"Should we fear the disrespect this will insinuate for Canopus?" he asked.

"They are being invited as well, though they will certainly be the wild card. Elvy and Zoe are sending Blaz as their emissary with the invitation to come. We hope that he can form an opinion or negotiations around them before they join us in Sirius."

"They're letting him go alone?" I asked. I knew how fond Zoe was of Blaz.

"He understands the risks," Zadie answered.

"Let's hope the air elemental court respects Blaz, or Zoe will descend upon them with a fury they will not soon forget. It will not be good for any of us," he said, sighing.

"What are my orders?"

"I will go as the representative from our court. You will stay here to watch over Algol while I'm gone."

Zadie nodded, seeming to have already expected this.

Even I knew this was coming, but I still wasn't fond of the idea of being apart from him. Especially after last night. I felt... closer to him now. We all had our jobs to do, even though I wasn't entirely sure what mine was.

"I'll make my preparations. We don't have much time."

Zadie bowed, taking that as her cue to leave.

"If I could tuck you in my pocket and have you come with me, I would," Oleander said, turning towards me, though his eyes had really never left mine.

"I believe you."

"I would much rather you be able to come by my side."

"Maybe one day," I agreed.

"Can you hold onto that for me while I'm gone?"

"To what?" I asked, confused.

We were only a breath away from each other. His blue eyes made me lose all sense of reason and perception.

"Hope," he said, taking my right hand and placing it on his chest.

He wore his sleeves rolled up, exposing his star tattoos and immortal birthmark, glowing black today—not hiding it with its tattoo form. I always preferred him this way.

"I promise to be here when you get back." I didn't want to make a commitment I couldn't keep. Hope was fleeting in my eyes. My stubbornness was eternal. I'd be here. No matter what.

"I'll take it," he said, kissing me gently—much softer than ever before. It was as if he wanted to remember this moment and carry it with him.

I've never been kissed this way—with intention. It had always been full of lust and an unquenchable need. It took what little self-control I possessed to not leap into his arms now, just to be as close to him as possible. He had come to mean safety to me.

"Come back to me, alright?"

"Always," he agreed, giving me one last kiss before he was a ghost, only in my memory.

I'd never wanted to be the doting partner, sending my other half to war. I'd always planned to be right by him through it all. Not that I was his partner or his other half—but that felt like a lie on my lips. I knew this was more than just a fling, but the conflict within me would never settle.

Before I could spiral into anymore unhealthy thoughts, I leaned against the floor to ceiling windows to watch Oleander leave the transport zone. He gave Zadie some last-minute instructions, then headed for the shadows. He caught my eye as he unfurled his massive, black, translucent wings, shifting into his Shadowed form.

"Hope," he mouthed.

He gave me a final wink and disappeared into the darkness, headed for Vega.

22

Converging

ZOE

"*L*ittle bear," The Archer whispered through me.

I knew suddenly that I was dreaming as the familiar beach of Saint Andrews manifested in front of me. My heart longed for my mortal home. The Archer appeared from the shadows in the form he had only just recently revealed to me. His skin was weathered from too many days by the saltwater, and he wore what I considered too casual clothes for a child of a celestial. Those same green eyes stared back at me with only love and concern for his daughter. The wounded inner child within me wanted to lash out, but I tucked her away for later when I needed her protection. Right now, in this moment, she was safe.

"You are going to Sirius?" he asked.

I nodded, not elaborating. I didn't need to. He knew all.

"Perhaps you should stay on course to Arcturus. These political games serve no purpose in the grand scheme of the universe."

"Was it not political games between the celestials that caused all of this in the first place?"

"You only prove my point, little bear."

"We need them to rally the courts to our side. Hesperia can't gain anymore supporters."

"Those who have already chosen Hesperia have chosen. There is nothing you can do to change that now. Without my bow intact, we will lose."

"What do you mean by 'those who have already chosen?' If you mean Arcturus, they came back to our side."

The Archer shook his head. "Seraphina and Kai had not decided in their hearts, little bear. Their dragon's lust for power corrupted them briefly. They came back to themselves with the power of the simargl."

"You speak as if you've been planning this since the beginning."

"I have anticipated certain things—yes. So have you, little bear."

"Who has chosen Hesperia?" I asked again.

"You already know," he said, pulling me into a hug. I didn't fight it and embraced him back. My inner child craved my father to be a safe harbor. "If you must go to Sirius, then go, but do not lose sight of the course you must stay on."

I nodded, holding onto his form with a death grip.

"Is June still alive?" I asked, half scared of the answer.

"She is, and she remains in Saint Andrews for now. She's been keeping an eye on your place should you ever wish to return," he said, smiling. "June may not look like a warrior, but I assure you she is. She is doing what she can to protect Earth from what is going on here."

The ache for simpler times grew, but they hadn't felt like simple times while I'd still been mortal.

"And Mom?"

"Your mother is out of both our reach, little bear. She would not want you to mourn her."

Too late for that.

"Am I going to get Freyja back?"

"That remains to be seen," he said, stroking my hair from my eyes. "I can't tell you what I see or know. It'll change the outcome."

I nodded, realizing that to be true.

"I messed up," I said, head hanging in shame. The faces of the immortals I had slaughtered flashed through me in a never-ending tidal wave.

He tilted my chin so that I met his gaze.

"Yes," he agreed. "And you offered them freedom."

"What do you mean?"

He shook his head and placed a gentle kiss on my forehead.

"I've made many mistakes because I acted too rashly. Do not repeat my choices, little bear. Whenever the truth is revealed to you, just know that I love you. I have always loved you."

"What truth?"

He shook his head again, eyes filled with grief I didn't understand.

"There is no part of you that is a mistake. You were born with intention and in love."

I could almost swear that the emerald of his eyes glowed with fire before turning into a pool of black. And if I knew my father, his words and actions served a purpose. I didn't get the chance to ask him what he was trying to tell me.

"Sleep, my charming child. Dream of better things," he said, and I followed his command, letting his voice soothe me into a peaceful sleep.

★★★

"It's time to go, starlight," Elvy said, teasing me gently from my slumber. "I have your favorite. Courtesy of Octavia."

Coffee. I'd get up for coffee.

"Thank you," I said, with sleep still in my voice.

"You really should let the other healers work. You weaken your reserves too much."

"I am not depleted," I countered. "Just a little tired. I still feel the well of magic within me. I'm good."

He handed me the mug of coffee and pulled me into his arms. Jelly jumped up onto the bed and wiggled her petite body between us. It's easy to forget that a fiery beast lurked within her.

"Who am I to say otherwise?" he asked, holding me firmly across his chest while giving Jelly her head scratches.

"Your worry for me is endearing, flame," I said.

"It annoys you," he said, laughing softly, but I disagreed.

"How long was I out?"

"Just a few hours. We are about to leave for Sirius. Clove and Imelda got your things ready for you."

"Stars bless them," I said, downing the last of the coffee.

I gazed into his storm-gray eyes, and the memory of The Archer's visit flashed through my mind. Discernment circled me, but wouldn't quite land in my grasp.

"What do you know about your family curse?" I asked, wondering if I stared long enough, his eyes would change to black.

He shrugged, pursing his lips. "Not much, really. My father had the curse, too. And his father before him. My parents did their best to keep me contained as a child, but… accidents happened. Before I learned to control my magic, I killed a few immortals—five to be exact. It was just one lapse in control."

My heart sunk. No wonder he carried this gift like a burden to be hidden away. I leaned my head back against his chest, looking for the words to say.

"Does that change—" he started, but I silenced him.

"No. It doesn't change how I see you or feel about you. If anything, Elvy. You should be angry with me. My flame—my shadows—they call to that part of you... I feel like I'm eclipsing the goodness that you are."

He tilted my chin gently so that my green eyes met his gray.

"I'm no saint, Zoe. I told you a long time ago that I will never fear you, and I don't fear us together. You are my mate for a reason—perfect for me in every way," he paused, kissing my forehead. "We are cataclysmic together, but we get to decide if it is good or bad."

"You've been thinking about this?" I asked. He'd always shied away from his shadows when mine were present.

He nodded. "I can't believe there is any part of you that is evil, and if I can believe that about you, then why shouldn't the same be true for me? We were both gifted something, and I refuse to believe it has to be something feared by those we love."

"The darkness isn't always bad," I whispered the familiar mantra. "The shadows serve us."

"I've come to believe that is true," he agreed. "I still think caution is good until you've had more practice, but... maybe we should start listening to what our shadows are saying instead of fearing them. Just because my family hated the shadows doesn't mean they were right to do so."

I smiled, kissing him deeply. There was nothing about Elvy that I didn't love. That would always be true for me. We saw each other for who we really were, and no force in the entire realms would ever take our bond away from us.

"Time for a quick shower?"

He swept me into his arms and did as I asked.

***

"Everyone ready?" Elvy asked as we all converged around the shadows that would transport us to Sirius.

Delmira, Clodovea, and Finn would stay behind. We had resumed the emergency evacuation for the immortals in Vega to Musterion.

Blaz and Imelda stood on either side of Elvy and me. Blaz had already returned from Canopus with nothing much to inform besides that they would be there, which didn't feel promising. Jelly settled in between me and my flame. Seraphina and Kai were astride their dragons. The rest of their Shadowed Wing would go back to Arcturus to await our arrival once we finished with our mission in Sirius.

We all nodded, unfurling our wings, morphing into our Shadowed forms. The roar of the black and brown dragons was magnificent. I almost wanted to dare Hesperia to come at us now, but I vanquished the thought as soon as it came. Tempting fate didn't seem like the brightest of ideas.

"Let's go," Elvy said, pulling me into the portal of the cosmos. What had once seemed overstimulating was now a welcome sensation. I let my *sight* take over my senses as my flame guided us towards Sirius. The dream from The Archer was a warning. Someone at this meeting was not on our side. I just had to figure out who.

The options seemed limited. It had to either be the air elemental court or the King and Queen themselves. I strained my magic, pulling on the threads of Algol—the source of my power. No path was clear for me, which likely meant the decision had not been made yet, or they were good at deceit. Sometimes I resented that I could only *see* what the celestials wanted me to.

Canopus was the next stop after Arcturus, according to the permanent map on my arm. Getting into a court that didn't want us there would be tricky. Deadly even.

I opened my eyes, glancing over at Elvy. He nodded, seeing what I had through our bond. We'd sent word to Oleander through the iris, warning him there would be resistance somewhere. Finnian had stashed a few more irises in our packs for the Court of Rigil when they arrived. It's a wonder the courts survived this long with so little communication between them.

"There was no reason to," Elvy said through the bond.

"Why?"

"After Algol was severed, and I suppose really before then, when the celestials required us to swear to one star, we just kind of stopped. We were taught to separate—think ourselves better than the other elementals."

"Needlessly cruel," I agreed. *"And a breeding ground for hatred and mistrust."*

I didn't have time to wonder if Hesperia's contempt for the realms began right there—at the separation. The swell of power in my gut let me know I was on the right track for that. What was her real motivation for all of this? It's more than just her desire for devastating chaos. I hated to even think about having sympathy for her—but who had wronged her in the past to drive her in this direction? What was her purpose in all of this? If we could figure that out, maybe we could use it to our advantage. I added that to my ever-growing, impossible checklist and followed Elvy across the barrier into Sirius.

23

Kingdom of Canis

ZOE

Sirius was as stunning and otherworldly as the other elemental courts.

The night sky glistened with what felt like billions of stars, even more than in the elemental realms except the realm of Nova where I'd completed my trials for the Emerging. Nothing would truly compare to that domain, but Sirius was a close second.

The moonstone castle was nestled within the city center and shimmered in the light of the stars and the moon. I didn't expect there to be a city here and was shocked to see such a vibrant one. Somewhere in my mind, I'd just pictured two old monarchs sitting on their thrones, doing nothing of consequence.

"It's the High Astral Court," Elvy explained. "This is the one place that there is a mix of elementals. To live here, you must submit to Sirius. Their elemental magic is limited, from what I'm told."

"So Sirius is the Papa Star and all the celestials are misbehaving children?" I asked for clarity.

"Well," Elvy laughed. "That's one way to put it."

The city was smaller than the other courts, but by no means tiny. By the looks of it, I could walk the entire city in half an hour. All the buildings surrounding the castle in a circular format seemed to be made of the same glowing stone as the vast castle.

"We're landing on the steps of the palace?" I asked, suddenly a little nervous.

"They are expecting us," he reassured me.

Below us, heavily armed guards waited. If the King and Queen were down there, I couldn't make them out.

With one last deep breath, I landed my feet on solid ground as the rest touched down with soft thuds around me. Jelly took her position between Elvy and me. Blaz and Imelda were on either side of us. Seraphina and Kai dismounted from their dragons and sent them away. Hopefully close by if we needed them.

Oleander landed right by us. He'd come alone. It was probably best not to bring Tiergan—the rebel leader—into the heart of our government. I made eye contact with his brilliant blue eyes, and he nodded discreetly toward me. Something was off about his expression, but I didn't have time to ask him what was troubling him.

Sierra and Terran of the Court of Rigil landed next. They'd come with a handful of their Shadowed Legion, whom I recognized from the battle in their realm.

We all politely acknowledged each other, but did not address each other as the friends we were. There was no sense in showing our cards to Sirius yet.

The last pair descended upon us. They had bright white wings with subtle hints of pale blue, like a robin's egg. Their uniforms mirrored their wings in many ways.

"That's Lord Astral Abel and Lady Astral Aura of Canopus," Elvy offered through our bond.

I nodded slightly, opening myself up to the discernment within me. Nothing malicious hit me, but nothing *right* flooded through me either. I was instantly wary of them.

Abel had long, dark hair with the Shadowed silver and was conventionally handsome by beauty standards. His immortal mark was a soft glow of white. He was tall with dark skin. There was something about him that I didn't trust. Aura had beautiful brown skin with raven-dark hair. A feather hung in her hair—the symbol of her court. My gift sang to me, but I couldn't discern what the lyrics said or what the melodies were trying to reveal to me. There was something… pure about her. I noticed their body language was stiff—cold. There was little love there.

"Welcome to Sirius," one of the guards said, pulling me away from Aura. My heart wanted to reach out to her, though. Something just felt strange, and my spirit was unsettled.

"We'll watch her," Elvy murmured through the bond, sensing my feelings.

"King Aldrich and Queen Farron are pleased to have the elemental courts in our realm once again. My name is Grayson—advisor to the High Astral Court."

Not a guard then. I got the sense he was a brown-noser. I disliked him immediately.

"Please follow me to the gallery for cocktails before dinner. The King and Queen will see you all then."

"What kind of power-play bullshit is this?" Blaz muttered under his breath, so low I could barely hear him. I stifled the chuckle that threatened to escape my lips. The games had begun.

We followed Grayson's retreating form through unnecessarily large and intricate doors. Each section of the door represented one of the five elemental symbols. The castle was brighter than I imagined it would be, and the gallery was exquisitely designed for showmanship.

Servers were dressed in white coats and black slacks, much like I'd expect to see in the Earth realm. Apart from the events my family made us go to, I preferred the hostel life when I traveled on my own or with Freyja.

The glasses on their trays were empty, which confused me a little, but I took one anyway, following Elvy's lead. The moment my fingers brushed the rim of the glass, it filled with water and lemon.

"As you can see, the drinks will fill to what you desire," Grayson said, waving his hands smoothly in the air. Gentle music played as we all assessed our opponents or allies.

My eyes kept drifting towards Aura, observing the pair's movements. My discernment wouldn't allow otherwise. She moved to please him—to keep him satisfied. When I was still mortal and people avoided me because they feared my 'crazy,' I became more attentive to people's actions and their motivations.

Emma—my late therapist—had told me it was part of having trauma. My mind would swing between hypo-arousal and hyper-arousal—a never-ending pendulation of torment of lows and highs. That state of mind remained until Elvy came along. And Oleander and the rest of the Luminaries. That didn't mean my struggles were suddenly gone, but I knew how to ground myself better now. They had given me hope when I doubted my worth.

Something was wrong with Aura. I noticed her wince when he touched her arm in what appeared to be a gentle manner. She made herself small, and my darkness wanted to come out to play with Abel.

I closed my eyes, calling upon the deep pool of power that Algol had gifted me. I pulled on the life force that was now anchored to me alone. Elation filled me instantly.

"Not here, flame," Elvy murmured through our bond.

"The darkness protects the innocent," I said through gritted teeth, though my mouth did not actually move. I did not think that my shadows could always tell the difference between innocence and guilt, but I was certain they knew Aura to be good.

"If you show those eyes, we will lose this cause before it even begins," he countered. *"I will help you. We will help you. Never alone. Never again."*

I listened to the steady beat of his heart. We may get kinder to our shadows, but that didn't mean the rest of the universe would be nice. He was my rock against the storm when the ocean could not bring me the solace it once did. With each beat, I gently nudged the power down into the stores until I was ready to call upon her again. Not the time. Nor the place.

"You're supposed to be practicing, love," Oleander said, whispering behind me.

"We have," I countered. "I just… it was so intense. I didn't even have a moment to think before she took over. The shadows seem to want to protect and slaughter anyone who could be a threat."

"That doesn't sound like a bad thing, Zoe. And you talk like your magic is something separate from you," he said, observant, as always.

"She's still me. A part of me, anyway."

Elvy nodded in understanding. His darkness was a mirror to my own, though his was arguably more deadly, and he'd had years of practice controlling it.

"Everything alright?" Sierra asked, dressed in the green and brown tones of her court—Rigil. Terran stood behind her like a shadow in an olive-green suit.

In fact, we were all dressed in formal wear, and it set me on edge, making me feel exposed in this midnight blue dress.

"You look beautiful," Elvy smiled mischievously. *"But I know what deadly weapons are underneath that dress."*

"Stop undressing me with those eyes and focus."

"Yes," I said, smiling and taking a swig of my water, letting it settle me further and cool off the unexpected heat. Elvy always knew how to distract me.

"Things were looking a little… tense there for a moment," Terran said, always nosy.

"I don't like the way Abel looks at Aura," I said, not bothering to hide my disdain. Let it be known to all the realms, for all I cared.

Sierra followed my gaze discreetly and sighed. "I'd hoped the rumors were false."

"What rumors?" Elvy asked.

"Ah, yes, I don't suppose you would have heard about them. Nor you Oleander with all the strife of both your courts and our new Emerged immortal."

Blaz, Elvy, and Oleander looked ready to kill. Now, I'll have to be the reasonable one.

"Not here, boys," I said, pulling their attention back to our group.

"She's pregnant. Aura," Sierra informed. "Recently so… one of her lady's maids broke the silence on the abuse that's been hidden for years."

"Years can mean centuries for an immortal," I said, fuming.

"What happened to her lady's maid?" Oleander asked.

"Executed, I believe," Terran answered.

"A lady's maid?" I asked Elvy through the flame.

"All courts used to have them, but Canopus is the only Astral Court to continue with the tradition."

Somehow, that only made me dislike him more, though I was glad Aura had someone to go to battle for her.

Imelda was circling back to us, bringing Seraphina and Kai of the Court of Arcturus with her.

"I'll kill him," Blaz said, taking a step in Abel's direction, but I pulled him back.

"Who are we killing?" Imelda asked, not looking particularly upset by the prospect. Playing delegate to the Lord and Lady Astral, who had just recently betrayed us, could not be easy.

"No one today," Elvy said.

"Today?" Blaz asked.

"Fine. This moment," Elvy rephrased, which seemed to pacify Blaz only slightly.

"While we are here," I said, pitching my voice low. I felt the hum of Oleander placing a shield around our group discreetly.

I quickly handed Sierra and Seraphina an iris and explained how to use them.

"Where did you get something like this?" Sierra asked.

"No questions," Elvy said, and they nodded despite their curiosity and hid them away.

"We need to go talk to them. Some of us, at least. They are the only court by themselves," I said, nodding towards Abel and Aura. "Introduce me, Elvy."

He nodded, placing his palm on the small of my back. Oleander followed on my other side, inviting himself and diffusing the shield. Jelly, of course, trotted behind us, swishing her tail along.

"Lord Astral Abel," Elvy began. I noticed he was more formal with him than with the other Astrals. "I haven't had the chance to introduce you to my wife and flame, Zoe Eferhild."

Abel looked me up and down, and my skin consequently crawled with little invisible bugs. The male had a death wish.

"I don't believe we received a wedding invitation," Abel said, taking my hand and placing a too-wet kiss on my skin. It felt… wrong. Sickening. My gut clenched. This male was all kinds of corrupt.

"We had a small ceremony. On Earth," I said.

"Surely you heard about the attack at the joining," Oleander said, brow raised, taunting him to deny it.

"Yes, I heard the rumors," Abel replied.

"Not rumors," Elvy said. "It was very much real."

"I am sorry that your wedding day was ruined, but it is no concern of mine."

I was going to punch him. Or stab him. Yes—stabbing would do. My hand cautiously moved closer to one of my blades.

"Hesperia's war is everyone's concern," Oleander said.

"Why would I trust an immortal from Algol?" Abel spat.

This was getting nowhere fast, so I tried a different tactic. Abel had not bothered to introduce Aura to me. It was probably to keep her isolated. Over my dead body.

"Hello, and you are?" I asked her, holding out my hand.

She glanced at Abel *for permission.* Oh, this gentle female. I wanted to tuck her into my arms. He nodded, but she still seemed scared to touch me. Ever so gently, she took my outstretched hand. My gift responded with vicious fervor.

The magic of Vega sensed her injuries that were well hidden from the public eye, but my magic could not be deceived. I sent in my healing magic while I continued to talk to her. I was careful not to remove bruising for fear that it might get her into more trouble.

"Hello, my name is Zoe, Lady Astral of the Vega Court. What may I call you?"

"Au—Aura," she said, stumbling over the words. This sweet, fragile immortal. I sensed a fighter within, though. The touch of silver in her eyes was her thank you to me, even though she was wary all the same of my help.

"Nice to meet you, Aura," I said, smiling. "Come join us girls. Let the Lords do whatever they do when we aren't around."

I gently pulled her arm, not asking for permission. Abel stopped her, but Elvy and Oleander were ready.

"A round of alchemy?" Elvy asked.

I briefly wondered what the hell alchemy was, but decided I'd find out later because, whatever it was, Abel took the bait.

"Think you'll actually win this time?" Oleander taunted, increasing his voice so Terran and Kai heard it. "We all know spirit is the superior element."

"Alchemy!" Terran shouted, racing towards us with Kai in tow.

Abel seemed to relax and joined the guys on the adjoining balcony of the gallery. The servers did not look thrilled by whatever game they were playing.

I reached the rest of the ladies who had gathered around the fireplace and settled into the too-stiff sofas that forced you to have proper posture—my nightmare.

"Boys," Sierra said, rolling her eyes.

"Even you like to play the game if I recall," Seraphina said, sitting by Imelda, likely in an attempt to make amends.

"It's been too long since I've played," Sierra said wistfully.

Jelly sat between my legs while Aura sat next to me on the sofa, across from Imelda and Seraphina.

Then there was Blaz. Relaxing with us girls.

"Comfortable, Blaz?" I asked.

"I prefer the ladies' company," he said, shrugging.

I tasted the lie in his words. Blaz wasn't sure he'd control his anger around Abel.

"Is someone going to explain alchemy?" I asked, taking a generous sip of water.

"It's a school game. Those of us born in the star realms grew up playing it. It's a test of the elements to see which is the strongest by creating a new, more powerful element."

"Creating new elements is just a school game?" I asked. "What happened to kickball or Red Rover?"

"Red-what?" Imelda asked.

"Red Rover? Two separate teams link arms, and the opposing team tries to run through them. It gets bloody."

I bet Delmira played it while she was mortal. She was the unnecessarily violent type.

"Your school games get murderous?" Aura asked, piping up, relaxing somewhat when no longer under the scrutiny of Abel.

"Different worlds, I guess," I said, laughing, missing Freyja. She would love this.

Blaz seemed mildly intrigued, but he said nothing.

"That's the thing about being mortal. We know our time is limited. Our spirits thrive in the anarchy of that fact," I said, driving the tone more serious than a simple game.

"High risk, high reward," Blaz said, nodding appreciatively.

"Care to challenge the former mortal?" I asked, smiling as an idea formed.

"What are the stakes?" he asked.

The girls had gone silent, with interests piqued.

"Anything goes. Whatever it takes to break through."

"You're on," he said, standing up.

"What, right now?" I asked, laughing.

"Us girls can have fun, too," Sierra said, following Blaz to the opposite balcony that the Lord Astrals were playing alchemy. They still seemed caught up in their own game.

Elvy's face looked particularly serious.

"Everything good over there?" I asked through the bond.

His reply was instant, always waiting for me. *"Just trying not to flay Abel alive."*

"We can't have that. Not today, anyway," I agreed.

"Beating him will have to do. Where are you going?" he asked, but his gaze was still focused on the task at hand.

"We are going to knock Blaz on his ass," I said with no explanation, and he didn't ask for it.

"Don't go easy on him."

We'd all gathered on the opposite balcony, and they seemed to be waiting for my instructions.

"Two teams. The first will call for someone on the opposing team to run through the linked arms of their own side. If the runner is successful in breaking through the linked arms, they get to bring one of the other players back to their team. If they fail, they have to join their opponent's team. Got it?"

Everyone nodded, and we divided into two teams. My team had Aura and Imelda. Blaz had Sierra and Seraphina. Aura's frame trembled, but there was a part of her that seemed excited to let some energy out. We all looked a little ridiculous in our formal wear, but none of us seemed to mind and hiked up our dresses where necessary for easier movement. Jelly sat perched as our informal referee, just as she had when we played volleyball on Earth.

"Are you okay, Aura?" I asked. I was pretty sure that her pregnancy was a secret. She wasn't showing any physical signs other than a slight bump, and I wasn't sure if it was the same process as a mortal. I assumed the mechanics would be the same.

"Is it dangerous?" She clutched her stomach in a protective gesture instinctively.

"It can be," I said, nodding. "But you don't have to play, Aura. Blaz and I get a little… excitable."

"No, I want," she began, stopping herself, as if she were afraid. "I want to. It's just…"

"You don't have to explain yourself," Imelda said gently.

Moisture formed in her eyes, and her lower lip quivered.

"The Court of Vega is very kind," she said.

"We're waiting!" Blaz shouted, and I sent him a look to shut his trap. For once, he actually did.

"Us girls have to stick together, right?" I asked, taking her hand in mine. My magic surged again, wanting to heal some of the invisible inflictions—her emotional pain. But I wouldn't. Not without talking to her about it. I didn't know what emotion might keep her alive. It was too risky.

She nodded, squeezing my hand in a vice grip, as if I were the last link of hope to her. I was reminded of the time I'd taken away some of Madison's pain at the lagoon when I was still an Emerging mortal. She'd lost her daughter and husband in a house fire. It would be so easy to take a little away, but then again, I didn't know how it might affect me. I'd cried for ages after helping Madison, not that I regretted it. Right now, I needed my wits about me, but I felt selfish even thinking the words.

"How about you keep us honest?" I suggested. "Referee with Jelly?"

"I can do that," she agreed with a small smile.

I made a vow to myself right there. She would know me as her friend from this moment forward. I would be there the minute she decided her pain was great enough to leave. If the stars were on my side, it would be sooner rather than later.

"You understand the rules?" I asked, and she nodded.

"Great," I said, positioning her, so she had a good view. "I won't let anything happen to you."

She said nothing else, but I caught the quiet sigh of relief in the settling of her chest. Jelly easily won her over and wagged her tail with Aura's head scratches.

"Three against two?" Blaz asked as Imelda and I linked arms.

"Afraid of losing again?" Imelda asked. "I know you're still sore about the volleyball game."

His nostrils flared, linking his own arms with Sierra and Seraphina.

I glanced over at Aura, wanting her to understand that I protected my team—that I would protect her. Closing my eyes for a brief moment, I called upon the power of Algol, and reinforced the link between Imelda and me. Nothing would penetrate this shield without my permission.

"Red Rover, Red Rover, send Sierra on over!" I bellowed, and she did not hesitate.

I'd give it to the Lady Astral of Rigil. Her magic was unique. She transformed her form into the rock of the ground element, which essentially made her entire body a battering ram. This was going to hurt.

Just before she collided, Imelda and I both shot out our water element like a tidal wave, slowing her movement just enough to lessen the blow. She didn't make it through.

Blaz was pissed. He was going to work me over at our next training session. The bragging rights were worth it.

Sierra linked her arms with Imelda, laughing good-naturedly. Aura waved her hand, drying Sierra off and the stone of the balcony.

"Your turn," I said sweetly to Blaz.

"Red Rover, Red Rover, send Imelda on over!" Blaz shouted.

Imelda gave her best effort, but could not break through the strength of Blaz and Seraphina.

On and on it went. Each team would gain a player, only to lose another. Bursts of magic lit up the night sky. Seraphina's fire magic singed the white stone beneath us, and Imelda and I worked to wash it away with Aura drying it. It was probably in our best interest not to damage the castle of our monarchs.

"What is going on over here?" Terran asked, trailed by the other Lord Astrals. Both Oleander and Elvy seemed amused by the chaos of the game. Blaz was irate by this point, and my egging did not help the situation nor Imelda's. As Abel crossed the threshold, Aura's frame shrunk, making herself less of a target.

I turned my head to keep my expression neutral, and the darkness tamped down. The longer I held Algol's life as part of my own, the more intense and separate from my true self I seemed to become. Or maybe I was just afraid of embracing all that I could be. Maybe I didn't trust myself.

"Finally!" Blaz shouted. "Come join us. This is way more fun than your stupid alchemy!"

"Can we join?" Elvy asked, slinging an arm around my shoulders, but my eyes were on Aura's. Abel had slunk to her side, and I silently prayed for her to make eye contact with me. *Come on, Aura.*

Ever so slightly, her gaze met mine. '*You are not alone,*' I tried to convey. She didn't nod or acknowledge it, but in my heart—in my gift—I knew she understood.

"Of course, Blaz needs the help," I said, laughing as if the moment between Aura and me had never happened.

"I'll help Aura," Abel said, with a firm grip around her arm.

The rest of the Lord Astrals picked sides, and the game continued with the same pandemonium as before, with the males adding their own elemental flare.

Not too long after, a voice permeated the crowd, causing a heavy, pregnant pause in the fate of destiny.

"The King and Queen will receive you now."

The shot heard around the realms. The real game had just begun.

24

Their Royal Highness
ZOE

"Their Royal Highness King Aldrich and Queen Farron!" Grayson boomed.

We all stood behind our assigned chairs, and we simultaneously bowed or curtsied the moment their footfalls crossed the threshold into the room. Elvy had instructed me to remain submissive until they verbally told us to do otherwise. Thankfully, my training had me used to being in uncomfortable positions for extended periods of time.

My eyes averted down, so I couldn't see them or what they were doing. However, I heard them slip into their chairs and scoot forward with the screeching of a chair leg against stone. That sound would have sent me into a panic attack a year ago, before… all of this.

"You may rise and be seated," a soft, feminine voice said. Her tone was kind, with a hint of authority. This was much different from the dinner with Hesperia, who played her power with cruelty. Immortals feared her, but the immortals here seemed to only respect the monarchs. I held onto the hope that they were good and incorruptible, though I feared everyone had a breaking point.

Queen Farron had blonde-brown hair and hazel eyes, with glowing cheeks. Her skin was the typical flawlessness of every immortal I knew. Her energy reminded me of a warm, sunny day. I found myself drawn to her. I was curious about her power—her element.

"Fire," Elvy answered through the bond. *"The King and Queen were once the Lord and Lady Astrals of the Court of Arcturus."*

"How are the next rulers chosen?"

"The Trials of the High Astrals," he responded.

My stomach dropped. I didn't care to ever go through another trial in the star realms again, if I had any say in it.

"Not to worry," Elvy said, clasping my hand discreetly under the table. *"Their rule is still considered young at this point. The next round of trials will be awhile yet."*

I squeezed his hand, relaxing a bit. Jelly positioned herself closer to me so that her fur brushed against my leg.

King Aldrich had beautiful black skin and dark eyes. His dreadlocks were pulled back at the nape of his neck with a red ribbon. They both wore subtle crowns that had flames engraved throughout the gold. However, there were flashes of jewels that were green, blue, black, and white to represent the other star realms they served.

"Don't forget they are flamed," Elvy said through our own bond.

I hadn't forgotten, and I wondered what they said to each other now.

"Welcome to our home," King Aldrich said, raising his glass. We all followed suit. The goblets acted on the same magic as the glasses during cocktail hour, so mine filled with coffee this time. I figured the caffeine would do me some good.

"It seems we have much to discuss," Queen Farron said. "We intend to hear all of your concerns and will not leave this table until there has been a resolution."

They seemed sincere, and that gave me hope. I would make them understand, but they would have to earn my trust first.

"Let's begin," King Aldrich said, snapping his fingers as food was brought out to us. I didn't really care what it was, as long as it was edible.

"I see we have one of the lost simargls with us," the queen said, gesturing towards Jelly. My companion perked an ear in her direction with a lopsided tongue hanging out.

"Yes, Your Majesty," I said, petting Jelly's ear.

"At this table, it will be Farron, please," she said as chatter began around the table. We sat the closest to her. Oleander was on the opposite side and conversed with Aldrich.

"Farron," I corrected.

She requested a plate for Jelly, and once she saw my protector take a bite, she looked back at Elvy and me.

"You've been keeping her hidden from us, Elvy," she said sweetly. It wasn't an accusation. Her tone was more that of a reprimanding mother who reminded me of June, though Farron looked the same mortal thirty that the rest held. June must have been ancient to actually show her age at all.

"We've been meaning to come sooner," he said apologetically. "I fear our hand was forced otherwise."

"Oh?" Farron asked, but I knew she was more than aware of what was going on in her own kingdom.

"I won't insult you by pretending you are unaware of what is going on in the star realms," Elvy said, holding her gaze.

"No, you wouldn't, would you?"

"We must rally together," I said, surprising myself.

"Zoe Eferhild, Realm-Healer—Emerging of Legends. That's what they are calling you," she said. The chatter surrounding us had gone quiet.

"Yes," I said, meeting her hazel eyes.

"And you cannot defeat Hesperia on your own?" Aldrich asked.

"I'm not meant to," I said, voice level.

"Then what exactly is your role in all of this?" she asked with curiosity in her voice. She hadn't figured it out—my true purpose. It was vital to her own safety, as well as the security of the realms that she remained blind to it. "You have not registered your magic yet, right? What is it exactly that you can do?"

I swallowed. "She is a healer, Farron," Elvy said smoothly. "We planned to register her magic during this visit if that would be okay, your grace?"

She nodded with a smirk. Farron undoubtedly knew Algol's gift had touched me as well, but she didn't press. She was perceptive, and perhaps she knew there was a good reason for my silence.

"I am the Realm-Healer," I said, taking my time to meet the eyes of every immortal at the table with intention. Elvy, Blaz, and Imelda showed me their love. Sierra and Terran nodded their support. Even Seraphina and Kai bowed in thanks for what I had done for them with Jelly. Aura's face was in a practiced neutral expression, but Abel seemed irate. He would not dictate this future. Oleander's eyes I met last. In them, I only saw loyalty to me and the cause we must complete together.

"Algol began dying the moment Hesperia severed the tethers to Sirius. I am certain you felt the ripple effect it caused in the star realms. It was even worse on Earth. Mortals are inherently wild, but they are good and hopeful. The damage of spirit… it has had devastating consequences for my people."

"Are the immortals of Vega not your 'people' now, Emerging?"

"Have you forgotten our oath to protect the peace of all realms?" Sierra asked boldly. "The mortals are our people, not just the immortals of our star realms. Their lives are not forfeit because they are different from us."

There was a reason Sierra and Terran had become such close friends with Elvy over the years. Their views were the same. In fact, so was Oleander, but they were too stubborn to see past their differences before I came along and made them.

My *sight* convicted me. Farron asked that question with intent—she was assessing us. My thumping heart eased… she was good.

"Are we to be their keepers forever?" Abel questioned.

The darkness that lived within me wanted to snap. It needed to have blood as payment for the vulgar things he was thinking… the things he had done and the things yet to be. My nostrils flared, but Elvy's steady, beating heart kept me grounded. This was real. I was safe right now. I couldn't kill him. Not yet. Aura sat beside him. Silent. Her gaze met mine, and there was sorrow in her eyes. She did not hold the same views as her husband and the father of her child.

"What purpose would there be without them?" Terran asked. "We are meant to serve. That is why we were created."

"So the stories say," Abel said. "Nothing more than myth to serve an agenda that no longer suits our way of life."

Abel wanted to die today, after all. Blaz's arms were crossed, muscles rippling across his forearms. He was fuming. Imelda whispered to him in an attempt to keep him leashed. Diplomacy had never been his strong suit, and he'd confessed that to me himself. That's why Clodovea and Delmira were second and third, though Delm's temper could rival the anger of Blaz.

"What you are saying, Abel, is bordering on treason," Farron said seriously. Aldrich studied Abel. I wondered what he saw there. I leaned into my own gift, trying to *see* what would happen next. Much like a game of chess, there were too many variables. The future was not set yet. I sensed foreboding, though. We needed to change course, or nothing good would come of this moment.

And moments were all we really had—all that mattered in the end.

"Zoe, you said Algol had been dying… what did you do to it?" Farron asked.

"Can you not feel it?" Oleander questioned, taking a sip of his drink.

Sirius was the star and realm at which all five courts connected before sending the power of the elements to the mortal plane. Aldrich and Farron could feel the healing more-so than the other courts, even though the tether was broken.

"You healed Algol," Aldrich said.

"Realm-Healer, indeed," Farron agreed. "But…"

They each closed their eyes, and I silently prayed that they would not announce to the entire table that I was now the tether to Algol if they sensed it. They may not be able to or would have sense enough to keep their mouths shut.

"What is it?" Kai asked, on the edge of his seat. Seraphina punched him in the arm. I felt she was the one who kept him honest—kept him on the side of good.

Farron gave a knowing half-smile. "Nothing."

"Then our issue is resolved?" Aldrich asked.

"No," Elvy said simply. "As long as Hesperia is breathing, the realms are in danger. I implore you to take that to heart."

"Perhaps we should hear what she has to say," Abel said, tracing the rim of his glass.

Then I felt it. The discernment. Her energy. She was here.

Before I could utter the words in warning, Hesperia burst through the dining room doors with Grayson's detached head in her hand, and a cruel smile on her face. Poor Grayson. His face was frozen in panic. I shuddered at the bodies that were likely scattered throughout the castle. Had they not prepared?

"This will not be forgiven," Farron spat towards Abel. He'd so clearly been the one to tell her about the meeting time and place.

"I won't need your forgiveness with Hesperia as my court's true queen."

What a delusional moron.

Blaz and Imelda now stood behind both Elvy and me. They would die defending us, but I would not allow either of them to do so. Jelly's hackles rose, but her flames were not lit yet.

Sierra and Terran were on their feet, poised for a fight. Kai and Seraphina's eyes were closed, and I imagined they were calling for their dragons. Oleander remained seated, studying our new playing field. He would not be quick to react, nor would I. If Elvy and I were not careful, we might unleash destruction on those it was not intended for—always teetering on the balance between life and death.

"Come now," Hesperia purred, slinking her figure towards Farron and Aldrich. She released Grayson's head, letting it roll down the stairs loudly. "I only want to talk. As a ruler of a star realm, I should have been invited to this, of course. I'll forgive the careless mistake."

"There was no mistake. The recognized Lord Astral of Algol is present," Farron said, gesturing towards Oleander.

"Oh, so now you recognize Algol?" Hesperia asked, cackling like a genuine maniac. "Convenient."

The Shadowed Legion of Sirius had surrounded the walls of the dining hall. Hesperia truly was insane if she thought she would win this fight… no. She knew this was a fight she would not win. She was here for another reason, but I had no idea what it was.

"We have always recognized Lord Astral Oleander. It was you we did not," Aldrich said with the authority of a king.

"Oleander serves me. He is on my side," Hesperia said, running her fingers through Oleander's white hair.

I knocked on the door of his mental shield instead of breaking through on my own. He allowed me to enter.

"Just say the word, and my shadows will slice her in half," I said, letting him know he was not alone.

"No, Zoe. You cannot do that. That's what she wants to happen. For them to lose faith in you. Besides, she cannot truly harm me. Not where it matters."

I wanted to argue the point, but Elvy interrupted.

"And prove that she can get to us. Even in the heavily guarded palace," Elvy said, joining us through our bond.

"Then what do we do?" I asked.

"I'm figuring that out. Just follow my lead," Oleander instructed.

The black and brown dragons landed on the balcony, eyes focused on Hesperia. Good. They could incinerate her if necessary.

"I have only ever pacified you to keep the immortals under my rule protected," Oleander said, looking bored. Inside, his heart raced.

"Why would they need protection from me?" Hesperia asked with mock offense. "I only want to make them better. Isn't that right, Abel?"

If only we'd gone to Canopus first. Maybe we could have prevented this. I leaned into my gift of discernment and realized that would never have made a difference. Abel's intentions were always going to lead him right here. His heart was dark and corrupted with a true lust for power, which was why he wanted to keep Aura submissive. He got off on the authority. If I had to guess, his wife's magic was stronger than his. Hesperia was his means of gaining that power. She—alone—meant little to him.

"Yes, Your Majesty," he answered, stroking her ego like the pet he was.

"Zoe seeks to take power from the star realms," Hesperia said, casting her voice so all could hear. "Do you think she only healed the celestial Algol? Where do you think Algol's life force lives now?"

The room was silent. Deafeningly so. She'd figured it out. I hadn't expected it so quickly, which meant all of Algol was in danger if she lashed out at me... but it also meant she knew where I was most vulnerable. The bigger question was why she had never attacked the bond? It made no sense.

More than concealing this from Hesperia, we wanted to keep this secret to protect the immortals of Algol. It seemed this card would be one we'd have to show.

"Algol's life is now bonded to my own," I confessed. I didn't explain any further, not even that I would return it to Sirius when it was safe. No one could know about the bow and what I intended to do with it.

"And she can do it to your celestial powers, too," Hesperia said, eyes wide with fear she did not really feel. "Absorb them. Take them for her own."

I guess in some twisted theory I could sever the tethers and bond them to me in the same way I did Algol… but that seemed impossible. I was only able to take in Algol because I was a true Daughter of Algol. It was part of the reason for my creation. To take in the others… the balance would likely destroy me, but the power… I would be unmatched. Even more than I am now.

Then I realized what Hesperia might want from me. Why she was so desperate for the darkness within me to come out. She wanted me as her weapon.

She could not have me.

"I am here to heal the realms. Restore them. I have no desire to take from the other Astrals or celestials," I said, voice clear. There was no shake or fear.

"Then why has your court come into alliance with Tiergan—the Sublunary leader?" Hesperia questioned, holding a rich pause afterwards.

There was an audible gasp from one of the Lord Astrals, but I didn't bother to see which one. Farron looked at me with a brow raised. She wanted an answer to this question. So did Aldrich.

"When was the last time you spoke to the Sublunary?" I asked, tone unwavering. "Do any of you even know why we supposedly hate them?"

"Because they will not swear allegiance to the stars!" Abel screeched. His voice grew unpleasant, and my shadow self wanted to slice him in half.

"And you have been loyal to your own?" I inquired viciously. "Do you really think your betrayal is what the Celestial Canopus would want? Have you all forgotten that the celestials are very real and live in us and for us? They are sentient beings who play a role in our lives."

I looked into Farron's eyes.

"The celestials are just as imperfect as you and I," I said. Comparing myself to Abel or Hesperia was not my intention.

Tiergan had been right. Whatever The Archer had been made to do… it had caused the immortals to forget the old ways. Except the Sublunary. They knew the truth.

"Because they never swore allegiance. Their rebellion has been since this all began," Elvy said through our flame.

"So they were not subjected to the spell… or whatever happened back then," I answered.

The wave of my power from Algol washed through me like a tidal wave, so powerful I almost collapsed back into my seat from where I had stood in defiance to Hesperia.

"You will burn, Zoe Eferhild." The words of Nova whispered through me again.

I had burned. Many times over, but I wasn't finished. I would be the lantern to guide them out of this, but it would do no good without The Archer's bow. I desperately wished my father would just tell me the whole truth, but I wouldn't hold my breath on that desire.

I refocused on the present. Hesperia seethed across from me, still near Oleander. All eyes were on me. Waiting. For what, I wasn't sure.

"Here's the truth," I said, swallowing down my fear and leaning into my conviction, though I did not know if this hunch was a certainty. "Hesperia intends to use me as a weapon."

Her smile dropped and was replaced with a sneer.

"Lies," she hissed.

"I'm her best option," I continued, ignoring the comment. "But I am not her only choice. She plans to use blood magic from all five star realms to reverse the tethers from Earth. This would kill the mortal plane. Hesperia plans on creating a new dominion in her own image—to be the sole ruler."

She smirked as if she'd just gotten away with murder. I'd gotten something wrong.

"Those who come with me will have their place by my side," she disagreed.

My magic felt the lie on her lips.

"This will not stand!" Aldrich said, rising from his chair and placing both palms firmly on the table before him.

"You are charged with high treason, Hesperia," Farron said, standing next to her husband. "The punishment is death."

The Shadowed Legion had begun moving in, surrounding her. She would not get away. Abel shrunk behind Aura—the coward.

"I have no intention of dying today," she said, laughing and unsheathing a knife. "What fools to gather together?"

With those parting words, the room went as dark as the abyss of a black hole, and a familiar mist stole all the starlight from the room.

Then the screams began.

25

Tethers

FREYJA

"Something isn't right," Zadie said, pacing in front of the blue-green fire in the well-loved parlor.

"I know," I said. "I feel it, too."

"Oleander should have checked in by now."

She held the iris in her hand as if it carried the life force of her Lord Astral. Zadie and I still had never really bonded, but we had a mutual understanding that we cared for Oleander.

The crystal glowed with the hues of the rainbow, and we both gathered around to hear what he said… only it wasn't Oleander. It was Finnian.

"Evening Star was at the palace," he said over the stone. "Be prepared for anything."

"Not good," Zadie said, leaping into action. "I need to get to our wards. I don't know what kind of damage she can do to Algol tethered to Zoe, but if she gets through… Their fates are intertwined. Brace yourself, Freyja. Anything could happen."

My sister needed me. I wanted to help, but there was very little a ghost could actually do to help. Maybe if Hesperia couldn't see me, I could go spy on her… I could make myself invisible. Even to

Oleander and Zoe. I just had to lean more into the *otherside*. It was a risk I was going to have to take.

"Are you okay here?" Zadie asked, gearing up to do her duty while I went to do mine.

"Yes," I said. "Go. I'll be fine."

"Just stay here. His magic will protect you."

"Thank you," I called after her retreating form, not agreeing to stand idle.

I sent up a silent prayer that I make it through this. Oleander would kill me all over again if anything happened to me. Zoe would be right there with him. But she couldn't always be the one risking herself, and technically, I wasn't endangering myself at all. Might as well take some of the few advantages of being dead.

Closing my eyes, I listened to the song from the *otherside*. It was sweet and warm, like a sunny day at the beach in Saint Andrews. I think most mortals feared what was there, but I didn't. Peace seemed to rest beyond the realm if I would just cross it. I centered myself, calling on every bit of strength I had to stay present. I just needed to dip my toe in the water of the *otherside* to act as a tether between there and here.

It'd been a while since I'd done this willingly. I also needed a tether to remain here in this world. Zoe's face emerged, and I leaned into the love I had for her. The promise in her green eyes, and the resolve she had to stay and embrace this life in a radical kind of way. She would ground me here. With one last nudge, I disappeared from the view of anyone in the realm of Algol. It was almost as if a cloud surrounded me. As long as it remained, no one could hear or see me.

Now, to see what that witch was up to.

***

I was flying by the seat of my pants and wasn't quite sure where I was going, but I had a feeling of where Hesperia might be. I'd never been outside the protection of Oleander, but I'd been observant, always listening.

My gut instinct led me to a cavern deep within the onyx castle walls of Hesperia's stolen home. No one saw me, and I moved freely around the halls until I reached the cavern, where Algol's power was fueled by the celestial. A thin, fragile string jetted out from the pool of darkness. No one else could seem to see it, not even Hesperia. She seemed to sense it was there, though, as she paced back and forth in front of the pool of black.

I realized that the silver strand was the link to my sister, keeping Algol alive from the time she'd healed it. It seemed to fade. The magic weakened over time. No wonder Zoe had to find The Archer. She'd never be able to unite the realms with her essence alone. Could this kill her? Did she know the price of this magic? Of course she did. Such a martyr.

Oleander had said she'd grown more… chaotic. Like she spiraled into the darkness more. She was going to have to find another tether soon, or she might be lost to all of us.

Hesperia scraped the pointed end of the knife she was holding into the side of her temple, drawing blood. Her jaw clenched, and there was a male immortal dressed in white with her. I didn't know his name.

"Did you get what we needed?" he asked.

"Yes, I got the first part anyway," she spat, holding up a vial of dark liquid… blood, I realized. In her other hand, there was a vial of bright light. "At least we know she doesn't know what I plan to do with her, but how did she know about the blood magic?"

"Maybe she doesn't. Maybe it was a bluff," the male offered, pulling Hesperia into his arms. I wanted to violently recoil from the sight. How anyone could show her affection was beyond me. I guess it took all kinds.

Please don't make out in front of me, I pleaded to the universe. Thankfully, they didn't. She walked closer to the swirling mass of black, and a wicked smile crossed her face.

"I want to make her scream. You cannot possibly understand how much I long for her death. She had her chance to join me willingly. I have given her too many opportunities… But that self-righteous female will never join me. Not without the right pressure. Or by force."

"Why don't we just kill her?"

"It's not time for her to die," she said unhappily.

That sounded personal. Perhaps more personal than we'd assumed. What was Hesperia's deal with my sister?

"Then let's make her wail," the male said.

"The moment my blade touches Algol, we won't have long before Oleander's Shadowed descends upon the castle. We'll need to move our operations elsewhere. To Canopus."

He nodded, apparently okay with her line of thinking. He must be connected to that realm.

"Is her pain worth that?"

"Her suffering is worth everything, Abel," she said, slicing the knife into Algol's energy. I watched in horror as the thin silver line waned and buckled as if it were writhing in agony. My sister was in trouble, and right now, all she had was me to stop it. I would not fail her.

"Forgive me," I whispered, removing my tether to the *otherside*. I knew what Hesperia could do to my spirit after what she'd done to my mother. But there was no hesitation in me. I was already dead… I would just cease to exist.

I only had a second of surprise, and I used it. I launched my spirit form around Hesperia's head, distracting her enough to focus her attention on me, not Zoe.

"Abel!" Hesperia shouted. He lashed his magic out wildly, unable to see me, but I was suddenly in a tornado of power, incapable of moving.

Hesperia straightened her hair and strode towards me.

"Well, hello, darling," she said, holding the knife up to my throat. I wasn't sure why, since I felt nothing. "And who might you be?"

"One of the dead?" Abel asked. Hesperia ignored him.

"Who do you belong to?" she demanded again, and I said nothing.

Another immortal came into the cavern, whispering something in Abel's ear.

"They've breached the borders of the grounds!" Abel shouted. "We need to go!"

"Oh no," Hesperia said, smiling with all her teeth. "We won't be going anywhere. I recognize you, my dear. You were on the beach the day of Elvy and Zoe's joining."

No.

"Are you mad?" he asked.

"Don't call me that," she said, pouting. "Bring her with us to the front gate. We're going to see just how valuable she is."

"Why don't you just end her?"

This guy had one excitable trigger finger.

"I will if needed, but I have a feeling she is more useful to me like this."

I swallowed, true fear coursing through me. I'd screwed up, that was certain, and Abel's magic was keeping me from doing literally anything. Rage coiled within me. How was I captured by someone who couldn't even see me? Fate was feeling spiteful.

"This night may be saved for us yet," she said with wild giddiness, and I knew my interference would come at a price, and either Zoe or I was going to pay it.

26

Submit

ZOE

I was quite literally moving at the speed of light, but it still didn't feel fast enough. *Freyja.* She had my sister. Oleander informed us immediately after he'd received word from Zadie. We'd barely cleared Vega when an excruciating pain ripped through me, causing me to plummet to the ocean below. The kelpie had been waiting to carry me back to the surface of the water. I'd been in too much agony to swim myself. Elvy and Blaz had dove in after me to carry me the rest of the way. I think Imelda had flown ahead to get help.

It felt like a knife was carving up my insides. Even when the sharpness of the pain had ceased, I still felt the ripple effects tingling throughout my nervous system. I hadn't even had time to process what had happened at the palace—what Hesperia had taken from everyone. The only thing we knew for sure was that she'd taken blood from all of us. I'd forgotten what taking a breath felt like.

Zadie hadn't been able to explain to Oleander how Freyja had gotten captured. She'd made sure she was safe before she left to defend the wards, which meant Freyja had likely left of her own accord. I wanted to wring her neck, but I knew in my heart that it had been her to stop Hesperia from hurting me. She hadn't realized that I could pull from Elvy to help heal me when this happened. We'd anticipated something like this taking place when Hesperia discovered the truth. We knew she wouldn't kill me. Not likely, anyway. Killing a celestial outright wasn't quite that simple.

Freyja had stopped her from hurting me. No matter what obstacles came now, I would not lose sight of the sacrifice she'd been willing to give for me. I would save her from this. The stars owed me that much.

I landed beside Oleander's pacing form with Jelly, Elvy, Imelda, and Blaz behind me. Delmira, Finn, and Clodovea had to stay behind to protect Vega and help Aura, who had chosen to come with us after Abel had fled with Hesperia. The future was too uncertain to risk otherwise.

I didn't have to ask where my sister was. Hesperia had her on display for the entirety of her realm to see. Freyja's face was calm, resigned to whatever fate lay before her. She would not meet my eyes. Whether that was to offer me further protection or because she was ashamed of being caught, I didn't know.

"What does Hesperia want? Has she figured out who Freyja is to me?" I asked Oleander.

"Your arrival has likely confirmed her suspicions," he answered, pulling me into a hug.

"I'll get her back," I said, my voice cracking on the last word.

"That's what I'm afraid of," he admitted. "But I'd expect nothing less."

Elvy, Blaz, and Imelda could not see Freyja, so they looked towards me for orders—answers. "She's got Freyja trapped in some kind of air magic to keep her spirit from flying away."

"Do we know why she hasn't…" I trailed off, incapable of finishing the thought. I didn't want the image of her spirit incinerating at the hands of Hesperia. My mother's fate would not be hers.

"No," Oleander answered, voice stiff.

"What do we do?" Elvy asked, pulling me against his solid form. "You're not alone in this."

"I'm so sorry, Zoe," Zadie said with silver in her eyes. "It's all my fault."

"No, Zadie. Freyja gets it honest," I said, staring at the playing field. "My family is just a bunch of self-sacrificing lunatics. We're used to getting the short end of the stick."

"But you always rise," Oleander said.

I turned my head towards him, then to Elvy.

"Give me some time," I said. "And retrieve Aura from Vega. We need an air elemental we can trust."

"Aura's fragile right now," Blaz said, genuine concern in his eyes. "We just got her safely into Vega."

"I don't need to be reminded of that," I snapped. The stress was getting to me. "She's stronger than you think. Tell her that our lives are defined by moments. It's time for her to have hers."

"Are you sure?" Imelda asked.

My gift swelled within me. Aura would come.

"Yes," I said confidently. "Take a squadron of the Sublunary with you. You might need them."

Hesperia would likely send some of her immortals after them, but I couldn't worry about them right now. I was about to piss a few celestials off. What was new?

"I'm not going to try to convince you otherwise," Elvy whispered, holding me close. I knew he saw what I was going to do.

"Just know I am with you always. To whatever future, as long as you're there with me."

"No goodbyes," I said seriously. "I'll see you soon."

"What insanity are you about to do?" Oleander asked, royally pissed off.

"I need time, Oleander. Make sure I have it," I instructed. He nodded, resigned to trusting me.

I pulled Elvy's lips to mine, memorizing the feel of him and the smell of saltwater that never quite left him. I would come back to my flame. His eyes said the same. He would be waiting for me. No matter what happened now. He would send all he had through our bond to see this mission through.

"I will find my way back to you. Always," I promised, then disappeared to find the place to meet my fate, with Jelly following dutifully behind me.

***

I didn't know how I knew where to go, but a path of light was steady in front of me. I didn't question whether I was safe or if Hesperia's army would come for me. They wouldn't. I was right where I was always going to end up. In this moment. The feel of Jelly's wings brushing alongside my body kept me in the present, even though I felt somewhat in a trance, like the strings of fate were guiding me home.

The path of light led me to a cavern deep within the heart of Algol—long forgotten by the immortals who resided here. I doubted even Tiergan knew of this place. The darkness provided me comfort, as if welcoming me home after waiting so long for me.

I felt his presence before I saw him. Only this time, he wasn't in my dreams. He was really here. The Archer. My father.

"Zoe," he breathed, stepping out of the dark abyss. He looked the same as he had in my dreams. I wanted to weep at the sight of him. With little thought, I wrapped my arms around my father, and I seemed to remember the feel of him from when I was a toddler. Before he'd left us—to save us. Only my mom hadn't been saved. She'd done the saving.

Jelly circled around him, sniffing him. She didn't raise her hackles and came back to sit at my side. The Archer had bowed politely in acknowledgment of the power of the guardianship of the simargl, but his eyes had remained on me—his daughter.

"You knew I would come," I said, breathing in the scent of him. It was familiar to my inner child. Liquorish. He'd always smelled like liquorish. I wasn't sure I had any true memories of him, but that one was strong, grounding me to this reality.

"Yes, little bear," he said, stroking my hair. "I am so sorry for the pain you have experienced. If there were any other way… I would have—" he paused, voice heavy with guilt.

I looked back into the same green eyes I had and shook my head.

"You are just as much a victim in this as the rest of us," I argued.

"I don't know about that, but I am honored by the faith that you have in me. You don't know the whole story, little bear. Nova. She tried to warn me long ago when this all began. If I had only listened to her," he said, eyes flashing back to a different time.

"We'd still be right here," I said with conviction in my words. "Some things just are. Were. And will be."

He seemed to age before me, cupping my cheeks in each of his warm, calloused palms.

"My fate was always this," I whispered.

"It didn't have to be if I had chosen differently… you are wise beyond your years, my child," he said, placing a kiss on my forehead. "I don't have much time."

"I know," I replied, feeling him slipping away already. He was not meant to be here.

"Take what you need from me," he said, laying me on the stone table at the heart of the cave. There was an opening at the top, about one hundred feet up. The light was barely enough to provide enough to see.

"Will I survive?" I asked.

"If you play your hand right," he said, kissing my cheek. "I've brought some familiar faces to watch over you while you are away."

The familiar scent of lilies wafted through the musty smell of the dark cave.

"Hey there, Zo," June said, eyes bright. She looked the same as she always had, but there was an air about her I hadn't noticed as a mortal. Phoebe—the old gypsy woman who had given me my first prophecy—was behind her, quiet, knowing I needed this moment.

I wrapped my arms around June's neck. She had always been there for me, taking me under her wing when I felt like I didn't belong anywhere. But I'd always belonged where she was concerned. She was one of the last souls to see my mother and Grant alive. June had buried them for me. My very own guardian angel.

"Thank you," I said, voice breaking slightly.

"You kept on bloomin', Zo," she said, pushing my hair out of my tear-soaked eyes.

"It's not over yet," I said, letting the fear I kept hidden out.

"No, honey. It's not," she agreed. "It's only just startin'."

"Am I ever going to get to make those mistakes?" I asked, remembering the advice she'd given me the last night of my mortal existence.

"I'd say you've pissed a few people off," she said, grinning. The Archer and Phoebe laughed at that, too.

"I wish I had time to ask you all the questions on my heart," I said as images of Saint Andrews flooded my mind.

"I know. And that's why you have to make it back, kid," she said seriously.

"It's time," The Archer said, holding my other hand.

I nodded, taking a deep breath from my diaphragm. Jelly leaped up on the table with me, covering my body with her own in protection. Nothing would get through her. I'd never felt more sure—more safe in what I was about to do. This was going to work. Even if I burned for it.

"I'm ready."

"It'll be just like the trials. Nova will be waiting for you."

I reached out to Elvy one last time before my spirit left this realm.

"I love you, flame. Make sure Aura comes. My plan won't work without her," I instructed through our bond.

"We won't let anything happen to Freyja," he swore. *"Come back to me—to us."*

"Are you afraid?" my father asked.

"Fear is useless," I said, shaking my head. "What must be done, must be done. Fear will not change that."

"Fight ferociously, little bear."

"Jelly and I will see you on the other side," June promised, as The Archer pulled a piece of his essence from his core and slammed it into my body, sending my astral form soaring through the cosmos to the realm of Nova.

27

Embrace

FREYJA

I'd seen Zoe embrace Elvy before running off to… I didn't know where.

She hadn't abandoned me to this fate. I felt that in my gut, even though I wouldn't blame her if she did. If I had just stayed put, nobody would be in this mess. Hesperia would have zero leverage against them, and they would have secured Algol's connection to my sister.

But I'd screwed that up. Big time.

It didn't matter that my intentions had been pure, and I'd thought I was saving my sister. I'd probably do it again if I were being honest with myself. I tried not to look at Oleander, though I felt his eyes burning right through my translucent form. The air magic Abel was using had calmed down some, but I remained caged—locked in this torment. I assumed it wouldn't hold forever. He would eventually need sleep, or they could just get another air user, I supposed.

I would just need a moment of weakness from them. One slip, and I'd be gone. Maybe straight over to the *otherside*, but beggars couldn't be choosers.

Zoe and I were like the Winchester brothers from one of our favorite television shows, *Supernatural*. One of them was always dying, and the other was always sacrificing himself to save the other. Except now I felt like Bobby. The ghost who wouldn't go away and move on when I was supposed to. Instead, I was wreaking havoc on everyone else.

We'd always had different tastes in books and cinema, but that one show we both went a little feral for. Maybe it was the bond between brothers that we, as sisters, had loved so much. She'd always favored Dean, and I'd been devoted to Sam. As the supernatural was currently all around me, I made a vow to myself right here and now.

The moment I could break free of this trap, I would go to the *otherside*. I wouldn't let my sister sacrifice another thing for me. I wouldn't upset the balance of death any longer. Oleander would hate me for it, but he'd get over it. He had quite literally forever to find a new plaything.

I glanced at him as I said the cruel, untrue words, and his blue eyes held mine. I winced as if he knew what I'd thought. One thing was absolutely certain about Ander. He did not see me as some toy. He cared about me deeply, and I him. More than I wanted to admit to anyone. His eyes seemed to tell me to hold on. They had a plan.

Well, so did I, and it did not involve anyone else doing something stupid and irreversible just to save me. I'd save my own ghostly self and put it right where it belonged.

"Come out, come out, Zoe Eferhild," Hesperia chanted like a children's song. "Come play with us."

Hesperia's eyes had grown darker, sick with madness. Her entire army seemed... unwell. Like she truly had some kind of hold on them. Not all of them, though. Some simply had chosen to be evil—like Abel. His greed for power was evident in the way he walked. Others seemed to sweat with defiance. This intel might make things a little tricky moving forward. How honorable was it to kill someone who was not acting on their own mind? Could they be sick with her very madness?

"Maybe we should go slice and dice her some more!" Hesperia shouted with glee.

Not good. I didn't think it'd matter where Zoe was… she'd feel that. And I couldn't stop it now.

No one could. This stupid legion wasn't going to move in to stop Hesperia, so long as she had me. My sister would have given that order before she ran off, and I had no doubt that Oleander would enjoy flaying anyone alive who moved against me.

"New game!" Hesperia cried out, mania consuming her. "How about every hour Zoe stays hidden, one of you dies?"

Did she actually think she could take on the Shadowed Legions of Vega and Algol? Not to mention the Sublunary, who were just as large?

"Oh, silly me," she said, smiling. "I forgot to mention that some of my subjects were not exactly… *willing* to join my cause, but I made them see reason."

A group of men and women stepped forward. They were the sweaty ones—the immortals that did not seem to sincerely serve Hesperia.

"These immortals who are truly loyal to you, Oleander, will die one by one until Zoe Eferhild comes forth. They all die immediately if you come an inch closer."

No.

Oleander's eyes flared, and a wave of darkness settled over his features. He was the embodiment of the Lord Astral of Algol, Commander of the Shadowed Legion. He would not take this lightly, and Hesperia knew it.

"And if I go through all of them… I can always rid this world of this sad little spirit," she said, glancing towards me.

I swallowed, knowing her threat to be very real.

Elvy and Tiergan joined either side of Oleander, ready to defend those innocent immortals, but none of them made a move. How could they? No matter what they chose to do, someone innocent was going to die. I hated to even think this way, but if they waited… if by some miracle I could escape or if Zoe pulled off another defiance to the stars… some would survive. Were some lives better than none?

"It's up to us, Zo," I whispered so low no one could hear me, but I prayed the message got through to her somewhere in the cosmos. "You or me."

28

Take a Bow

ZOE

Unlike the first time I'd arrived in the realm of the stars, I did not collide with the ocean like a flailing newborn bird. I guided my wings to the beach along the shoreline where Nova waited for me, just as The Archer promised.

"Welcome back, Zoe Eferhild, Realm-Healer—Emerging of Legends," she said, as I landed upright on my feet. Nova looked the same as the last time I'd been here in my trials. Her translucent skin was covered in a language I didn't know, and her eyes swirled with an infinite glitter of stars.

"I guess you knew it was always going to be a possibility for me to come back here," I said, arms crossed.

"I knew it was one conceivable course of fate amongst a myriad," she agreed, holding out her hand to follow me. "I understand we are on a bit of a time crunch."

Freyja.

"Yes, we are," I said, following her with purpose in my steps. "Will you be going with me?"

"I think it wise that I do."

She led me into the palace I'd called home during my trials. The nostalgic part of me wanted to see if it was still the same, but we didn't have time for that. If I didn't pull this off, my sister would be lost to me forever. I knew she would cross over indefinitely, and I simply refused this fate for her.

"I won't ask you if I will succeed," I said, walking along her silent form. My footfalls were the only sounds in the moonstone palace. "I just want to know if it is possible."

Nova stayed silent for a while, leading me deeper into the heart of the palace. My ears popped from the pressure change, and I opened my mouth, trying to clear them. She looked at me curiously. I guess such things did not bother her.

"It is not likely," she admitted. "But impossible? No, Zoe Eferhild. I won't say that."

That was enough for me. I just needed to know that it was within the realm of possibility. I'd made an oath, and I didn't intend to break it.

She led me to a large stone that was quadruple the size of me. There was a swirling rune carved into the white rock, and Nova gently laid her hand on it, causing it to light up with violet magic.

A portal opened, unlike anything I'd ever seen before. It wasn't the typical shadows we used to transport between the fissures of other star realms. This gave off the same energy as the orb I'd latched onto in my final trial—the time I'd defied the stars.

"The Realm of the Celestials," Nova said, holding out her hand. I laced my fingers through hers and took a steadying breath. "I cannot protect you once we cross. Your fate is your own."

I nodded. I preferred it that way. If I died—if I failed—I'd prefer it to be of my own accord.

"I'm ready."

"So you are, Eferhild," she said, pulling us through the glowing light.

***

There was no sense of falling or the rush of stars flying past us. This was… quiet. I'd almost argue it was tranquil, but I didn't dare give much power to the thought. This would not be peaceful. But it was an important moment. Perhaps one of the most critical of my existence.

We both kept silent as I followed her to a stone table that seemed to comprise all five elements. The base was the trunk of a tree that looked like clay layered and twisted together. The top of the table was circular, with each section having some form of the element it represented. In the center of the table was a fire pit with a blue-green flame.

The fire took me back to the first moment I'd spoken to Elvy and daringly asked him who he was. Even then, my soul needed to know my flame. The mortal moment that everything had changed for me.

I refocused back to the table and found five massive chairs that correlated with the section of the table they were at. One section was covered with moss and a seemingly tiny terrarium. Another had an ocean encased in sea glass. Spirit was a swirl of shadows that never stopped moving. Air had multiple tornadoes going through it. The last section had flames of varying colors encased beneath the impenetrable surface of the table.

Our hosts weren't here yet. Whether that was a power play or not, I didn't know. I was certain they didn't care to be summoned by the likes of me, but I didn't really care about what they wanted. They needed to want what I needed them to.

There were two chairs that were much less intricate and nestled between Algol and Vega's place.

"Do we sit?" I asked.

"If you'd like to die," Nova answered, standing eerily still and patient.

"No sitting then," I agreed and took up a stance with her.

A few moments later, the celestials descended upon us in flashes of light, so fast it was as if lightning struck each place they came from.

The celestials were easy to identify. Algol and Vega looked the same as they had when I met them in the trials. Vega was turquoise and gold with little orbs of life wanting to leap from their form, while Algol was a whirl of darkness with orbs of light clinging to their core. Somehow, they still had identifiable features that made them appear more familiar. Their elements formed facial features for them to appear more like mortals or immortals.

Arcturus seemed to be made of cooled lava; however, orange liquid glowed beneath the cracks in the black stone. Like Vega and Algol, they were neither male nor female. They just were. Their forms were the past, present, and future.

Rigil's form was probably my favorite. They were made of nature, with tree bark, flowers, and moss defining their facial details. Rigil seemed like the safest target to secure to my side. If I could win them over, maybe the rest would follow.

Canopus was the brightest celestial of them all, with a never-ending tidal wave of wind flowing over its body. They seemed kind, but I knew firsthand how ferocious the wind could really be. So much destruction by something we couldn't always see, and we certainly couldn't control the forces of air. Freyja definitely did not appreciate the clutches of the magic now, that's for sure.

Nova and I still stood on the outskirts, waiting to be summoned. I didn't dare speak, following her lead.

"It's been too long since we've convened," Rigil said with a… happy expression. They seemed to be joyful about seeing their fellow celestials.

Algol humphed and rolled their eyes. I had half a mind to slap the celestial. If it weren't for me, they would be dead. Maybe they should be reminded of that.

"It is good to see you all again," Vega said, which seemed to make Algol even angrier. I guess I got my attitude honest?

"Why is it that every time we meet, it's because someone else is forcing us to?" Canopus asked, siding with Rigil. Hopefully, I could use that to my advantage.

"Ah, yes," Arcturus responded, glancing towards where we stood. "We do have guests, don't we?"

Nova bowed, and I followed suit. My pride would not ruin this.

"Please, come sit," Rigil said, standing and gesturing to the two empty chairs. They had been the only ones to stand.

I tried to keep my breath from shaking. It was as if I'd run up several flights of stairs. Diaphragm breaths, I coached myself. This was nothing. You've already pissed them off once. I'd be reasonable if they would. But I wasn't afraid to anger them again if they forced my hand.

"Nova, it's lovely to see you again," Arcturus said with a smile, and I realized their teeth were made up of rocks. Was their tongue a flame? No, that must have been a trick of the eye.

"Do not lie to me," she said, annoyed.

"I would never lie to you, Nova," Arcturus responded gently.

What in the world was going on with these two? I shook my head. I could not get side-tracked right now.

"Zoe, I'm glad you survived the Emerging," Vega said, putting the focus on me. Algol seemed to seethe on the other side of Nova.

"Yes, I am, too."

"You've found Vega to your liking?" the water elemental celestial asked.

"It feels like home," I agreed.

Algol clenched their fists. What the hell?

"You'll have to excuse them," Vega said apologetically. "Algol is… prideful."

"What she did is forbidden. To serve two stars," Algol said, tone angry. I must have gotten their mystical voices during the trials. This was all a little too real.

"I did warn you," Nova said, voice raised. "You did not heed me."

"You're right. We didn't," Arcturus agreed.

"Agreeing with me does not earn you my favor," she said.

Arcturus seemed to like the challenge, no matter how cold Nova was to them.

"Maybe we were wrong," Vega said, cocking their head in my direction.

"It is time, Algol," Canopus said, folding their hands in front of them. "To get rid of this arbitrary law."

"No," Algol said, voice tight. I was going to stab them before this meeting was over. No wonder I had daddy issues. My own father had them.

"Must we continue this feud?" Vega asked. "We cannot change what happened with my Astral line—"

"Silence!" Algol said. "You must not speak of it."

"It does not change the balance, Algol," Rigil said gently.

Algol seemed to only grow angrier, and I tucked that information away for later when I had time to make sense of it.

Vega sighed, turning back towards me. "Why have you come, Zoe?"

"My sister," I began, but Algol interrupted.

"More favors. More defiance," Algol muttered, but I ignored them. "Is Hesperia really causing you that much trouble?"

"She certainly seemed to cause too much trouble for you," I said, taunting. "But I guess it's only okay for you to ask for help?"

If looks could kill, Algol would have ensured my death in that moment. I wasn't sure what force kept them from smiting me alive, but I sent my higher power my never-ending thanks. Unfortunately, my mouth wouldn't seem to stop talking without my permission.

"Yes, my sister is being held captive by Hesperia. You should be able to have empathy for her, right, Algol?" I asked, raising a brow. If they wanted defiance, I'd give it to them.

They only clenched their fists tighter. The swirls of darkness grew even bleaker, more chaotic. It was difficult to remember that Algol had chosen me, just as Vega had. They didn't seem to choose me now.

"Why can't you free her on your own?" Canopus asked.

"She's being held by one of your immortals," I stated. "His magic is keeping her trapped. One wrong move and Hesperia will end what's left of my sister."

Canopus' cloudy brows furrowed. They didn't seem to know how to feel about one of their own doing this.

"You forgot to mention that she's dead," Algol pointed out.

I nodded.

"You're right," I agreed. "She died in my place on the night I was supposed to meet my maker. If it weren't for her, I never would have had the opportunity to Emerge."

"Your realm-healer could not have saved you, Algol," Arcturus said.

"War demands sacrifice," Algol scoffed.

My darkness grew irritated. My shadow self loved Freyja just as much as the part of me that lived in the light. She was a little more unhinged, but still good… I think.

"We are only in this war because of what you made my father do!" I shouted, tired of the games the celestials played.

Vega looked at me curiously, as if they could see the darkness swelling, writhing within me to unleash on them. I wasn't sure what damage I could really do to a celestial, but I wasn't opposed to trying.

"Is it really fair?" Rigil asked, tilting their chin softly. "To bring one back goes against nature. It could have a ripple effect you do not want."

At least they asked a somewhat intelligent question.

"I don't care about fair," I said, voice much calmer than I felt. "Every choice we make has consequences, whether those are good or bad, is entirely up to us. The way I see it, you all decided to rip away the connection of immortals, forcing them to choose which parts of themselves to love the most. Forcing families apart for no reason other than to stroke some ego that none of the immortals care about. Not to mention the memories you took from them, which they are all starting to figure out, by the way. If you want to talk about going against nature, start there. Own your choices. Freyja will not be collateral damage in a mistake *you* need *me* to fix."

The black tendrils of Algol were a breath away from my neck, ready to choke me. It seemed I had struck a nerve.

"You all made the wrong choice back then. Will you repeat history all over again?" I asked, voice steady. "All I'm asking for is a fighting chance to mend the tethers in the Kingdom of Canis. Let me restore the dominion as it was always meant to be."

Nova bit her lip, as if stifling a laugh. The celestials would probably not take kindly to being laughed at and called out in their own realm. Her face turned serious once more.

"You did not listen to me nor The Archer last time. I'm imploring you to listen to Zoe now. You cannot imagine the depth of regret you will face should you choose pride over grace," Nova said, pausing for effect. "Choose wisely."

The celestials looked at each other. Canopus spoke first.

"I am sorry one of my Lord Astrals has lost his way," he said, pausing. "We will take responsibility for what was done in the past to lead him to his dark heart. I call upon the council of the celestials to vote on the fate of Freyja."

"I second this notion," Vega agreed. "I will give her a grain of my essence, which will restore her to her mortal state."

I was likely going to regret the next words, but they fell out of my mouth before I could think better of it.

"Not good enough," I said seriously. "Her mother—our mother—was murdered by Hesperia, and her spirit incinerated from the universe entirely. Her father was slain right along with her. She has no one on Earth. The star realms are her home now. You will make her an immortal—a Shadowed."

"You selfish little—" Algol began, but Nova raised her hand to silence them before they said something that would end us both.

"Grant Freyja the right of the Emerging, Algol. Give her the option to go through the trials," Nova suggested. "Let it be her choice. Let her prove her worth."

Algol twiddled their thumbs, and I could *see* that they would not do this. Their pride was too great. The rivalry between Vega and Algol was too much of a conflict in their eyes. Since I couldn't force them into an 'I will get along t-shirt,' drastic measures would have to be taken.

I looked to Nova, and she bowed her head, knowing what I was about to do. This was a pivotal moment, and that's what this world was about. It was up to us to make them count. This time when I chose death, it would be out of love for my sister, not a desperate plea to end the pain of my mind. I was a warrior, poised to pay the ultimate sacrifice, as so many Shadowed before me had.

Without hesitation, I unsheathed one of my knives and pointed the blade to my carotid artery, pulsing in my throat. I pressed in enough so that blood trickled down my neck, staining my skin burgundy.

"I implore you to make a different decision, Algol," I said, gritting my teeth. "Or you and I will both go meet our makers together."

Silence.

"Get ready, Elvy," I whispered through our flame.

29

Rigid

DELMIRA

Blaz had escorted Aura to me before they'd immediately left for Algol.

I'd wanted to talk to Blaz and apologize for dipping out on him and for the headbutt, but he'd stunned me into silence. The truth was, he hadn't left my thoughts much, and I didn't like that at all. I'd just wanted things to get back to where they had always been with us—best friends.

He didn't want that.

"I know what you're going to say, Delm. Just stop," Blaz said, pulling me onto a secluded balcony. "Stop *thinking* so much."

"But—"

He cupped my cheek in his rough hand.

"If you really don't want this, then stop me," he said, and I knew he'd meant it.

I didn't stop him—didn't want to.

He softly kissed me, taking in my bottom lip, pressing me up against the stone wall. My body's reaction to him was immediate. I took us further, exploring his mouth with my tongue. He tasted divine, and I lost all sense of reason.

I didn't want it back. I wanted to leap forward into whatever he was offering.

He broke the kiss, nuzzling against my neck.

I wanted him.

"I have to go," he said, eyes darkening.

A breeze blew away the fog of Blaz.

I nodded, straightening my uniform and hair.

"Of course," I said, back to business.

"Delmira," he said, placing an arm above me, eyes piercing through my nonchalant facade.

"Yes?" I asked, sounding more confident than I felt.

"We can talk when I get back, okay? Just don't talk yourself out of it—us—while I'm gone."

"They're waiting for you," I said, stepping away from him. Feelings in times of war were fatal. And I didn't want him to die.

I left him standing there, and I didn't look back.

***

"Delm?" Clodovea asked, pulling me from the memory. She'd asked a question, I think.

"What is it?" I asked, running a hand through my hair. I could not spend time stressing about Blaz.

"Aura. She's strong, don't you think?" she asked again.

In all honesty, she looked weak at first glance, but appearances were deceiving. I'd been mistaken as weak many times before as a mortal. Their mistake. Aura, Octavia, and Finnian sat around a fire in one of the private studies in the manor. Finn and Octavia laughed with Aura about something I couldn't hear. I was glad they could find something to smile about in times such as these.

Finn and I had continued using our gifts. I had mostly used my influence of thoughts to keep the immortals in Musterion settled. Only slightly. With such a vast population, I couldn't influence them much. Just enough to take the edge off their worry. Finn had still been monitoring for any traitors, but so far, we hadn't found any.

My gift was much easier to wield than his. Pulling thoughts from others proved to be much more difficult than influencing them. Mortals and immortals alike were very guarded creatures.

Finn and I had gone back and forth on using his gift to check Aura's thoughts. He'd eventually relented, only verifying that she was on our side. I knew it ate at him to violate the privacy of others, but it frustrated him even more that he couldn't get into Hesperia's mind.

"You're distracted today," Clodovea noted.

"Just a lot on my mind, Clove," I brushed off.

"Want to talk about it?" she asked.

"No," I said firmly. It came out harsher than I'd meant it. "Sorry."

I leaned back in my chair, staring up at the stars through the skylight.

"How do you do it?" I asked. "Manage a relationship and your duties?"

She perked an eyebrow at me, but she didn't ask the question I could feel burning beneath her. I wasn't exactly known as the relationship type. I was more of the casual hookup to get my needs met type. Not that my needs were actually met very often.

"It doesn't feel like I'm having to 'manage' anything. Especially not Imelda," she said. "She makes everything clear for me. When everything else sucks... she doesn't."

"But how do you care about someone that much?"

It was a strange question. I knew I cared about Blaz enough to push him away for his own good. It was more than that, though. I wasn't sure I was capable of... *feelings*. I'd never been in a relationship, even as a mortal, before Finn and I had Emerged. It's not like I hadn't been pursued or found others attractive. All of that was there, but I'd never bothered to add emotions into the mix. Sex served a purpose, and once it had been fulfilled, I moved on.

Until Blaz. He *knew* me. I couldn't hide from him. He was my best friend.

"Where is all this coming from, Delm?" she asked. "Talk to me."

I pressed my lips into a thin line—silent.

"Sometimes, love just chooses you in a disastrously intense way. I never had a chance when it came to Imelda," she said, smiling softly—secretly.

"You wouldn't go back to before? When it was easier?" I asked, trying to sort out my thoughts.

"Who said before her was easier?" she asked, amused. "This immortal life would be meaningless without her. Just a void. That sounds much harder to me."

Hell. That does sound terrible.

Speaking of... Evander came through the double doors, with Blaz and Imelda trailing behind him.

Clodovea and I were up from our seats in a heartbeat. We weren't expecting them to be back here so quickly. Especially not alone.

Finnian looked just as perplexed. We hadn't received anything through an iris.

"Report," I demanded. It sounded more like, 'what the hell is going on?'

Evander stood off to the side, and Blaz and Imelda stepped forward, pitching their voices low. Finnian had come to join us. Octavia offered some coffee to Aura, which she declined, staring at us.

"We need Aura to come back with us," Blaz said.

"What for?" Clodovea asked, giving Imelda a once-over, making sure she was in one piece.

"I'm pregnant, not deaf," Aura said, striding towards us. Octavia chased after her, offering her some tea instead of coffee, which Aura pushed away again. You couldn't deny that Octavia tried.

"Well, go on. Answer Clodovea," I said, directing the question at Blaz.

"Abel is using his magic to hold Freyja hostage," he informed. "Zoe requested a trusted air user."

"You want her to face the male who has been abusing her for centuries?" Finn asked, hatred in his expression.

I echoed the sentiment. I knew Zoe well enough that she would not want us to force Aura's hand.

"It's your choice, Aura," I vowed. "Whether you choose to go back with them, you have a safe place in Vega until it is safe for you to return to Canopus."

"Zoe told me to tell you that life was defined by moments, and this one was yours," Blaz said with conviction.

I felt him staring at me, but I kept my attention on Aura.

"I always knew it would come to this," she said, swallowing as if to settle herself. She rubbed her tiny, almost non-existent bump in thought. "I will face him. The Court of Vega offered me sanctuary without a second thought. I will help Zoe in whatever way I can."

I nodded, smirking at the fighter I'd seen deep within her surface more fully.

"And I hope I can rely on Vega to help me reclaim Canopus when this is over," she said pointedly.

"I have no doubt that Elvy and Zoe will honor that desire," I promised.

"We will need to leave immediately," Imelda said, looking at Clodovea sadly. Another goodbye for them.

Not so easy now, is it, Clove?

"Go," I said, nodding. "We will be here, waiting."

I felt like I was always waiting these days.

Imelda said her goodbyes to Clodovea, and I couldn't ignore Blaz any longer.

"Are you avoiding me, Delm?" Blaz asked.

I kept my expression neutral.

"No, Blaz. Not everything is about you," I snapped. "I've got a realm to protect."

"I didn't mean—" he started, but I cut him off. I couldn't hear whatever he was going to say because I didn't trust myself to.

"Evander!" I called.

"Yes, Commander?"

"Please take a squadron with these three on their way back to Algol. Now," I ordered.

He nodded and left without hesitation, just like any Shadowed would.

I felt Blaz hovering over me, but I didn't look up from the paperwork I was looking through.

"This isn't over, Delm. Not by a long shot," he promised.

I felt him leave, and my eyes lingered on his retreating form until I could no longer see him.

My twin stood next to me, arms crossed.

"Why are you giving Blaz the cold shoulder?"

"It's complicated," I answered.

"Is it?" he asked, brow raised.

I went to snap at him, but he raised his hands in surrender. "None of my business."

"No, it isn't," I agreed. "Come on, we have work to do. "

30

Sisters

FREYJA

For the first time since I'd died, I felt tired. Sleepy. I was more than ready to go into an endless hibernation, if that's what the *otherside* was.

Hesperia had stayed true to her word. Five of the warriors she held against their will had been slaughtered by her hand. She'd slit their throats after immobilizing them with her black magic. More innocent blood on my hands. If I'd just stayed in that parlor… Better yet, if I had just crossed over when I'd first died, I would have saved everyone a lot of heartache, including Zoe.

But I'd been selfish. I hadn't been ready to let go of her. She'd always thought that she'd been the one keeping me there, but that had never been true. I stayed because I was scared to go. What happened to Zoe that night had been my fault. Yes, I'd died, but she'd met a fate worse than death, in my opinion. Yet, she had been the one to carry so much shame over it.

At least I'd gotten to see her happy with Elvy again before I was lost to her forever.

In the end, I guessed I had a role to play when The Archer had come looking. I'd agreed to help Zoe without hesitation.

Movement near Oleander and Elvy caught my eye, and I saw a beautiful girl with raven-colored hair and dark skin arrive with Blaz and Imelda. She wore the colors of the Court of Canopus, but I didn't know her name. I assumed she was someone they had been with on Sirius. She looked… fierce. Like she was ready to take on her greatest enemy.

For a split-second, the air keeping me trapped wavered, but not enough to let me escape. I glanced down at Abel, and his eyes burned toward the new woman.

"Do they seriously think I care whether Aura lives or dies?" he asked Hesperia, who had come beside him.

They were both morons if they thought Elvy or Oleander would hurt someone else just to get me. I knew it killed them every time Hesperia executed one of the immortals under her control. They also wouldn't bring her here without a purpose.

"Don't worry," Hesperia said, running her fingers up and down his bicep. Gross. "I'll take care of her."

Abel smiled at that and kissed Hesperia sloppily. I assumed it was to put on some sort of display for the woman named Aura.

I turned my attention back to her, and she didn't seem to care about them. She looked determined, though. Like she had something important to do here.

Somehow, I knew Zoe was involved in this. The Dean to my Sam, always figuring out some way to rescue me.

Oleander's eyes found mine, and he furrowed his brows, trying to convey some message to me with facial expressions alone. I shook my head in confusion, not knowing what he wanted from me.

He didn't give up and mouthed two words, "Get ready."

Get ready? Did I read his lips right? I had gotten familiar with those lips of his, so I was pretty sure that's what he'd said. For what, though?

31

Defiance

ZOE

"Stop!" Algol shouted, as I pushed the blade deeper into my throat. One centimeter further, and I would puncture the vital vein that would spill my life's blood and Algol's life force right along with it.

"I tried to be reasonable," I said, though it wasn't entirely true. Nova had offered a good compromise, though.

Algol stepped closer, and I moved back.

"You don't need to come any closer," I said. "Grant my sister the Emerging or I'll end us both. I'm not one that loves ultimatums, but since you celestials force all immortals into one, how does it feel to be on the other end of that choice?"

All the celestials seemed perplexed by the question, truly seeing this for what it was. What they had made The Archer do was rooted in a baseless ego that ultimately meant nothing.

"See reason, Algol," Vega said, resting a hand on their shoulder. "Let this hatred for my Astrals end."

"We must bestow the Emerging for Freyja," Canopus and Arcturus said in unison.

"In payment for our mistakes," Rigil agreed.

"It's a good start," I said with a death wish, apparently.

Vega said nothing and paid my snarky comment no attention.

"Fine," Algol conceded. "We will return the girl to her mortal form and grant the trials."

"Nova, how far away is the Winter Solstice?" I asked, having lost track of time in the realm of the stars.

"One month," she said, smiling at my question. I wouldn't let them win on a technicality.

"You will permit Freyja to stay in the star realms until then," I added. Deals had to be precise.

"I will add that to the essence I gift to her. One month only. If she fails the trials, she will die," Vega said. "Our aid ends here."

I bowed, slowly moving the blade from my throat. "Deal."

Vega reached their hand to my throat, pausing before touching it. "May I?"

I nodded, and they sent their healing magic through me. Algol and I both sighed in relief.

"Thank you," I said, glancing at Nova.

"You have somewhere you need to be, child of the cosmos," she said, gesturing for me to follow her.

"Yes, I do," I said, sheathing the blade and taking a step in her direction. I didn't bother wiping the blood from my neck. Let it serve as a reminder of the lengths I would go to save those I love.

"The moment you reunite with your body, Freyja will be mortal once more," Vega said intently. "I will give her the dignity to be whole once again. Her death will be marked on her no longer."

"Thank you, Vega. I'll make it count," I promised, running after Nova's retreating form.

Thankfully, she moved with haste back to the internal cavern that had portaled us to the realm of the celestials. She quickly waved her hands around, and the swirl turned black with the essence of Algol.

"Good luck, Zoe Eferhild, Realm-Healer—Emerging of Legends."

"Thank you, Nova," I said, then stepped through the shadows to fulfill my oath to my sister.

★★★

"Zoe?" June asked, gently moving the hair out of my face.

Jelly licked my nose frantically, and I leaped from the hard as rock stone table. My body was sore from the time it'd spent lying there.

"How long was I gone?"

"Ten hours," she informed, and I winced, *seeing* what Hesperia had done with that time.

"Did I succeed?" I asked, turning to Phoebe, who was waiting in the darkness.

Her eyes glazed over. "You must hurry."

I didn't need to be told twice.

"Come on, Jelly. We've got to fly," I said, unfurling my massive wings. Something was happening on the battlefield, and I prayed it was going the way I intended.

Jelly and I sprinted out of the cavern and launched ourselves into the air the moment we could see the light of the moon. The flickering of blue lights and swirls of darkness were like a beacon to me, and I flapped my wings harder than I ever had before.

My sister was waiting for me. A mortal in the realm of the stars—something that had never been done before. Freyja would be a legend in her own right.

The trees cleared, and the battle was before us. Aura had shown up for us and was facing off with Abel bravely. Freyja was unfortunately caught between the pair, swept up in a tidal wave of the power of wind. But—she was Freyja. Beautiful dark brown, flowing hair and fair, glowing skin. She was whole once more. Her light blue eyes found mine, and there was a mix of fear, confusion, and perhaps tears of joy streaming down her face.

"I'm coming! Just hold on!" I screamed, flying towards her. Jelly's flames ignited beside me, and we launched into the fray below us.

We didn't bother landing, and I slit throats from the air as I made my way to Elvy, Oleander, and Blaz, who were the closet to Aura and Freyja. They were shielding Aura from Hesperia's Shadowed Legion. I didn't have time to feel bad about the innocent immortals they killed. I would grieve and feel guilty later.

My eyes eventually found Hesperia, who was looking at me like a piece of meat, but for the first time, I saw some fear in her, too. She'd lost her leverage over me, and I refused to allow her anymore. It was time I ended this. Right here. Right now.

Hesperia glided towards us, eyes focused on me—her prize. Not today. Jelly and I had reached our target, and we landed. I rolled into a somersault, unsheathing one of my knives along the way and launched it into the nearest enemy.

"Tell me what you need!" I screamed towards Aura, who was drenched in sweat, but her expression was all concentration. She would not relent.

"A distraction would be nice," she said, nodding towards Abel. Gone was the feeble female, bowing to the whims of her abuser. There was no judgment from me. We all found our ways to survive… until our pain was too great. Then we emerged as our true selves. And her truth had arrived.

"On it!" I said, and Jelly and I worked our way towards Hesperia.

Imelda joined Oleander and Blaz in protecting Aura's back as she worked her air magic to free Freyja's mortal form.

"I am with you," Elvy said through the bond, the calm in the surrounding storm.

A few seconds later, I felt his figure reach my left, and he ran towards Hesperia and Abel. She looked absolutely delighted at this turn of events.

"We must end her. Tonight," I demanded through our bond.

"Agreed," Elvy said.

There were so many things I wanted to tell him, but it would have to wait, which meant we both had to survive. The way I loved him… it scared me.

I shook my head at the thought. Not now. Hesperia's palms filled with the magic of Algol. Abel's strength waned. He was just as soaked as Aura, and that fact seemed to piss him off. If I had to guess, he had never truly known her. Abel had been clueless about the true power of his wife.

There were no pleasantries as we met our enemies. Jelly transformed into the full might of the simargl and launched herself at Abel. He couldn't fight both Aura and my protector at once if he wanted to live. The scent of burning skin reached my nose, and I tried not to notice as I faced Hesperia. I couldn't worry about

Jelly's fight. I had my own very lethal one before me, and I trusted Oleander to secure my sister.

I wasted no time in unsheathing a knife, and I sent it towards her forehead. Her magic stopped it, and she smiled with wicked delight. Elvy lifted his sword, expertly slicing towards her spine, but she rolled, dodging the blow.

"I like this dance," she said, transforming her magic into weapons. They were short swords. I'd seen Blaz work with Shadowed who used them, but I couldn't remember their name.

I loosened two more knives that were longer than the rest of my blades and centered my spirit. This was not a fight I could afford to lose. Elvy readied his own sword, positioning himself behind her.

In perfect unison, we unleashed ourselves on Hesperia… and she was good. Fantastic even. Much better than I thought she would be, and I felt the surprise in Elvy's bond. But we were good, too.

She met us point for point, making it difficult to find an opening. Much to my dismay, she found one with me and sliced her dark blade across my stomach.

"Fuck," I said, wincing at the pain. Elvy sent his healing magic through our flame, not requiring physical touch to heal me.

That seemed to piss Hesperia off, and I smiled.

"How long can you do this?" I asked her. "Because we can keep healing and restoring ourselves. How long before you succumb to fatigue?"

Her sneering face wavered for just a moment. She knew the truth in my words. If she wasn't careful, she would die tonight.

Jelly trotted up beside me, snout covered in blood. A lot of blood. I didn't dare take my eyes off Hesperia, but I assumed Abel was out of the picture. Or gravely injured. Jelly's flames burned brightly around her. She poised, ready to attack on my command.

"Blaz and Imelda are coming," Elvy informed through our bond.

Hesperia glanced behind me, eyes becoming frantic—desperate.

"This isn't over," she promised.

I formed my water magic into an orb, sending it towards her head in an attempt to drown her, but she used her shadows to dodge my attack. *No.* Not again.

Seeing she would not win, Hesperia transformed into a tornado of shadows, picking up Abel's broken body—what was left of it, anyway. I didn't think he'd come back from that, but I wouldn't put anything past Hesperia, either.

The rest of Hesperia's Shadowed Legion unfurled their wings and disappeared into the shadows. Cowards. How many times were they going to run from us? How many times would Hesperia get away? We would never know peace until she was stardust.

"Where are they going?" Blaz asked.

"Canopus," I said, knowing it to be true.

"Not good," Blaz said, sheathing his weapons.

"Nope," I agreed. "Hopefully, Tiergan will know some way to get there unseen."

I traced the map of the stars that was hidden beneath my uniform. We had to go back to Arcturus first. Then we'd have to face Canopus.

"And we have to figure out how to get the bow to work," Elvy said, answering my thoughts aloud.

I nodded. "No pressure."

"So what the hell happened?" Imelda asked. "Where did you go?"

"Later," I said, standing. "I need to see my sister. Elvy, Blaz, Imelda, I have someone very special for you to meet."

32

Always

FREYJA

I didn't know how Zoe pulled it off, but I was me again. Human, I think. I just prayed she hadn't made some deal with the devil. *Winchesters.*

I had been so close to giving in to the call of the *otherside* the moment the air had stopped whirling around me, keeping me trapped.

But then a figure had appeared beside me—the size of a building. No one else seemed to be aware of the massive entity. They had different shades of blues and golds, with shimmering lights, trying to leap off their form. They smelled of the ocean—like home.

"Don't be afraid," it said. "I am Vega. I come on behalf of one who loves you."

"Zoe," I said.

Vega nodded and reached into their core, taking out what looked like a grain of… them.

"Zoe has bargained for your life, Freyja. The celestial council has agreed to grant you the right of the Emerging. My essence will make you mortal once more," they explained.

"Right of the Emerging?" I asked. "The trials? Like what Zoe went through?"

"Yes, child," they said. "Algol has agreed to permit you in their realm until the trials."

"To be an immortal in Algol? Will it be their star I'm sworn to?"

"Yes. When you enter the realm of Nova, Algol will touch your spirit to initiate the trials. Oleander will be instructed, as he was with your sister."

"But I could fail and die a mortal death, right?"

"Yes, Freyja," Vega answered. "It is time."

They placed the seed of their essence right over my heart, and my entire body felt like I was on fire. I was too excited to actually *feel* to be upset by it. The pain only lasted a few minutes, and then I was whole again.

Then I'd seen Zoe flying like a bat out of hell towards me with Jelly right beside her—my saviors. Oleander's eyes were wide, but he raced towards me with the female named Aura. Elvy, Blaz, and Imelda were right behind them.

★★★

I pulled myself from Oleander's arms and turned towards the castle to find Zoe staring at me with tears in her eyes. Tears already dampened my own pale cheeks.

In my periphery, there lay broken bodies, and the ground ran wet with blood and Vega's water magic. My mortal heart ached at the devastation, but my eyes couldn't stop staring at my sister. She'd kept her promise against every odd.

Just like in the movies, we sprinted towards each other, ignoring the dead immortal's bodies around us and the smell of battle permeating the air. It was as if the rest of the world went out of focus, and all I could see was my sister—the one who loved me.

Finally, we reached each other and slammed into one another with too much force, yet not enough. We both crumpled to the ground together, crying—weeping—with joy and all the fears we'd both held back. The wet ground seeped through my clothes, but I didn't care, welcoming any and all sensations.

"You're here," she said, breathing me in and touching my face. "You're really here."

The tears continued to flow down both of our faces.

"Because of you," I said.

"I promised you I'd find a way," she said, pulling me back into a powerful hug.

"What did it cost you?"

"Nothing," she said, laughing softly. "Just pissed off a couple of celestials. Almost killed one. No big deal."

The Dean to my Sam. Always.

"I love you, despite how hard-headed you are," I said, laughing through my tears.

"My stubbornness has saved us more times than one," she said, gripping her neck. There wasn't any marking there, but dried blood caked the skin.

"Seriously, we've got to stop this cycle. It's not healthy," I said pointedly.

"It wouldn't be us if we did," she said, kissing my cheek. "I'm glad you're back."

"Me too," I said, hugging her tightly again.

"Do you think somewhere mom is smiling down on us?" she asked, fear in her voice, as if she was afraid to hope for that.

"I don't know, Zo," I admitted. "But it's hard for me to believe she could ever truly leave this world completely."

She clung to me tightly, as if I'd fly away from her, and I had no desire to let her go.

A wet nose nipped at my hand, and Jelly's face came into view. I was still marveling at all the senses I was privy to now.

"Hey, good girl," I said, scratching her ears. "Are you okay?"

Her nose was stained red, and Zoe cast some water magic to clean her up.

"She is," Zoe answered. "The other guy, not so much."

We both laughed at the marvel of it all.

Slowly, we emerged from our bubble of sisterhood, remembering that we were not alone. The Court of Vega looked at me curiously, seeing me for the first time. Tiergan and Oleander stood with them, both seeming to enjoy this moment of happiness amongst so much death.

Oleander seemed to burst with… *something*. He held it back, giving Zoe and me our moment.

"Want to meet him?" she asked. "Formally, I mean."

"Of course," I said, standing up with Zo.

She laced her fingers with mine and pulled me over to her court.

"Elvy, this is my sister Freyja," she said, smiling proudly, as if I were her favorite person in the world.

"I cannot adequately describe how happy I am to finally meet you, Freyja," he said, bowing, then pulled me into an unexpected hug. I embraced him back, excited to have a brother.

"It's nice to meet you, Elvy," I said, squeezing him.

He pulled away, and Zoe's eyes glazed with just a touch of silver.

"My two favorite people finally meeting," she said, choking on the words.

"Hey now," Blaz said, holding out his hand to me. "We all know I'm the favorite. I'm Blaz."

"Good to meet you, Blaz," I laughed, and Jelly barked.

I turned to the last member of the Vega court that was present and grinned.

"Imelda," she said, meeting my smile with her own. "It is an honor."

I was suddenly nervous as I turned back to Oleander. I'd felt his eyes on me the entire time. They'd burned into me, and I didn't mind it.

"What now?" I asked.

"Algol is requiring you to remain in their realm until your trials," Zoe said, frustration clear in her voice.

"Of course, you are welcome in my court, Freyja," Ander said, glancing at the Court of Vega. Zoe's lips pursed and one of her brows raised at Oleander. Oh, no. Please don't give him the whole 'what are your intentions with my sister talk.'

"The Vega court is welcome to rest, too," he offered to them, but his eyes were still on me.

"We'd love to recharge before traveling," Elvy said, thanking Oleander and pulling Zoe's attention back towards him. He gave me a wink and a knowing look. I'd have to thank my new brother later.

Zoe circled her arms around me once again, holding onto me for dear life.

"I'm really here," I whispered. "You did it."

She nodded and moved back towards Elvy.

They all unfurled their wings, and Ander held out his arms for me, as he had done for Zoe while she was still mortal.

"Come on, sweetheart," he said, smirking. "I know you want to."

The stubborn part of me wanted to walk all the way back just to spite him, but he was right. His arms were right where I wanted to be.

I nodded, and he scooped me up snugly against his chest. Then we were flying.

33

Tears

FREYJA

Oleander carried me into my bedroom, ignoring Zadie's shocked cries of, "What the hell happened? Freyja?!"

I didn't blame her. I would have freaked out to see a spirit in the flesh once again. Natural reaction really. Ander had not stopped touching me, and I wasn't complaining. My senses were flooded with *everything*. Smells, sounds, taste, but, most of all—touch. The warmth of skin against mine. I'd forgotten how comforting it could feel.

He slammed the door behind him and placed me on the bed. His breath was frantic—feral—with nostrils flared. I'd never seen him in such a frenzy before.

"Ander?" I asked, cupping his cheek and staring into his ice-blue eyes.

"When you call me that, I feel like I belong to you," he said, leaning into my palm, as if I were the most important thing in the cosmos.

I didn't know what to say, so I said nothing. I might be flesh and bone again, but my spirit was the same. There was a fear that still lingered in getting close to him. What if I didn't make it through the trials and hurt him? What if he hoped too much?

Another part of me challenged that thought. What if I hoped *too little?*

"Do you understand that I could die in the trials?" I asked, needing to hear it.

Ander pulled my chin up so that my eyes met his gaze.

"For immortals, this has been one of the most vulnerable eras in our very long existence. More now than ever, death is a near reality," he said, swallowing. "But, Freyja—you are my moment."

I was too stunned to say anything else, so I just stared back at him in wonder.

"I will make every one of them count with you, sweetheart. There will never be a moment in time when I feel like it is enough. Not with you."

Tears pooled at the brim of my eyes.

"I—I," I stumbled. I felt a tidal wave of emotions—love, desire, fear…hope. It appeared I was no longer a viper with my tongue. I couldn't get any words out.

"I've got you," he said, pulling me onto his lap and resting us against the headboard of the bed.

A tsunami of tears flooded my warm cheeks, and I dug into Ander's chest, hiding my face. I'd always loathed crying in front of other people. Even Zoe sometimes.

"I'm—I'm back," I said, sniffling and most assuredly leaving snot on his black shirt, making it incredibly obvious. He didn't seem to care, and ran his fingers through my hair. It felt so good, but my back kept buckling as a new onslaught of tears took control of my body.

I'd still felt emotions as a ghost, but they weren't quite this intense. My stomach rumbled, echoing through the room like the call of a whale to its mate.

My face heated even more, and I hid further into Ander's arms. He'd been so patient with me, and here I was, a bumbling mess with liquid coming out of various orifices and weird sounds. But I was starving—truly.

"Let's get you some food," he said, continuing to rub his hand over me soothingly.

"I don't want to see anyone," I said through the last of the tears. I prayed they stayed gone. My ego couldn't handle anymore.

"I'll call for some," he said, closing his eyes.

I took the moment to study his face. He truly was handsome. His Adam's apple bobbed as he swallowed, communicating with whomever he was. His chin was sharp with stubble showing, which was unusual for him. He was typically meticulously clean-shaven. His hair was my favorite, though. I'd once tried to color my hair like that when I was still mortal, but it'd turned out yellow. His was the perfect platinum and silver that humans spent a lot of money trying to achieve.

"I can feel you staring," he said, smirking.

Can he read my thoughts now that I'm a mortal?

He smiled.

No.

"Can you read my thoughts?" I asked.

"No, Freyja. Just your future intent. But I can break into your mind and sift around in there."

"Don't," I pleaded.

"I won't… until you ask me to," he promised, opening his eyes. "Food will be here soon."

My head rested comfortably on his chest, and I relaxed as I listened to the rhythm of his heart.

"Zoe is still here, right?"

"Yes, they are staying for at least one night. Maybe more. I'm not sure."

"I'd like to see everyone… later? To be honest, I have no idea what time it is," I admitted.

"It's late. I could have dinner for everyone if you want, or breakfast. Whatever you'd like."

Breakfast was my favorite meal.

"You'll enjoy breakfast. So will I," he said, getting up.

"Where are you going?" I asked, heartbeat increasing.

"Food is here," he said, opening the door to a cart full to the brim with some of my favorites.

"Lord Astral," a male immortal bowed. I'd never seen him before.

"Sorry to wake you so late," Ander said apologetically.

"It's no trouble."

"We will be hosting breakfast for our guests from Vega in the morning," he informed and thanked the immortal again.

Ander pushed the cart towards me, and my mouth watered. A burger had never looked so good in my entire life. The fries were crispy, too. Mozzarella sticks? I was going to gorge myself.

"I thought immortals only ate healthy stuff?" I asked, biting into the gloriously fried cheese.

"Why would you think that?"

"That's all I've seen immortals eat. Lean meats, fruits, and veggies. I didn't know what half of it was, but it definitely was not french fries."

"Mmmm, I guess there is some truth to that. We do value our health, but that doesn't mean we never indulge. What's the point of a long existence if we don't have a few pleasures now and then?" he asked.

I nodded, munching on the cheeseburger.

He let me eat my fill of food before he began eating with me. He didn't quite indulge himself the way I had, but he seemed to enjoy it all the same.

With a full belly, I was suddenly very fatigued.

"Tired?"

I nodded.

"Let's go to bed," he said.

"I need to brush my teeth and clean myself," I mumbled, eyes closing.

I felt like a toddler. I'd cried. I'd eaten. Now, I wanted to sleep. I was a barely functioning baby right now.

"Come on, sleepyhead," he said, swooping me into his arms.

"I'm awake," I argued. "I can walk."

I didn't bother fighting him on it, and knew I was lying. He handed me a toothbrush, and I put it in my mouth on instinct. I hadn't done this since I was mortal, but it was easy to pick up on the routine again.

Oleander busied himself with starting a bath for me. I wasn't going to be able to sleep until I was clean again. Even when Zoe and I had been traveling in tents and hostels, I always had to find a way to take a bath or shower before sleeping.

I held out the toothbrush, and Ander took it from my hand.

"Can you take a bath by yourself?" he asked.

I opened my eyes again, and I was so tired, it physically hurt to keep them open.

"I don't know," I admitted.

"Do you want help, sweetheart?" he asked, lifting my chin to meet his gaze.

"Okay," I agreed, holding up my arms.

He made quick work of my shirt and bottoms and lifted me in his arms again. I was briefly aware that he was naked, too. His skin was soft against the marble statue that his body seemed to be. He gently settled us into the hot water, and he held me against his chest.

"That feels nice," I whispered. "The water."

"Mmmhmm."

He poured water over my hair and scrubbed it gently with some sort of shampoo that smelled like flowers I couldn't pinpoint. The steam in the room kept me warm, and I sighed content. Just like a soothed child.

Not being able to stay awake any longer, I drifted off to sleep in the safety I felt in Ander's arms.

34

Goodbyes Come and Go
FREYJA

I was in a bed.

I hadn't fallen asleep in one, though. There was a heavy arm wrapped around me, and I nestled nearer to Ander. He pulled me closer to his sleeping form. I assessed my surroundings and found myself in an oversized, long-sleeved, black waffle shirt, and I wasn't wearing anything else.

The night sky shone through the windows, and a blue-green flame flickered in the fireplace. The snow-capped mountains glistened beneath the cosmos. Everything was quiet and still. I'd made it back. Zoe had found a way to bring me back and give me a second chance at life.

Ander's breathing changed, and I knew he was awake.

"Good morning," he murmured.

I turned to face him and wrapped one of my legs around his, tangling myself with him.

"Good morning."

"You seem happy… more settled today," he noted.

"I had just been brought back to life. I think I was owed a night of wallowing," I said, pressing more of my body flush against him.

He brushed a strand of hair out of my face.

"Indeed," he said, voice lowering.

His arousal pressed against my stomach.

"What are you doing?" he asked.

I pressed my lips against his, sucking on his bottom lip. His body froze for just a moment, as if in a state of shock. It didn't take long for him to come back to me.

He met my fervor and kissed me as he never had before, slipping his tongue to meet my own. His groan vibrated between us, and he rolled over so that I was beneath him.

"Let me worship you… let me remind you of *all* the things you can feel now."

I swallowed, challenging myself to be brave. "I need you, Ander."

He nodded, lifting me up to take his shirt off me, exposing my bare body to him. This felt completely different from when he'd cared for me last night. Now… he wanted me. He'd slept in the nude, and Oleander was no shy male. It was evident how much he needed me.

He leaned up on his knees, gazing down at me with unabashed desire.

My libido was finally satisfied, that she would soon get what she had been wanting for so long. He didn't seem to be in any hurry, but I felt like I was bursting at the seams for him. If he didn't touch me right this second, I would burn.

"I need you," I pleaded, and he raised an eyebrow. "Please, Ander," I said, squirming beneath his piercing gaze.

"You never have to tell me twice, sweetheart. And you certainly never have to beg. I was simply admiring the view," he laughed, leaning down to kiss my neck, sending chills all the way down my spine.

"Tell me what you like," he said, kissing me up and down the length of my torso. His lips moved lower, and my skin prickled in anticipation.

For the life of me, I couldn't remember what the hell I liked. I'd never been with anyone long enough to explore that much, really. I'd had some decent lovers on my travels, but they'd just done it, never asking what I preferred.

"I'd still love to know where that mind goes, Freyja," he said, brushing his smooth lips against my skin. He gently unsheathed his teeth and bit me, sending a pulsing groan through me. My toes curled in response, and I gripped my fingers in his hair.

"It's safe to say you liked that," he laughed. My skin warmed against his breath as he went lower... and lower.

I felt like my entire body was burning, on fire for him—for us.

"Do you want this?" he asked, hovering above the most sensitive part of me.

Incapable of words, I just nodded, gripping the silky sheets for dear life. I couldn't see his smile, but I felt it against me.

He wasted no time in eliciting glorious pleasure from my body with his mouth and fingers. My eyes were closed, but I saw stars. I needed more.

Ander was generous with himself, bringing out sensations I did not know resided within me. I was drenched, writhing beneath him. He was in full control, and I didn't mind it one bit.

Gasping, I braced for the wave of pleasure that was about to be released through me. He moaned in response, sending more friction to my throbbing body.

I broke for him—for me. He saw me through the pulses of pleasure, but I wasn't finished. One look at him told me he felt the same.

He leaned back up on his knees, licking his fingers.

"You taste divine, sweetheart," he said, smirking.

I started to sit up, wanting to taste him, too, but he gently pushed me back down.

"If you don't mind, I'd really like to make you come again," he said, keeping all the attention on me.

Settling back down against the pillows, I waved my hands and said, "By all means."

"Mmmm," he murmured, pulling my body closer to him so that I lay flat against the bed. He pulled one of my legs across the other and settled himself in between them, gripping my hip with one hand, and I closed my eyes as he trailed his fingers along my body, bringing out goosebumps where his fingers lingered.

I'd never been with someone as big as Ander, but there was no doubt in my mind that I would have him. My body trembled as he slowly shifted inside me, and it brought me even more pleasure as his eyes gave away how much he enjoyed the feel of me.

"Freyja," he said, breathing heavily. "You're so perfect, sweetheart"

He opened his blue eyes to meet mine, as he teased at my entrance.

"Come on, Ander," I panted. "I need all of you."

"I don't want to hurt you," he said, but his resolve weakened.

"More," I said, pulling on his arms to bring him closer.

His eyes fell on the way I bit my lip, and he pulled out. Then, much to my delight, he shifted swiftly into me, filling me. I cried out in pleasure at the feel of him joined fully with me. Ander was not one I would ever tire of.

I started moving against him, as he dictated our rhythm. He leaned over so that he could trail his mouth along my overly sensitive body while I held on to him, rocking through the waves of pleasure he brought out of me. I was going to combust from all the sensations flooding through me. Just yesterday, I was dead, and now, I'd never felt more alive. The friction of our two bodies moving in harmony with each other was too much.

Ander brought out another wave of pleasure from me, and I cried out in bliss. Ander flipped my body over so that I was on my hands and knees for him. My legs felt like jelly from the pure desire he brought out of me, but I wanted to keep going. He moved with me, gripping my hips tightly, and I welcomed his needs as my own.

"You're perfect," he said with heavy breaths. "Come with me. One more time."

His fingers knew my body as if he had been studying me for centuries, and I knew it wouldn't take long for me to lose all sense of reason again. If I had to guess, he didn't have much longer left, either.

"Come for me, sweetheart," he said, and my libido obeyed.

He spilled into me as we both fell into oblivion together. Ander held onto me as we clung to each other through the pulsating vibrations of our pleasure. Lying down beside me, he pulled me close to him so that my back was against his chest.

He trailed his fingers down my side, sending a shiver down my spine, and a sudden realization hit me at the same time. I just prayed I wasn't ruining the moment, but I had to ask.

"Ander?"

"Mmm?"

"Do we need to worry about…" I trailed off.

"Worry about what, Freyja?" he asked, turning my gaze to meet his.

"Unwanted consequences," I said, sighing.

"You don't have to feel weird asking that," he said, kissing my hairline. "I take a monthly tonic, so we are good."

I settled in next to him again, and we just held each other as our breaths steadied, letting the rest of the world fade away from us.

***

"So glad you could join us, Freyja," Zoe said, laughing. She had a knowing look, but my cheeks didn't flush with embarrassment. There was nothing to be ashamed about—not when it came to Ander.

I laced my fingers through his and embraced the 'just had sex hair.' Oleander chuckled beside me, but he was all smiles, too.

"Please stop smiling, Oleander. It's weird," Blaz said, in a joking tone. "You look much better brooding."

"I'm glad you are so invested in my appearance, Blaz," Ander said, winking. "Do you dream about me, too?"

"You wish I did."

"Always a pleasure, Blaz," he replied, sitting down on one of the benches around the breakfast table. He pulled me down next to him, closer than was necessary.

Elvy smiled politely at me and said, "Good morning, Freyja."

Zoe looked at him, eyes glistening with such powerful love. She had wanted her two favorite souls to be in each other's lives for so long… to finally see it was overwhelming for her.

"Good morning, Elvy," I said.

Oleander started to pour me a coffee, but I stopped him. "Ew. Gross."

Everyone looked at me as if I had three heads, except for Zoe. She knew I hated the stuff.

"She doesn't get it from me," Zoe said, laughing. "Trust me. I've tried to get her to like coffee."

"Then what will it be?" Ander asked.

"Any kind of juice will be fine," I said, eyeing the orange juice.

Imelda joined the crowd with sleep in her eyes. Zadie trailed behind her, looking as if she'd been awake for several hours. I guessed someone had to run the realm while Ander had been… occupied.

"Good morning, Lord Astral. Freyja," Zadie said, nodding to us both. The energy was different between us now. I was sure she was still pissed at me for running off the way I had, but she, at least, knew I was alive now.

Once everyone was seated, the food was brought out, encompassing typical breakfast foods. I snagged a couple of waffles and bacon, but there was something for even the pickiest eater. I'd expected us to get down to business about what we were doing next, but I think we all needed the normalcy of having breakfast with the ones we loved the most in life, just for a moment.

Zoe's eyes gleamed with genuine joy. Not a trace of darkness. Her friends—her family—kept her grounded. As long as she had them, and as long as she never became isolated from us, Hesperia would never own her.

However, as Zoe had proven many times over, she would give anything… become anyone she needed to for those she loved. I looked around at all the immortals sitting around me and knew in my heart they all would do the same.

Oleander squeezed my knee, bringing me back from my thoughts, and I took another bite of a waffle.

"I'd still like to know where that mind goes," he whispered in my ear.

"Just thinking about how fragile this all is," I answered, voice high enough that Zoe and Elvy heard it.

"This is what we fight for," Zoe said as a matter of fact. "We must always remember the magic in the ordinary, everyday moments."

"Way to rally us to war," Blaz said, holding up his glass.

They all laughed, but the tension could not be hidden.

"We'll need to make our arrangements," Elvy said.

"Tiergan should be arriving soon," Zadie offered, sifting through some papers in front of her. I didn't know enough about battle or strategy to discern what it said.

Elvy laughed at something Zoe said under her breath, and I looked at her curiously. "I'll fill you in later," she promised.

"Where will you go next?" Ander asked.

"Arcturus," Zoe said.

"Is that wise?" he asked.

"Doesn't matter," she said, shrugging. "We have to go."

"Any word from King Aldrich and Queen Farron?" Blaz asked.

"Not since the mad dash out of Sirius," Elvy said. "Farron told me they would be moving the High Astral Shadowed around Sirius and closing their transport zones."

"I get that it's the last defense for the mortals, but it seems a little shady to shut down the realm and not offer more help," Blaz said.

"They may know something we don't," Zoe offered. "Either way, it's the hand we've been dealt."

"I'm more concerned about Canopus," Imelda admitted. "How the hell are we going to get in there with Hesperia taking over?"

"Between Aura and Tiergan, we will figure something out," Zoe said, face determined. "Not going isn't an option."

"Tiergan will what?" the male himself asked, joined by Aura, who looked exceptionally fragile on his arm.

"Help me conquer the world, of course," my sister said, smiling fondly.

"As you wish, Realm-Healer," he said, smiling so widely I could actually see the white of his teeth beneath his mustache.

"Can the Sublunary help escort Lady Astral Aura back to Vega?" Imelda asked.

"We will," Tiergan promised.

"When did he get so friendly?" Blaz muttered under his breath.

Tiergan seemed to be glowing. It appeared he was taken with Aura.

"Pregnant immortals are sacred to the Sublunary," Oleander explained, and Tiergan nodded.

"As they should be cherished," he said, smiling. "And not forced to choose their star or between their magic."

Zoe nodded, agreeing with the sentiment.

A male Shadowed I recognized only by face entered from a hidden door and whispered something to Zadie. Her face paled, and Oleander noticed immediately. She seemed to convey the message silently, and he nodded.

"What's going on?" Elvy asked, ever observant.

Ander ran a hand through his hair, sighing.

"Some immortals that Hesperia said were loyal to me were left behind in her departure. They're in a sort of coma. We'd hope to ask them how she'd controlled them or influenced their actions. However, it seems whatever magic she worked was extensive. We're not sure they will wake."

"We can send more healers," Elvy offered.

Zoe's brows furrowed in concentration. I could see her trying to connect the invisible dots.

"We will take the help," Ander said, and Zadie shrugged in relief.

Elvy nodded and turned towards my sister. The stars alone knew what the pair said to each other.

"Will I see you again before the trials?" I asked Zoe, wanting to ease her worry.

"Yes. I promise," she said, rising from her seat. We all followed her lead, preparing for yet another goodbye. I was tired of them.

I embraced her, trying to memorize the way she felt... the way she smelled. I didn't want to take this moment for granted.

"I'm sorry I have to go," she said, voice breaking slightly.

"Don't be," I disagreed. "We all have our parts to play—even me," I replied, even though I didn't know what that looked like yet. "There's something you should know before you go."

I paused, hesitating. I hadn't forgotten what I'd overheard Hesperia say before she'd captured me. All eyes were on me, waiting.

"You haven't figured her out," I said. "She was surprised you knew about the blood magic, but she seemed happy that you hadn't figured out her purpose for you."

"Maybe she knew you were listening?" Zoe asked, turning to Elvy. His brows furrowed in concentration. I knew they were all nervous about understanding Hesperia's endgame. It was hard to prevent something when you didn't know the means or the bigger picture.

"No, it was before she knew I was there," I said, shaking my head.

"I was afraid of this," she admitted. "When I'd called her out during the battle, she seemed pleased. Like I'd gotten something wrong. This only confirms that I did."

The weight of the world was back on her shoulders.

"It seemed... personal, Zo," I said. "Like she has it out for you specifically."

"Why would she?" Elvy asked in frustration. "Hesperia was well before Zoe's time."

"Just focus on the trials," she said, voice too casual. I'd rattled her, and she didn't want me to worry about what she considered her fight. "We'll figure out her angle."

There was something Elvy and Zoe were hiding. I knew my sister too well, but I also trusted her.

"I don't suppose you could give me a little hint?" I asked, playing along.

Ander perked up at this.

"Nova said it would be useless. Each trial is unique to the soul who enters," she answered, pausing. "She also said that both our lives would be forfeit if I revealed too much of my experience."

"I guess I'm on my own then."

She shook her head, disagreeing. "You are never alone."

Jelly pawed at my leg, demanding that I give her attention.

"No, I'm not," I agreed, bending down to scratch Jelly's ears.

Elvy wrapped an arm around Zoe's waist. "Seraphina and Kai are expecting us soon."

Zoe nodded, turning to Aura and Tiergan. "Are you sure you don't want us to go with you to Vega first?"

"Smaller numbers are easier to hide," he said. "She will arrive safely. You have my word."

"It's alright, Zoe," Aura said, sounding stronger than she looked. "I'll make myself useful in Vega."

"I think we are more worried about you resting," Blaz said gently.

"I've done enough resting," she said, black eyes serious. "I need to help."

"Delmira and Clodovea will put you to work," Imelda said reassuringly.

We all stood in a circle, staring at each other for a few seconds before we all dispersed to fulfill our missions. One by one, each party left, disappearing into the shadows, leaving just Zadie, Oleander, and me.

"I'll be in the castle, sifting through Hesperia's mess. Hopefully, we'll find something useful," Zadie said, leaving us alone.

Ander laced his fingers through mine and kissed the back of my palm.

"What are we going to do now?" I asked.

"I'm going to teach you to fight, sweetheart," he said, smiling viciously.

35

Branded

ZOE

I didn't think I'd ever get used to the massive size of dragons.

We flew behind Seraphina's black dragon and Kai's brown dragon. His dragon appeared more bronze under the light of the stars, and Seraphina's dragon's scales glimmered with the reflection of the moon. They expertly landed them at the cave system from our previous visit. The dragons hadn't even come to a full stop before the Astrals leapt off the beasts.

I bowed to the dragons, and they seemed to blink in some kind of recognized acknowledgement. I didn't speak dragon, so I was just living on a prayer.

I'd spent the flight to Arcturus analyzing the facts of Hesperia, trying to make sense of it all, and the mysterious magic of Algol that evaded me at every turn. The answers were right in front of me, but I couldn't seem to force all the evidence together. Why would someone hate me so deeply? Was it truly just because I was destined to heal the damage she'd done to the star realms? If my greatest magic was my ability to heal, what could she truly want from me and my magic? My shadows weren't connected to my healing ability, though.

And much to my dismay, I didn't have time to focus on the whims of Hesperia. I had to find the next piece of The Archer's bow, so I refocused on the present.

Jelly morphed into her true simargl form, with flames engulfing her body and wings unfurled in a display of power. *Please don't piss the dragons off.* Jelly's body was now the size of a small horse, but she was no match for a dragon.

Then, the oddest thing imaginable happened. The dragons bowed to Jelly, so low that their monstrous snouts touched the ground. If they opened their jaws, they could swallow her whole.

I moved to step forward, but Seraphina held me back. Blaz looked ready to behead her if I commanded it, but I shook my head.

"You have much to learn in the way of the simargl," she whispered. "They are the most revered guardians in Arcturus—masters of all creatures of fire."

"Why would you just now tell me this?" I hissed.

"My dragon lust," she started, but shook her head. "I will tell you everything that I know. I swear it."

It stunned me that the dragons would bow to my Jelly. My protector.

"Mine," I heard a soft, angelic voice ring through my mind.

"Did you say something?" I asked Elvy through our flame.

"No," he said, but there was confusion in his voice.

"Mine," the sweet voice rang through me again.

"Your eyes, Zo," Elvy said. The startle in his voice was evident.

Are they black again? I checked my shadows, and they were tucked in deep within me.

"They were orange," Elvy answered my unspoken question.

Jelly turned to face me, eyes boring into mine.

"Mine," the voice—her voice—whispered through my mind.

I dropped to my knees.

"Yours," I said.

A piercing burn flashed across my chest, and I ripped my shirt open to assess the damage, only to find… a tattoo? No. A brand.

"The Seal of the Simargl," Kai breathed.

In the dead center of my chest, there was a figure of a dog with wings and flames forever branded in red. It no longer hurt, and the healing power my flame sent me was needless. It had already settled.

Seraphina had tears in her eyes, and her black dragon gave a thunderous roar. I would have pissed myself if there had been any liquid in me.

"Can you hear me?" I asked, directing my thoughts to Jelly.

"Yes," she said.

"Why now?" I asked.

"I'm a young simargl," she said, her voice lovely. *"The full range of my powers ignited on our second pass through Arcturus."*

Elvy looked between us, perplexed.

"You continue to shock me, Zo," he said, smiling genuinely. "Leave it to you and Jelly to bring dragons to their knees."

Blaz and Imelda looked equally astonished.

"I need rest," she said, yawning.

With those words, she extinguished her flames and transformed into the dog I'd always known. Just Jelly.

"She's tired," I said, and she barked to drive home the point.

"I'm sure she is," Seraphina agreed. "Follow us."

★★★

Everything in this place is red. I was sick of the color. It plagued my nightmares, and I didn't care to see it when I was awake.

We sat in the living area of the Lord and Lady Astral's home. Jelly snored soundly next to the fire. I wondered if anything could surprise me anymore?

"As I said when you were mortal, you're good with strange," Elvy said through the bond.

"I feel like I need to up my bar for what is odd."

"Perhaps," he said, chuckling. *"And perhaps I should join you."*

Seraphina watched us, as if she knew we were conversing with each other. At least she had the decency not to ask.

"What do you know of the simargl?" I asked.

Seraphina looked at Kai, and he nodded.

"No lies," Elvy said.

"And leave nothing out," Blaz said, crossing his arms.

Imelda and Blaz sat on the burgundy chairs on either side of the couch. Seraphina and Kai did not bring any of their Shadowed Legion in here with us. I took that as a good sign of faith that they would be honest.

"There are many laws between the creatures of fire and the immortals here in Arcturus. Some say we were created from the fires of Arcturus."

"Not wanting to elevate immortals above the animals Arcturus created, he made it so that we lived in harmony with each other," Kai explained.

"Then why are the simargl gone?" I asked.

"We betrayed them," Seraphina said. "Our celestial charged the simargl with the task of protecting the heart of this realm."

"Our dragons are good, but their lust is their downfall. Too many of us bonded with dragons and forgot about the simargl. There were many battles over land and… gold."

"There have always been whispers of skirmishes in Arcturus," Elvy said. "But no one outside of your realm thought it was anything that serious."

"We kept it that way," Kai confirmed.

"And the times I've come here for trade agreements?" Imelda asked, as the emissary to the fire realm.

"We were—are—desperate for resources," Kai admitted.

"Arcturus is a cunning celestial. He made the simargl the protectors of seed, plants, and life," Seraphina said, glancing at Jelly's sleeping form. "They were created to bring our world warmth… and we abandoned them for greed. For nothing."

"When we were in Rigil, we saw shipments of food destined for here," I said, putting the pieces together, though I'd not thought much of it at the time.

"The land is barren," she said sadly. "We were so desperate… that's why we initially accepted Hesperia's offer."

"I'm sure turning to evil would bring the simargl back," I said, venom in my voice.

"Why didn't you ask for help?" Imelda asked, voice turning furious. "I gave you every opportunity."

"We would have helped you," Elvy confirmed.

"A dragon's pride is its ultimate destruction," Seraphina said. "We were too embarrassed."

"So you let your immortals suffer over your pride?" Blaz questioned.

"They were just as stricken by the dragon sickness," Kai explained. "Seeing the simargl—Jelly—she gave us hope. Conviction."

"Our dragons can't fight off their own lust and pride without them," Seraphina added.

I looked over at Jelly in awe of the might that lived within her. At her heart, she was man's best friend—inherently good. Incorruptible. There lived no purer soul than that of a dog.

"She can't stay here," I said, voice firm.

"We know," Seraphina said. "A guardian cannot be without their bonded for very long."

"She gives us hope even still," Kai said.

"Can she always hear my thoughts?" I asked quietly.

"She can always hear the thoughts you want her to hear. Just as we can with our dragons."

"I'd imagine it would work similarly to the flame you and Elvy share," Kai said.

They wouldn't know since they are not a flamed pair.

"Will my eyes always glow orange?" I asked.

"No, that only happens the first time a simargl chooses its bond. Your mind has a door that is just for your guardian," Seraphina explained. "You can leave it open or closed."

Just like a shield.

I nodded, closing my eyes and centering myself. I felt the familiar presence of Elvy. His energy was warm and safe. The door was always open to him. I concentrated a bit harder and found my link to Jelly. Her essence was powerful and soft all at the same time.

I opened my eyes to find everyone staring at me as if I were going to perform some parlor trick.

"She's sleeping, but I felt her," I confirmed.

"What else do you need from us?" Kai asked. His attitude had shifted drastically from the first time I'd met him.

"We need access to travel your lands unbothered," Elvy said. "We need to find something."

"Do you know what you are looking for?" Seraphina asked.

"I'll know it when I find it," I said, not offering anymore.

"Carry this with you," Kai said, holding out a small stone with the Lord Astral's sigil. "It will grant you any access you need should you run into any trouble."

"Thank you," I said, slipping the sigil into my satchel. "Should we expect trouble?"

They shook their heads.

Elvy and I stood, followed by Blaz and Imelda. Jelly perked up at the rustling and trotted over to my side.

Seraphina and Kai rose, leading us back out the way we'd come.

Once outside, I breathed in deeply, wanting a bit of fresh air. Unfortunately, the air was tinged slightly with the smell of sulfur. I longed for the ocean of Vega.

"May you be successful on your journey," Seraphina said, nodding.

"Do not lose the conviction you possess now," I said, leaning into the discernment. A small smile surfaced at what I *saw*. "You may find it crucial that you don't."

I kept the knowledge I'd just received to myself, hoping the Lord and Lady Astrals would heed my warning. I had a role to play in it coming true.

Closing my eyes, I dug deep into my discernment, calling on the power of Algol to show me where The Archer's next bow piece lay hidden. After a few moments and a little sweat, an invisible path of light emitted in front of me, and I led the group in the direction it went.

In the distance, I heard a dragon roar, as if rallying the forces of destiny to our aid, and I welcomed the vibrations of hope within me.

36

Training

FREYJA

Sweat poured down my back and into my backside.

I'd never felt more disgusting in my life, and I'd showered barefoot in a hostel before. This was worse.

"Go. To. Hell."

"There she is," Ander said, circling me with a training sword. I had one clutched in my aching fist. My hands bled from the new calluses, trying to form. Being brought back to life had removed any trace of my scars or imperfections, which I didn't totally hate until right this second. "My sweet little viper."

I wanted to tear out his throat, and the smirk he was giving me told me he knew that.

"I feel like we skipped a few steps," I said, breathing heavily. To say I was fatigued and fading fast was an understatement. "What happened to building up my strength and stretching and all that?"

"No time," he said. "We're in the middle of the worst war of our immortal existence. You need to learn to fight and fight well. Your muscles will build. Your endurance will increase. It's going to hurt like hell, but you will do it because you are a fighter."

I swallowed. I'd wanted to give up, though. Before Zoe had miraculously brought me back, I was seconds away from answering the call to the *otherside*. I was too ashamed to tell him that. So I snarled instead. Anger had always been easy for me to hide behind.

"I'll make sure to stretch you out real good later," he said, teasing me.

The bait worked. I swung the fake blade at him. He easily blocked me.

"Quit telling me what you're about to do," he coached.

"I'm not saying anything!"

"Your face gives everything away, and so do your feet," he countered. Little did he know.

I sighed, looking up at the moon, feigning my defeat.

"I'm tired," I said, voice cracking just where I wanted it to.

"I'm sorry," he said, fumbling just slightly. "I'm pushing you hard after…"

"I just got brought back to life?" I asked, eyes brimming with tears.

He stepped closer.

Got him.

I swung, piercing his gut.

He grunted, not expecting the blow.

"Little viper," he purred. "Reminds me of when you used to threaten my life on Earth."

"Fun times," I said, laughing. I dropped the training sword, truly tired. I didn't have anything left in me.

He let his own weapon fall, and gently cupped my cheek in his hand. His eyes fell on my lips.

I answered his want and stretched my toes to plant a feverish kiss on my Ander. His body responded to my need and lifted my body so that my legs straddled his waist.

"Never," I said, still kissing him, as he walked me through a hallway I didn't recognize. "Apologize for pushing me to my potential."

He said nothing, and moved his lips to my neck, biting down just enough to send a thrill through me.

"Promise?" I asked.

"I swear it," he said, breath sending flames to my core.

He closed the door behind us. I'd become so lost in him, I didn't care where we were going.

I looked around the space, trying to gather my bearings.

"My room," he answered.

I'd never been in his room. All my time in the Court of Algol, and I'd never been here.

"I don't let anyone in my space," he said, setting me on the bed that was covered in the softest midnight-colored blanket.

"But you're letting me?" I asked.

"Yes," he answered, sitting beside me.

I took my time looking around the room. The walls were black, and his furniture was in different shades of gray. There was a blue-green fire that flickered as the focal point of the room. The onyx canopy bed was competing for the attention in the room. The floor was smooth stone with black rugs, warming the place some. Above us was a massive skylight that took up the majority of the ceiling, displaying the stars and moon beautifully.

"Can anyone see in?" I asked.

He shook his head. "It's spelled so that we can see out, but no one can see in."

I nodded, examining the room further. There was nothing that seemed personal in the space. No trinkets or anything that designated the space as his.

"What's up with the stars?" I asked, pointing to the display above.

"For a long time, my hope lived in them. I guess this room is a representation of what my life felt like during that time. Everything was bleak. Except when I looked up. Algol chose me as the Lord Astral. It was unprecedented to change the bloodlines of the Astrals. I put a lot of faith up there," he said, following my gaze upward.

"You say it like you don't believe it anymore."

He pursed his lips. "Right now, my hope lives in what is right in front of me."

Ander's eyes bore into mine, as if I were the one his life source was connected to. I was mad for him. I couldn't deny that to myself, but to have him need me in the same way... I wasn't sure that I was ready for that.

Somehow, he saw that in my eyes and held my hand, stroking soothing circles with his thumb. "I'd really like to know where that mind goes."

"I'll tell you one day," I said.

"One day may never come in times of war," he said gently. He didn't mean it as a threat or to coax me to say anything I didn't want to. Ander spoke only the truth. We didn't know if tomorrow would come or not. Everyone had to live with that knowledge, but did we let it dictate our choices—our fears?

"You are important to me, Ander," I conceded, willing to say that truth.

"As you are to me, sweetheart."

He smiled warmly, pulling my lips to his again. It was an instant flare of passion that consumed me. The kiss grew fast, hungry. I needed him, and he needed me. We needed this moment. Together.

A knock came at his door, and he growled, frustrated.

"No one would knock at this door if it wasn't important," he murmured against my forehead.

I nodded in understanding.

"Hell," he said, looking down. His arousal was clear against me.

I couldn't help the laughter that escaped my lips, and his eyes darkened.

"Zip up your top," he said.

I bit my lip to stifle my laughter and began zipping up my training uniform, and he groaned.

"Me putting clothes *on* gets you going?"

"Everything about you turns me on," he said, pulling me in for another kiss.

I threw up my hands, exasperated.

The knock came again.

"For the star's sake," he snarled.

He tossed a throw blanket around me and closed his eyes, breathing in deep breaths as if his life depended on it. I wasn't sure about his life, but the immortal on the other side of that door may not live if they knocked one more time.

After a few moments, he settled himself.

"You're coming with me," he said.

I dropped the blanket before he whisked me away and slung the door open.

"What is it, Zadie?" he asked.

She seemed startled by my presence. I guess everyone knew he was usually alone here.

"I wouldn't bother if it wasn't urgent, Lord Astral."

"I know, Zadie. Did one of Hesperia's immortals waken?"

"No, but we found the spell Hesperia plans to use to reverse the tethers—the blood magic."

"And?"

"We're in a heap of trouble," she said frankly. "Come with me."

Ander and I looked at each other, then followed her retreating form.

37

The Flame of the Hearth
ZOE

Everything was barren.

Most of the land was rock, and the grass we came across was more or less a fire waiting to happen. The realm was incredibly dry. It'd remind me of a desert if there was one to be found.

I'd checked Jelly's paws several times, worried about them burning on the hot surface, but she just rolled her eyes at me, saying she was a creature of fire. It could not hurt her. I'd almost leapt out of my skin when her voice coursed through me again.

We'd tried flying initially, but the smoke coming from the mountain was too dense to see through. On foot it was, and Blaz was grumpier than usual about it.

"I need water," I said, mouth sticky.

"Let's rest a bit," Elvy agreed.

We found a few decent-sized rocks and leaned against them. It wasn't the most comfortable, but it gave my aching feet a rest. Ely handed me a water bottle that never emptied. Pretty neat magic.

The moment the elixir of life touched my lips, my energy felt restored, and my magic sang its siren song within me. Imelda poured some into a bowl so Jelly could drink.

Everyone seemed brighter after the refresher, our magic humming. It was a strange feeling to be in this realm. My magic felt almost suppressed here.

"I've never enjoyed coming here," Imelda admitted, stretching. "I always feel on edge, like my magic is ready to burst out."

"I feel it, too," Blaz agreed.

We all did. It was an uncomfortable sensation.

"Can you see how much further we have, Zo?" Imelda asked.

I leaned into my gift, calling its power to me. I couldn't be sure, but I'd guess a few more miles until we got to the cave system.

"Maybe three miles until the cave," I said. "Looks like it'll be a similar process."

Imelda winced. Her partner—Clodovea—had been tortured last time to get the bow.

"Don't worry," Elvy said. "We have the five elements with us now."

"Oh?" Blaz asked.

"Elvy and I found a pendant for air in Musterion," I explained. "With Sierra's ring for ground, Elvy for water, Jelly for fire… and me for Algol."

"Good thinking," Blaz commended, and Imelda nodded her agreement.

"It's weird, isn't it?" I asked, looking around the terrain. "Vega is so full of life. So is Rigil. You can always hear the birds, frogs, and other animals. Here… it's glaringly silent."

"We'll need to help them," Elvy agreed. "It seems like the simargl put a curse on the land… I'm not sure our magic can restore it unless the simargl allow it."

Jelly looked at each of us, but said nothing. She was still a pup when it came to her lineage in the simargl. I didn't really know what she knew or if she could feel what I would assume would be her pack. If she wasn't offering the information, then I wasn't going to ask.

"One thing at a time," I said, standing. "We need to keep pressing on."

Elvy slung the satchel on his back, and the others stood, steady on their feet.

"Just a few more miles," I whispered, heading off in the direction my magic sent us.

★★★

A few miles had turned into twelve miles.

"You are terrible at land navigation," Blaz said, painting angrily. The sweat and dirt coating his skin gleamed in the moonlight. We were all soaked through.

"You're not wrong," I said, breathing heavily next to him.

"Settle down, Blaz," Elvy growled in warning. He got exceptionally protective when he was cranky.

"She's only following the light," Imelda said, trying to keep the peace.

"I misjudged the distance," I admitted, but sighed in relief at the caverns coming into view. The air was thick with smoke, and the rock beneath sent shooting pains up through my spine.

"Oh, really," Blaz said, and Elvy whipped around.

"Take a breath," I whispered through the bond. *"He doesn't mean any harm."*

Elvy's frame trembled, and his eyes darkened for just a second. He was fighting for control of his magic—the shadows feeling protective. I knew the sensation all too well and took either side of his face in both my hands.

"I've got you. I'm okay. Everyone is okay," I said, bringing his forehead to my own. He took several deep breaths and opened his eyes to reveal them as the gray that I'd grown to love.

"Thank you," he said, nostrils flaring with each breath.

"Sorry, brother," Blaz said, shifting his weight between his feet.

"Way to piss off someone with death magic," Imelda said. "Idiot."

It was odd to hear Imelda say it out loud. The Luminaries were the only immortals who knew of his power. Even Oleander and Freyja were not privy to the information.

"Sorry to give you such unstable leadership," Elvy said, himself again.

"Yeah, we're kind of terrible," I agreed.

"Shut up. Both of you," Imelda said, hands on her hips.

"Now who's pissing off the wrong immortal?" Blaz asked.

"No one is pissing anyone off," I said, glancing at Elvy. His opinion seemed to differ from mine.

Mercifully, the arguing ceased as we came to the end of the light that led straight into an ominous cave that was so dark it looked like black liquid.

Jelly's tail wagged, which I took as a good sign. If there were something bad in there, her hackles would be raised.

We each cast our starlight so we could see enough to navigate the twisting tunnels that were sure to come.

I took one last deep breath and crossed the threshold into the cavern. It was enormous. Even the starlight did not illuminate the ceiling or show just how big this place was.

We trekked forward carefully. I'd hate to fall off a ravine. Logically, I knew my wings would catch me, but I didn't care to experience it either.

We came to a fork in our path. My gift gave me no sign of which way to go, but Jelly did.

"Follow me," she said, leading us down the tunnel to the right.

"Jelly says to follow her," I said, leading the entourage behind me.

The further we followed Jelly into the cavern, the weirder things became. The air went from bone dry to moist, as if we were approaching a stream or a body of water.

"Is that a light up ahead?" Elvy asked.

"Difficult to tell with the pollution from the starlight," I answered.

"Wait," Blaz said, his footfalls stumbling. "Do you hear that?"

The sound of a waterfall was close by.

"Birds," Imelda said, confused.

The chirping of birds could not be mistaken.

We came to the end of the tunnel, and there was a door carved out of the stone. The symbol for fire and the mark of the immortal seemed to be scorched into the door.

"Last time, there was only the mark of the immortal," Elvy said.

"This feels different," I admitted. "But I know whatever we are looking for is behind there."

I removed the glamor from my mark and held it against the identical burned mark on the door. Jelly engulfed her body in flames and placed a paw on the symbol for fire.

Once together, the door moved down, and I hid my eyes from the glaring light that emitted from the cavern that was now in front of us.

"What the hell?" Blaz asked, stepping up to get a closer look at what was hiding behind the door.

In front of us was a… grove. It was lush and green with trees, and the moon and stars shone brightly above. Whether that was magic or reality was lost on me. The most incredible thing of all was the species that seemed to occupy the gardens as their home—the simargl.

There were about fifty of them, and all of their eyes were on us.

"They've been expecting us," Jelly said through our bond. *"Come."*

We each extinguished our starlight and moved lightly, following Jelly. I trusted her to bring us where we needed to go. There were two simargls standing on a stone dais that I recognized from our time in Rigil. The next part of the bow had to be within the stone, but I certainly wasn't going to tell them to move.

The larger simargl resembled a true wolf that was as black as the night sky. The one standing beside the dark wolf looked more like a labrador with a beautiful golden coat that shimmered in the moonlight. Each of them had beautiful gray wings closed at their backs.

Jelly bowed to them, and I took that as my cue to take a knee. Elvy, Blaz, and Imelda did the same. I didn't think disrespecting them would go well.

I opened the link to Jelly to understand what was going on, but the pair of simargls didn't seem to need the brand to converse with us.

Their presence flooded each of our minds. At least, that's what it felt like. It was as if we were all linked by some magical stream of light that none of us could see.

"Immortals, many moons have passed since we allowed you into our grove," the dark wolf spoke. Male. *"I am Skoll. This is my mate, Tala."*

"You are simargl but not… What are you called?" Tala asked. Her voice was sweet, motherly.

"I am Jelly, Guardian of Zoe Eferhild, Realm-Healer—Emerging of Legends."

"A pup guarding Eferhild?" Skoll asked.

"I am not a pup," Jelly answered, voice going lower.

"You smell young," Tala said kindly.

"Where did you come from? All simargl were ordered to the grove many years ago."

"My bond made me," Jelly said, chest puffed out in pride.

Tala and Skoll came closer to me, and I kept my eyes averted with my head bowed. I would not rise until they invited me to do so. If I'd learned anything in working with animals, it was to respect the ways of all creatures, no matter how big or small.

"You made a guardian?" Skoll asked, voice perplexed.

"I didn't know that I was creating a simargl," I admitted to the alphas. "I just knew I couldn't leave her behind."

"You have great love for this pup," Tala said, smiling, if dogs could smile.

Jelly humphed, unhappy at being called a pup again.

"I do," I confirmed.

"You all may rise," Skoll said in a stern voice.

He let out a howl that permeated throughout the grove, gathering the simargls together.

"We want to hear your story," Skoll said. *"That is the payment required. Then you may collect what you came for."*

"My story?" I asked.

"Yes, the story of the Emerging of Legends," Tala confirmed. *"If we deem your tale untruthful, there will be a punishment."*

"I have nothing to hide," I whispered. "Not to you who guard life."

Four little puppies with tiny wings gathered in front of Skoll and Tala, looking up at me expectantly with tongues hanging out. They were each uniquely mixed with the breeds of Skoll and Tala.

"Now those are pups," Jelly muttered. I didn't bother reminding her that she often looked the same.

I looked over at my entourage, and Elvy sent me his support through our bond.

"Then a story you shall have," I agreed, sitting cross-legged in front of the mighty alphas and started from the beginning. A blue-green flame flickered to the side of us, giving the feel of a campground. Elvy sat beside me with Blaz and Imelda on either side of us—always protecting our backs.

"There once was a little girl who looked up at the stars, always feeling more connected to the night sky above than the grass beneath her feet," I began, revealing the truth in my heart. "She longed for her father, whom she thought had abandoned her. The young girl would wish on every shooting star that he would come back, but he never did. She grew to believe she was not worthy of his love."

I'd never admitted that secret. It was true that I had no concrete memories of The Archer, but I remember feeling waves of sadness. Sometimes the waves crushed me, and sometimes they didn't. All any little girl wanted was for their father to find them captivating.

"Then one day, the little girl's mom brought her a new dad. She knew it wasn't her real father, but he was nice to her and loved her like she was his own," I said. My throat felt like golf balls were lodged in there, but I swallowed them back down.

"Not long after, the little girl's sister was born. Freyja. She loved her as fiercely as only a child can. It was a pure love. She vowed to be her protector. The little girl did not want her new charge to ever feel lonely like she had."

"As they grew, they went on many adventures together, chasing the unknown and unexplored lands. They found crystal-clear waters, snow-capped mountains that glistened beneath the moonlight, and exquisite canyons with the colors of the Earth. The sisters never said no to good food, even when they had no idea what it was. They were fearless and wild. The promise of freedom lived in their spirits."

I paused, bracing myself for the pain that would follow the next part of the little girl's story. Elvy laced his fingers through mine, sending me his infinite, unconditional love.

"Then one of their adventures led them into danger. They were all grown up now, and no one came to save them. As several of the evil men hurt one sister, she cried out for the father who had left her. She wanted to believe he would save her—that he would come for her."

Tears welled in my eyes, but I continued, not finished with my story. Jelly laid her head on my lap, nuzzling her snout into my stomach.

"When her father didn't come, the evil men killed the sister she'd sworn to protect with the heart of a child. But before the men could kill the now grown little girl, someone did come to save her."

I stilled, clearing my mind. I'd never told my story like this and leaned into the gift of discernment. Just on the periphery of my blurred vision from that moment stood a familiar stature I'd know anywhere. She'd been there. She'd been the one to call for aid… but she hadn't made it in time. The guilt that must have eaten at her… though I placed no condemnation on June. I shook my head, returning to my audience.

"The sister did not want to live without her best friend. Her pain was too great. She lost her spirit and the will to carry on. So, she decided to join her sister in death."

Skoll and Tala looked at me with reverence. Like they were living my pain with me. The pups perked up their ears curiously, and I wondered what they asked the alphas. Whatever it was, they did not share it with me.

"Only when the sister's soul passed on, two of the stars she used to wish on gave her the chance to become an Emerging. The heart of the little girl who loved fiercely agreed, and she was brought back to Earth. There, she learned her sister was still with her—only in spirit."

Almost there. I noticed out of the corner of my eye that the blue-green flame now shone a more radiant white and had doubled in size.

"Then, the sister got her companion, Jelly," I said, scratching her favorite spot. "There were no adventures for the three of them anymore, fearing the world too unsafe. Until one day, the sisters and Jelly went to the beach to watch a volleyball game."

I turned to Elvy, and he wore his love openly on his face.

"And the sister's heart fell right there for the gray-eyed man, but she didn't know it yet."

The flame grew brighter, pure energy. It was my truth. I'd fallen for Elvy from the moment I'd seen him, which I thought was the most irrational thing to ever happen. But here we were—loving each other through it all.

"The sister eventually went through the trials of the Emerging. There she learned to embrace herself and believe she was worthy." I didn't elaborate on what the trials were in case Nova chose to smite me from existence. "But when the girl came back from the trials, she could not leave her companion behind, so she transformed her with magic she barely understood."

"The elixir of life," Skoll said, and I nodded.

"What happened to the sister?" Tala asked, and the pups looked at me as if they might bite me if I didn't answer them.

"Not on my watch," Jelly said, growling in a low warning.

"I brought her back."

"With magic?" Skoll asked.

"Um, no," I admitted. "I threatened a celestial's life."

Tala and Skoll looked at each other, probably questioning what maniac they'd let into their sacred place. Maybe they were just impressed. Who knows?

"Now you seek an object in our grove?" Tala asked.

"Yes."

"You are not the first to want something from us," Skoll said.

I briefly wondered if he was referring to Kai and Seraphina, but he pressed on.

"The Archer left something hidden here long ago," he said. *"He said his daughter would come one day to collect it."*

"Yes," I said, bowing.

"You have proven your heart true," Tala said, nodding her towering head towards the now white flame. *"Gather what you need."*

"Thank you for your generosity," I said, bowing my head.

They said nothing else, and my entourage all stood, ready for my instruction on the dais the simargl had just dispersed from.

I felt like I was inside a terrarium with the juxtaposition between what was inside here and what lay just outside. Silently, I wondered if I should push my luck in asking the simargl to give Seraphina and Kai a chance to make things right.

I shook my head of the thought and refocused on the task at hand.

"Ready?" I asked my companions.

"Ready," they said in unison.

38

Bonded in Fire

ZOE

Elvy stood on the sigil for water. Jelly sat on the mark for fire. Blaz held the ring of Rigil since it was too small for him to actually wear. Imelda wore the necklace with the pendant for air. I hovered over the seal of Algol. Time to shed more blood. I wondered how much I would give by the end of this war.

All of it if I had to.

"Just like last time," I said, slicing my hand and moving to Blaz first.

He placed the ring on the carved stone, and I let my blood drip onto the ring. Starlight erupted from the stone and moved to Elvy, who had already released some of his magic onto the carving.

I slit my hand again and let my essence drip onto the seal of Vega. The starlight drank up the offering with fervor, then moved to Jelly, who was already engulfed in flames and in her simargl form.

"Good girl, little dragon," I whispered, and tried not to notice the other simargl beyond the dais staring at us.

My hand was aching, but I sliced through it again, letting more of my blood act as payment for the ritual. The flames and blood collided and sent the starlight toward Imelda.

She placed the infused pendant onto the sigil for Canopus, and I squeezed more blood onto the necklace. The starlight drank greedily, then moved to the center of the stone, and I followed.

The starlight encircled me, encapsulating me in its energy. I couldn't leave without more blood payment, and no one could cross the barrier to rescue me if things went wrong.

I cut my hand yet again while letting my dark tendrils touch the mark of Algol. My darkness took that as an invitation to come full force. I tried to embrace them, shoving them into the balance of acceptance and fear of them. I was still present with myself now, but my nostrils flared, trying to keep me from fully shifting into my shadow self.

I whirled around, looking for Elvy's eyes. I quickly found them and focused my attention on him, as the magic of the sigil drank greedily from my essence. His frame was solid, but even his eyes struggled to remain gray. It was as if his shadows answered the call of my own.

After what felt like hours, but could have only been a few minutes, the magic ebbed and the starlight was gone. My body slumped, and I felt lightheaded, as if I'd lost a lot of blood. I guessed I had.

Elvy raced over to me, pulling me up into his arms while Imelda and Blaz circled protectively around me. Jelly laid her head on my legs, trying to ground me to this moment.

"Well, that sucked," I mumbled. "It took way more from me than last time."

"I could tell through the flame," Elvy said, voice level, but his eyes gave him away. He was worried, but it was the gray eyes that gave me peace. He was okay, and so was I.

He sent his healing magic through the bond, healing the cuts on my hands and filling my stores in the way only my flame could.

"I've got you," he mumbled.

"I know," I said, smiling weakly, but I was beginning to feel a bit stronger.

"Did we get it?" Imelda asked, looking around.

I finally felt well enough to sit up, and I tested my footing to find the place solid and no longer spinning.

In the center of the dais, a stone had risen, revealing the next part of The Archer's bow. I was no archery expert, but it was definitely a piece of what we were looking for. The curved part of the bow to which the string would attach to if I had to guess.

"It's the limbs," Blaz said, peering down at the silver metal.

I picked it up to find it much lighter than I'd expected. It was beautiful and felt… right. Just like the wooden grip that we'd found at Rigil, this bow answered to the call of my blood as The Archer's daughter. I pulled out the grip and situated it between both limbs—a perfect fit.

Then the parts flew away from each other. So much for 'perfect.'

"What the hell?" Imelda asked, and I shrugged.

"Hell if I know," I answered. "The pieces definitely go together, but there might be something we are missing to make them stick."

Elvy sighed, pulling me against him, needing to feel my presence—my assurance. We were all ready for answers instead of more questions.

"We'll figure this out," I whispered through the bond.

"I know," he murmured back, kissing the back of my neck lightly. *"I'm more concerned about what you'll have to do with it once we get it together."*

"One step at a time, flame."

He didn't answer but hugged my waist tighter, and I slipped the limbs and grip into my satchel.

Skoll and Tala looked at me expectantly, and I led the group over to the alphas of the simargl.

"You were found worthy, Daughter of Algol," Skoll said.

"Do you know anything about The Archer's bow?" I asked, curious.

"Of course, I do. The simargl have not forgotten the old ways."

"But it is not for us to explain them, Shadowed," Tala said, joining her mate. *"It is our job to protect them and punish those who do not heed them."*

I got on my knees before them, lowering my eyes to show them the respect they deserved. I just prayed they wouldn't bite my head off for the next words that came out of my mouth.

"The immortals of Arcturus are suffering," I began. "I have spoken with the Lord and Lady Astral. They have sworn their allegiance to me in reverence to her." I pointed to Jelly, who was not bowing. Too much alpha in her. Her chest was puffed out, demanding that the alphas listen to her bond.

"They will fight alongside us to rid the star realms of this evil, but they cannot do it living off barren lands and poisonous air."

"Did the dragons bow?" Skoll asked. *"Are they still infected with dragon lust?"*

"They bowed," Jelly answered, voice low—dangerous.

"It seems it was broken with Jelly's presence," I offered.

"We will commune with the elders," Tala said, bending her head.

I wanted to push for more, but Elvy shook his head slightly. Pushing my luck on this may cost us our lives.

"Thank you," I said.

We all stood up to leave the peace of the grove. At the entrance, I turned a final time to Skoll and Tala, looking them in their eyes. I would speak my truth.

"This war isn't about territory or power," I said, voice strong. "It's about good and evil. If we lose, evil wins. There will be nothing left for you to protect or punish."

I tossed Kai's stone to the ground before them. "As a reminder."

I didn't wait for a response, not that I thought they'd give me one. My heart raced as the stone door sealed behind us, leaving us in the darkness once again.

39

Blood Magic
FREYJA

I hated this room.

We stood in the chamber deep within the castle Hesperia and her army had vacated. The swirling mass of black kept me in its trance. I couldn't seem to look away from the darkness and secrets it held. And if I made it through the trials, I would become a part of Algol. That magic would run through my veins. The thought terrified me, but not surviving the trials petrified me even more.

Oleander, Zadie, and Tiergan pored over some stone tablets Hesperia hadn't been able to take with her. In fact, she'd left almost everything behind when she'd fled to Canopus. Materials didn't matter much to a female like her.

"Did Aura get to Vega safely?" I asked. She'd been instrumental in saving my life. Fighting against Abel had been one of the bravest acts I'd ever witnessed.

"Of course," he answered. His mustache was so overgrown that his mouth didn't fully move.

"Good," I said, moving closer to them. "How bad is it?"

"Terrible," Oleander said, running his fingers through his hair. He always did that when he was stressed.

"Finn has been looking into this magic since all of this began. Maybe he'll have something useful to counteract it," Zadie said. Her voice sounded uncertain. It wasn't any doubt in Finn, but in the magic's depth. "The Hall of Memories led him to believe there was no stopping this magic once she started, but every spell has a weakness. We just need to exploit it."

"So, what are we looking at?" I asked.

"She needs blood from all five elemental courts," Zadie said.

"Which I am pretty sure she has," I replied. "She showed the vial of blood before she had Abel trap me."

Oleander nodded. "That was her intent when she came to the King and Queen's palace. It was never about attacking. It was about distracting to get what she needed. I'm just pissed the witch cut me."

That makes two of us.

"And what purpose would the blood have for her?"

"It looks like a binding spell," Zadie said. "Finnian could help sort through it, but from what I can tell, she will use the spell to bind the blood to her own essence, essentially making herself into a vessel for all five elements. Once completed, she will be the most powerful immortal in all the star realms. There's no doubt about that. As long as her body can manage hosting that much magic."

"You said everything has a weakness," I said, clinging onto a sliver of hope for dear life.

"It looks like this process will make her weak," Oleander said, eyes analyzing something I couldn't see.

"She'll have to touch each star's power source to bind the blood magic, which means she's going to have to travel to each of the realms and steal a seed from the star."

"Every time she absorbs a new element, she will weaken until the process is complete," Zadie said, agreeing with Ander's assessment.

"That's what was in the other vial," I said, whispering. "It was Algol's starlight."

"I want her head," Oleander said, seething. "Tiergan, we will need the Sublunary to deploy to all star realms to help guard their connections to the celestials."

"Canopus will be tricky," Tiergan replied. "Logic says she's already gotten what she needs there with Abel's aid."

"That only leaves three," I whispered. "But what happens once she possesses all five seeds of elemental magic?"

"She will be able to reverse the tethers to Earth for starters," Zadie said, voice shaking.

"The mortal realm would cease to exist," Oleander confirmed.

An unsettling feeling crept over me. It just seemed like a lot of work for what? To make herself a god? It just didn't sit right with my spirit. Her reasoning must go deeper than we think.

"Hesperia wants Zoe still. For what reason?" Tiergan asked.

"She'll need Zoe to form new bonds to another mortal world," Zadie said, painfully honest. "Hesperia wants to be worshipped. If I had to guess… if the new mortals don't accept her as a new god, then she'll wipe them out, too."

"So, she'll just go killing everyone who doesn't bow?" I asked.

I wanted to vomit at the purely vile heart of Hesperia. She would bring chaos to the entire universe if we didn't stop her, but there was a nagging feeling that said we were missing something.

"What you are saying is something Zoe has always assumed—that Hesperia wants her to bond to another mortal realm. That's only because we can't think of another use for the bow. But I don't think that's it. Hesperia said she was glad Zoe hadn't figured that part out."

"Somehow, that is much scarier," Zadie admitted. "But why would anyone need that kind of power?"

I couldn't help my pacing steps, as we all tried to psychoanalyze Hesperia. Everyone except Tiergan. He seemed lost in his own thoughts, but I was too frustrated to call him out on it.

"And I'm supposed to worry about going through these trials in the meantime!" I shouted at no one in particular. "It just seems so pointless."

"That's exactly what you are supposed to do, Freyja," Ander said, pulling me into an embrace, not caring who saw. "You survive to fight another day."

"Zoe won't do it," I whispered, knowing my words to be true. "She'll die before helping Hesperia. Whatever her true motives are."

"We know," Zadie said, hands on her hips. "And she's literally holding the life force of Algol in her hands. If she loses, Algol will die. We will die."

I swallowed the golf ball-sized lump in my throat. I glanced at the shattered orb that was supposed to hold the life force of Algol. How Hesperia had gotten her hands on the arrow was beyond me, but she knew the devastating consequences of her actions and did it anyway.

"It won't matter, Zadie," Oleander spat. "Zoe is keeping us alive so that we have a fighting chance. Get that through your head. She was made for this war. This is her purpose. And if she fails... if we fail... it's the entire star realms gone. Not just Algol."

Zadie closed her eyes, breathing deeply. She was hurting, needing to direct her anger somewhere tangible. I understood her grief.

"We're in this together, Zadie," I said.

"It is essential that we are all united against a common enemy," Tiergan answered. "Or we don't stand a chance."

"What do you need, Zadie?" Ander asked.

"I am sorry, Freyja," she began. "I need to speak with Finnian and find a solution. A fail-safe if everything goes wrong."

"Keep it between the two of you," Oleander commanded. "Don't tell me. Don't tell anyone."

Zadie nodded and left the room, whipping out her iris to call on Finn.

"I will prepare the Sublunary for departure," Tiergan said before leaving.

It was just Ander and me in this wretched room. I needed to get the hell out of here.

"Now what?" I asked, eyes pleading.

"We keep training," he said. "You don't have the luxury of doing otherwise."

He hadn't said it harshly, but it still stung all the same. Part of me wished to go back to my room and wallow in all the bullshit, but that would accomplish little for me right now. I needed to become stronger because the moment I got back from the trials, war would be on our doorstep.

"How long do you think we have?" I asked. "Before she tries to collect the next piece."

"She'll need time to recover from the loss here, but it's hard to say. We're going to need to send out patrols. We'll need to get someone on the inside to send us information about her movements, but until we figure out how she was controlling our immortals, that's too risky."

"That's only a couple of things. Easy," I said, laughing half-heartedly, then turned more serious. "They haven't woken yet?"

"No," he said, voice low, as if he was personally responsible. "Elvy and Zoe sent their best healers, but the damage is extensive internally."

I wrapped him in my arms, wanting to provide whatever comfort I could.

"I'll get in touch with Elvy. We'll figure it out," he murmured.

"It's weird seeing you two be nice to each other," I admitted.

"I assure you, it's stranger for me. Life seemed so much easier when my only desire in my existence was to gut him."

"I'm sure the feeling is mutual."

"You're probably right. He's much darker than I give him credit for," he said, lips in a thin line, as if he were in deep thought about something.

I had a feeling he was right.

I wrapped my arms around him, allowing him to hold me until his spirit settled enough to let go for a little while. I didn't even mind when he inevitably turned into trainer mode and knocked me to the ground in the practice room until I was black and blue.

40

Dreams

ZOE

"*Little bear,*" *my father said, manifesting in front of me. He looked exhausted, as if the weight of the universe lay only on his shoulders, but we both knew that wasn't true. His expression was haggard, but his green eyes smiled back at me with the same twinkle my own held.*

"Archer," I said, nodding, feeling like he looked.

Even in the world of dreams, my arm ached from the power of the magic in the star map. The star of Canopus was the next to sear itself into my flesh. The moment the stone door of the grove shut behind us, the magic of the map on my flesh lit my arm on fire. It'd been even more painful than the first time. None of us had been thrilled to be sent to Canopus next, with Hesperia lying in wait for that very thing. We'd have to regroup or figure something out before trying.

"Something troubles you," he said, sitting down beside me on the beach that wasn't really there, yet I heard the crash of the waves, letting me know this moment was real even if it was just in my head. Perhaps my perception of what was real and what wasn't had changed since I was mortal.

"What doesn't trouble me is the better question?" I asked, sighing. My arm hadn't hurt this long after we'd collected the grip from Rigil. It was like an ever-constant thrum of energy pulsating through me.

"It will only get worse," he said, with genuine sadness crossing his face. "I wish I could promise otherwise."

"Will it kill me?" I asked, not out of fear, but to prepare for what was to come.

"You will burn," The Archer said, voice steady.

"So I've been told," I agreed. "I'm burning as we speak."

"I know," he said, offering his arm.

I leaned into him, letting him cradle me like I'd always longed for my father to do. I didn't want to fight him or blame him. Peace was all I craved in any place I could have it. The lingering feeling of discernment sang its song in precarious warning.

"I feel like there is something you're not telling me."

"Yes," he agreed.

"And you aren't going to tell me."

"Not yet," he said. "Can you trust that some things need to be learned in time? At the right moment?"

I paused, thinking back to the time I'd met Elvy. He'd said something similar before I learned what he was. I didn't know what I would've done if he'd told me everything right away. The hospital would have been my new home, probably, but I don't know. He'd always felt right to me.

"Yes," I said.

"You're strong, little bear. You will prevail in this fight. When the time comes, you will do what you must."

"I will give anything to protect those I love."

"I know," he said, kissing the top of my head.

"You all have really made a mess of things," I said, sighing.

He laughed softly, not disagreeing with me.

"Can't you tell me what Hesperia's magic is? Why is she doing all of this? I feel so alone in this sometimes."

The laughter was gone, and his expression was troubled again.

"You already know what it is. It's all right there, little bear. I made sure you would not face this alone," he said pointedly.

There was protest on my lips, but The Archer silenced me before I could voice it.

"Get some rest. I just needed to see that you were in one piece."

***

I woke with a start, bringing my consciousness back to awareness. Strong arms circled around my waist, and the rise and fall of a firm chest was at my back. Elvy's legs were tangled in mine, and his heartbeat was steady against me. The stars and moon flickered in the skylight of our room in Vega, and the blue-green flame of the fire created a peaceful atmosphere.

No, I was never truly alone, and I was grateful for him—my flame.

No one would be waking for a while, and there was no way I could lure myself back to bed. Part of me wanted to wake Elvy up to get lost in his distractions, but he looked so peaceful. Now, how to get out of here without waking him?

I threw up a silencing shield around my body and rolled gently out of the bed. His arms reached for me for a few moments, but settled on a pillow before he eventually drifted back off to sleep. Jelly, however, caught me red-handed. Her ears perked up, letting me know she was going with me.

"What about the Lord Astral?" she asked through our branded magic.

I still startled when I heard her voice, but quickly shook it away.

"He needs rest," I said, leading us down the hall and down the stairs.

"So do you," she said, tail wagging.

It was hard to believe an ancient beast lived within her petite border collie form.

"I'm wide awake, unfortunately."

She said nothing else and followed me. If I turned left, that would lead me to the small training room in the manor, but if I turned right, that would lead me to the library. Both sounded enticing.

I turned left, knowing I was too on edge to get lost in a book right now. The moment I crossed the threshold, the lights flickered on, and Blaz emerged from the other door across the room.

"Couldn't sleep either?" he asked, moving towards us.

"No," I admitted. "My sleep was interrupted."

"Spare me the details," he said, laughing.

"Do you see Elvy with me?" I asked, rolling my eyes. "He's still asleep. The Archer came for a visit. And I just haven't been sleeping well. Most of the time, my dreams are just a replay of watching my mom die. Sometimes I prefer his visits. At least I don't have to watch her die over and over again." I was too worked up to hide behind a mask tonight. Vulnerability it was then.

I felt a smidgen of relief in confessing this to Blaz, and his expression was sincere.

"I'm not going to tell you things that you already know, Zo. My offer still stands. I'm here for you. Always."

"I know," I said, stretching my muscles.

"Did The Archer say anything useful?" he asked, setting up the practice dummies

"Just wanted to check on me like the doting father he is now," I said, shrugging. "And that he hasn't told me everything yet."

"So, no?" he asked.

"No," I agreed.

"Useless."

I nodded and picked up a handful of knives from the wall full of weapons. Blaz scratched Jelly's belly, and her leg was going nuts. He'd found the right spot.

"It's weird how quiet it is, right?" I asked, launching a knife into the center of the chest. Spot on.

"It is the middle of the night," he said.

I started to clarify what I meant, but he stopped me.

"I know what you mean. With most everyone in Musterion… it just feels weird."

"Hopefully, it serves its purpose in protecting their lives," I said, sending a second blade through the middle of the forehead.

"Wish we could figure out a way to move the connection to Vega down there," he said

"I guess Finn tried?" I asked.

"Yeah, no luck. I think Zadie is arriving later today. Said she needed help with something about the blood magic Hesperia is using."

"Sounds promising," I said, firing another knife into the shoulder. The blow would have severed the labrum, rendering the arm quite useless. "I wonder how much longer we can keep Musterion from her… and Oleander. I really don't know why we haven't shared it with them."

"Because your duty is to the immortals you serve. Security measures are in place for a reason," he said gently, likely knowing I didn't like keeping this from them. "She'll be briefing us on arrival. Oleander and Freyja are staying behind."

"I figured. She needs to focus on the trials, though I wish she could come. I'll send her a message today," I said, refocusing on my target. The next knife sliced through the carotid artery in the neck.

"You've become lethal with these things."

"In war, you either learn to fight or you die, right?" I asked, digging the blades out of the fake target.

"Yes," he said. "But you never forget the *why*."

I closed my eyes, picturing every face that meant something to me. "They never leave me, Blaz."

He nodded, as if he held my pain with me.

"Let's practice with the bow," I said.

He didn't ask why, and I didn't offer an explanation. We weren't gathering the pieces of The Archer's bow for him. No, I'd be the one using it.

Blaz lifted one bow from the wall and grabbed a few arrows. Jelly lay beside me, observing his every move.

He handed me the weapon, and it was heavier than I'd imagined. My training had made me strong, though.

"These curved parts are the limbs. The middle there is the grip, or some call it a riser."

"Does the string have a special name, too?"

"Nope, it's just the string," he said, laughing. "Hold it like this."

Blaz moved my arms into position, and it felt… natural. Like I'd always be right here in this moment with Blaz.

"Good, now we'll notch the arrow here, and then just pull back," he said, letting me get used to the resistance of the string. It was difficult, but not impossible.

"And I just let it go?" I asked. My arm still throbbed from the mark of Canopus, but it was more of an annoying, dull ache.

"Aim and let it go," he said.

I let the arrow fly, and it was like watching it move in slow motion. It was as if the arrow flew exactly where I wanted it to go. My eyes held onto the arrow until it met its mark in the chest of the practice target.

"That's unusual," he said, cocking his head.

"It felt… effortless. Like the bow and arrow answered to me. My vision latched onto the arrow the whole time, but time moved slowly for me."

"You are The Archer's daughter," Blaz said.

"Again," I said, grabbing another arrow.

For the next hour, Blaz gave me more and more ridiculously tough targets to hit, and I never missed. I ignored the pain in my arm, and I found myself laughing at the giddy feeling.

"You're unstoppable," Blaz said, cheering.

Then, he worked on doing knife and archery move combinations to integrate them more cohesively in battle.

"You can't throw all of your knives. Obviously, your aim is great, but you don't have an unlimited supply of knives or arrows. Pick up the ones you can and reuse them. You have to get more comfortable with close hand-to-hand combat with knives."

I nodded, soaking up his advice. Blaz had trained the greatest warriors I knew. It'd be foolish not to listen to what he said.

"And don't forget my magic," I said, grinning.

"Yes, don't forget that," he agreed, punching my shoulder.

One of the training doors slammed open and someone shouted, "What the hell is going on in here?"

Delmira. She looked seven shades of pissed off.

"Hey Delm," I said, waving. "You okay?"

"Oh, sorry," she said, nodding slightly. "I thought it was just Blaz in here losing his mind."

"So you were coming to yell at me some more?" he asked, nostrils flaring. "Or were you going to give me the silent treatment? Can't make up your mind?"

"You know… I'm getting tired," I said, beginning to back away.

"Stay right where you are, Zoe," Blaz ordered. I froze, not wanting to anger the beast.

I was trying hard not to laugh at my two friends. Jelly stood beside me, tongue hanging out at both of them.

"You want to come busting up in here with that attitude? Then you get to help train Zo," he said, arms crossed.

"Fine," she said, pulling two knives from her waist in less than a second. Her violet eyes held no mercy.

I was not about to get in the middle of whatever was going on between them.

"Wake up!" I shouted through the bond at Elvy, and I felt his consciousness respond immediately.

"Where are you?" he asked frantically.

"In the training room. Blaz and Delmira are trying to use me to punch out their problems."

"Start with that bit of information next time," he said, laughing. *"I'll be there in a second."*

Moments later, Elvy joined my side while Delmira and Blaz continued to seethe at each other, expecting my presence to somehow diffuse the situation.

"What's going on with you two?" Elvy asked. "I can't have my second and my general at each other's throats. Not in these times."

"Nothing," Blaz said, closing his eyes to center himself, no doubt.

"We're fine," Delmira said, coming out of the statue her posture had become.

"Whatever it is, get it together," Elvy said.

They both nodded, hearing the command of their Lord Astral.

I yawned, growing more tired, but not ready to lie back down. The world of dreams was not a place I cared to be right now.

"Thanks for the help, Blaz," I said, offering a small smile. I handed him the bow, and he walked away, placing it back on the wall rack.

"Sorry, Zo," Delmira said, eyes focused on Blaz. Delm was not one to ever say sorry, so whatever was going on was truly bothering her. My gift wasn't hinting at anything yet, so I would have to find time to talk with her later.

I led Elvy and Jelly out into the hall in search of a less exhausting distraction.

"Sorry to wake you," I said, lacing my fingers through his.

"I'd rather you always wake me when you need me," he said pointedly. "I don't mind getting up with you. What made you wake up, anyway?"

"Long story short, The Archer paid me a visit, and I don't know, it sent me into a frenzy. It's like my magic is pulsating through me, trying to figure out what The Archer isn't telling me. Whatever it is, there is a reason he doesn't want me to know it yet… which means it's probably bad."

He squeezed my hand, grounding me to reality once more. "You never have to face these things alone. Talk to me, Zo."

"You were sleeping," I argued. "I know you're tired."

"We're all tired, flame."

"Well, what good is it for both of us to be tired? If one of us can get enough sleep, then maybe it'll make a difference."

Elvy whirled me into his arms, tilting my chin so that his gray eyes met my own. "I love you, Zoe Eferhild. Don't you understand there is nothing I wouldn't endure for you—with you?"

"I know, but—" I started, then paused. All he wanted from me was to let him in. I would want the same from him if the roles were reversed. But what if there was something that I had to hide from him? What if my role in this war ended in my death?

"Together," he said. "Always together."

"To whatever future," I said, suddenly feeling those words more strongly than anytime I'd muttered them. He would have to be with me to my end and accept that.

He seemed to watch the thoughts cross my mind even though I'd shielded them, but in my heart, I knew there was nothing I could hide from Elvy. He said nothing, but kept his eyes on me, as if begging me to tell him what I was thinking.

I glanced at our now-joined hands, reading the story of our love in the stars. Mates, bonded by something greater than ourselves.

"I feel like we're on the cusp of something," I murmured. "And I'm not sure we're going to like the end result."

"You have theories?"

I nodded, but I wouldn't elaborate. Not tonight, when my mental state was fluctuating between sane and numb and panicked.

"Can you trust that we'll talk about it later? I don't want to even think about it right now. That's why I came out here in the first place."

"I always trust you," he said, pressing his lips to mine.

"Come on," I said, leading him into the library. The disappointment from him was palpable, but he didn't press, understanding what I needed. Whatever was coming, we'd face it then.

There was only one soul in the library, and I smiled a greeting at her.

"Lord and Lady Astral," she said, bowing. "And Jelly."

"Hey Octavia," I replied. "I'll need to get with you soon. I have a lot to tell you about the simargl."

"I'd love to," she agreed. "I want all the knowledge we can possibly have to be here. For everyone."

"I have a feeling when this is all over, you and the other Keepers will have much history to restore in our archives," I said.

"That's what we are here for," she agreed.

"Tiergan would be of great help," Elvy offered, and I nodded my agreement.

"I'll make it a point to come by before we leave," I promised, leading Elvy and Jelly to my favorite reading spot in the library.

"There's a fresh brew of coffee by the table," she called after us, and I beamed at that.

I pulled a book from the romance shelves nearby, and Elvy opened his arms in invitation. Jelly nestled by the crackling flames of the fireplace. There was something about the smell of a library that just brought me peace. It smelled the same as any library in the mortal world. It smelled like home.

"Come here," he said, wrapping me in his arms. He pulled the fuzzy blanket over us and massaged my scalp while I cracked open the first page of the book.

It didn't take long for me to settle into an easy reading rhythm, and I forgot all about The Archer's visit and the nightmares that plagued my sleep as I listened to the steady breathing of my flame to keep me safe.

41

It's Complicated

DELMIRA

Zoe and Elvy hadn't been able to get away from us fast enough. I couldn't blame them, yet I was pissed at them for leaving me alone to deal with Blaz. More honestly, I was angry that I now had to deal with myself.

We stared at each other, each daring the other to make the first move.

Fine, I'll do it.

"Elvy has a point. We can't let what's going on between us affect the Luminaries or our duties."

"Is there something going on between us, Delm?" he asked, arms crossed. The muscles in his forearms wavered, and I quickly looked away into his brown eyes. Nope. That was not any better.

I ran a hand through my violet hair. It'd grown long enough to keep it tidy in a braid. I didn't want to have this conversation, but I had no choice but to.

"You're my best friend, Blaz. You know that," I said, trying to lighten the mood.

"Then why are you avoiding me?"

"Because—" I started, but I didn't like any of the answers that came to the forefront of my mind.

"Let me lay it out there for you," he said, stepping in closer to me, but not so much that he was touching me, which somehow felt even more intimate. "You piss me off a lot, but you're the only one I feel like talking to most of the time. You're my best friend too, Delm. I'd never really thought about pursuing you as anything else because I never thought you'd give me a chance. Having you in my life was more important than what I might feel."

He clenched his jaw, and a muscle rippled through his left cheek.

"Then *you* kissed *me*. Not the other way around. If you don't feel that way about me, then just say that. You aren't responsible for sparing my feelings."

Before I knew what I was doing, I wrapped my arms around his neck and kissed him recklessly.

His body started to respond to me, but he pulled away and held my wrists to his chest.

"No, Delm. Not like this. I want to make one thing very clear," he said, pausing to make sure I was listening to him.

I tried to shove down the sting of rejection, transforming my heart into ice once more. Trying and failing.

"I want to pursue you," he said. "But not unless you want me to."

I stayed silent because I didn't know the answer.

"And if you want this—," he said, gesturing to what had just happened between us. "Then, know I don't do friends with benefits."

I stood in stunned silence. He was going to deny us this?

"So when you figure out what you want, then you let me know. I'm not going anywhere."

"Got it," I said, letting my pride fill me as I walked away from him yet again.

He didn't follow me.

"What the hell is wrong with me?" I asked the universe, as I paced the training grounds, daring someone to approach me.

Tears fell from my eyes, and I tried in vain to suck them back in. Surely, I was more powerful than puny little tears.

"What's going on, Delm?" a familiar voice said from behind, startling me.

I whipped around, holding my blade at my twin's neck.

"No need for theatrics," he said, moving the sword down, and I let it fall.

"How did you find me?" I asked.

"Your thoughts are loud tonight," he said, shrugging. I was the only mind he could almost always hear.

"I don't know, Finn. I feel like I self-sabotage everything."

I plopped down on the grass, staring up at the stars. He joined me on the ground and bumped his shoulder against mine.

"You're just figuring things out," he offered. "We had dreadful lives for a long time."

"You know I don't like talking about our mortal life," I said, wincing.

Growing up dodging the foster care system didn't exactly lead to an easy or happy life. Let's just say vile went down.

"It seems to still affect you, though, Delm."

"We've been immortals for centuries. And you're perfectly normal with a healthy relationship, right?"

"Are you actually admitting to liking Zadie?"

"Hell no," I said, laughing at his smirk. "You know, if Zoe pulls this off, you and Zadie could have a real future together if you wanted. Neither of you would have to change which celestial you serve."

"Aw, Delm. I knew you cared," he said, winking.

"I'm just saying you seem to function, and I want a happy ending for you. I'm all trust issues and self-doubt with a mask of fake confidence."

"And you camouflage it well. Maybe too well," he pointed out. "And things haven't always been easy for me. I just eventually worked through it, is all. And you will too. In your own time, and in your own way."

"I think I may have just lost my best friend," I said, voice more vulnerable than it had been in a long time. I hated feeling weak to my emotions.

"I don't think that's true."

"Keeping people at a distance seems easier," I admitted.

"It is until it isn't."

"So what do I do, oh wise one?" I asked, wiping the snot from my nose.

"Gross."

"Shut up," I said, threatening to touch him with my contaminated hand.

"I'm no expert, but I'd think about what you really want. Are you letting fear control you? Are you scared of being vulnerable because you are giving up control of all the variables, and that means you aren't safe?"

That struck a nerve. I did like being in control. It was the way I kept myself and Finn safe. Leave it to my twin to call me out like that.

"Some immortals deserve your trust, Delm."

"You read too many books," I said, smacking him on the back of the head.

"Hey! I'm trying to help," he said, holding up his hand in defence.

"I know," I said, standing up and holding my hand out to help him up.

"Zadie is coming tomorrow?"

"Yes," he said, giving a genuine smile. "Though I don't think her visit will be particularly pleasant. Hopefully, we can put our heads together and figure something useful out."

"We will," I said encouragingly. "Come on, let's get a couple of hours of sleep before she arrives."

He nodded, and we walked in comfortable silence back to the residential wing of the manor.

42

The Origin of Poison
FREYJA

Zadie had left for Vega a little while ago and had informed Oleander of her safe arrival through her iris.

At least that was one good thing, and we needed more good things. Surely if we collected enough of them, we'd win, right? Good was supposed to always win against evil, but the more I faced evil itself, the more I questioned the validity of all the superhero stories I'd watched on television. Everyone could be wicked. The term 'villain' was subjective to the person telling the story. Who was Hesperia's villain—if not Zoe? Why would Zoe truly be her enemy? It just didn't add up. Everyone seemed to think that it was just Hesperia creating chaos, but I had my doubts. No one hates someone that much for no reason—no motive.

"Oleander, can you send Zoe a message?" I asked, and he paused his training.

My jaw dropped to the floor as he strode towards me with no shirt on, drenched in sweat. My eyes followed a drop of sweat down his rippling abs until it disappeared beneath the waistband of his training leathers. I had been so lost in the ramblings of my mind that I hadn't seen him take his shirt off. Not that I hadn't seen him without it before, but a girl could be appreciative, right?

Oleander waved his immortal mark against the iris, charging it with his magic. He nodded when it was ready to send a message.

"Find Hesperia's true villain, Zo," I murmured, and the crystal rainbows disappeared to deliver it to Zoe.

"What's that about?" he asked, wiping the sweat from his brow.

"I don't know," I said. "Just a hunch, I guess. I know I need to focus on the trials, but I could be gone for months with those. Zoe needs my help now. As much as I can give it. Anything big or small could be the one thing that will give us the advantage."

"So you think Hesperia is doing this for what? Revenge against a lover?"

"It's deeper than her ego," I said. "What motivates someone to have that kind of power?"

He thought for a moment, then answered, "To have control over someone?"

"No," I said, shaking my head. "To show someone that they are powerful."

Oleander took out his iris that was filling with rainbows. Zoe's voice came across the barrier, saying, "We're already looking into her history. We'll let you know if we find anything. Focus on your training."

"And not one 'I love you,'" I laughed.

"She's not wrong," he said pointedly.

I placed my hands on my hips and smiled sweetly.

"I'm sure there are more optimal ways to spend our time," I said, unzipping my fighting leathers to my navel.

Ander's eyes darkened, and he moved his body to become flush with mine. He leaned down, kissing my neck. I braced for him to bite my ear, but he chuckled softly instead.

"Nice try," he said, zipping me back up and kissing the top of my head.

"Seriously?" I asked with mock surprise.

"Nothing is worth you missing out on training," he said. "Once you get back from the trials, you can have all of me anytime you want."

"What if we don't have that time when I get back?"

"I haven't lived such a dreadful existence to find you and lose it all, sweetheart. I reject that notion."

"I didn't take you for an optimist," I said, smiling half-heartedly.

"It's not about optimism. It's just the truth."

"You can't just will your want into existence," I said, exasperated with this male.

"The stars can certainly try me," he said, completely serious.

I believed he would take on the stars for me—for us. Stubborn male.

"Now quit stalling and climb that wall," he said, pointing behind me.

I turned around and gulped.

"I thought this was for, like, decoration or something."

"Why would we have something like this for aesthetics?"

"It's a literal wall made of rock, and there's a waterfall. It's all slippery," I said, wiping my hand against the stone. He's lost his mind.

"So you're not even going to try?" he asked, arms folded across his chest.

"You can climb this?"

"Of course. Every male and female in the Shadowed Legion has climbed this wall."

"But they have wings to catch themselves if they fall."

"I'll catch you, Freyja," he whispered against my ear. "Always."

I wanted to turn around and punch him, but I swallowed my fear. I'd climbed hundreds of rocky cliffs before. Granted, I'd never been an alpinist, but I was no novice at climbing rock walls either. I stepped back from the wall, examining different routes in my head. Anything too close to the water would cause me to slip, but the routes furthest from the falls would require some fairly technical maneuvers. My strength was likely not what it used to be, or maybe it was the same? I didn't think there would be any statistics on climbing success post being brought back from the dead in an immortal star realm.

"Technical maneuvers it is," I murmured.

Luckily, there was some chalk, and I covered my moist palms in it, testing my grip. I'd lost all of my calluses from years of adventures while I'd been mortal. Something about being brought back had cleared all of that from me. In fact, my hands were covered in blisters from wielding the mirage of weapons Oleander was making me train with. They would eventually turn into calluses, but this was going to hurt.

I took one more deep breath in and began my ascent to the top of the towering wall with nothing more than my stubbornness and a bag of chalk strapped to my waist. I'd been through worse things and came out on top.

"Good luck, Freyja," Oleander called, and I silently flipped him off.

"You got this," I whispered to myself and made the first purchase against the stone. "Just like riding a bike."

★★★

It was not like riding a bike.

I'd only made it a third of the way up before my grip failed on one of the most difficult maneuvers on the entire route. Ander had caught me as promised, which seemed to just piss me off even more.

Bruises covered my body, and I was tired—hungry. I didn't know which one I needed to address first. Perhaps I could eat while showering? Why wasn't it possible to eat while sleeping?

"Come with me, Freyja," he said, gently grabbing my shoulder to direct me to his room.

Wincing with every step I took, I let him guide me to his quarters.

"I've already called for some food to be brought up. Let's get you cleaned up."

I unzipped my leathers, slipping them down past my hips. I flinched, trying to get them all the way down, but I was too sore to bend over to finish the job.

Oleander got on his knees in front of me and placed both of my hands on either of his shoulders.

"I've got you," he said, pulling them all the way off. Any thought of seducing Ander had long left my mind, and he seemed to know that.

"Ouch," I said, examining my body in the mirror. My hips and arms took the worst of it. There were a couple of scrapes on my knees. My hands hadn't stopped bleeding and had a throbbing ache pulsing through them. I desperately wished for Zoe to heal me, but then I wouldn't develop the calluses I needed. I'd just have to endure it.

"This will sting a bit," Oleander stated before placing a salve on my aching hands.

I grimaced, but the pain ebbed some.

"Shower or bath?" he asked.

"I'll rinse off in the shower, then soak."

He nodded, turning on both, and I slipped under the water of the shower to scrub myself of the grime and blood. My stomach growled, demanding that I fuel it soon.

Just as I settled down into the boiling water of the bath, Oleander brought in a plate of food. Cheeses, fruits, nuts, and crackers were placed beautifully on a wooden board, and I began picking at it immediately.

"The chef will bring something more substantial later."

"This is fine, thank you," I said with a mouth full of cheese.

"You never make it easy," he murmured, staring at me.

"Huh?"

"May I?" he asked, hand on his belt.

"Oh, sure," I said, scooting forward in the water, averting my eyes. Watching him strip would do things to me, and I wasn't in the mood to fight my traitorous little libido.

He settled in behind me, allowing me to use his chest to rest against. The silence was comfortable, but my mind wanted answers.

"I have questions," I said, pausing.

"You've never been one to hold back on those."

"Well, they're about you. I wasn't sure if you were in the mood to talk about you."

"I'm rarely in the mood to talk about me," he admitted. "But what do you want to know?"

"You mentioned that you've had an unpleasant existence..." I trailed off, unsure of how or what I was asking exactly.

"What's the question, Freyja?"

"You've never mentioned your family... we all know Elvy's tragic story. I've never heard yours."

He was silent for a long time. I didn't think he was going to answer, to be honest, and I was okay with accepting that. Whatever his truth was, it was his to share in his own time.

"I don't know my parents," he said, voice quiet. "I was raised in a group home."

"Immortals have those?"

"There are never very many immortal children born together," he began. "But even immortals don't want their children sometimes. There were only two other children in the home. The caretaker was a nice female. It wasn't a traumatic experience or anything. I just wasn't wanted."

My heart stilled and grieved for him in that moment. It was hard to imagine Ander vulnerable, and to think of him as unwanted... unloved. I couldn't stand the thought at all.

"When I came of age, I learned who they were. It's not that hard to find out amongst the immortals with so few children born. My mother was a servant in the palace of Hesperia and her then-husband Janus. My mother's name was Isla. She was involved with one of Hesperia's consorts. They were apparently in love. Janus tried to help my mother, but Hesperia found out."

I swallowed and kissed the back of his hand.

"From what I learned, Hesperia killed the consort. I don't even know his name. My mother hasn't been heard of since, so I assume she's long dead."

I didn't know what to say, so I said nothing and held him close to me. Knowing what Hesperia had made him do with her… it's a wonder he can even stand to be touched.

In my heart, I felt that his mother and father wanted him very much. But perhaps there was something in him that needed to believe that.

"Hesperia killed Janus eventually. Just before she severed the tethers."

"So it wasn't a fit of rage from her?"

"No," he shook his head. "Janus and Hesperia had no marriage of love. At least, that's what the rumors say. It was his bloodline that had held the Astral title, not hers. She would have been nothing without him."

I laid my head against his chest, listening to his heartbeat.

"I'm glad you're here," I said, foregoing the condolences. What good did sorry do for something like that?

"Me too, sweetheart," he said, running his fingers up and down my arm, lost in thought.

Neither of us said anything else while we let the still hot water melt away our worries of the past, present, and future.

43

A Meeting of Shadows
ZOE

"You wanted to see me, Lord and Lady Astrals?" Zadie asked, escorted by Finnian.

"Yes," my flame answered. "Before you brief us on what you've learned, there is something we need to inform you and Oleander of."

Finnian unsuccessfully tried to hide his smile. He'd been campaigning for Zadie to be briefed on Musterion since we'd found it, so she could help him better, but we'd denied it until this point. My gift had seen Zadie as true, and no harm would come to our immortals by sharing this with her and Oleander.

But precautions would be taken, nonetheless.

"Before we tell you, a blood oath is required to our court. Breaking it will end in death."

"And since Oleander is not present, your oath will extend to him. If he breaks it, your life will also be forfeit."

Finn's expression had become firm, but he understood the risks.

"That serious, huh?" Zadie asked.

"Yes."

"Alright, give it here," she said, sighing and holding out her hand. Elvy handed her the blade that would solidify her oath. She slit her palm, letting blood drip on the seal of the Astrals of Vega. "I swear with my life that I will keep the Court of Vega's secrets and will pay with my life should I or my Lord Astral break this oath."

The seal flared with starlight, and her fate was now tied to her vow.

"Thank you," I said, taking the blade back. "Finnian, you may share all that you need to about Musterion."

"We will meet you both in the manor shortly," Elvy said, pulling me from the room. Zadie and Finn both bowed before our exit.

***

"So if we keep Hesperia from taking the star seeds, the blood magic won't work?" Clodovea asked.

We all sat around the familiar table on top of the manor in the secure meeting room. The view of the ocean brought me just a little peace. Every ounce of space was being utilized in Musterion, and most of the Shadowed Legions were stationed above ground. Finnian stated that the kelpies were coming by the dozens, which wasn't a good sign, in my opinion. Any change in wildlife indicated that something big was happening soon.

"That seems to be the case," Zadie confirmed. She'd arrived not long ago. Finnian was by her side, reading over the texts Zadie had brought with her.

"Finn?" I asked.

"Seems right," he agreed.

"She can't possibly think she can take on all the remaining three star realms, right?" Imelda asked.

"Oh, she absolutely does think that," Blaz said. "She'll become the shadows themselves to get what she needs."

"Delmira?" Elvy asked.

"I've already reinforced security around Vega's orb. If there were a way to move it to Musterion…"

"I haven't found one," Finn said, dismissing the idea. "I haven't found any material on how the celestials created them."

"So, the Shadowed will surround it, making it an obvious target," Imelda said.

She wasn't wrong, but there was no other option. Creating a ruse in the hopes she would be tricked was too risky if she didn't go for it. No, this was the hand we were dealt.

"She likely already knows where the orbs are," Blaz said. "Her palace was above Algol's. It would be natural to think every Astral's home was covering their star's power source. What better protection?"

"Tiergan is sending Sublunary forces to provide extra aid. They should be arriving in a day or so."

"What about Canopus?" Clodovea asked.

"It's been deemed too risky to save right now. The Sublunary would likely be killed the moment they landed in the realm," Zadie explained.

"How are we supposed to go there undetected?" Blaz asked.

"Doesn't matter," I said. "We have to go."

"Tiergan sent coordinates for the back door," Zadie said, handing them to Elvy.

"We should expect a fight," Elvy said, looking over the coordinates of the shadows.

Jelly paced around the room as if she felt the anxiety coursing through the air. I suppose she probably could, though she chose not to speak her mind right now.

"We still have some time," I said. I wasn't sure if I was trying to convince them or myself. "My gift has been quiet since she went into Canopus. We've got time to be smart about this."

"I agree," Elvy offered. "This isn't the time to make hasty mistakes."

Besides, I needed time to figure out who Hesperia's real enemy was and what she truly wanted from me if it wasn't to bond to another mortal realm. I just needed… time. Time to figure out a way out of this where everyone lived and got their happy ending.

"I'll monitor her daily," I confirmed. "I'll give us the most time that I can."

"Let's not waste it," Elvy said. "Dismissed."

Everyone nodded and went their separate ways. I wanted to pay Aura a visit today, but first I needed to put in some practice. The kind only Elvy can help with—my shadows.

I latched myself onto Elvy, and Jelly followed behind us silently. I was on the edge of exhaustion, but fatigue was all I ever truly felt anymore. Learning not to break under any circumstance when it came to Hesperia was more important than anything. She could not get her hands on my shadows.

Elvy sat me on the floor in front of the fire while Jelly nestled in close beside me.

"You sure about this right now?" he asked, grabbing both of my hands. "We could wait until you've slept."

"I'm sure," I promised. "Sleep and I don't get along these days."

That didn't seem to reassure him, but he didn't argue either, always allowing me to choose my way in life.

"I need to test a theory with both of our shadows."

"Alright," he conceded. "I trust you."

We both took mind-stilling breaths. The reality that his own darkness would come to meet mine was all too real.

Closing my eyes, I focused on the well of power from Algol that lurked within me. I called it to my consciousness, and it felt like roots clawing through my core up to the surface of my skin. Painful, yes. Divine? Absolutely.

I stifled a groan. Why did they have to feel so good?

Licking my lips, I opened my eyes to find Elvy staring back at me with gray eyes.

My nostrils flared in need.

"Zoe?" Elvy asked, squeezing my hand.

"I'm still me," I said, voice lower than normal.

"Focus on embracing your shadows. Talk to them," he coached. "Welcome them into your space. They are a part of you that serves an integral purpose."

I nodded my head, more in control than I ever had been in wielding my shadow self.

"Welcome," I murmured. "Thank you for coming to me."

They swirled in my bloodstream, living in my veins. I sighed, twitching for something… anything.

Elvy's thumb rubbed soothing circles on the back of my hand.

Soft fur pawed at my exposed thigh. Jelly. My protector. And she was not afraid.

"Thank you for the times you have protected me," I said, leaning into the darkness. They were a part of me. A destructive, bloodthirsty part. But a part nonetheless. A part that protected and served me.

A pain shot through me. Hunger. My shadows were hungry for vengeance and violence. My face heated with rage as I recalled the image of my mother's face in death and the sacrifice she'd made.

I embraced their hatred, encouraging them to hate Hesperia the way my light despised her.

"Justice," I said, throat burning with thirst.

"Not yet."

"Now," I countered, eyes heated. "Hesperia will answer to me."

"Yes," Elvy agreed, voice trembling.

"Join me," I said to his darkness. "Executioner."

Elvy's frame went rigid.

I smiled, feeling the instant connection of shadows through our flame.

Dark eyes met my own.

"Flame," I purred, forgetting about my earlier bloodlust. My shadows were delighted to see their mate.

His eyes darkened even more, but he said nothing.

I leaped into his lap, shoving him to the floor so that I straddled his hips.

I barely noticed Jelly's swift exit from the room and refocused on my bond.

"I'm still me," he said, voice shaking, as if he was concentrating with great difficulty. "I need to know you are still with me, Zo."

My quivering hand stroked the silver-brown curls from his dark eyes.

I swallowed. This was a part of me. Not all of me. She wasn't bad or good. She just was.

"I'm still Zoe," I said, welcoming the darkness between us. "And she's with me."

Shadows shot from my hands as the urge to release power enveloped me. The surrender encased me in euphoria.

"Still painfully beautiful," he whispered.

I leaned down, kissing his jaw, and worked my way up to his lips. A groan escaped him as I ground against him. My skin was on fire with the absolute need for friction. If my shadows couldn't kill, they wanted something else.

I was in control, and so was my flame. We'd just invited every part of us into this moment. To truly be seen by the other. To be known...

Breathing in his scent, I grinned at the familiarity—Algol. His shadows smelled of Algol.

"Mate," I said. "In every way."

I slipped my pants off as he unbuckled his. Dark eyes locked with mine as Elvy filled me.

"Mate," he said, growling, flipping me over on the rug. He ripped my top off, exposing my bare body to him.

He moved inside me, and I whimpered, clawing at his back. It was as if my soul was crying tears of joy to finally be fully joined with its perfect bond—true soulmates.

I saw Elvy for all that he was—all that he feared—and I loved him even still. My shadows loved him as his loved me.

"Mine," I said, claiming him with my mouth, and he snarled, unsheathing his teeth to bite my all too willing skin against my neck. I moaned in satisfaction.

"More," I demanded, and he tore his shirt off so that there was nothing separating us now.

His fullness left me as he moved his tongue down my body, setting my body on fire where they collided. His mouth and fingers brought pleasure and expertise that my shadows and I both appreciated. With his delicious pace guiding us, I lost myself in divine elation.

The room was filled with black tendrils protecting us from the outside world. In this moment, it was just us, surrounded by darkness. Our darkness.

Our love eclipsed the fear that threatened to take us away from each other.

"You are everything to me," he said, nipping at my thigh, and I could take it no longer. I came for him violently, grinding against him, as he continued to tease me with that sinful tongue.

He sat my hands on the fireplace so that I kneeled with my backside in front of him. My knees trembled with the power that radiated from us both, and our bodies joined together, moving in a perfect rhythm.

"I love you," I said through labored breathing, leaning back on his chest as we moved in harmony.

"I love you, Zoe," he answered, and I felt something cool against my skin.

I looked down to find his shadows teasing my body, and I cried out. He swallowed my cries with his lips. Sweat poured down us both, but we kept going.

"It'll never be enough. Not with you," he said, groaning.

"I need you, flame," I said, and he gripped onto my waist as he released his pleasure in me.

I was a convulsion in his arms and didn't possess the strength to move. Elvy kissed my neck gently and slid me off him so that I faced him.

His black eyes were still staring back at me, and I knew my shadows met his.

"Algol," I murmured, holding his hand against my cheek. "It's not a family curse. Algol is just in your family's bloodline."

"It's both Algol's and Vega's magic."

With tears in his eyes, he wrapped a blanket around both of us as our shadows settled more. They didn't have to be something we feared. We could learn to be allies with them.

As our room claimed its usual form with the shadows dissipating, we were startled by what sounded like a battering ram at our door.

"What the hell?" a voice said, bursting through the door.

Control. Gone. My shadows took the driver's seat.

My shadows didn't hesitate to ensnare the male who interrupted me and my flame.

"Zoe!" a female voice screamed. She had violet hair. Odd.

"What the hell are you doing!" my flame screamed at the intruders. "We were fine!"

ers. "We were fine!"

The large brute of a male turned purple against my shadows.

"Come back to me, starlight," my mate whispered through our flame.

"They are a threat," I said back, squeezing my shadows tighter.

"No, they aren't, Zoe," my flame said reasonably. *"Look at me."*

I turn to find gray eyes staring back at me.

"Let go. We'll face it together," he promised.

"Tell her to stop!" the violet one screeched. My shadows wanted to silence her just for the annoyance.

"Silence," my flame said firmly.

With every ounce of light and willpower I possessed, I let the shadows fall. The pressure was almost too great as I ordered the shadows back into the well for safekeeping.

With trembling hands, I dropped to my knees in horror at what I'd done to Blaz.

Maybe Elvy and I didn't have to worry about the shadows harming each other, but anyone who they deemed a threat had much to fear.

Jelly came to me, and I hugged her neck while Elvy dropped right down beside me.

"Get him out of here," Elvy said, anger palpable.

Delmira nodded and helped Blaz to his feet.

"I'm fine, Zo," Blaz mumbled, but I wouldn't meet his eyes. "I'm the idiot who got between you."

I stared at the floor, holding on to Jelly for dear life. Shame reddened my cheeks, and I just wanted to crawl into a corner.

I didn't look up until I heard the door shut behind them, and then I let myself break down.

My tears had me buckled over in the fetal position. I couldn't talk, and I didn't care to be reasoned with.

"I've got you," Elvy murmured, holding me and wiping the tears away as they came.

He didn't tell me it was okay. I didn't want to hear that, and he knew it. Logically, I knew Blaz was fine, but we'd discovered my limits. My shadows recognized Elvy as mine. Claimed him. They would protect him at all costs. How were we supposed to be on the battlefield together? He seemed so much more in control.

"It's taken years of practice, Zoe," he said, answering my loud thoughts. "Even so, they can be unpredictable, but you have just helped me understand them so much better. To know what this power really is… I'm not cursed."

"I always knew that," I said, snuggling back up to him under the blanket. He'd managed to slip his pants back on with the outburst, but I was still completely naked.

My gut swelled with discernment.

"What if that's how she'll get to me?" I asked, heart racing. "It's got something to do with our shadows, but what the hell does she want? What if her own tendrils connect with my shadows like they just did with yours?"

I was in the mood to be pessimistic. I'd earned as much.

"I don't think that's it," he disagreed. "Our shadows are bonded, just like our flames."

The unsettling feeling would not go away.

"Well, it makes sense why Algol hates Vega," I murmured, thinking back to the celestial's animosity.

"Why is that?"

"Vega has an Astral bloodline with a death magic that is made possible by the combination of both Vega's water magic and Algol's spirit magic. Algol doesn't think it's right. But it means that the Vega Astral line had Algol users on the throne at some point."

"It's a wonder that we lost that history, but it seems like that is what the celestials intended from whatever they did to us."

"But you could never see Freyja?"

"No," he said, shaking his head. "I didn't have that part of Algol's gift, I guess. Just the darkness."

"I don't know how, Elvy. But it's all in the shadows. Hesperia." My frame shuddered at the truth of my words. "I don't want to be scared of that part of me any longer. I refuse to let her make me fear them."

Elvy pulled me closer to him, stroking my hair.

"I'm not going anywhere, starlight. Remember, I might get afraid for you, but I'm never afraid of you. Hold that in your heart. Always."

"It doesn't seem *you* have anything to worry about from my shadows," I said. "Just everyone else."

I was on the verge of turning my sorrow into rage. Elvy didn't deserve that.

"I'm sorry," I said, taking a deep breath. "I just can't believe I hurt Blaz."

Jelly was still lying next to me, consoling me in the best way she could when her voice entered my mind.

"I should not have gotten him. The shadows… I thought you were in trouble. They didn't feel right," Jelly said through our bond.

"It's okay, Jelly," I thought back. *"You were trying to protect me."*

"I made things worse. Maybe I am a pup," she said, whining.

"Not a pup," I said, holding her close. *"You have the heart of a warrior, brave little dragon."*

That seemed to pacify her, and she said nothing else.

"I think I'm actually tired," I admitted, body exhausted from the power it'd wielded.

"Do you want to nap or push through until tonight?" Elvy asked, still stroking soothing rhythms through my hair.

"I'll sleep for an hour, then we'll do all the things," I said, eyes already closing.

"Sleep, beautiful. I'll be right here," he promised.

For the first time in a while, there were no nightmares of my bloody wedding or visits from The Archer. The shadows lulled me into a dark, deep sleep.

44
Finding the Unseen
FREYJA

"There you are," a familiar voice called from the door.

I was in the palace archives looking for something useful. It would be helpful if I had any idea what I was looking for, but I didn't, so here we were. I've read anything from animal migrations, the best areas to plant a variety of crops, and the most promising—the lineage of the Lord Astrals. The latter was the most interesting, but not all that helpful in learning much about Hesperia's secrets, since she was not of the bloodline.

"Do immortals have birth records?" I asked, sifting through more records.

"Not really. Nothing like what you had on Earth."

I gave him a pointed look. I never thought I'd wished for anything in the realm of bureaucracy. Birth records would have been useful, though.

"Maybe we should start them," I suggested.

"We?" he said, smirking.

He leaned down to kiss my neck, and I swatted him away.

"Don't distract me, Ander."

"Are you sure? My distractions are rather enjoyable."

I glared at him. He grinned wider.

"Fine, fine. No distractions," he conceded, sitting down next to me. "What exactly are you looking for?"

"Literally anything that could help us get the advantage on Hesperia. She had to come from somewhere."

He looked at me as if I'd gone mad, which made me want to punch things.

"What?" I asked.

"Apart from the Lord and Lady Astrals, we just don't really keep track of those things. Living as long as we do. I guess we don't think we need it."

"Then where did she come from?"

He scrunched his eyebrows together in thought, sifting through who knows how many years of history.

"I'm not sure," he said finally. "I can't recall hearing anything about her, but I wasn't alive when she was made Lady Astral."

"But someone knows," I said. "Tiergan, maybe?"

"We could ask. I'm not sure how old the male is."

"Let's go," I said, standing up. Ander stood up with me.

"Training first," he said, brows raised. "You were supposed to start an hour ago."

"Oh, hell. I never know what time it is here."

"Training first. Then we'll go talk to Tiergan. Your job is to get through your own Emerging trials. Zoe will handle Hesperia."

"You're completely daft if you think I'm not going to do every-thing in my power to help her before I go."

"I'd expect nothing less," he said, voice softer. "She needs you to come back, too."

"I don't even have magic manifesting yet," I said, my insecurity showing strongly. "Zoe was healing turtles and stuff by this point."

"I think it was Elvy who healed the turtle. Zoe healed the sea lion."

"Point missed, Ander," I said.

"Zoe had been going through the Emerging process for two years," he said, voice still calm and steady. "You've been Emerging for what? Two seconds. You're an incredible female, Freyja, but that's asking a lot of yourself."

"So we focus on what we can train now," I conceded.

"Yes, sweetheart," he said, cupping each side of my face with his warm, rugged hands. "We focus on what we can control, not on what we can't."

"Kiss me," I breathed. I wasn't even sure if I'd said the words, but he didn't hesitate, placing a tender kiss on my lips.

It was softer than normal, but it fired up my core like anytime Ander kissed me.

He pulled back, placing his forehead against mine.

"Are we good?" he asked.

It wasn't a question about our relationship. We hadn't had any formal declarations of a relationship, but I didn't feel like we needed one either. We just were. He was asking if I was okay, because if I was, then he was.

I nodded, taking his hand in mine as we headed down the winding passageways to the training room.

★★★

"Yield," Oleander said, pinning me down on the black mat beneath us.

He'd spent this training session teaching me how to use my body weight against an opponent. So far, I had been losing.

"No," I spat, but he had me locked down.

"Bridge your hips," he coached. "You can get out of this."

"I thought you wanted me to yield!" I screamed through labored breathing. Sweat poured into my eyes, but I did not concede.

"I know you better than to expect an easy defeat," he murmured in my ear.

I placed both feet firmly on the mat and thrust my hips into the air, trying to take back control of the situation.

"All you have to do is tap twice, and this will all be over," he promised.

"Forget it," I said, gritting my teeth.

"There's my girl," he said with pride in his voice. I still wanted to smack the hell out of him.

With every ounce of strength I possessed, I strengthened the bridge in my hips and rolled, finally getting him off me.

"Now use your body weight to keep my knees from bridging."

I flopped myself on top of him, but I forgot about the top half of him.

"You're supposed to cover my shoulders, too," he said, laughing.

"You're massive," I said, frustrated.

I wasn't short by mortal standards and was much taller than Zoe. Even so, there was no way I could cover all of Oleander with my body.

His eyes darkened, and he pulled me onto his hips, so that I straddled him on the floor.

"Divine," he said, kissing my neck.

He was already hard beneath me.

"Ander," I said, laughing. "We're supposed to be training."

"Training over," he said, slipping a hand into my shirt, exploring my body.

My hips ground against him without any coaxing. It was just a reflex at this point.

"Someone could come in here," I whispered, as he unzipped my leathers to get better access.

"No, they won't," he said, sending his shadows to cover the door while throwing up a shadow shield around us. "Complete privacy."

I pulled his shirt over his head and slid my hands over the ridges of muscles lining his back. How did one body contain so many? Moving my hands to his platinum hair, I gripped him tightly, bringing his mouth to my lips. He slipped his tongue inside, moving in a steady rhythm. One of his hands explored my bare body while the other ensnared my hair in his grip.

I needed him. Now.

I shoved him down to the floor and swiftly undid his pants, exposing his arousal for me. Somehow, I was already ready for him, and we'd barely done anything. His touch did that to me, though. Maybe training was my new favorite foreplay.

Positioning myself over him, I slowly inched myself onto him, reveling in the sensation of him filling me.

"*Freyja*," he said, gripping either side of my hips. His eyes closed the further down I moved.

He filled me in the way I needed, and with one final shift down, he was all mine. I groaned and began moving, needing friction between us.

"Bridge those hips, Ander," I said, smirking.

"As you wish," he said, and began meeting my pace, and I cried out in pleasure.

I bit my lips as his hands found ways to bring bliss to my aching body. All for him.

Ander's eyes moved from my lips then lower, seeming to savor where his eyes lingered. He gave himself willingly over to every need and desire I possessed for him.

In one quick movement, I was suddenly on my back with Ander never losing his rhythm. His lips moved all over my body, eliciting euphoria from me. The pressure built, and I scratched his back, nearly there.

He rose, gazing at me seriously.

"You're all I'll ever need, Freyja."

He bit my lower lip, and all the sensations brought me to oblivion, and I cried out his name.

Ander saw me through the pulses of my pleasure, drawing it out with his movements, promising me the next. My legs trembled.

He grabbed my hands and slammed them above my head, and with one more shift forward, Ander found his release in me.

We both had labored breathing, staring at each other. It was as if my very essence called to him, and there was no one else I wanted to answer.

Trailing kisses down my body, he savored me as if I were something he worshipped regularly.

Slowly, he pulled himself from me, and I moaned.

"Ander," I whispered.

I opened my eyes to survey the situation. We were both in varying states of undress, neither completely naked. There had been no time for that. My leathers were ruined until it could be cleaned, but I didn't really mind.

"Come on, sweetheart," he said smoothly, eyes kind. "Let's get cleaned up. There are extra clothes in the locker room."

I nodded, taking his outstretched hand. He swept me into his arms, carrying me into the adjoining showers.

"I can walk," I chastised.

"I know," he said, turning on the water. "I just didn't want to let you go."

45

Legends

FREYJA

"What do you want to know?" Tiergan asked, sitting across from us in his living quarters.

Ander and I had finally made it from the showers, but it was not without great effort that we left each other's arms. Even now, the warmth of his skin permeated through where our bodies touched. I leaned in as close as was socially appropriate.

"The Sublunary seem to remember things the rest of us have forgotten," Oleander said, with annoyance in his voice. I didn't think it had much to do with Tiergan, but that something was taken from him and his fellow immortals. "What do you remember about Hesperia rising to the position of Lady Astral of Algol?"

Tiergan sat back in his chair, crossing his legs. A hand was on his chin in thought, but something about it felt staged, as if he wasn't sure he wanted to say.

"I was there at the ceremony," he admitted. "It broke my heart. Shattered me."

"Why would that break your heart?" Ander asked.

He switched legs, looking down at a piece of lint that wasn't on his very leather uniform.

"Janus—the Lord Astral—and I were lovers," he said, and my heart swelled with compassion. "More than that. We'd planned to marry."

"I'm so sorry, Tiergan," I said, though the condolences felt empty compared to losing someone you loved.

"That would have been quite sensational, right? A known rebel leader marrying a Lord Astral… It made little sense, but we loved each other despite that glaring difference. Until the day Hesperia showed up."

"What happened, Tiergan?" Ander asked gently.

"Janus went from the love of my life to someone I barely recognized. He became cruel, dark—indifferent. Prior to Hesperia, he was going to meet with the other Lord and Lady Astrals to help the Sublunary become part of the realms again… give them more rights while respecting our beliefs about the stars."

"Then he just stopped?" I asked.

"Yes," he confirmed, eyes saddened. "Hesperia got her claws in him, and he was never the same. I begged him to leave her, even if he didn't want to be with me anymore. For his own sake."

"You'd never heard of her before then?" Ander asked.

"No. When I realized how corrupt she truly was, I looked into her. I found no one who knew her. The oddest thing was no one seemed to care that she seemed to rise from the shadows themselves. From nothing. All except the Sublunary. It was no coincidence that we gathered to Algol in anticipation of something happening, Oleander. No one could tell me what her magic was. I even broke into the archives in Sirius after they married… the Algol court was in a broken state by that point."

"You broke in because the Lord and Lady Astrals have to register their magic in Sirius," Ander confirmed.

Zoe's own magical registration had been interrupted while they had been on Sirius.

"Exactly, but there was nothing of note. Only chaos."

Oleander and I looked at each other, and we knew all too well that those records could be manipulated. Zoe had planned as much during their visit, but she'd never gotten the chance.

"All I know is that Janus was a loving, compassionate immortal. Then he was unrecognizably ruthless the more he was with her."

"But he helped my mother escape?" Ander questioned.

"It's odd, isn't it? I even helped him do it. Your mother was lovely, Oleander. I guess the idea of executing unborn children brought back some sense of decency briefly. He looked awful, tired. Physically ill. There were a million words said between us during that one moment, but the only words he got out were, 'It was always you, Tiergan.'"

Oleander had gone quiet, and I could sense the questions he wanted to ask Tiergan. He kept silent, though.

Tiergan adjusted in his seat once more. "I don't know what her magic is, Oleander, Freyja. But I know that it is powerful. Strong enough to make someone turn into the worst of themselves. I'm sorry I can't be of more help."

"You said he looked unwell? Like he was sick?" I asked, remembering the way Hesperia's legion had looked when I'd been trapped in the vortex created by Abel.

"Yes, like he had a horrible fever," he agreed, eyes in a memory we couldn't see.

"Thank you," I said. "Everything helps right now. She didn't come from thin air. We'll figure it out."

He stood, leading us to the door. Apparently, he was done talking about this, and I didn't blame him.

"Thank you, Tiergan," Ander said, going out the door first.

I paused, turning back to the rebel leader. I threw my arms around his neck, ignoring the tickle of his mustache.

"I am so sorry that you lost Janus," I whispered.

He grunted something I couldn't quite make out, and squeezed me hard.

When he pulled back, he caught my gaze and turned a bit serious.

"Don't be sorry. But do me a favor and never let fear keep you from loving Oleander fully. Real love is everlasting, Freyja, but life is fragile. Especially in these times. You have a second chance. Use it."

My eyes silvered at his words.

"I promise."

He seemed satisfied that I took his words seriously and let me go.

"Can you do me a favor as well?" I asked, and he raised an eyebrow. "Go easier on Oleander. He's a good male."

He paused, considering my request. "So he is. It was just too painful for so long. Every time I saw him, I was reminded of the last words Janus ever spoke to me. I don't guess that was entirely fair to Oleander."

"He's appreciative of your alliance and far more understanding than he's given credit for," I said, and he bowed slightly.

I waved a last goodbye before joining Oleander outside.

"Were you listening?"

"He's got a very distinct voice. I could hear it miles away," he said, lacing his fingers through mine. "I didn't realize how kind he could be, though. But I'm glad to know why he's always been difficult with me."

"Not only do you remind him of those last moments, but the last Astrals of Algol screwed him over in the worst way possible. The love of his life chose someone else."

"It makes sense now," he admitted.

"It doesn't give him license to be mean to you, though," I said, squeezing his hand, but my thoughts turned to everything else Tiergan had told us. "I have a feeling her magic did something to Janus to make him like that."

"We need to tell Zoe," he said, pulling out his iris.

His magic quickly charged his iris. He told her everything Tiergan had, and I mentioned my observation of the similarity between Janus looking ill and those that she executed on the battlefield. The rainbows disappeared to find their mark, and I longed to go with them to see my sister.

"What are the chances I'll see Zo before I leave for the trials?"

"I have no idea. Everything is unpredictable right now."

I sighed, knowing that to be true, and I took his hand back in mine.

"Why didn't you ask Tiergan more questions about your mother?" I asked gently.

He pressed his lips tightly together. "Because it would make her too real. It's been easy to keep myself numb to it... but to know she suffered at the hands of Hesperia... Knowing I did what I did to keep my immortals safe. I fear my mother would be ashamed of me. I just can't deal with it right now."

I wrapped him tightly in my arms, and he embraced me fully. I wanted to tell him that none of his thoughts were true, but it would take more than me saying it for him to believe it.

"Let's go get some food, sweetheart. That always seems to make you feel a little better."

He wasn't wrong, but I wasn't the one who needed to feel better. He did, but I followed him anyway.

We walked in silence back to his palace, both lost in our own thoughts. I focused on the smell of the pine trees and the feel of the ice biting my nose, making my cheeks flush red. I relished the feel of everything, and I wasn't sure I'd ever take these sensations for granted again. Oleander's warm hand contrasted with the frigid air around me, and I didn't even notice how cold it truly was with how warm my core pumped when I was around his very energy. My home.

46

The Luminaries

ZOE

We were no closer to finding Hesperia's origin than when Freyja and Oleander had sent us the message about Tiergan's story a week ago. My heart broke for him. How many mortals and immortals have suffered at the hands of this miserable female?

"Let's face it, we're not going to find anything in the Musterion archives. Not about her," Blaz said, standing from the table as Finnian and Zadie joined the rest of us from the Hall of Memories.

"Anything?" I asked.

"No," Finn answered. "They revealed nothing about her history, but I think I made some headway on The Archer's bow."

"Well, that's something, at least," I said, grateful.

"We wouldn't have to waste resources on the bow if your father would just tell us what we needed to do," Delmira said, stabbing one of her knives into the table.

Clodovea looked up from her stack of papers to glare at Delm, but she didn't bother to look her way. Imelda placed a loving arm on Clove to help settle her. We were all stressed and on edge. Hesperia could try anything at anytime. Anyone would be exhausted trying to anticipate her moves.

"I don't think it would work if he did," I admitted. "The user has to earn the bow to wield it."

"I think you're right, Zo. In part. The archer must be of Algol with all four elements infused into the bow."

"The limbs from Arcturus, the grip from Rigil… something is in Canopus," Elvy said, writing the list down on parchment.

"The string, I'd guess," Blaz said. "Those are the three main parts."

"That accounts for three of the elements: fire, ground, and air," I said. "What about water and spirit?"

"The wielder is the spirit element," Zadie said, and Finn nodded, coming to the same conclusion.

"Water… we haven't quite worked out yet," Finn admitted.

"Wait. Didn't the pieces fly apart when we tried to put the grip and limbs together?" I asked, a theory coming together.

"Yeah, they did," Blaz answered.

"What if the water element sealed it all together?" I asked. "Can water magic do that?"

"Yes," Elvy confirmed. "The magic itself may be all that is required to make it whole."

"I'll feel a little better once we have the bow," Imelda said, lacing her fingers through Clodovea's.

"Getting the string is going to be the most difficult one," Clove said. "We need to speak with Aura."

"We'll be asking her to betray those she is sworn to protect," Elvy said. "We will not force her to give us information. The immortals there are not responsible for Abel or Hesperia."

They all nodded, though I felt confident she would help after her very public display against Abel. In fact, I had been doing regular healings on her since I'd been back. It was taking its toll on me emotionally, but it didn't last too long. I was slowly healing some of the emotional damage she had experienced at the hands of her abuser. It was taking much longer than her physical injuries.

"With the realms united again, do you think her power will weaken?" Delmira asked, pulling me from my thoughts. "We haven't heard anymore from King Aldrich or Queen Farron."

"They await word from us," Elvy said. "But they cannot leave. None of them. Even the High Astral Legion. They are centered on Sirius. If the courts should fail, they are the last line of defense to the mortal realm."

Elvy pulled his hair back into a hair tie, a new sign that he was trying to focus.

"I don't know… she doesn't seem weakened at all. Even when Algol was dying. And according to Zadie, she should weaken when she absorbs the star seeds, so maybe she hasn't started," I pointed out. "I don't know what it is, but there's something we're missing in all of this."

My gift of discernment swelled within my stomach. I knew I was right, but I couldn't get the magic to focus enough to let me *see* what we were truly up against. Maybe fate didn't want to give me too much of an advantage.

"Lay it all out, Zo. Talk it out, and let's see the bigger picture," Elvy said, squeezing my hand reassuringly.

I embodied my best Hercule Poirot and tried to fit the evidence together. Knowledge was power, and we had a heap.

I paced around the room and began speaking in a free flow.

"We know Hesperia has a hidden magic, and that she wants me for some purpose. In particular, she wants me in my shadow form.

We think that might be to help her tether to a new mortal plane, but we aren't really sure. In fact, I don't think that's her endgame, though maybe a means to an end. Given what Tiergan witnessed in Janus's change of behavior, her subjects she slaughtered when she took Freyja, and the immortals I killed during the Vega attack… the one common factor is they all are of Algol—shadow magic. Even my mother's spirit was technically of Algol when Hesperia…" I trailed off, not wanting to be reminded of her fate.

Elvy brushed my hand gently in encouragement, and I refocused.

I paused, thinking back to the night I'd sliced those poor souls into ribbons. They'd given a warning.

"There was a black mist during the attack on Vega right after I killed those immortals. Elvy, do you remember what I said? Did I mention Algol?"

He swallowed, eyes piercing right through me. "Yes, and that was the first time…," he trailed off, switching to communicating through the bond.

"That was the first time my eyes went dark for your shadows."

"She saw us. The mist was Hesperia, or some connection to her, anyway. That's where she learned Algol was linked to me. She had been biding her time all those months. But why?"

"Wanna clue us in?" Delmira asked, pulling me from our conversation.

"Hesperia's gift," I began. "I think I know what it is."

"What, Zo?" Blaz asked, rising from his seat.

My eyes hadn't left Elvy's as the unsettling realization fell on me.

"The shadows. She controls the shadows," I said, voice full of righteous fear. "That's why she wants me to go dark. Not because of who my shadows would make me become, but who she would force me to be. And if she controls me..."

Elvy held me close.

Everyone was silent, unsure of what to say.

"Where did this female come from?" Blaz asked, breaking the silence.

"There's no history on her… she just popped into existence. There's nothing in the Musterion archives, the Hall of Memories, or the records in Sirius. Why wouldn't there be? I know immortals don't keep tedious records, but someone somewhere would know about her."

"Maybe she isn't immortal," Elvy said, brows furrowed.

"She has the mark," Blaz said.

"Which can be faked," Delmira said, sitting up in her chair.

"Or maybe half-immortal?" Finn asked. "I mean, Zoe, even you are a little different from most immortals as a direct descendant of The Archer."

"So, she's one of the celestial spawns?" Blaz asked.

"Let's say she is. What does that mean?" I questioned.

"Makes sense how she knew about the arrow in the first place," Zadie offered.

"It means she's stronger than we initially thought," Clodovea added.

"Even more than all that," I said, voice shaking. "We don't know her true motivation—we still don't know who the villain is in her story."

"It seems to be you," Delmira said, stating the obvious.

"Which doesn't make any sense," I said, anger growing.

"Which means this goes much deeper than wanting to be a god," Finn said. "She could have something to prove and nothing to lose."

"I'll see if I can get The Archer to tell me anything," I offered. "If he won't, maybe Phoebe or June will have sympathy."

"Nova?" Elvy asked.

I shook my head. "No, I don't think Nova will intervene, but she is on our side."

Elvy paced around the map in the center of the room, searching for answers that weren't there.

"Let's focus on what we have control over. Blaz, go get Aura," Elvy said. "We need a better plan than the one we have."

Blaz nodded, leaving.

I sat back down in my chair from which I'd risen without even realizing it. Jelly placed her head on my lap for me to scratch her ears, and I tried to focus on the feel of her fur. This whole situation was frustrating. Why was it always up to someone else to clean up the celestial messes? Even in Greek mythology or with any gods, their children often suffered for the actions of their divine parents. Personally, I think we should form a club and have a pity party or start a riot. I could go for either at this point.

Everyone chatted around me, and prior to my Emergence, the noise frequencies would have sent me into a panic attack by now. Delmira was yelling at Finn about something or nothing, probably. Finn stormed off towards Zadie. Delm had an anger in her… and it had only grown since I'd known her. Something was going on. She was executing her duties well, but maybe there was something else we could do to support her.

Imelda and Clodovea were lost in each other, tuning the rest of us out. The pendants I'd gifted them flashed on their wrists, and guilt washed through me at keeping them apart for as long as we have in our collection of the bow. I knew neither would truly complain, committed in their duties to the immortals of Vega.

"And to you, Zoe," Elvy said through our flame.

He sat down next to me, from where he'd been conversing with Finn and Zadie. They were huddled over some more papers, as if they were hoarding some secret.

"They're up to something," he said, tucking one of my stray hairs behind my ear.

I leaned into him, catching his storm-gray eyes.

"He wouldn't tell you?"

"No," he said, shaking his head. *"He has his reasons, and I trust him."*

"I do, too," I confirmed.

Elvy wrapped a muscled arm around my frame and petted Jelly's other ear. If dogs could smile, Jelly was.

Moments later, Blaz walked in with Aura's timid frame, but the strength was there. She was the epitome of resilient. Her affect was a little brighter after the healings I'd done, but we still had a long way to go. But I'd face her trauma with her any day. No one should walk that journey alone. I smiled at her discreetly. I was certainly no Emma, but I hoped I was helping.

"Blaz said you needed my help?" she asked, sitting beside him and returning my smile.

"Yes, we do, Aura," Elvy said. "We need to get into Canopus without being detected."

"For what purpose?" she asked, holding her pregnant belly.

"There's something we need to collect to win this war against Hesperia," I said. "We will lose if we don't."

"You're not there to start a war?" she confirmed.

"The war has already begun," Elvy disagreed. "But no, our goal for this visit is to get in and get out without anyone knowing we were there. We can face Hesperia another day."

She nodded in thought.

"Do you know where you need to go within Canopus?"

"I won't know until I get there," I said. "My gift will lead me to it."

"Tiergan gave us coordinates to a transport zone that is out of the way. We just need help navigating from there," Blaz said.

"Let me see," she said, holding out her hand, and Elvy gave her the parchment.

"Good, this is beyond the wards of the main city. Abel won't feel you arrive," she confirmed. "You know the city is essentially a scattered floating mass in the sky, right?"

"We know," Blaz confirmed, as the emissary to air. "I've only been on the one that holds the city center."

"The only way to get from each section is to fly," she said.

"What about the immortals who aren't Shadowed?" I asked.

"They have to ask someone who is," she said, frustrated. "I've been pushing to have bridges built, but Abel has stopped me every step of the way."

"We'll make it happen with you… when all of this is over," Blaz said, with everyone nodding their heads at him. We'd all agreed to help her reclaim her rightful place in Canopus, and we would honor that.

"Do you know of any older parts of Canopus?" I asked, grasping for some location or hope that we could avoid the city center.

"The capital city is Canopus' oldest section that I know of."

"Of course," I mumbled, but maybe my gift would lead us far, far away from there when we arrived.

"Is there anyway to navigate without being on the streets?" Clodovea asked.

"The waterways underneath downtown would be your best bet, given your gifts," Aura suggested. "And don't wear your usual leathers, of course. Wear white or light blue."

"They connect to everywhere in the city?" Finn asked.

"Yes, the floating landmasses are their own ecosystems in the sky. We have small rivers and lakes, but a lot of our waterways for our immortals come from the rain we collect."

Finnian opened his mouth to probably ask quite detailed questions about all of their systems, but Delmira stopped him.

"Now's not the time, Finn."

"Right," he agreed. "Can we discuss this more later, Aura?"

"Sure," she said, yawning. "I'm sorry. I've been so tired since…," she said, waving to her tiny bump.

"Thank you for your help," Elvy said, smiling. "Go rest."

"Good luck," she said, standing. "Not everyone agrees with Abel. Remember that."

"We will," I promised. I didn't plan on losing any lives on this mission. Enough blood had already been spilled.

Ever the gentleman, Blaz left with Aura on his arm.

I turned to find Delmira shooting daggers at them.

"What gives, Delm?" I asked, moving closer to her and throwing up a shield to give us some privacy. Elvy looked at me curiously, but I shook my head for him to stay put. He nodded and resumed his conversation with Finn and Zadie.

"Nothing."

"Liar."

She glared at me, but said nothing else.

"Look, you don't have to tell me if you don't want to. I just want to help. You seem upset a lot lately. Is Musterion too much?"

"No, everything in Musterion is fine. My duty is the only thing that makes sense to me anymore."

"I'm here if you want to talk," I offered.

I sat with her in silence as she seemed to wage war within herself on whether to confide in me or not.

"No one can hear?"

"Nope. I've got a shield up."

"Blaz and I… it's complicated."

"Let's see if we can make it less complicated together."

"We've been—I don't even know what to call it," she said vaguely. "I wanted to start having sex, but he wants more than that."

"Kind of wondered if that would ever happen between you two," I said, laughing softly at how blunt she was being.

"That's the thing… we've only kissed. I don't know. Maybe war heightens the pheromones or something."

"So, is it not good or something?" I asked, trying to figure out what was going on with her.

"No. He knows what he's doing," she admitted.

"Which seems to piss you off?"

"No… what pisses me off is Blaz trying to complicate it by expressing his feelings."

"Oh…" I trailed off. "And you don't feel that way?"

"It's not that," she said, taking a deep breath. "You don't go declaring feelings in the middle of a war when you feel pressured to because of the doom of the world and all that."

"What if he really feels that way, though?"

"He doesn't."

"Why?"

"Because he's Blaz!" she said, as if that point weren't obvious.

"Maybe he's ready to settle down," I suggested. "He's a good male."

"I'm too busy running Musterion to figure this all out right now."

"So is it that you're too busy, or that he expressed how he feels about you in the middle of a war?"

She glared at me, making me feel small in the way only Delmira can.

"Both."

"I do understand, Delm. I didn't tell Elvy that I loved him until we made it back from Algol the first time. I had my reasons, but I hate knowing that something could have happened to me, and I'd never taken a moment to just tell him how I felt. Love isn't always on our time, you know? Sometimes, we just have to put our heart all out there and trust someone with that. Then you'll know either way. Don't let fear of burning stop you from something great," I said, glancing at Elvy—the greatest part of me.

"It's more than that. I'm not sure I'm good enough—healed enough. I feel broken."

I wrapped my arms around her, understanding all too well how that feels, even though I didn't know her exact story.

"I can't tell you what to do, Delm. But maybe digging deep into your courage is exactly what you're supposed to do."

"We could all die," she said, with a hint of fear in her eyes.

"Dying is easy… inevitable. Even for us," I whispered. "Loving someone… that's what makes dying terrifying."

"When did you get so philosophical?" she asked, rolling her eyes.

"I've got daddy issues for days," I said, shrugging.

She laughed with me, and the tension seemed to fall from her shoulders.

"Only you know the answer to what you should do, but Delmira, you have never let fear be your master. Why start now?"

"I hate you," she said.

"I love you, too," I said, dropping the shield.

"Thanks, Zoe."

"Anytime," I said, rising from the chair. "Go find him."

She rolled her eyes at me again, but left through the door.

Elvy came up behind me, wrapping his arms around me and kissing my neck.

"Is Delm okay?"

"She will be," I said, arching my back to him. "Figure out what Finn and Zadie are up to?"

"Nope," he murmured next to my ear, sending chills down my spine. "He said it was a matter of security that I do not know, so I didn't press him."

It was hard to miss that we were suddenly alone with everyone dispersed on their missions. Even Jelly had gone off somewhere.

He slowly unbuttoned my casual shirt while continuing to kiss up and down my neck, biting and teasing.

"Can anyone see us?" I asked through the bond, as I stared through the glass wall at the ocean.

"Hell no," he answered, unclasping my bra from the front.

His hands explored my bare body, sending goosebumps across my skin. Flipping me around, he lifted my hands above my head and placed my fingers around a wooden beam.

"Hold on to that," he instructed. "No moving."

I nodded, barely breathing.

Elvy kneeled in front of me, slipping my pants off. I was completely exposed to him, and I'd never felt sexier than I did under his admiring gaze.

"You're my gravity—my sun in the eternal night," he said, kneeling back down. My heart warmed as I was reminded that he used to feel like my personal sun when everything else felt dark.

He unsheathed his teeth, biting the thin fabric of my panties, pulling them down my leg, past my knees, and down to my ankles. *Oh.*

"I love being on my knees for you, Zoe," he murmured, before making me gasp with his mouth. "Only you."

It took every strand of willpower I could muster to not fist my fingers through his curls, but I held onto the wooden beam for dear life as Elvy brought me into oblivion with his tongue. I needed more. Always more with him.

"I've got you, starlight," he said, lifting my body into his powerful arms and pressing my back against the cool glass. He slid into me with one dominant shift forward, filling me in only the way my flame could.

He gently placed my shaking arms around his neck and tilted my chin to look into his eyes—his black eyes. The darkness screamed within me to meet its mate, and I embraced it.

"Control, Zoe," he said, still sounding like my Elvy.

His brows furrowed as he continued to move, and I clawed my nails into his back. He blinked a few times, returning his storm-gray eyes to me. My own darkness settled, but somehow seemed a little miffed at the denial.

"I love you. So much," he said, laying me against the table so he could see more of my body. His eyes gazed over me hungrily.

"I will always find you, Elvy," I whispered, suddenly feeling as though he was slipping away from me.

He guided me through my fear, kissing away every worry. He was mine, and I was his. Endlessly.

47

Vulnerability
DELMIRA

Part of me wanted to turn right back around and tell Zoe that she'd lost her mind, but the part of me that was both defiant and curious kept pressing on to find Blaz.

He was coming from our guest quarters, head bowed in such deep thought that he almost passed me until I was right on him.

"Delm?" he asked, startled. "Is everything okay?"

His eyes scanned behind me for danger, and I suddenly lost every bit of my nerve.

"Sorry," I said, turning around to walk away from him yet again, but he grabbed my arm.

"Why did you come find me?" he asked, eyes curious.

The words caught in my throat. I did not know what to say.

"Come with me," he said, lacing his fingers through mine, and my legs followed him without my brain giving them permission.

He led me into the massive ballroom that hadn't seen a party in ages. I felt even more exposed in here as the moon shone brightly down upon us.

"What are you doing?" I asked, watching him move to the corner that held the large gramophone.

A beautiful melody filled the empty room, and he held out his hand in invitation.

"What are you doing?" I repeated myself.

"Asking you to dance," he said, raising his eyebrow as if he wasn't sure my brain was entirely functioning.

"Why?" I asked, taking his hand against my better judgment.

"Because when we talk, we argue. And I'm tired of fighting with you."

Fair point.

Blaz was a graceful dancer, just like he was when he was fighting. It was easy to follow him, and I found myself lost in the warmth of his brown eyes.

"Were you looking for me?" he asked, breath on my ear.

A shiver coursed through my frame at his closeness.

Zoe's question flashed through me. Would I let fear become my master?

"I was," I admitted.

"You found me," he said, twirling me around.

My cheeks flushed with embarrassment, but he kept our bodies moving around the dance floor.

"I'm going to say some things, and I just want you to listen," I said, voice shakier than I wanted, but I kept going.

He nodded, slowing us into a comfortable sway as the music changed.

"I'm afraid of losing you as my best friend if things don't work out… but even more than that… I'm not sure I'm capable of giving you what you want, assuming you want something more with me."

I swallowed.

"And that has everything to do with me, and nothing to do with you."

I averted my gaze to somewhere behind him as he pulled me closer so that my head fit snugly into the space between his chest and shoulder.

"You're not the only one who wears a mask, Delm," he said, kissing the top of my lilac hair.

I'd grown to know that Blaz often used humor to deflect. Because I knew him. Really knew him.

"I want you to kiss me," I mumbled.

He cupped my cheek in his hand, making me meet his eyes.

"I don't want you to do anything you don't want to do," Blaz said, pausing. "I'll take whatever you're willing to give. If you just want to have sex, then I'll do it. As often and as much as you'd like."

He was sincere. Blaz would be whoever I needed him to be. He always morphed into what the universe needed from him, but who did he need? What did he crave in life? Who was there to let Blaz be his authentic self?

I shook my head. "I don't want that."

"Tell me what you want, Delm," he pleaded, holding my hands in his firm grip against his chest.

"I just want you for you," I said, pausing for a breath. "But I can't promise anything. I just don't know what I'm capable of."

"Then I'm yours. In whatever way you will have me," he said, leaning in to kiss me with unabashed passion.

I leaped into his arms, wrapping my legs around his waist, needing to feel as close to him as possible. I slid my tongue into his, sucking on his bottom lip. His body responded to me, and I ground myself against him. Neither of us could hide what we wanted from the other any longer. I wanted this. More than that—I needed him. The one who knew me—could see me—for all that I was.

I didn't know what the future held, but I refused to be afraid. We'd figure out the rest.

"Let's go to my room," I said, breathing heavily.

"Mine is closer," he argued.

"I have fun things."

His eyes dilated even more, and he didn't have to be told twice.

We dodged any prying eyes on the way to my room, and I quickly locked the door behind me. I turned around to find him leaning against my bed, watching my every move.

"Is there anything you don't like?" I asked, moving towards him.

"Haven't found anything so far," he said, unbuttoning his shirt, exposing his olive skin. He really was beautiful.

"And you're not going to judge me?"

"Oh, no, Delm. I'm more than happy to delve into your fantasies."

"Are you on a tonic?" I asked, even though I was on one, anyway. No surprise babies for me.

He nodded, and I moved to the locked cabinet and motioned for him to join me. I held my breath as he took it all in, fearing he'd be scared off. Of course, he wasn't.

"Do you have a favorite?" he asked, wrapping his arms around me and kissing my neck.

There was a variety of textures and 'toys' in front of us. A collection of restraints that were leather, metal, and velcro hung above a box with drawers with an assortment of vibrators, and I pulled out my favorite and grabbed my violet leather cuffs.

He smirked, holding out his hand for the vibrator, and I raised an eyebrow.

"This doesn't hurt your masculinity?"

"I'm a secure male, Delm," he said, voice serious. "Show me what you like."

I handed him the toy and locked eyes with him as I unzipped my leathers, exposing my lilac bra and panties. I leaned against the side of the bed and motioned for him to come to me with my pointer finger.

He moved forward and kneeled in front of me, eyes devouring every inch of my body.

I knew I was sexy, and he made my core light up.

"Do you have a safe word, or does 'no' work?" he asked, jaws clenched, as if he was ready to pounce.

"You wouldn't be in this position if I didn't trust you... or think I could take you," I said, biting my lip.

"I need to hear it," he said seriously.

"No will work," I agreed. "Now, take those and attach them to the bedposts," I said, motioning to the leather cuffs.

He expertly and quickly locked my wrists in the restraints and stood up, examining his work. His arousal was evident against his leathers, and my legs squirmed in need.

"Do you do blindfolds?" he asked, eyes darkening.

I grinned and nodded my head toward the cabinet.

He retrieved a lilac satin mask, slipping it over my eyes and pulling my lips to his.

"You are so beautiful. You bring me to my knees, Delm. Always have."

He trailed his lips down my neck, unclasping my bra from the front, baring my skin to him. Goosebumps flooded my skin with the sudden breeze, and if I were being honest, being under his gaze did more to me than the breeze, even though I couldn't see him.

His mouth moved to my neck then lower, and the warmth sent a shudder through me. With his other hand, he skirted my panties out of the way, using his fingers to bring out sounds of pleasure from my lips. He quickly found out just how much I wanted this—wanted him.

"Delm," he breathed, moving his mouth lower to my apex. He swiftly ripped my underwear off—so long, lilac thong.

Not being able to see him sent a thrill through me every time he touched my body. The hum of the vibrator started, and he held it against the most sensitive part of me as he used his other hand to elicit euphoria from my body.

I cried out, squeezing my thighs together, trying to brace against something. I pulled on the cuffs as the pressure built, and I felt like I was about to explode.

"Blaz!" I cried as he continued his steady, unforgiving pace.

"Come for me, Delm," he said, biting down on my thigh, and I screamed in elation and ground against his fingers as the ebbs of my bliss came in waves.

"More," I said. "I've thought about this for so long."

"I've got you," he promised, and I heard him slip out of his uniform.

The warmth of his full arousal pressed against me, and I internally begged to be filled by him.

"Ready?" he asked.

I nodded.

"Let me hear it, Delmira."

"Yes. All of you," I panted, and he spread my legs open from where I'd clenched them in my need for him.

He shifted into me, inch by inch, stretching me to take all of him. *Oh.*

I heard the vibrator start up again.

Blaz took his time adjusting himself so that he filled me so completely that I thought I might lose myself in the feeling of him. He moved the vibrator against my apex again. He groaned, and I needed to feel him.

"Take the cuffs off," I said, breath labored.

He unbuckled them, but never stopped his rhythm. I removed the blindfold so I could take all of him in.

His eyes found mine, then moved down to my body as he continued to bring me to the edge of ecstasy again.

I shouted out as the sensations shoved me right off the edge, and he swallowed my cries with his lips.

I wrapped my arms around his neck, and he tossed the vibrator to the side as he lifted me in the air so I was now on top of him. He moved his hands up my needy body as I took him all the way in, meeting his pace in perfect harmony.

"I'm going to come," he grunted, and I was determined to follow him.

"Hold on," I said, gripping my hand on his ripped abdomen, as pleasure built up in me again.

"Delm," he said, as I felt him fighting for control.

We both let go at the same time, and I moaned as he emptied his desire within me.

Legs too weak to function, I collapsed onto his broad chest, and he wrapped his arms around me.

"That's what we've been missing out on?" he asked, laughing, and I joined in with him.

Any trace of fear was gone. I didn't know how long that would last, but right now I'd never felt closer to or safer with another soul.

48

Discernment of Dread

ZOE

Elvy, Jelly, and I snuggled together in our bed in Vega. The stars winked at us through the skylight, and the fire provided a calming ambiance.

"The Archer won't respond?" he asked, twirling a strand of my hair aimlessly.

"No. He hasn't," I said, voice heavy with fatigue—dread. "No word from June or Phoebe either."

I was tired from making decisions and analyzing an uncertain future. I just wanted to pretend that I was living my happy ending.

"What do we do, Elvy?" I asked. "The other courts don't know about your death magic. I hate lying to Oleander and Freyja. It was hard enough to keep Musterion from them as long as we did."

"I know," he agreed. "Perhaps we should tell them. Just in case."

"It feels like a betrayal to keep it from them any longer. Now that we know the true risks."

Jelly nuzzled in closer to us, feeling both of our distress.

"Then we tell them," he conceded.

"When?"

"After Canopus. Let's not add to the stress of the mission."

He pulled me closer, kissing the top of my dark curls.

✦✦✦

"Can you *see* anything?" Blaz asked.

I shook my head in frustration.

"No, I can only tell you that we have to go to Canopus and there's a sense of… grief," I admitted. "I can't *see* what's going to happen. The Archer never answered me. June and Phoebe were nowhere to be found, either. I assume they are under the direction of The Archer. Whatever is supposed to happen, he doesn't want anyone to interfere."

"That blows," Blaz said, and Elvy squeezed my hand again. He knew how disappointed I was that my father abandoned me when I thought we were getting closer.

"Hesperia could collect what she needs from the other courts any day. We know where she is now, so we must act," Clodovea said.

Elvy looked at me with a raised brow, waiting for my confirmation. We were in this together, no matter the outcome.

I nodded, but in my heart, I screamed a resounding no. The grief I felt was so overwhelming, I had to fight the tears that threatened to come to my eyes, yet the call to go to Canopus was too strong to ignore. My chest ached with sorrow I didn't understand and prayed I never would. I felt like I was leading someone to certain death. I looked into each of the Luminaries' eyes, loving each of the immortals that were my family now. The only truth I could hold on to now was that Freyja would live.

She was only a week from the trials, and she would prevail. That had been my most recent message to her through the iris. *"Find the strength to live."*

She'd sent back a snappy comment that I had better be there to greet her when she got back. There was nothing I wanted more than the truth.

"Check your weapons. Find your center. We leave in five," Elvy said, jaw clenched.

I counted the hilts of the four knives strapped across my Shadowed uniform. I decided not to take the bow due to the difficulty of concealing it. This was a stealth mission, not a battle. We all wore packs that contained more appropriate attire for the Court of Canopus once we emerged from the waterways below the surface. None of us wanted to be without our fighting leathers, though.

There was no hiding Jelly. A glamor could only last so long, but we would try to conceal her for as long as we could. She was going to ride in my pack as much as possible, but she would likely eventually be spotted. She was too well-known. Too different. Yet, it was essential that she come along.

I flared both of my magics to life, testing their well of power. It was nearly infinite. Tethering Algol to me had its perks. I was surprised Zadie hadn't argued for me to stay behind, but she hadn't. I guess she had come to learn that I would not risk it if I didn't have to. Yet a secret part of me also knew I'd risk it all—if it was for those I loved.

My love for Elvy was reckless. I had no shame in that.

Clodovea embraced Imelda in a passionate goodbye, and I hoped beyond hope that I was not leading Clove to her death. Delmira and Blaz seemed to be in a heated discussion, and I could spot a lover's quarrel when I saw one. I quickly averted my eyes, letting them keep their secret between themselves.

"Ready?" Elvy asked through our flame.

He tilted my chin so that I could see his gray eyes. There was only love there. No fear. An unyielding faith in me. In us.

"I'm scared," I admitted.

He placed a gentle kiss on my lips, steadying my center. Once we crossed into the cosmos, I didn't have time to be afraid. Fear got me killed.

"One moment at a time, Zo. We'll face them as they come."

"Together."

"Endlessly."

"It's time," Elvy said aloud.

The resounding pause seemed to permeate through my very bones. My soul mourned what was to come. I just didn't know who my spirit already knew to grieve. At least Freyja was safe with Oleander. Two fewer to worry about in this moment.

I wove Elvy's fingers through mine as we lifted off into the cosmos.

***

I'd expected sewage and a rancid smell underneath the city center of Canopus, but the water was relatively clean with whatever filtration system they used. My gift lit up the moment we landed outside the city wards. Much to all of our dismay, the path of light led straight to the main building in the heart of Canopus. Aura informed us it was the oldest building that she knew of, and it functioned similarly to our Hall of Memories, which sent a chill through my bones. I loathed the Hall of Memories and its lifeless silence.

"With any luck, there will be an access to the building under here," Blaz mused.

None of us sloshed through the water as it parted with our footfalls, keeping our feet dry.

"I don't believe in luck," Clodovea said.

"How morbid of you, Clove," Elvy said to my right. Jelly trotted on my left.

The tunnels were large enough to fit three of us comfortably across.

I kept silent, calm in my storm. The discernment raged inside me, demanding to be felt. Yet the song of fate… of destiny propelled my feet forward. One foot in front of the other. I—we—had to keep pressing on, but I couldn't ignore the sinking feeling that I was leading the ones I cared about to their execution.

"We know what we signed up for, flame," Elvy said, tracing soothing circles on the back of my hand.

"That does not assuage the guilt I feel," I argued.

"The stars set our paths long before your existence, Zoe. If we must die to save the star realms, then we shall. But you must live. That is your fate."

I didn't argue with him because I felt the truth of his words. No, my fate would be far worse than death. It would be to watch them all die should I fail.

"We're getting close," I murmured, as the searing pain in my marked arm lit up. I grew tired of the stars and their suffering.

A few hundred yards later, we stood before a moonstone door that was oddly out of place against the dark walls of the waterway.

The sigil of the air element was engraved into the stone, and the pulse of fate pounded behind the door.

"This is it," I confirmed, but my body was frozen. I didn't want to move forward, but I did anyway.

"Here," Elvy said, handing me the pendant infused with the air element.

I stilled my trembling hands and took the pendant from him, placing it against the mark on the moonstone door. The stone rolled away with a groan, as if it were angered at being awakened after so many years of slumber.

We all shared glances with each other, confirming that we all had each other's backs.

One foot in front of the other. I lived moment by moment, not thinking of the past or what awaited in the future. Right now was all I could handle.

I plunged through the darkness with my family behind me.

***

We eventually emerged into a spacious cavern, much like the first cave system we found in Rigil. This one had been more of a winding, confusing tunnel system, but my gift kept our course true.

The ebb of energy flowing from the remaining piece of the bow permeated my soul. I steadied my racing heart, feet heavy. I felt like I was in a nightmare, with part of my essence racing towards where it needed to go, but my body stayed behind.

"Ever forward," I whispered, finding myself standing over the mark of Algol.

Jelly sat on the sigil for fire and nodded her head low when I caught her eye, but she remained silent. Elvy stood above water, jaw flexing with tension. We all knew this had gone too easily—too well. Blaz stood over Canopus with the air pendant, and Imelda stood resolute over Rigil with Sierra's ring.

I didn't fear the pain that would inevitably come when I sliced my hand. The torture that would burn my arm alive seemed insignificant to the dread I felt coming. How cruel of the stars to gift me with sight, only to obscure the details. The desire to rip this feeling from my core was almost too much to bear, but bear I must.

"Be ready," I said, unsheathing one of my blades to slice the skin of my palm.

Starlight flooded through the stone as it had the last two times, following the payment of my blood. Imelda placed the Rigil ring on the sigil, and I let my blood fall, binding my soul to the ancient magic here. The agony shot through my arm, making it so heavy I could barely lift it. The starlight wrapped around my arm, searing my flesh along the way.

I moved to Elvy next. My eyes found his, and I tore through my palm again, letting the blood magic serve its purpose. There was only love in his gray eyes. My calm in any storm. My center that eternally holds.

"I'm with you. To whatever future," he reassured through the bond.

I nodded in too much pain to respond with words.

Jelly shifted into her true simargl form, igniting flames on the starlight stone.

"I will protect you," she said in that angelic voice of hers that still sounded young to me.

Blinking away the tears, I bent my head back to her as the starlight consumed my arm, creating a new mark of the cosmos.

One more, Eferhild. One more.

I shifted my feet before Imelda, and she placed the air-infused pendant on the sigil, and I let my blood feed the magic here. She had become my sister, and I loved her fiercely.

My arm was painful dead weight, but I pressed on, hovering over the last sigil in the center of the room—Algol.

Instead of cursing my father, I called upon his strength. "Be with me."

I sliced my hand one last time, letting the blood magic flood my body. The stone bit my knees as I fell to the cavern floor, and I gripped my arm, trying to find some solace in the movement. None came. Tears filled my eyes, but I clung to the hope that this would end soon. I was briefly aware that the stone floor shifted upward, revealing the string of the bow. At least it hadn't been for nothing.

Eventually, strong arms found my body, wrapping me close to his heart. Soft fur nudged me gently. The pain was releasing, like my arm was waking up from sleeping on it wrong, but a hundred times worse. I was too afraid to open my eyes to see the mangle of my arm.

"How bad is it?" I asked, breathing heavily, my body drenched in sweat.

"Your arm is fine," Elvy whispered, his voice echoing against the cavern.

My eyes fluttered open, examining my arm for myself.

Smooth skin was all that remained. There was no remnant of the scar from my mortal life and no flowing constellations from my Emergence.

"You completed the task," Elvy murmured, rubbing the surface of my skin.

It felt surreal, knowing The Archer had made this possible, and I feel like he somehow had Vega's help in crafting the magic from the very beginning. He had been intentional.

"Here," Blaz said, handing me the string for The Archer's bow. "You earned it."

"I'll say," I said, holding the string in my hand. It almost felt metallic, unbreakable.

"Can you *see* a way out?" Elvy asked.

The dread flooded my senses again.

"That cavern door wasn't open before," I said, pointing behind them. A path of white light led straight through there. "We have to go that way. I think it'll lead us up into the city center. I'm pretty sure we are underneath the archives."

They all nodded, even Jelly.

"This is going to get ugly," I said. "I can feel it."

"I've been itching for a fight," Blaz said, turning his neck.

"You don't want this fight," I whispered, voice deadly serious.

He stilled at that.

"Get changed," I said, tossing on my light blue tunic and linen pants that were baggy enough to obscure my fighting leathers underneath. I didn't see the point of even trying to hide, but if there was even a small chance it would help, then we would take it.

Jelly begrudgingly got into my pack, and I hoisted her behind me. She laid her heavy head against my shoulder, comforting me as she always tried to do.

"I can't protect you like this," she huffed.

"The moment there is danger, I'll let you down," I promised.

She seemed satisfied enough not to say anything else, and I turned to the rest of my family.

"We keep Zoe alive," Elvy commanded. "Above all else. Swear it."

"You know we will," Imelda said, eyes determined. Blaz held the same oath. In this moment, I hated both of them for it, but I also knew there was no point in arguing with them.

"Let's go," I said, taking the first step into whatever the string of fate had in store for me.

49

Dark Flames

ZOE

The streets of Canopus were busy, full of life, yet I felt exposed and under a microscope. I couldn't shake the feeling of being watched, and June had always told me that meant I was, which meant we were being followed.

I clutched Elvy's hand, leading us beyond the wards where we could transport without being detected.

"Just a couple of miles," I said through the bond.

He nodded, keeping his eyes forward. Blaz and Imelda flanked our right and left sides. Their eyes scanned the crowd before us, ever analyzing the next move. That's all we had to do. Make the next right choice to keep ourselves alive.

My hands twitched for the blades strapped to my chest. Even now, it was hard to hold on to the hope of the stars. I preferred taking the reins of my own fate.

Sweat dripped down my back, and my heart fluttered unsteadily the closer we got to the transport zone.

My head was suddenly in a fog, and my surroundings seemed to blur.

I clutched my stomach painfully. She was here.

"It seems our fate is intertwined, Zoe Eferhild," a voice called from behind us. I'd know it anywhere.

"Hesperia," I said, turning, letting go of Elvy's hand.

The street had cleared of immortals, and I wondered briefly if they had all been some elaborate illusion.

"I grow tired of our dance," she said, letting her magic seep from her. Abel stood behind her, looking brand new from the last time I'd seen him. Well, that wasn't good.

"Then end it," I suggested, letting Jelly down from my pack as promised and shredding my disguise. Jelly immediately shifted into her flaming simargl form.

"I plan to. Right here today."

My darkness swelled within me, begging to come forth to shield me—to protect me. I answered the call, letting the darkness become one with me, but I made sure I was still in the driver's seat of my magic. I couldn't let Hesperia get her magic on mine.

"Are you still there, Zo?" Elvy asked, eyes still the beautiful gray I know and love.

"I'm still me."

"You've learned some control," Hesperia said, laughing with mania in her eyes. "That's cute."

It would come to blows between her and me. Shadows against shadows. Failing was not an option.

"I'll make you a deal," she said, gliding closer. Blaz and Imelda stepped forward in unison, getting in front of Elvy and me only slightly. "Give me the bow, and I'll let you walk away from here."

Why would she want the bow? Only a true Daughter of Algol could wield it.

"No deal," I said, shaking my head.

"I have just as much right as you," she said, moving closer.

My heart sank, eyes going wide. I thought back to my conversations with The Archer and his notable absence recently… and there was no immortal record of her anywhere. *No, no, no.*

"Hello, sister," she said, and my world stopped—paused—just for a moment.

The ripple of shock coursed through Elvy, Blaz, and Imelda. My head was spinning, but I refused to let the shock consume me.

"Whatever monologue you're about to give, I'm not interested," I said, voice darker. Shadows twisted around my arms, aching to be released to fight for me.

"Don't you want to know how The Archer betrayed his first daughter?" she asked. "Don't you want to know what this is really all about?"

I shook my head. The Archer was not a perfect father, but he would not have wanted this. No, this was only about her lust for power, disguised by daddy issues.

"Having crap parents doesn't give you the right to be evil," I said.

"I'm the only reason you were created," she seethed. I flinched at the harsh words, but remained resolute in my stance.

"Then I promise you I plan to fulfill my purpose," I said, voice strong—unyielding.

"Sorry, sister. I've got my own plans," she said, releasing her black tendrils towards us.

Then all hell broke loose.

I released my own shadows to meet hers, allowing my darkness to face its match. My shadows were good, but I always remembered in the back of my mind that Hesperia could manipulate them. I felt her magic trying to take control of my shadows, but they would not answer her. They belonged only to me, and I did not fear them.

"My magic answers me. Only me," I said, laughing and unsheathing my longest blade. I wasn't sure if it was because we shared a father or my ability to embrace my shadow self, but that part of her magic did not affect me. Not now. Maybe it would have at one point. That didn't mean it wouldn't affect Elvy.

"Keep your shadows locked down!" I shouted through the bond.

"Got it," he said, impaling one of Hesperia's followers on his blade.

Blaz was locked into battle with Abel, and Imelda was holding her own against three of Hesperia's followers. They were all fighting at my back, protecting me as much as they could. As much as I wanted to focus on them, I returned to my own enemy. Jelly circled Hesperia with me, body engulfed in flames.

We worked in unison to get closer to her, but Hesperia also seemed to want this.

I sliced my blade across her chin, narrowly missing her neck. With my other hand, I twisted my shadows to encircle Hesperia's throat, but her shadows kept them from choking her. I hated to admit that she was strong.

"You will not win this fight," she said, trying to call on my shadows to meet her once again.

"I told you, they answer only to me," I spat.

"Everyone has their breaking point," she said, eyes bright with the thrill of this fight.

We circled each other for what felt like far too long, both gaining an inch, only to lose it the next round. She was covered in cuts from my blade, but none of my strikes had hit their lethal mark. My body was bruised from the onslaught of her magic, but she was burned in several places from Jelly's flames.

No one had attacked from my back, so Elvy, Blaz, and Imelda were keeping Abel and the rest of Hesperia's army off me.

A searing pain suddenly coursed through my arm, and I stumbled to my knees. Hesperia didn't hesitate in grabbing my hair and holding her own shadow blade to my neck.

Jelly growled and launched herself onto Hesperia, but her shadows knocked Jelly to the ground. The sound of whimpering broke my heart, but she was alive.

"Stop!" Elvy yelled, covered in blood. He had Abel poised for a death blow. The rest of Hesperia's followers were either dead or had fled. "I'll kill him."

Hesperia laughed. "Go ahead. What's it to me?"

Abel's eyes widened in shock as Elvy beheaded him in one swift swing of his blade, then aimed it at Hesperia. So long Abel.

"Let her go," he said, as Blaz and Imelda moved forward with him. "You can't win this fight."

"When will you all see the bigger picture?" she asked, sinking the blade a little further into my skin, drawing blood.

"Don't play into it," I said, sending my tendrils after Hesperia again, but she didn't budge. I tried to keep my eyes calm, but I was frantic inside.

Elvy's eyes were going darker. I had to distract them.

"Why didn't you force my hand?" I questioned. "That day on the beach? You could have secured my shadows then. You had the power to take me in that moment. Why didn't you?"

"Because, sister. I have always hoped you would be by my side in the end. Without me forcing you. I'd hoped you would choose me."

Just for a moment, there was vulnerability in her eyes, and I felt her pause even though I couldn't see her very well from this angle… But maybe this was something I could use against her. Her expression went dark again, and her voice returned to the chaotic mania I'd grown used to from her.

"Give me the bow," she demanded.

"No," I said, convicted in my choice. Something was off about her demand. I just didn't know what it was.

"Let's find your pressure point," she said, dragging the blade across my skin. I didn't flinch. "No, you are all too happy to die and be a martyr…"

She looked at Elvy. "But you would do anything for him."

I swallowed, taking deep breaths.

She poised her blade to cleave into my neck.

"I love you," I whispered through our flame.

"I can't let this happen, Zo. They won't stand for it," he said, eyes full of love and terror.

Through the fear, his eyes blackened with his shadows, needing to protect their bond.

"No!" I screamed, but it was too late.

Elvy's eyes were dark, and he was launching himself towards Hesperia.

She released me from her grip to focus her magic on my mate.

In one moment, he was no longer mine. In one second, Hesperia had control of my flame—my shadow's bond. My heart threatened to stop, no longer finding the strength to beat.

"I think I'll have fun with this one," she said, clutching his bicep in her grimy hands. I was going to be sick. "He'll prove quite useful, don't you think?"

"Let him go," I begged.

"Call for me," she said, moving towards the transport zone. "Call for me when you're ready to give me the bow and submit to me, little sister. In the meantime… let's see what trouble the Lord Astral and I can get into."

Before I could move a muscle, they were gone. My frame trembled with… rage, grief, love.

"I will find you," I said, sending all the love I had through the bond and flame—they were one and the same.

Strong arms found me and cradled me to his chest.

"We'll get him back," Blaz promised.

I couldn't move. I couldn't breathe—didn't want to. My starlight. He was gone, and any sense of hope left with him.

"I've got you, Zo," Blaz said, lifting me into the air, with Jelly and Imelda flanking us.

I didn't shed one tear. My chest swelled with empty sobs. I was too numb to feel anything anymore.

50

Emerging

FREYJA

"**W**hat am I supposed to say to her?" I whispered, clinging to Oleander.

Elvy was… gone and in the hands of our greatest nemesis. And Hesperia was her *sister*. The Archer hadn't answered any of Zoe's demands for a meeting. I prayed it was for a good reason.

"How am I supposed to tell her it will all be okay when I have everything I need right here?"

"Be there," he answered, stroking my hair. "Don't try to fix it or console her. Just sit with her. Even if she doesn't talk… sharing your energy with her is useful."

"But she's always fixed everything for me!" I shouted, standing up from the comfort of his arms. I didn't want to be comforted when I knew my sister was breaking… burning without her flame.

"Freyja…"

"No, no. I refuse to just be helpless in all of this. She threatened the life of a *celestial* for me. She's given too much."

"Once you get through the trials, we will get him back. We will do whatever it takes," Oleander promised, circling around my waist. "You have to make it back to us, though."

"Failure isn't an option," I agreed, allowing myself to lean into him.

Zoe would be arriving momentarily to see me off for the trials. Oleander's staff had decorated the place for the solstice, but it seemed a little too jovial given everything that had happened. Evergreen trees adorned with twinkling lights and ornaments were in almost every room. I'd expressed a desire to tear it all down, but Ander had talked me out of it. It had been an irrational thought, anyway. I had been so excited to celebrate our first Winter Solstice in the star realms.

As much as I wanted to see her, I'd expected Zoe to stay in Vega after what'd happened with Hesperia. True to her nature, Zoe had insisted on being here despite my protests. Her voice had been calm over the iris, but there was no life to it. It was as if a part of her was dead, and I guessed it probably was. I didn't expect her to have her act together.

"Finnian told Zadie that Zoe has thrown herself into Vega, taking over all the duties of the Astrals. She's strong."

"Distraction will only last so long, Ander," I said, sighing. "Then she'll break."

I felt her the moment she entered the room. Zoe's presence demanded to be felt.

"I have no intention of breaking," she said, voice… different. The tone seemed forced. Blaz and Imelda stood beside her, with Jelly in tow. Even she seemed sad.

I didn't try to apologize or explain myself. I meant what I said with the love I had for my sister.

"It's good to see you," I said, wrapping my arms around her. Her frame was rigid—unyielding.

No, she wouldn't break, but she might shatter at the right pressure.

"Of course. I wouldn't miss your Emergence," she said, smile not quite meeting her eyes. Swirls of darkness flashed in her green eyes, but they were gone as quickly as they'd come. My sister was a ticking time bomb.

Blaz discreetly shook his head when I met his eyes, and I stopped myself from pressing Zo. They knew how far my sister was willing to go to save those she loved. But they didn't really know her strength's limits. She could hold out for a long time… until she couldn't.

"I've missed you," I said sincerely, motioning for her to join me on the couch.

The blue-green flame of the fire crackled beneath the cosmos, shining through the floor to ceiling windows. It was a calm setting for my journey to the realm of the Emerging.

"Have there been any breaches in the other realms?" Ander asked, sitting on the other side of Zoe. He crossed his legs diplomatically, but if I knew Ander, he was trying to get a read on Zoe. And if I knew my sister, she was going to be pissed at his prying.

"Don't bother trying, Oleander," Zoe said, smirking. I was thankful for the playful moment. I'd expected her to snap at him. "My shields are impenetrable."

"Oh, how I long for the days on Earth when you were a mere mortal," he said, chuckling.

"I miss them too sometimes," she said, looking down, serious.

Oleander and I both wrapped our arms around her, and she went rigid again. She didn't push us away, though.

"To answer your question, Oleander, no. Delmira spoke with Sierra and Seraphina earlier, and they reported nothing back," Imelda said.

"They've reinforced their wards as much as they can, but we don't think they'll be much of a match for Elvy…" Blaz said, trailing off.

The silence was deafening.

"I'm going to stop him," Zoe said, determined. "I just need to reach him."

"Stop him?" Ander asked.

"That is, in part, why I have come tonight," my sister said, standing up from the couch.

Blaz, Imelda, and Jelly stood protectively around Zoe. Zadie came to stand by Oleander, but something in her expression gave her away. She knew whatever she was about to confess. They must have granted Finnian permission to clue her in.

"What's going on, Zo?" I asked.

Zoe cast a shield around our small group, sighing deeply.

"What I'm about to share with you is the greatest secret of the Vega Astral bloodline," she began. "It is imperative that you never breathe a word of this to anyone."

Ander sat up from his casual stance, listening intently.

"I expect you to have discretion, Oleander, while we navigate how to inform the other courts, if at all," she said, voice formal.

"I'm on your side, Zo," he said, brows furrowed. "You know that."

"You may not be after what I tell you," she admitted.

Zadie nodded in encouragement for Ander to trust Zoe.

"I swear I will protect this secret," he agreed.

"There's a reason Elvy knew how to teach me to alter my magic during the registration of my Astral magic in Sirius—not that I got the chance. His family has been doing it for generations."

She shifted her gaze to the fire and turned back to us.

"But before I tell you Elvy's secret, you should know Hesperia's," Zoe began. Blaz and Imelda both shifted on their feet.

"Yes?" Oleander asked.

"Hesperia's magic. It's controlling the shadows. The very magic that rests in every immortal of Algol," Zoe began. "What I can't figure out is why she never tried it with you, or did she?"

Oleander sat up straighter, running a hand through his tousled hair. "You're certain?"

"Quite," Blaz said, crossing his arms. Zadie nodded in confirmation.

"My shield, maybe?" he suggested. "I've always had it up around her."

"I don't think so," my sister disagreed. "If she's ever been exposed to your shadows directly, you were at risk of her taking control of you. Just like she did to your immortals. Have any of them woken?"

Zadie shook her head. "They haven't, but their bodies are perfectly fine."

"It's their magic that has been damaged—their spirit. I will see them before I leave. I'll do what I can."

"So every immortal of Algol is at risk of Hesperia's control?" Oleander asked.

"Yes," Zoe confirmed. "Her magic has limitations. Maybe that's why she never got to you. She was already controlling too many to take you on with the amount of power you wield. She had to choose between one large prize and an army."

"This is the worst-case scenario," Oleander said, and I couldn't agree more, which made me hate all the more that I had to leave this realm. "And Elvy?"

"He was able to be captured because he has shadows, too. My shadows bonded with Elvy's, and we learned they are Algol and Vega—a combination just like me. His true gift is death," she said, voice breaking.

Ander's face paled. "Death? On what scale?"

"Larger than you can shield," Blaz said, and Imelda nodded in confirmation.

"Swear to me you will not harm him," Zoe pleaded. "If he has to be—if he has to be killed. I will be the one to do it."

I wrapped my arms around her trembling frame. For once, Ander had no idea what to say.

"Swear it, Oleander," she demanded again.

He nodded his head. "No harm will come to him by my hand unless he is an immediate threat to Algol."

She nodded, resigned to accept his compromise. "Thank you."

The three of them relaxed slightly.

"Are you going to tell the other Astrals?" Ander asked.

"It's uncertain what would be more helpful or harmful," Imelda offered. "We can't have the courts fighting one another right now. We've equipped them all with an iris. They are supposed to call for us should he cross into their realm. We've told them that he has been compromised and is dangerous and that a wide berth should be taken if he is seen."

"What if he kills everyone?" Zadie asked, noticeably silent this whole time.

"It won't come to that. I won't let it. I suggest in the meantime, we gather every immortal who has the power to shield and move them to the front lines," Zoe said.

"We'll begin immediately," Ander said.

"I know this is a heavy thing to bear," she said, sitting back down. "Thank you."

"Have you tried to reach him through your flame?" Ander asked, eyes moving rapidly in thought.

"It's… cloudy. I think he's blocking me. Or maybe she is. I don't know. But I will break through."

"Maybe there's a reason he's keeping you out," I said gently, leaning my head on her shoulder.

"I'm sure he's trying to protect me, and when I get him back, I'm going to have words with him," she said, sighing.

Jelly trotted from Blaz's side and placed her head on Zo's lap.

"Good girl," I said, scratching behind her ears. "You'll have to take extra care of her when I'm gone."

She nodded, and I smiled, wishing I could hear her the way Zoe could.

"Any advice for the trials?" I asked, trying to change the subject in the last few moments I had with her.

"You know I can't tell you," she said. "Nova would smite us both down."

"Are you going to be okay?" I asked, fastening her hand in mine.

"Focus on your trials. We will all make sure you have the star realms to come back to," she promised. Everyone nodded in agreement with her. Even Zadie, who was now tucked away in a corner, reading yet another ancient tome.

The clock struck midnight, signaling that it was time for my Emergence. With every chime, I felt a piece of my fate solidify in the stars.

Ander, Zoe, and Jelly escorted me to my bedroom, and I lay comfortably on the bed.

"Just be you," Zoe said. "And never forget who you're fighting to get back to."

"I won't," I swore. She kissed me on the cheek and stepped back with Jelly.

"You ready?" Ander asked, holding my hand.

"I am," I said, more confident than I truly felt.

"Be a viper," he whispered, placing a kiss on my lips.

"Always," I promised.

He reached into his own essence and produced a glowing black orb to send my consciousness to the realm of the Emerging where Nova would greet me. At least, that's what we assumed, anyway.

"I'll see you soon," I said.

"I know, sweetheart."

I gave one last look to Zoe, and she mouthed, "I love you."

I nodded back, scorching her love within my very soul.

Oleander plunged the orb into my spirit, and then I was soaring into the cosmos.

51

Saint Andrews

ZOE

It smelled of books and saltwater.

I dropped my keys into the bowl on the table by the door, like I'd done a hundred times as a mortal. This time it felt foreign, but the smells let me know I was home.

I opened a window so that I could hear the waves crashing along the shoreline. This was real. But I wasn't safe.

The white Jeep Wrangler was still in the driveway. I doubted it would even start up now.

My chest felt hollow and like it was going to explode all at the same time. I wasn't sure what had called me back to Saint Andrews, but my soul longed for the one place I'd always felt safe.

I needed to break, and I couldn't do that in Vega where my family and my immortals were depending on me to lead them. It was difficult to sneak away from the solstice festivities, and I knew I wouldn't have too long before one of the Luminaries found me. Jelly had probably already alerted them to my absence.

But I couldn't be in the star realm where my flame was not by my side.

Elvy.

I crumbled to the floor in the fetal position and let the tears I'd been holding in fall in waves. My body convulsed with every sob, and the tears blurred my vision. I didn't want to see anyone or anything, anyway.

Maybe it was a mistake to come to this house where our love had grown. There were too many memories here, and they flooded through me all at once. But I also felt irrevocably empty.

I was a shell—an empty hearth without a flame.

I'd brought my sister back just to lose my soulmate.

Except she wasn't my only sister. Fate had to give me an evil one, too.

I wanted to simultaneously burn my father to a crisp and let him comfort me. He'd tried to tell me in his own way. Rationally, I knew he had a good reason for not telling me. But now he owed me an explanation, and he had been radio silent.

When the tears had emptied, and I had nothing left to give, I flipped on the TV to a random channel, not having the energy to read a book.

Dean Winchester's face greeted my own, and it would be one of the most gut-wrenching *Supernatural* episodes of all time that was on. The finale of the eighth season had always torn both Freyja and me up when Dean reassured Sammy that he would always be there for him. I understood the weight of that responsibility all too well. And Sam revealed his greatest sin. It was enough to get my tears flowing again, and I welcomed them.

I just needed one day to wallow. One day not to be the Lady Astral of Vega. I didn't want to make any decisions. I needed to let go… just for a little while.

I was three more episodes deep when the knock came at the door.

"Go away," I said, curling up further into my burrito blanket.

"Zoe, let me in," Oleander said through the door.

"No," I repeated. "I'm not interested."

"I brought coffee."

I sighed.

"Fine. Come in, but no questions."

"Promise," he said, letting himself in the door. I hadn't bothered locking it. Mortals were no longer a fear of mine, and anything immortal could easily bust it down.

I was certain I had puffy red eyes and a tangled mess of hair, but he didn't say anything.

"You can't just leave without telling anyone," he said gently, handing me the coffee, and I took it greedily.

"I know," I admitted. "I just got so overwhelmed. My body reacted. I was here before I even thought it through."

"I know, Zo," he said.

Another knock came at the door, and I recognized him immediately.

"Come in, Blaz," I said, pitching my voice loud enough for him to hear.

Blaz and Jelly burst through the door, and she jumped up on my lap. He carried a bag of tacos in his hand as an offering. He held out the bag as if I were a frail animal who might bite him.

"Thank you," I said, taking a couple of tacos from the brown bag.

"We were worried. You shouldn't leave without me," Jelly said through our brand.

"I know, little dragon. I'm sorry. It was selfish of me."

Jelly laid her head in my lap, wings closed on her back. Half her body was on Oleander, but he didn't seem to mind.

"Be selfish today," Oleander said.

"I shouldn't. Not when he's… stars only know what she is doing to him."

Blaz sat down in front of me, taking my hand in his. "We won't solve it now, but we will get him back. Take care of yourself today. Wallow. Be pissed. Cry. Whatever you need to do. We'll be with you."

Oleander nodded in agreement.

I wasn't at peace. I never could be until my flame was by my side. He wasn't letting me in through our bond, and I loved and despised him for it.

I'd take the day.

Then I would burn the star realms down to nothing but stardust myself, if that's what it takes to see my flame again.

I would be the darkness that eclipsed every ounce of starlight if anything happened to him.

I would *burn*.

52

Epilogue
ELVY

Sweat trickled down my back, and my leathers clung to my skin uncomfortably. Zoe had been trying to fight her way through the door I'd slammed shut on our flame the moment Hesperia had taken me. I was still me, but she controlled me like a puppet. Without a doubt now, that was her power. To control the shadows and darkness, but she hadn't been able to control Zoe's. So she'd gone for me to torment Zoe into doing her bidding. I preferred it this way. Hesperia would not lay a hand on her ever again.

So I kept Zoe out. My flame. The starlight of my life. The bond that lived in my veins. I wouldn't let her see what this vile female was doing to me. It was tempting to lose myself in Zoe. If I visited her mind, I would be free of this torture, but she might feel my pain through our flame. Not to mention Hesperia might get to her through our bond. I couldn't risk it. No, I was on my own.

My arms ached from hanging in the chains in the ceiling above me, but I hadn't given her what she wanted. Not yet. My feet were frigid against the cold, damp stone beneath me. My torso was bare, and all I had for clothing were the pants of my fighting leathers she'd allowed me to keep on. I was in a constant state of hypothermia, but my immortal healing kept me from succumbing to it.

I lifted my aching neck to catch a few drops of water on my desert-dry tongue. The small drops from the cavern ceiling seemed to rejuvenate me just enough to keep going. My water magic swelled happily at the contact. My neck slammed back down, too weak to stay up.

Footsteps echoed through the cave, and I recognized Hesperia's gait immediately. I cringed away internally, but focused on my mask in front of her. She had some control over me, but it couldn't last. No one's magic was eternal.

"Elvy, darling," Hesperia purred, tracing a clawed nail down my exposed chest.

My flame recoiled from any touch that was not its mate.

My dark eyes answered her, though, and I wanted to vomit. My only hope was that it didn't seem happy about it. I don't think it appreciated being controlled anymore than I did. I had a true sense of fear for what she might make me do. If Hesperia commanded my death curse… we were all doomed.

Hesperia's beady eyes stared back at me with a feline grin. She seemed less and less immortal with every moment I was around her.

"Still not talking to me?" she asked, summoning her black, smoky blade.

This was going to hurt.

"All you have to do is open that little bond of yours. Call your mate here. Bring the bow," she said, sounding reasonable.

I'd heard the speech a hundred times by now, and I'd never said a word.

"My patience is growing tired, I'm afraid. You know the consequences, Elvy. If Zoe does not come for you, I will activate your fun little parlor trick."

My frame trembled. Part in rage. Part in fear. I remained silent as my eyes were made to follow her form.

"Your choice," she said, stabbing the blade into my thigh.

I was consumed with ice and fire all at the same time, contrasting with the warmth of my blood as it slid down my leg, dripping to the floor at my bare feet.

Silent. I would remain silent. I would endure this. No, I *had* to bear this.

"It's a simple choice, Elvy," she said, slicing into my ribs.

Silence.

"You have to choose between everyone else… the immortals you swore an oath to serve and protect… or your flame."

Silence. Speaking would not help.

"You're going to sacrifice the many to save the one?" she asked, carving into my flesh. "History won't remember you kindly."

Silence. It was the only power I had.

"So be it. We'll paint the cosmos red," she said, tearing into me again as my silent screams filled my soul.

Acknowledgements

There are so many people who have believed in me throughout this journey of publishing The Zoe Eferhild Chronicles. I have felt your cheers across the globe, and I hold them in my heart.

To my Heavenly Father for all the ways He has been there for me—seen and unseen. For giving me the gift of storytelling.

To you, the reader, I am humbled that you chose to read The Zoe Eferhild Chronicles. I hope you have felt seen amongst the stories told and feel comforted by the words written on the pages. I am in gratitude for you always.

To my Mimi and Mom, who are always the first to read my books and listen to my ideas. To my Mom who instilled my love of 80's movies to this very day. To my Mimi who never says no to an adventure and taught me to do the same.

To my husband, who listens to the world in my brain with deep interest and love. I'm so glad to have found such support and belief in my dreams from you.

Thank you to my long list of friends who have cheered me on from the beginning. Your excitement for these characters and their fate has kept me going when the imposter syndrome tries to take over. Two special thank you's to Lisbeth and Kelby. Your enthusiasm never wavered.

To my four dogs, whom I could always count on to snuggle beside me when writing. Your snores were a nice sounding board, and you always listened to my ideas. (Though your feedback was minimal).

To the entire Indie Author community and the readers who support Indie Authors, you have been such a light in this overwhelming process. You amaze me always.

About the Author

E.C. Lawton is the author of The Zoe Eferhild Chronicles, which is her debut series. She writes books about mental health with a magical twist in an easy-to-read fantasy world. E.C. is also a psychology adjunct professor and therapist. When not writing, she can be found nose-deep in a book, adventuring outdoors with her husband, drinking too much coffee, listening to true crime podcasts, and hanging out with her wolf pack.

Make sure you subscribe to E.C.'s newsletter at her website, authoreclawton.com to stay up to date with new projects. E.C. is releasing a six-book contemporary romance series in 2027. Stay tuned!

Connect with E.C. on her socials at ec_lawton or via the QR code.

Also By

The third and final book of the Zoe Eferhild Chronicles trilogy is available now, titled *Embracing*.

E.C. is currently developing a new high fantasy series, anticipated to come out in 2028! E.C. also has a six book small town romance series in the works for 2027. Make sure you are following her on all social media at ec_lawton to stay up to date. Subscribe to her newsletter at authoreclawton.com to learn about ARC and Street Team opportunities.

See where it all began with Emerging: Book One of the Zoe Eferhild Chronicles!

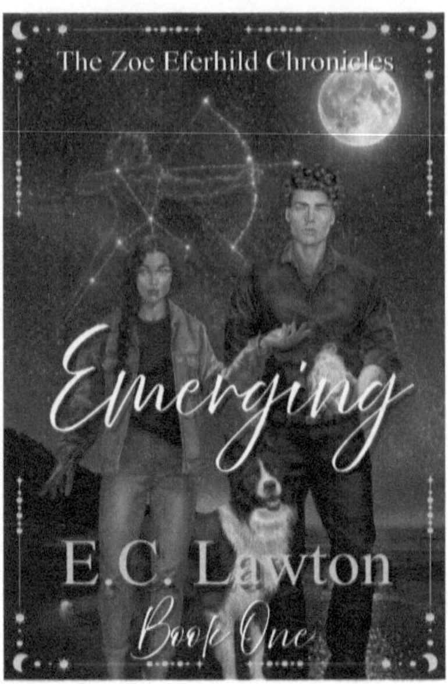

Read the Finale now!

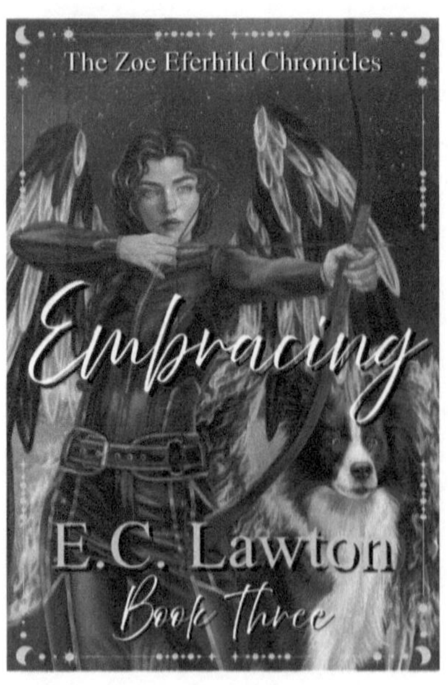